ALICE ARCHER

EVERYDAY HISTORY

For everyone who dares to love in truth.
Thank you for inspiring me to do the same.

CONTENTS

Consciously, we teach what we know;
unconsciously, we teach who we are.

D. Hamachek

PART I
THE YEAR

THE HISTORIAN
RETREAT

THE EXPLORER
APPROACH

THE HISTORIAN
RETREAT

AUTUMN | BOSTON

Every fall I begin the first class of the school year the same way. I'm not fool enough to think the students entering the Boston Museum of History's internship program—high school seniors selected for their drive and intelligence—won't want to test me. So I offer them a challenge. They always leap, assuming they'll win. They won't. Not the way they expect to.

My glasses and bald head, the way I dress—in tweed vests and ironed shirts, like a stereotype of a museum curator—work in my favor, keep me from being a threat. I stand behind my desk, hands clasped at the small of my back, suppressing a smile as the students enter the classroom for the first time, stealing looks at me, loud and boisterous to cover their nerves. They goof around, point at the unusual art I've packed into the room, and peer into the empty inkwells built into the tops of the old desks.

I want to smile because I know something they don't, something they think they already know. They're here because they think history is interesting. But I can make them fall so in love with history that the way they see themselves will shift forever.

Starting today.

Then he walks into the room with his arm around a beautiful girl.

His exuberance is incandescent. He doesn't simply enter the classroom, he radiates into it, vibrant with life, as though fueled by an energy source of pure dazzle.

His effect on his classmates is instantaneous. Girls shamelessly bat their eyelashes at him. Boys jostle and joke. They slap him on the back, vying for his friendship. At least one of the boys bats his eyelashes, but he doesn't seem to notice.

At first I think he's going to be a disciplinary problem, but he's the opposite. He holds out a desk chair for a pretty girl with red hair and then brings the other students into line by cajoling them into settling down and paying attention.

I blink, give myself a mental shake, and get down to business, starting with roll call.

His name is Ruben Harper.

I SPEND THE first ten minutes of class capturing their interest by sharing my genuine aversion to modern contraptions and answering their incredulous questions, shaking my head as they call out the names of things I don't know about and don't want to learn how to use—their beloved cell phones and computer programs and video games and fancy calculators. My unconcealed ignorance eventually stuns them to silence. And then I introduce the challenge.

"No way can you beat us on that thing, Mr. Normand," one of the boys scoffs when I propose a contest between their calculators and an abacus. I hold up my most daunting abacus, the wide one with ornate scenes painted on the red-stained wood of the frame.

"We'll see," I say with a casual shrug, like I have nothing to worry about. Then I make them wait for an hour, using the gift of their piqued interest to regale them with awe-inspiring aspects of the history of the calculator, including a brief demonstration of the slide rule. By the time I've made sure everyone in the class can do basic multiplication using the slide rules I passed around, they're obsessing over the clock, whining to get started with the contest.

"Okay. Who wants to be our impartial tester and referee?" I ask the class. A girl in the front row raises her hand first. "Sarah, right?" She nods. "Bring your calculator." I wave her up front to a freestanding easel with a large pad of paper on it and hand her a fat felt pen.

"Now do you all agree that it will be a fair contest if Sarah thinks up what to ask us and determines the winner?"

I get nods and grins from the students, and Ruben says, "Come on, man. Let's go. My trigger finger's itchy," which makes everyone laugh.

"A few ground rules," I say. "Sarah will write problems on the page in secret." Sarah takes the hint and turns the easel around so she can write without us seeing. "The problems can include addition, subtraction, multiplication, division, and combinations of any or all of those. When she's ready, she'll turn the easel around. As soon as you have the answer, raise both hands in the air. Sarah will judge the winner. If there's a tie, we'll do a rematch. Okay?" I look around the room and all I see are smug, eager faces. With the abacus on the desk in front of me, I nod to Sarah to begin.

Ruben comes closest to beating me. Closest, but I still wallop him in a conclusive, best-eleven-out-of-twenty challenge. By the time I've won the first nine matches in a row, the class is teasing Ruben for his determination to think he has a chance. They're also looking at me differently, as I knew they would.

Ruben is gracious in defeat. He gets up from his desk and walks to the front of the class, where he bows his head and presents his slain calculator to me on the palm of his outstretched hand.

It's obvious that he loves the attention.

———

OVER THE NEXT weeks, I catalog Ruben's effect on the people around him. He's not a selfish god. He acknowledges the attention of his classmates without overtly encouraging it, is carefully platonic, except with whatever girl he's dating, rarely initiates physical contact, and spreads his attention evenly—survival techniques probably already long practiced by the time he showed up in my class.

He's good-looking enough, but his beauty is in his energy. The wavy, dark brown hair that curls into his collar, his tall, solid frame, and his wardrobe are all only average. But the force field of his laser-focused attention, his contagious curiosity, his fluid movements, and the pure strength of his purpose are something else entirely.

I duly note the effect he has on the people around him, and then I use my observations of Ruben and his classmates to inform my lesson plans, to assist my reach for words and ideas that will capture their interest and motivate them toward an appreciation of history. I'm a teacher. I do what I do best.

I'm also human.

Over the progression of weeks and months, I succeed in dampening my reaction to Ruben. By early December I've grown accustomed enough to the discomfort to consider the issue resolved and reward myself with occasional self-chiding chuckles for having been a fool.

I behave impeccably, responsibly, irreproachably.

I behave so impeccably that I'm unaware of the escalating threat until it's too late.

When I notice the look, *that* look, on Ruben's face, that spark in his brown eyes, I have to fight to keep from turning around to see who's behind me. I know no one's behind me. The absurdity of that look being directed at me makes me laugh out loud. I turn the laugh into a joke about the next topic of my lecture and carry on.

But that first questioning smirk of Ruben's is followed by others. Over the next months, the looks he sends me evolve into confident flirtations, and his deep voice when he speaks to me takes on new subtexts of softness and danger.

Certain he'll outgrow his infatuation, I remain professional, watch the calendar, counting on time to save me. Inside myself doors close. Locks click. I turn away. Close my eyes. Try not to see.

But sunlight finds a way.

As Ruben grows to fully inhabit his curious desire... I wake up.

The feeling I wake to is pain, but I awaken. Even the *never* of our nonpossibility gives me an image, something to touch in my dreams, a warm pocket of flame in my cold bed, thawing me for a fleeting hour now and then. Those looks Ruben gives me reunite me with an old feeling of wanting something I can't have. Of *really* wanting something I *really* can't have. Will certainly never have. An exquisitely sad feeling that has always resided behind my sternum, even when I've managed to ignore it.

This feeling of awakening grows all through winter's fear and into spring's tortured taunt. By May's countdown to the end of Ruben's time as my student and his subsequent catapult away to college... I *require* him to leave. I *ache* for him to leave. To please *just go*.

ON A SPARKLING day at the beginning of June, on the last day of Ruben's internship, after our little ceremony in the museum's private drawing room with parents and siblings and museum officials, after the handing out of certificates and the polite sipping of sparkling punch from stemmed glasses, Ruben finds me alone, leaning against the window ledge in my office.

I'm watching white petals lift and float and drift onto the grass below from the apple trees that crowd against the windows. I'm imagining a life that is spontaneous and graceful. I'm praying in my own way, waiting for him to be gone.

Ruben places his warm palms on my back.

The shock of his boldness bows my head.

When I don't turn around, he leans his whole body against mine and whispers into my ear, "I'm away for the summer. After that, I'm not waiting any longer."

His fingers leave me in a soft fall down my spine and I listen to him walk away, blood pumping inside my ears until that's all I can hear.

I close my eyes and press my forehead against the window until I stop shaking.

It takes a long time.

But I've found a new prayer.

I lift my head and turn around to get my jacket.

He's right there, leaning in the doorway, watching me.

He stares, waiting, until I nod.

Then he finally, finally leaves.

THE EXPLORER

APPROACH

THREE MONTHS LATER | AUGUST

RUBEN ARRIVES BACK in Boston ready to party. After a long summer at his grandmother's farm in western Massachusetts and a sedating three-hour bus ride home, the need to move and talk and flirt makes his legs jump with impatience. He's spent most of the bus ride texting his friends to arrange a traveling party to reunite him with city lights and his favorite bars and local bands.

It's only when the bus turns the last corner and Ruben sees a posse of his friends waiting for him that he finds the courage to make the call, which goes immediately to voice mail.

"Mr. Normand... um, Henry?" Ruben clears his throat, regretting the question mark. "I'm back in Boston and wonder if you'd like to... if we could... if there's a chance you'd... *damn it*. Call me if you want to go out for coffee sometime." He leaves his number, hangs up with a frustrated sigh, and grabs his bag, more ready than ever to be swallowed by music and rowdy laughter.

Anything to distract him from months of silence from the man he doesn't want to want but can't forget.

CANDACE, ONE OF Ruben's buddies from high school, sidles up to him at the second bar, a small almost-dive with a low cover charge and a history of ignoring questionable fake IDs. She slides her hand into Ruben's and turns toward him until her breast presses against his arm.

"Anything especially exciting happen over the summer, way out there in the country?" Her delivery, full of breath and big eyes, makes the question a proposition.

Ruben mentally reviews his summer. The giddy feeling of graduating from high school. The hope of a call from Mr. Normand that would turn Ruben's long crush into something else—something hands-on with an invitation to call Mr. Normand by his first name. Endless busy days on the farm. Squiring farm girls to the village but excusing himself from anything more than chaste kisses on doorsteps. The shock of realizing it wasn't the girl stable hands his own age he was trying so hard to impress but the hands who were older... and men.

"Nope," Ruben finally answers, but he looks down at Candace and smiles to take the edge off his body's unwillingness to react to her. She must sense it, because she shifts away and pats his arm.

And that's when Henry calls.

PART II
THE EVENING

THE HISTORIAN
OPENING THE DOOR

THE EXPLORER
CLOSING THE DOOR

CLOSING THE DOOR

LATE AUGUST | BOSTON

RUBEN STARTS TO knock on Henry's apartment door, attempts to blame the tremor in his hand on the unseasonably early cold spell, then decides to pause for decompression. He sets down the brown paper bag he hauled up the stairs, shakes out his hands, and walks in circles around the welcome mat, but his nerves reject the attempt at a hasty scolding. If only he knew whether Henry considered this a date. God, Ruben hopes it's a date.

Three months without seeing Henry and… nothing's changed.

He's still got it bad for the object of his senior-year crush.

His high school teacher.

A *man*.

A crush unrequited for almost a year.

In a few hours—after dinner—maybe Ruben will stand in this exact spot and give Henry a good-night kiss to thank him for their date, if it even is a date. But he doesn't hold out any hope, not really—not after a school-year's worth of education regarding Henry's unspoken moral code and his frustrating resistance to Ruben's charms.

Letting go of hope calms him.

He picks up the bag and faces the door again.

With the sound of his knock reverberating in the stairwell, Ruben commands his lungs to take a deep breath. Then he stills his hands and waits, reminding himself that he's only there to scratch the itch of that seductive ache, left unrelieved over the long summer, and to dabble around the edges of his known sexual universe. He craves a little adventure before heading off to college, where he'll no longer be the most experienced student, where the girls will have become women, and a spicy tale about a man crush could sweeten his patter and close a deal.

That's what he's determined to keep telling himself.

At the belated "Come in!" he hears faintly through the door, Ruben tries the handle and walks through a small foyer and into a room wider than it is deep, with a high ceiling and tall windows all along the wall straight ahead. At this level, three floors up, the windows reveal only trees, whipping hard in the strong wind.

Mr. Normand—*Henry, damn it*—stands in the open kitchen to the left. He smiles, says, "Hi. Sorry. Crucial moment," and keeps stirring something in a pan on the stove. It's all a bit poorly scripted and overly homey, considering the momentousness of the event, their first meeting since Ruben's graduation from student to former student.

Ruben nods, playing it cool, pretending he's more confident than he is. In truth he's dying to sprint around the room to burn off the nervous energy that roared back to life with Henry's smile. Ruben holds up the heavy bag and says, "Apples from my grandmother's farm," and sets it on the kitchen counter.

"Thank you. That's... that's really thoughtful." After another quick smile, Henry looks down at his cooking again.

Ruben stares at Henry's bowed head for too long, still surprised he has a crush on someone who's not only a man, but bald. Henry looks healthier and more rested than when they last saw each other. His pale skin is clearer and rosier, his lean body more muscled.

Before Henry catches him looking, Ruben closes his mouth and turns to check out the big room. It's somehow spare and packed with stuff at the same time. Everywhere he looks he sees something unexpected and interesting and thoughtfully arranged, which tells him he's had expectations, which he generally tries to avoid.

"Smells great," Ruben says. He unzips his coat and, because the room suddenly feels too small, makes his way around the end of the long couch to stand in front of the wall of windows and look out at the trees.

He hears Henry stop stirring and slide the pan off the burner. Leaning forward against the deep windowsill, Ruben discovers the gentle heat of a radiator against his knees. He presses his legs against the warm metal and waits, curious to see what will happen next. He imagines Henry growing jittery as he nears, the same as all the times at the museum when Ruben narrowed the gap without closing it all the way, doing it for the thrill of watching panic rise in Henry's dark blue eyes.

Before Ruben turns around—delayed by a fantasy that this time he won't rein in his desire, will allow himself to touch Henry's pale, concerned face—he feels the spread of Henry's palms against his back and involuntarily takes a big breath.

This is so not the first contact he's imagined.

He stands still against the pressure of Henry's hands.

Henry slides his palms slowly up and over Ruben's shoulders, gathers the edges of his coat front, and pulls it backward and off. *Shit. Smooth move.* After months of feeling like the headlights to Henry's deer, Ruben suspects he may need to reassess. He closes his eyes and tries to slow his breathing, which has sped up rather more than necessary for the simple removing of a coat.

Henry's hands land on Ruben's shoulders and move down his arms to his wrists, which Henry holds while he shifts his feet to crowd Ruben's legs together from the sides. Ruben's heart pounds. *Maybe I've been wrong all along about that timid look on Henry's face.*

When Ruben pushes his hips back in preparation for turning around, his bottom meets Henry's front. *Glad to see me?* An aroused rush sweeps over Ruben, making him giddy.

Instead of giving way to Ruben's backward push, Henry presses Ruben's hips firmly forward against the flat grill of the radiator.

Pressure and warmth front and back. Legs pinned. Henry's arms around him for the first time ever. Nothing said. Nothing thought. Nothing seen except hard wind in trees swaying like underwater creatures in a complex tide.

Henry bends his head to whisper into Ruben's ear, "I'm not waiting any longer."

After that last meeting in Henry's office, the day they passed out the internship certificates, Ruben had carried the imprint of Henry's solid back on his palms for hours. He had to take off his suit jacket to hide his erection until he could escape into his room at home. He'd toppled with a moan onto his bed and gotten himself off in a marathon of imagined variations on how things could have ended and the way the hard muscles under his hands had rippled and tensed. He remembered the tenderness he'd felt at the sight of the smooth skin at the back of Henry's neck, only a couple of inches from his lips.

Finally Henry's hands are on him for real, and Ruben can't help but squirm and lean forward in compliance because it feels incredible—getting hard because a man is touching him. It feels delicious and uncomplicated.

Henry, undisputed captain of this cruise, begins to untuck the front of Ruben's shirt.

We're having sex now. We haven't seen each other since June. I was here for thirty-seven seconds, we exchanged two words each, and now we're getting it on. Ruben had assumed that if a good-night kiss happened at all, it would be because he worked Henry up to it gradually over the course of the evening and frightened him through twelve stages of longing in order to get anywhere near that close.

Apparently not.

Everything about it is so unlike what Ruben had imagined that he feels dizzy and off his game.

When Henry's warm hand touches Ruben's bare belly, Ruben has to open his mouth to get enough air. They're the same height. What's leaning into him and where it's leaning as Henry presses his hips forward feels so much better than in Ruben's fantasies, even though their clothes are still on. It feels mind-bendingly perfect.

In the window's reflection, Ruben makes eye contact with his own serious face, a white ghost wreathed in leaves.

Henry's arms tighten around Ruben's, and any direction Ruben tries to move meets with resistance. Feet, legs, arms, back, bottom, pelvis, chest. It's adding up, building up, making him need to do *something*—to give in or push back.

He's strong. What if I don't have to be so careful?

He pushes back harder, his knees against the radiator for leverage, but Henry holds his ground. The solidness of him gives an inch without giving way.

Ruben starts to pant and shift within Henry's containment. He needs to see Henry. He sucks a deep breath past the restraint of Henry's arms and prepares to push back again, but in that still moment, in the pause before the push, he feels Henry's quick, hot exhalation against the back of his neck, and suddenly he doesn't want anything but exactly that after all.

Moving his arms down inside Henry's embrace, Ruben slides his palms against Henry's thighs and reaches back and around to pull Henry closer.

Those slender hands of Henry's—hands Ruben has, for months, dreamed of being touched by—slide down along the skin of Ruben's abdomen, past the top of his pants. Ruben sucks in his stomach, desperate to provide access for Henry's hand, which—*oh, God*—finds and then wraps tightly around his erection.

Henry stops breathing then, though his hand moves, and Ruben, holding Henry tightly against himself, pushes back to find space enough to push forward into Henry's hand, then back again... and again, and again, until Henry groans on a sigh and presses his lips against the nape of Ruben's neck as though they share the same fantasy about that day in Henry's office.

That simple gesture is all it takes.

As Ruben falls apart, memory fills the window in front of him with a swirl of petals.

OPENING THE DOOR

THE ROMANS BROUGHT apples with them when they invaded Britain. The Brits took them to America, but they also had to take along honeybees to pollinate them.

I save all the seeds.

At the kitchen counter with his apples and a pie pan, I play back recent history—the heat of the radiator, his energy bound and unbound.

After living his own story about my denial for so long, my boldness took him by surprise.

Now he sleeps like a fevered boy plucked from a wrecked ship.

As I slide the pie into the hot oven, I remember a small volume on the history of heating. I kneel on the floor to pull the book from a bottom shelf, then tuck myself at the end of the couch with the bottoms of his feet against my leg.

In St. Petersburg, Russia, Franz San Galli developed a radiator that he patented in 1857.

I imagine Franz's half-frozen, half-gloved fingers fiddling with cold metal parts and yearning, month after month, to bring warmth into his life.

My living room windows reveal blackness relieved only by the warm glow at my side.

I close the book and wait patiently for the next chapter to begin.

CLOSING THE DOOR

FIRST THE SOUNDS, small and new. Rain and wind beating against a wall of windows. The soft tic of the radiator. The distant click-whoosh of the gas oven cycling on. The turn of a page.

Then the smells. Baked apple. The indefinable scent of Henry, learned over the course of a year of internship at the museum, during heady seconds of devised nearness before Henry stepped away. A complex, natural smell, intensified in Henry's apartment.

And then touch. The heavy warmth of the blanket covering him. Dampness at the front of his pants. Tightness absent from his shoulders. Solid thigh against his feet.

The sound of another page turning.

The combined sensations of joy and sadness rising in Ruben's chest make him open his eyes and sit up.

"What's this?" he says. "Did I sleep through to our tenth anniversary? Who drugged me and turned me into a guy who naps after a first go?"

Henry laughs and says, "Good morning." A little joke, as it's pitch-black outside. Henry gets up to check on whatever's in the oven.

"What did I miss?" asks Ruben. "Wait... God, I'm starving. Damn it. I missed dinner, didn't I?" He sheds the blanket onto the couch and walks to the dining table, which is set for dinner.

"It kept," says Henry. "Here. Take this." They pass the warm dishes to the table—soup, rice, stir-fried chicken curry and vegetables. Henry points to a beer bottle and Ruben nods.

As he sits, Ruben notices the kitchen clock. Ten minutes after ten. Of course he's hungry. Ruben chats them through their nervousness as they eat. Wanting Henry to put his nap in context, Ruben makes sure to mention how much partying he's been doing in the few days since he returned home from his summer away.

He needs Henry to know how grown-up he is.

"That was... different," Ruben says, pushing his plate away.

"Thanks," says Henry, "I think."

"Yeah. The food is spectacular, and I'm looking forward to having more, but I'm talking about how you took control of my... welcome." Ruben leans back and studies Henry. "It surprised me."

"You don't know me outside my role at the museum," says Henry.

"No, but I wanted to."

"And now?"

"I've been dreaming about our first kiss for almost a year."

"And now?"

"I thought you were shy," says Ruben.

"I am."

"I thought you lacked initiative."

"I lack the desire to be fired."

"Right." Ruben stands up and says, "Stand up."

Henry sets his napkin next to his plate and stands. "And now?"

"And now I want that first kiss."

As always—at the museum in recently emptied offices or exhibit halls, on field trips, behind the museum cafe, anywhere Ruben could find Henry alone or arrange to get him alone—when Ruben steps boldly forward to close the gap between them, Henry looks right into Ruben's eyes and tenses.

As it always has, that look captures and fires Ruben's imagination.

But when the familiar first second of nearness flints Ruben toward impulsive action and, for the first time, Henry doesn't break the moment by turning or stepping away, it's Ruben who stops. That exact look on Henry's face has been burned into Ruben's memory... but a new interpretation forms.

It's not a heady mixture of nervous shyness and lovesick yearning.

It's much more suggestive.

All those hours of pleasure alone in my bedroom thinking about that look were based on a false read.

When Henry allows it to last longer than two seconds, Ruben sees mature hunger willed into suppression, longing and desire stoked past restraint... and yet restrained.

After what feels like decades of denial and waiting, Ruben is finally allowed to touch. His shaking fingers light up like matches against the soft, dark stubble along Henry's jawline. Henry stands completely still, his eyes serious and intent.

The kiss—bracketed by Ruben's hands on either side of Henry's mouth, to make sure he stays, to keep him still until Ruben is good and done with him, to finally touch his sweetness—begins with the scent of curry, immediately skips beyond the niceties, and turns Ruben's gentle hands into arms that try and fail to clutch Henry close enough.

Ruben can't get enough of the press of flat chests, hard thighs, and muscular arms. Of the beautiful ache of his cock against Henry's through their jeans. Of the end of refusal.

Henry slows the kiss, then slows it again, tormenting Ruben with degrees of denial. Hands firmly around the buckle of Ruben's belt to keep him close, Henry shuffles back, bumps into the kitchen counter, and Ruben gratefully presses him there.

Unhinged by freshness and friction, a new wildness suffuses Ruben, making him desperate for more. Desperate with the realization that he will never get as much of this as he wants. Desperate enough to moan. He hears himself and starts to care how he sounds, but moans again, presses harder against Henry hips, sinks further into the joy of Henry's mouth.

I'm not going to be able to stop. Please, dear God, don't let this end.

The kitchen timer dings.

The kiss goes on.

The kiss with Henry lasts long enough to burn the apple pie around the edges. If the doorbell hadn't rung, that pie would have burned to ash.

"I'm sorry," Henry says, pulling away from Ruben's lips and out of his arms, "but I have to answer. I'm not expecting anyone, but it could be a friend of mine who's been having a really hard time."

Ruben adjusts his trousers as he watches Henry walk to the intercom. *What about my really hard time?*

Henry presses the intercom button, and a man's voice says in an anxious rush, "Henry, I know it's late and I'm terrible not to check first, but the hospital called about Mom, and I got a last-minute flight and I wonder if it's okay if I've showed up a few days early?"

Henry says, "Of course. No problem. Come on up." He presses the door buzzer and turns back to Ruben. He opens his mouth to say something, but

Ruben doesn't want to hear it and asks where the bathroom is. Henry points to the hallway door at the other end of the living room.

In the bathroom, Ruben focuses on swabbing the crotch of his pants with a wet washcloth and untucking his shirt to cover the resulting dark spot.

By the time he opens the bathroom door, he's convinced himself he hadn't been about to cry.

THE INTRUDER'S NAME is Martin. When Henry introduces them, he says, "Martin lives in Germany, but his mother lives here."

Ruben hates the guy on sight.

"I'm so sorry to interrupt," Martin says. Yet he wheels his suitcase to the far end of Henry's living room and leaves it there, only a few feet from the open door to Henry's bedroom.

"No worries," says Ruben with a casual wave of his hand. He practices pretending he's already gotten what he wanted from his extracurricular forays at the radiator and into Henry's mouth. *That sure was fun. Mission accomplished. Time to skip along to college now. Tra la la.*

Henry watches Ruben closely.

Martin's suitcase is enormous. And his eyes are ridiculously dark, beautiful, and sad. Henry's apartment has one bedroom. Ruben checked on his way back from the bathroom. The bed is unthinkably huge.

Martin, his face flushed, pulls off his sweater and walks back to hang it on a hook by the front door beside his coat and scarf. When Martin reaches out to hug Henry, Ruben shoves his arms into his coat and says, "Okay. I'll be off, then." He feels like he might throw up.

Henry disengages from Martin and takes Ruben's hand. His firm grip makes Ruben desperate to get away from the tumble of more new sensations, yet Henry doesn't let go, so Ruben pulls him out the door and down the stairs to the front lobby.

"Are you sure you don't want to stay for pie?" Henry holds on tighter when Ruben tries to free his hand and escape.

"I should finish packing. I'm off to Amherst to settle in tomorrow."

"You'll let me know when you want to come back to Boston for a visit?"

Ruben finally looks at Henry and sees more than he wants to see—regret mixed with blazing desire and enough mastery over both to allow Ruben to disappear into the darkness beneath the trees.

"We'll see," says Ruben. *I don't know how to say good-bye without finishing hello.* To give himself the freedom to avoid more of that surprising hurt, he adds, "I might not be in touch for a while."

Henry releases his hand.

When Ruben opens the heavy outer door, the wind blows him back against Henry's chest.

Ruben's worst moment of the evening is Henry's good-bye kiss—a linger abbreviated to a loss.

OPENING THE DOOR

BERNARD SADOW'S INVENTION of the rolling suitcase in 1970 straightened postures, redefined packing, and increased independence for travelers.

It made leaving home easier.

And turned unexpected arrivals into rivals.

Martin's first food since arriving in Boston is a slice of my apple pie. He pushes the burned-edge bits to the side and politely asks for a second piece.

"Why aren't you having any?" he asks me. "It's incredible. Truly. Your best ever."

When Martin excuses himself and goes to the bathroom, I wrap the hot pie dish in a kitchen towel, shove it into a plastic bag, and push it to the back of the freezer.

I'm so angry it's all I can do to set the bedding for Martin on the couch instead of flinging it.

"Good night," I call through the bathroom door as I pass. "I'll see you tomorrow."

I close and lock the bedroom door.

After a short search through a thin volume of poetry, I find what I'm looking for.

> *When the Sun weeps a second time,*
> *and lets fall water from his eyes,*
> *it is changed into working bees.*
> *—Egyptian text, first millennium BC*

In a few days, I will go to the museum with my notes and begin a new year of training high school interns in the wonders of history.

In a few hours, in a college town on the other side of the state, a schoolboy's too-bold gaze will find all the grown-up independence it has yearned for.

My last kiss counted for nothing against the storm. Ruben's face blew from my hands.

He walked three steps and then ran into the rain.

CLOSING THE DOOR

BY THE TIME Ruben reaches the bus shelter, he's soaked. He can hear the bus behind him, rumbling closer, but he walks on past the lighted shelter, walks into the dark shroud of falling water, walks with determined steps away from the promise of the evening and how long he's waited and yearned to be alone with Henry.

Squelching along the dreary street toward the next bus stop, Ruben brawls with his conflicting emotions until one thing becomes absolutely clear.

High school is over.

OPENING THE DOOR

FIVE WEEKS LATER | OCTOBER

RUBEN'S SILENCE CONTINUES, as infinite as space. I try not to draw conclusions. I fail.

Martin will be gone in a week. If I add a couple of punishing workouts to my schedule, I can make it through the next seven days.

Would it have made a difference if I'd told Martin my history all those years ago? No. I think not. Would we find comfort now in comparing our empty, mother-shaped spaces? Definitely not.

My grieving houseguest leaves soggy tissues all over the apartment. I feel for him, but I'm beyond done.

I spend my time cataloging my transitions. From needing what's given to giving what's needed. From heat, aggression, and closed gaps to coolness, distance, and closed doors. From openings to empty space.

I am weary of walking beside the absence of myself. If only I could fold up the empty tent of longing and eliminate unwanted space in a collapse of walls. If only I could replace the void with something I've chosen. But the wily magnet of Martin's grief has found me unprepared and unprotected, reviving old burdens rather than shedding them. I shamble from day to day, lumbering lopsided under old and new grief too heavy to balance, too barbed to shrug off.

The mother-shaped grief from which I hatched has become tangled with the sorrow under the branch where the apple used to be. Temptation derailed by time.

After not sleeping most of the night, I've come up with a pact.

Like a seed, I will feed on my own self, trusting the process until something green grows from the absence in which I was planted.

I write in darkness and fall asleep with the pen in my hand.

PART III
THE WEEKEND

THE HISTORIAN
TELLING EVERYTHING

THE EXPLORER
NOT TELLING EVERYTHING

NOT TELLING EVERYTHING

ONE WEEK LATER
OCTOBER | FRIDAY EVENING

When Martin opens the door of Henry's apartment, Ruben barely manages to turn his snide smirk into a smile.

"You okay?" asks Martin.

"Sure." Ruben amps up his smile and offers his hand.

The asshat has a great handshake. Ruben can't let go fast enough.

Just make it through the next ten minutes.

"Come on in." Martin opens the door wider. "Henry said he'll be home around six."

Ruben resists saying, "I know," and says instead, "I'm sorry about your mom."

"Thank you." Martin sets his slippers bottoms-up in the suitcase that's open on one end of the couch. He walks to the foyer in his sock feet and picks up his boots while Ruben frowns at his back.

"Have you known Henry long?" asks Martin, his casual tone contradicting an apparent eagerness to explore the topic. He ambles back to the couch and sits, but when he bends to put on his shoes, his fingers seem to hurry to tie the laces.

Careful to betray no more than necessary, Ruben says, "I guess Henry didn't talk about me."

Martin shakes his head. "No, but he's extremely private."

"We worked together at the museum last year," says Ruben. *Oh, we "worked together," did we?* "Actually I was one of his high school interns."

"Interesting," says Martin. *Asshat.*

"How do you and Henry know each other?" asks Ruben, dreading the answer. Sure enough.

"We met at university in Germany. And were together there for a while."

Ruben moves away to the windows to hide the expression on his face. Whatever it is, it's more than he wants Martin to see.

But the window reminds him of the last time he was there, so he turns back.

"What happened?"

Martin takes a last look around the room, zips his suitcase, and lifts it off the couch.

"History," says Martin.

"What do you mean?"

Ruben beats Martin to the door and holds it open for him.

"You'll have to ask Henry." Martin smiles a sad smile.

Well, his mother died two weeks ago. Of course he's sad.

THIRTY MINUTES AFTER Martin leaves with his suitcase, Ruben is sitting on the couch pretending to do homework while resisting the urge to explore Henry's apartment. When he hears Henry's key in the door, he gets up and goes to the foyer, where Henry is trying to shrug out of his coat.

"Give me those," says Ruben. He takes the grocery bags from Henry's arms and the briefcase strap from Henry's shoulder. While Henry takes off his hat and scarf, Ruben hangs his coat on a hook.

"Thank you." Henry leans against the closed door to study Ruben, who'd gotten as far as the doorway to the living room but then turned back at the sound of Henry's voice. Under Henry's scrutiny, Ruben becomes aware of how much less hopeful he feels compared to his first visit. In an effort to reconnect with his usual confidence, he puts his hands in his pockets and leans against the door frame to study Henry back, but Henry's wary eyes only remind Ruben of what an ass he's been by not being in touch. His trim shoulders snug in a gray sweater, his rosy cheeks, and those dark brows furrowed over the midnight blue eyes only drive that point home.

"I'm glad you're here," Henry says, "but I'm also tired and I need you to tell me what you want."

Ruben exhales. What he *most* wants is to pick up *exactly* where they left off, but the shadows under Henry's eyes signal a need for caution.

"Let's see," Ruben says. "First of all I want to apologize for not being in touch sooner. I'm sorry." He makes himself stop there. Short and sweet.

"And then?"

"And then... well..." Ruben rubs the back of his neck but recognizes the nervous gesture and decides to be direct. He lifts his head, straightens his shoulders, and looks Henry in the eye. "I want to know what it's like to be with a man."

"I'm sure you've had plenty of chances over the past six weeks."

"Yeah. I explored a little, but I want to... cross the frontiers... with you."

"Why?"

Ruben shrugs. "Because of the excruciating foreplay. Because I can. Because I like you."

Henry nods and bends down to untie his boots.

"And you?" asks Ruben. "Why did you invite me?"

"You mean after not hearing from you for so long?"

"Yes."

"Because of the way you look at me. Because I can. Because I need a vacation."

"And?"

"That's it," Henry says.

"That's it? I always assumed you'd want more."

Henry kicks off his boots and straightens up. He steps closer, his expression inscrutable, and Ruben takes his hands out of his pockets. They stand a few inches apart. Henry's breath is slow and easy against Ruben's closed mouth.

Without permission Ruben's lips part slightly. He swallows. "I mean, more than sex," he whispers.

"I do. I want a lot more."

"Like what?"

Henry's expression shifts. He places the tip of a finger on Ruben's chest and says, "Commitment. Responsibility. Monogamy." With each want, Henry pulses his finger against Ruben's heart. "I want a *family*. With *someone*. Do *you* want that anytime soon?"

"You want someone mature. Like a real grown-up."

"Yes."

They stare at one another.

"I'm not...," Ruben begins, but his breath has quickened. "That's not me."

Henry nods as though Ruben's answer was expected.

Ruben stares at Henry and tries to figure out what he's just said no to.

"Not even a maybe?" Henry asks softly.

Ruben swallows and shakes his head, and as Henry's exhaustion and electric energy wash over him, Ruben finds himself wanting to wrap Henry up for safekeeping—though for Henry's safekeeping or his own, Ruben's not sure.

Henry takes an inch of a step closer, making Ruben take an inch of a step back to keep his balance.

"Are you saying no to *this* now?" asks Henry, and the fierce intensity of his dark blue eyes makes Ruben blink, makes the past year's ache condense into a single moment.

Instead of kissing Henry—because Ruben suspects this kiss will bring him to his knees—he hoists Henry by the armpits and walks him backward into the bedroom.

As Ruben pushes Henry down onto the bed, Henry finally laughs. Craving a distraction from uncertainty, Ruben bends down to swallow Henry's laughter.

THE HISTORIAN
TELLING EVERYTHING

HE PRETENDS HE'S in control. He's a young man trying to convince me he's a god, but he's grappling with a new map.

Despite, during, and beyond the learning curve, he's fearless. Instinctive. Majestic.

The animated heat of him spreads over me. The bright intensity of his personality reaches for me through his strong, hungry hands, through his wide shoulders and his long legs that curl around me, and in the smirk that remains in place even as he mutters and moans. He asks eagerly with his eyes, "Is this okay?" But he doesn't wait for an answer... or he feels my answer before I shape it.

He wants to do it right, his exploration of the new world that's captured his attention. But even more than wanting to do it right, he wants to do it *right now*.

The sparkle of him dazzles me.

After deliberately, greedily touching me all over with his hands and his mouth, he stops trying to learn and allows himself to fall down the well of desire.

I'm already there.

I've been waiting in desire's wordless, reckless, thoughtless swirl since the first time his expressive mouth smirked while his eyes said, "What is this you're doing to me?"

I was sure I would wait in vain. I knew I *should* wait in vain.

Incredibly, against all expectation, I haven't waited in vain.

But my pact, the seed timidly growing inside the blank space of me, requires more than Ruben's offer of less than.

And so in spite of the hot sunbeam in my bed, in spite of the crashing together of desires, the long-craved romp... after our weekend, I'm done.

I embrace my decision, only because arguing with myself about it—which I've been doing for a week, suspecting he wouldn't want more than our bodies together—only scorches the earth around me, and I need nourishing soil in which to grow.

Even with his arms surrounding me and his mouth on mine, intent on figuring out the code of me, I know I'm going to end it.

But... not quite yet.

For the moment I'll allow myself to educate Ruben wickedly, to concentrate the curriculum for the gifted student and store history for myself as time ticks us closer to the cliff of Sunday.

He'll fly. It's in his nature to fly.

It's in my nature to germinate.

As an unspoken thank-you to Ruben for waking me up over the past year, I am ruthless. I reduce him to begging breathlessness until he curls against me, exhausted. I watch his face as he falls asleep, his red lips curved into a smile.

NOT TELLING EVERYTHING

I DON'T WANT Henry to think I'm a jerk. That thought nudges Ruben awake and then keeps him awake for hours, lying on his side, pressed against Henry. His arm rises and falls to the slow rhythm of Henry's breath.

Eventually Ruben admits the truth to himself—that he needs to tell Henry why he wasn't in touch over the past six weeks. He knows it's a good idea because, after he thinks it, his shoulders relax and he can't stay awake any longer.

TELLING EVERYTHING

RUBEN SLEEPS ON, but I can't. I'm too busy reviewing all the glorious reasons he's so worn out.

Alone in the kitchen, I start to put away last night's groceries, but can't muster the energy. So I sit on the couch with a take-out carton of our forgotten dinner resting on my knee and watch the fog outside lift and drop in lazy whirls as the heat of the morning sunlight tries to break through.

The first few bites of cold food organize my scattered thoughts into a parade of questions.

What words will I use to tell him I'm done?

And when?

As I chew I imagine what it will feel like to feed the me-shaped space the nourishment of a no, to choose myself over the conflicting needs of a lover.

When I think back to locate the last time I did that, I feel sadness pull at my face with the heaviness of stone.

I decide I'll tell Ruben by noon the next day, allowing a strategic delay of the withdrawal of friendly forces.

How many hungry looks between now and then?

How many hammering heartbeats?

How much more history can I store?

The carton of food forgotten, I watch more questions rise up inside me, afraid of them even as I need them.

Do I dare tell Ruben my history, my worst thing, before I let him go?

What if I used the near absence of his presence to practice telling someone?

Does wanting more for myself justify using Ruben in that way?

What if I say the words out loud when someone might actually hear?

NOT TELLING EVERYTHING

RUBEN WAKES TO daylight shining through the bedroom windows. Lying in bed untouched feels wrong, so he reaches for Henry, only to find himself marooned on an island of warmth.

He sits on the edge of the bed for a while, staring at Henry's dresser. When he opens the drawers at random, he finds what he was sure he'd find—a perfect pair of gentleman's pajamas. They're pale blue and so soft. He puts them on and rubs his hands over his thighs, but stops immediately because they feel like Henry's hands and it starts to turn him on.

He's about to pass out from lack of food.

Seeing Henry slouched on the living room couch, wrapped in a blanket, eating from a take-out carton, looking generally wrecked, Ruben can't help but feel pleased with himself.

***

HUDDLED NEXT TO Henry on the couch, Ruben wolfs food like he hasn't eaten in a month. "Yum." One carton scraped clean, then another. He sets the last empty carton on the coffee table and lies back with his head against Henry's shoulder.

Ruben's body feels simultaneously flattened and hypersensitive. Every cell throbs. Muscles all over his body ache for relief, even though all he's doing is sitting, quietly taking one slow breath after another.

"Christ, Henry."

"Hmm."

"You *used* me so shamelessly." Ruben grins with joy.

"And?"

"Holy fuck."

"Amen to that."

"I think… had I known…" Ruben stops to beat back the flood of memories from the night before that threatens to distract him. "Had I known," he starts again, "I never could have waited."

Henry nods. "I know."

"You knew?"

"You and your naive escalations drove me nuts, Ruben. You ignorant, cocky, flirtatious bastard."

"Well, knowing what you knew, I can't believe you held out. You stoic, mysterious, self-disciplined bastard."

"Once again experience wins out over zealous theory." Henry lifts his almost-empty take-out carton in a mock toast.

Ruben laughs. "Yeah. Theoretically, in my own mind, I could have had you whenever I wanted to push it a little harder."

"The reality was always going to be different."

"So far I'm not complaining." Ruben waggles his eyebrows at Henry.

But Henry only studies Ruben's face for a drawn-out moment until Ruben's heartbeats shift.

Henry looks at Ruben's face like he's trying to memorize it.

"I'm right here," Ruben says and leans over to kiss Henry's eyes closed.

CIRCLING THE COFFEE table strewn with empty take-out cartons, Ruben wanders Henry's living room in the blue pajamas, touches Henry's belongings, and chats about nothing.

He continues to avoid saying what he needs to say.

Henry looks small and self-contained on the big couch. He follows Ruben's movements intently, but says nothing.

"Where's your television?" Ruben asks.

"There's one at work I could use if I wanted to. Not here."

"Right. I'm not surprised. And I know you don't have a cell phone." He looks around the room and gravitates to the desk in the corner under the windows. There's a small manual typewriter in the center of the desk and a laptop off to the side. "I'm surprised you have a laptop."

"Me too. I only got it when I couldn't avoid it anymore because of work."

"I remember that you and the digital world are not on friendly terms." He pats the laptop. "Do you have technicians standing by?"

"Something like that. The museum keeps trying to give me a cell phone, but constant availability seems like the worst kind of purgatory. They spring for a computer tutor for me now and then, but it never really takes. It's like that part of my brain forgot to evolve. I'd be more embarrassed about it if I weren't so grateful."

"You prefer to be left behind?" Ruben teases.

"I prefer to understand how things work. I spent a lot of time as a child around poor old people and their old things and their old ways—mechanical, old-fashioned, simple. The clatter of a typewriter. Turning the crank on an ice-cream maker. Conversation as entertainment."

"So now those things remind you of your happy childhood? I get it."

Henry snorts, but it's a humorless sound, and he doesn't answer the question.

Unwilling to push, Ruben brushes his fingers over the ends of the pencils standing in a pewter cup so he can hear them rattle. Every new layer Henry reveals intrigues Ruben more, and he thinks of several things he could ask, but then decides they're all too shallow, after the depth Henry's taken them into.

Anxious about what he hasn't told Henry, Ruben lapses into chattering again as he continues to study the objects on Henry's desk. He picks up a carved wooden bowl in the shape of an empty half of a walnut shell. Larger than life, the bowl fits nicely within the spread of his open palm. Tiny red and black seeds pooled in the bottom of the bowl skitter and clack as Ruben gently tips it back and forth. When he tilts the bowl into a ray of sunlight, the seeds blaze like miniature embers.

The sunbeams that slant in through the trees throw sharp-edged, shuddering leaf shapes onto the carpet. Ruben blinks against the glare. It reminds him that he wants to be open, to maintain the clear brightness he feels when he's around Henry.

He carefully sets the wooden bowl back on the desk.

When he clamps his mouth shut against his own blathering, a gap of silence stretches across the room. Before the space becomes too wide to jump, he says, "I didn't want to know."

Henry takes a deep breath and rubs his bald head with both hands, like he's trying to wake himself up or bring himself back to the present. "Know what?"

"I didn't want to know whether I cared if you and Martin were going to have sex." Ruben leans back against the desk and watches Henry. "Or whether I would miss you. So I decided I didn't."

Henry grins. "Chicken. Well, we didn't, if you must know."

Ruben tries to hide his relief.

"Go on, then," says Henry. "Tell me the whole story of the past six weeks. You started buying condoms in bulk. Right?"

Ruben laughs. "Yeah. Pretty much." He takes a deep breath and sees that Henry is smiling, which makes talking about it feel less serious. "I was like a conveyor belt. I propositioned every woman in sight, trying to prove to myself that nothing had changed."

"And?"

"Nothing had changed."

"Meaning?"

"Sex was the same as it's always been. I couldn't get satisfied. Believe me, I tried."

"So how's that reputation of yours coming along?" asks Henry.

"Oh, I win the campus slut award. No question."

"But?"

"But I didn't care, because something *had* changed after all. I had a new standard. And nothing I did with a woman even came close."

Henry's eyes widen. "Even though all we'd done was lean against a radiator and share one broken kiss?"

"Two actually, but let's not count the one down in the lobby."

"Agreed. But..."

"Henry, two seconds into our first kiss I had a new standard." Ruben walks to the couch, scattering leaf shadows, sits close beside Henry, and says, "Leaning into you and kissing you with all our clothes on that night was a million times better than any other kiss I'd ever had."

Henry stares at Ruben with his mouth slightly open.

Ruben rubs the back of his hand along Henry's soft morning stubble. "Being with a woman was *never* enough. It was never going to be enough."

Henry blinks and says, with an air of pomposity, "Well, quantity is certainly no substitute for quality." He quirks a smile that doesn't quite reach his serious eyes.

"Don't gloat."

Henry closes his eyes and leans into Ruben's hand. "I wouldn't dare."

THEY HAUL THE empty take-out cartons to the kitchen, put away the groceries Henry brought home after work the day before, and return to the couch. Henry says, "Go on, then. I know that's not the end of the story."

"Okay. Well, then I discovered something really interesting."

"*Men*. Ooh la la."

"Well, sort of. I already knew I was headed that direction. I mean, I've spent the last year having sex with women while imagining having sex with you."

"Yikes." Henry fans himself.

"That was my first revelation—imagining sex with a man satisfies me more than actual sex with a woman."

"Uh-oh."

Ruben raises a hand in the air. "Yep. More gay than not. Who knew?"

Henry snorts.

"Shut up."

"So you weathered dark days of sexual reassessment," says Henry with a teasing smile. "And then?"

"And then I started batting my eyelashes at actual fellas."

"Exciting. So... how'd it go?"

"Mixed. Well, actually not great. I kept floundering on the follow through."

Henry laughs. "I find that *extremely* hard to believe."

"And yet it's true. And it really pissed me off. A lot. Technically, yeah, stuff happened, but only up to a point. I thought it was because I was new at it, but that never stopped me with women, so I couldn't figure it out. Then I twigged to the fact that whenever I got into a promising tangle with a guy, I'd distract myself and ruin the mood by looking around for a window sill or a radiator or a doorway to shove him up against." Ruben ducks his head and looks away. "And I've eaten enough curry in the past six weeks to drown a Buddhist."

Henry laughs. "Aw," he teases. "You've got a crush on me. That is so sweet."

That's when it becomes obvious to Ruben that Henry's doing his best to keep their conversation light in spite of the topic. *Henry wants more than I'm willing to give, yet he's trying to make it easy for me to go.*

The disturbing sad-joy feeling rises up again, and Ruben takes a mental step back.

What he's not willing to tell Henry is that there was another revelation. Getting off while imagining sex with Henry was much more satisfying than trying to have actual sex with other men. Until this weekend. Until *actual* sex with *actual* Henry. Ruben squirms and feels his face flush just thinking about it.

If Ruben didn't know better, if he viewed his own tale as an outsider, it might look like the story of him falling in love with Henry.

That thought makes him excuse himself and head to the bathroom.

Door closed, sitting on the edge of the bathtub, Ruben takes stock.

But I don't do love. Not the kind that presumes a future. He's never been that kind of guy. "Sorry," he always says when someone falls for him. "Love would get in the way of sex." No amount of pity-me eyes or I-could-be-the-exception pleas ever made him want to change his tune.

Okay, that could be because, until recently, it was always women who wanted more. *Maybe love would be different for me with a man.* Over the past six weeks, Ruben has fended off two I-could-be-the-exception pleas from guys, and neither of them remotely tempted him to consider changing his policy... but they weren't Henry.

All along Ruben had considered his thing with Henry to be about the thrill of sex with a man. Couldn't it still be about sex? Henry is older and, Ruben assumes, more experienced than any of the other guys he has fooled around with so far. So maybe sex with Henry is so satisfying because of Henry's experience. And his exceptional skills as a teacher.

The crux of the matter is the siren call of the learning curve. Because of the proper education Henry is giving him, Ruben feels a new confidence. He's looking forward to giving the playing field of men another shot back at school. In fact he can hardly wait. He remembers a few of the hot, out gay guys he hasn't had the confidence to approach. They'd better brace themselves.

Let's review. I'm an eighteen-year-old male. I'm newly aware that I'm mostly gay. I recently moved away from home for the first time. I attend a large university, full of people my age who are also naturally hopped up on hormones. Is this a description of someone ready for commitment? No. I think not.

Case closed.

With an adjustment for gender, he renews his old policy—sex, please, hold the love—as his new policy. Pretending anything else would be dishonest. *Promising* anything else would be cruel.

Ruben slaps his thighs, stands, and nods decisively to himself in the mirror. He gives himself a lecherous grin to seal the deal, remembers to flush the unused toilet, and heads back to the living room.

As Ruben walks behind the couch, Henry leans his head back and smiles up at him.

Ruben has to close his eyes to remember what he just decided in the bathroom.

He'd been hoping to convince Henry to keep the door open for weekend flings, but a smile like that doesn't bode well for keeping things casual. He needs to do something to spare Henry the heartache of impossible expectations. Ruben's satisfied body, thrumming with delicious aftereffects, registers a complaint, but he overrules it in favor of Henry's welfare.

I'll have pity and break it off sooner. That will hurt Henry less.

Many months later Ruben remembers that moment and admits how obvious it was, even then, that he was trying to keep from hurting himself.

TELLING EVERYTHING

I MEMORIZE THE journey of Ruben's fingertips as he roams the room touching my belongings.

I am tempted to fall for Ruben as I watch him leaving his fingerprints, marking his journey through my life. My antidote is a thought. *I am nothing more than his safe way to begin.*

I am Ruben's starter kit. A short preface that will soon pale when his real story begins. An overture to the symphony he will discover beyond me, after me, without me.

I try to feel honored to perform that public service for the gay community at large.

To further distract myself from Ruben's graceful movements, I shift my focus to two clear goals I've formulated, which I repeat to myself like mantras, wards against darkness, defensive spells against caring for what I will soon abandon. *Use him to practice saying my worst thing. Send him away with a satisfied smile.*

A perk within a pain.

A temporary holy dovetailing of our rites of passage.

NOT TELLING EVERYTHING

STANDING AT THE kitchen counter, crafting and chomping sandwiches made from the assortment of options Henry has set out, Ruben hums a *yum* to himself as he chews. Each sandwich tastes better than the last.

Henry's shower-damp skin and freshly shaven face make him look ten years younger—closer to Ruben's age. He looks more vulnerable than Ruben has ever felt.

When Ruben came out of the bathroom after his little pep talk in the mirror and saw Henry smile up at him from the couch, he climbed over the back of the couch, pushed Henry onto his back, and wormed his way inside the blanket to kiss Henry from the top down, until they were both much too hot to need a blanket.

Eventually the sun's dip toward the horizon motivated Henry to stand up, clean up, and do something about their grumbling stomachs.

By late afternoon they're clean and dressed and fed. The plan is to walk down to the harbor for drinks on a deck before the sun disappears, and then dinner when they're hungry again.

Going out. In public. With Henry.

Ruben can't stop smiling about it.

"Almost done?" Henry starts putting jars back into the fridge.

"One more." Ruben spreads hot mustard on another slice of dark bread.

"Ever considered using a feed bag? It might be easier."

"Shut up. It's your fault for turning me on so much I keep having to do something about it."

"Do I look like I'm complaining? Eat up."

Ruben finishes making his sandwich and sits at the table to get out of Henry's way. He remembers the last time he sat there. *Curry dinner. First kiss. Martin. The asshat.*

"Hey Henry, how about telling me why you and Martin split up? I asked him, but he only said 'history' and to ask you."

"Jesus, Ruben."

"Yeah. I went straight for the jugular. Big surprise." He shrugs. "Well?"

Henry puts away the last of the sandwich things and leans back against the counter with his arms folded across his chest. Ruben thinks he's either deciding whether to tell or how to tell.

Henry touches one of the oven dials with a fingertip. "This is an oven." He raises his eyebrows to make sure Ruben is following along.

Ruben laughs. "Okay."

"You know how we sometimes looked at artifacts at the museum through the lens of everyday history?"

Ruben nods. "Yeah. Sure. What did the people who actually used this say to each other about it? What was going on around them as they used it? What did it mean to them in their everyday lives? All of that."

"Right. Top marks again for you. Those everyday histories we imagined at the museum were about things used by people who are long dead. But in our own lives, in the present day, we're surrounded by things we actively use. These things—our own things—have everyday histories too."

"Like that oven?"

"Like this oven. The first written reference to an oven is about one built of brick and tile in Alsace, France, in 1490."

"Um... okay."

"I could make that fact more interesting to us both if I knew some specifics about the lives of the people involved. And I'm willing to try to do that in order to bring history alive when I'm teaching at the museum. But I'm even more interested in *this* oven, because it means something to me personally. This oven has affected my life in ways that facts and stories about a long-ago oven aren't likely to."

"Okay. Interesting. So go on, then. What about this particular oven?"

With a hand on the stovetop, Henry says, "My uncle Scotty bought this stove new in 1958, a month after he and Aunt Janice married. They were living with her parents because they couldn't afford a place of their own, but Uncle Scotty wanted Aunt Janice to think of him when she cooked, to remember that he'd become part of her home, so he bought her this oven as a wedding present. She loved it. And him. And they never did move. They lived in that house and cooked with this stove until they were in their fifties.

"A couple of years before Aunt Janice and Uncle Scotty died, they gave the stove to their daughter, my cousin Jamie, as a housewarming gift when she graduated from high school and got her own apartment. I was nine then, and she babysat me most afternoons at her apartment, which was down the block from my school, in an ancient building that was horribly cold in the winter. We'd pull her little kitchen table right up next to the hot oven and play games while mouthwatering things baked."

"In this very oven."

"Yes. And she baked all the time to convince herself she could justify using the oven to heat the kitchen."

While Henry talked, a part of Ruben remembered how much he'd loved Henry's museum lectures. The stories Henry told about history, and the quiet, gentle, thoughtful way he told them, stopped his students' tapping fingers, doodling pens, and bored whispers every time. Ruben didn't know any other teacher who could do that. It was one of the first things that made him take a closer look at Henry.

"How did *you* get the stove?"

"Jamie gave it to me when she moved abroad."

Ruben stands to get a better view of the stove. "Is there more? Are there more stories about this stove?" he asks.

"Yes. Many. But that's enough."

"Was it enough for Martin?"

Henry laughs. "You've just listened to several paragraphs more about this oven than Martin ever cared to know."

Ruben thinks about how he was never jealous of guys who moved in on the women he was dating, but even the thought of Martin makes him want to punch Martin's face a few times. The feeling is so novel Ruben's not sure where to file it.

"Seriously?" says Ruben. "What was Martin's problem?"

Henry sits on a kitchen stool as though Ruben's question added fifty pounds to his shoulders.

"I'm not sure it *was* Martin's problem," Henry says.

"Whatever it was, sum it up. You're killing me here."

Henry rubs his hands across his face and says on a sigh, "I think the totality of me got in the way."

"Got in Martin's way, you mean?"

Henry shrugs. "He wanted something else."

"What kind of something else?"

Ruben watches Henry search for an answer. It takes a while. Ruben waits.

"I really *care* about my stove's story," Henry says. "I have a relationship with my stove that feels alive and real and important." He plucks a potholder from a hook. "Things, the normal, everyday things in my life, are like that for me. They're so full of the past and steeped with personal meaning that they're like... They're my family."

Ruben connects the dots. "Martin didn't care about your family."

A look crosses Henry's face that Ruben can't decipher. A haunted, almost feral look of panic. It comes and goes in a split second, but Ruben knows he didn't imagine it. It makes him sit on the stool next to Henry and make sure their thighs are touching.

Henry studies the potholder in his hands. "All around me are reminders of stories about normal, everyday people who are also brave, interesting, thoughtful, kind, and amazing. Because of these *things*, this everyday history, I have a connection to them that I can touch." He smooths the potholder flat against his thigh. "I find that incredibly... comforting."

Ruben takes the potholder and smooths it over his own thigh. "Henry... this is really interesting. Why didn't you ever talk about this kind of everyday history with us at the museum? We would have totally gotten into it."

Henry doesn't answer.

"Was it because of Martin's reaction to you and to your... family of things?"

Henry stands so abruptly his stool scrapes on the floor. He retreats to the living room, where he stands with the backs of his legs against the coffee table, facing the windows, his arms folded tight across his chest.

"Come on," says Ruben, following him. "Tell me what Martin said?"

"I forget."

When Ruben gets close enough, he sees the pain in Henry's eyes.

"Henry," Ruben says gently. "We both know you didn't forget."

Henry's pain seems too raw to be about a breakup that happened years ago, so Ruben backs off and reverts to a temporary diversion to give Henry a chance to compose himself.

"Martin's an asshat," Ruben says. "Obviously. I saw that right away."

Henry exhales a shaky laugh and takes a big breath.

"Go on, then. Tell me the entire history of the oven."

"No."

"Yes," says Ruben, putting his arms around Henry. "And afterward I'll tell you a little story about the radiator."

THE HISTORIAN
TELLING EVERYTHING

Why *haven't* I talked about everyday history with students at the museum?

I allowed Martin to shame me into believing the devotions embodied in my personal belongings are unworthy of being shared.

Okay. I get it now. I see the twisted conclusion my psyche drew to protect me. *The more meaningful it is, the harder it is to share.*

A sad conclusion that reverberates through my life.

Consider the case in point. Ruben stands in front of me with more concern on his face than I ever saw on Martin's. It's torturing me to send him off into someone else's arms, to accept that I must share him when I so want to keep him all to myself.

Staring into Ruben's intent eyes as my own threaten to brim and spill, I feel again the empty space of me reaching out to the real me standing beside it. That blankness yearns to close the gap and urges me toward a unity I imagine will heal me.

I need to turn toward myself. I have to tell someone. I have to heal.

Even if telling turns Ruben away sooner than I want.

NOT TELLING EVERYTHING

RUBEN TAKES HENRY'S hand and pulls him back to the stove.

"Well, if you won't tell me any more stove stories, tell me the history of this thing," Ruben says, plucking an apple corer from a kitchen shelf.

I'll give it a few more minutes. Then I'll sneak up on the main event—finding out whatever misguided asshat wisdom Martin foisted onto Henry.

Henry sighs.

"Come on, Henry. Humor me. I really do want to know."

"I suspect you know that's an apple corer." He pauses.

Ruben nods and says, "My grandmother has a few. I've never used one, though."

"Jamie bought it for me at a flea market. Here." He reaches for the device. "You clamp it to the edge of a counter or a table. Like this. The apple goes here, and you turn this crank, and it cores and peels an apple in no time flat."

"I want to try it."

Henry hands Ruben an apple from the bowl on the dining table and silently watches Ruben figure it out.

With his mouth full of peeled apple, Ruben says, "Okay. Go on."

"When I was nine, Jamie took care of me for a whole week. We got the apple corer on our way back from the hospital. I'd broken my big toe kicking Norville Hinkenblot after school."

Ruben laughs and puts a hand over his mouth. "With a name like that he probably needed a good kicking."

"Don't be mean. He was a big kid with big problems. Unfortunately for my big toe, he took his problems out on kids who were a lot smaller than he was."

"Like you?"

"Like a shy kid a couple of years younger than me. Lewis."

"So you stepped in."

"Yeah. Big toe leading. And got the crap knocked out of me. The broken toe, a black eye, asphalt burns on my elbows and knees, and a cracked rib. But it was enough. Lewis got away."

"Christ, Henry. I hope Norville got sent to the kiddie slammer."

"No. No one was there to see it happen but me and Lewis, and Lewis begged me not to say anything. He was terrified of bully backlash. But he ran toward the school, pretending he was going to get help, which was brilliant, because he knew it would make Norville leave. I don't think Norville would have stopped otherwise. When Norville was gone, I persuaded Lewis to go inside to see if anyone was in the school. He found a secretary."

"And you didn't tell the secretary who beat you up?"

"No. But not because Lewis asked me not to. Norville had been banned from the school grounds after sixth grade a few years earlier. The last thing he hissed at me before he ran off was that if I told anyone it was him, he'd do to Lewis what he'd just done to me."

"Hang on," says Ruben, standing up straighter. "You went after a fourteen-year-old when you were *nine* to save a seven-year-old?"

Henry shrugs. "Well… yes. I didn't think about it that way at the time. I just did it."

Ruben flashes again on a mental image of punching Martin in the face, but the vision has been amended to punching Martin and then Norville. He shakes his hands to rid himself of the sensation and focuses back on Henry.

"What happened next?"

"The secretary called Jamie to come get me, and when Jamie arrived, the secretary gave her a shrill earful, trying to convince Jamie to convince me to be more responsible and turn in whoever had beaten me up."

"Wow. Even back then you were a stoic, mysterious, self-disciplined bastard." Ruben shakes his head in half-mocking wonder. "Naturally neither of you cracked."

"No way. Jamie dug in her heels, her voice got really soft, and within about two well-crafted sentences, the teacher was showing us the door, her hands trembling. Seriously if you ever need a kick-ass cohort, Jamie's a good bet."

"Gratefully noted."

"On the bus back to Jamie's after the hospital, she spotted a flea market and decided we should stop so she could get me something to cheer me up." Henry laughs. "She insisted on carrying me off the bus and then deposited me onto a lawn chair someone was selling."

Ruben, engrossed, can picture it all so clearly. "So why the apple corer?"

"Jamie ran around the tables, choosing various things she thought I might like, convincing their owners to part with them long enough for her to jog them over to me for inspection." Henry smiles at the memory. "She wanted to make sure she got me something I really, *really* wanted. One of the things she brought over was this apple corer."

Ruben reaches for another apple and goes through the motions of peeling and coring, his movements faster than before.

"I remember the moment she put it into my hands," Henry says. "This bizarre-looking red contraption. I had no idea what it was. It looked incomprehensible and intriguing. I clutched it and refused to let go."

Ruben is grinning so hard his face is starting to hurt.

"That afternoon in her apartment, Jamie pulled the mattress from my bed into the kitchen so I could lie down and be comfortable and stay warm near the stove. We lay on the mattress and played Monopoly for hours and hours, making up ridiculous new rules to keep the game going. And she baked a gargantuan apple crisp, using apples she prepared with my new corer."

"She cored them? Not you?"

"Yes. I was only allowed to supervise. It hurt my cracked rib to turn the crank."

"An apple crisp baked in this oven," Ruben says. "You've told me another story about this oven after all."

Henry nods and pats the stovetop fondly. "It would take years to tell all my oven stories."

Not wanting to think about not having years to hear them, Ruben says, "Was it good? That apple crisp?"

"Oh *God*, yes. Even back then she was a remarkable baker. We ended up skipping dinner and just eating more apple crisp. We ate the entire thing before bedtime. It was absolute heaven. I woke up the next morning with a distended belly, a throbbing toe, and a race car imprint on my cheek from the Monopoly piece I'd slept on."

Picturing that little boy's courage, generosity, and pain, knowing that boy lives inside the grown-up Henry, makes Ruben beam at him, makes him grab him into a rough bear hug, makes him crave the mouth that told that story and tasted that apple crisp.

With a hand on the back of Henry's smooth head, Ruben kisses his way into Henry's memory.

IN THE BATHROOM to comb his hair and wash a spot of mustard off his sleeve, Ruben glares at himself in the mirror and struggles to choose the feeling he wants instead of the feeling he has.

Shit. Shit. Shit.

I'm not ready to fall in love.

It's too early.

I'm too young.

There are too many men I haven't yet met.

I can't.

I won't.

TELLING EVERYTHING

M Y A N X I E T I E S C O M B I N E with the mustard on Ruben's sleeve to pull up the memory of a conversation I once had with Jamie in a park in Paris.

The sandwiches Jamie had brought to our picnic were so delicious they made me dizzy. Everything she made seemed designed for my taste buds alone. Lying in the sun-warmed grass with my arms spread, I chewed the last bite of the last sandwich, lingering over the taste, and sighed.

Jamie entertained me with mustard lore.

Maybe, Jamie told me, the origin of the word mustard goes back to the Latin word *mustum*—new wine—because monks mixed new wine with ground mustard seeds to make a condiment.

One etymological legend she regaled me with involved a duke in Dijon and a dubious interpretation of the phrase *moult me tarde* to mean "I am impatient."

While Ruben's in the bathroom, I pace.

Missing the comfort of his questions.

The quirk of his interested smile.

Impatient for new wine.

NOT TELLING EVERYTHING

WHILE HENRY'S IN the bathroom brushing his teeth, Ruben struts around the living room, preening, pleased with himself for understanding Henry in a way Martin didn't.

Martin needs to get the fuck out of my head.

He shakes himself and continues his search for a family photo, which he's been trying to find since his midday ramble around the living room in the blue pajamas. Except for the stories Henry told about the oven, he's never said a word about his family, and now Ruben's dying of curiosity.

Where did Henry come from? Who created him?

Finally on the top shelf of the built-in bookcase in the wall opposite the living room windows, Ruben finds a small, framed photo tucked half behind a stack of books about the Celts. He takes the photo to the desk, sits down, turns on the desk light, and leans forward to take a closer look.

An older couple—mom and dad? grandparents?—and three kids. There's Henry for sure, maybe about seven years old, the youngest of the children, looking sweet and cute and so serious in his suit and tie.

When Henry comes out of the bathroom, Ruben walks the photo to him and says, "It was challenging, but I found it. I want to know the everyday history of *this.*"

When Henry sees what Ruben's holding, he pales, yanks the photo from Ruben's hand, and bolts from the room. Ruben stands stunned for a moment, then follows Henry into the bedroom. By the time he arrives, the photo has disappeared.

"You must know there's absolutely no way I'm going to let this go," Ruben says.

But Henry looks so distraught Ruben reconsiders. He opens his mouth to take back what he's said, but Henry surprises Ruben by sitting on the edge of the bed and nodding his head, his hands clenching and unclenching in his lap.

Ruben waits.

"Ruben, what's... what's the worst thing that's ever happened to you?"

THE HISTORIAN
TELLING EVERYTHING

Now is the time. *Right now.* I'm determined to find out what will happen if I tell someone.

Maybe Ruben will stick around until I'm done. It's a good sign that he was eager enough to know about my family to find that photo, which I should've gotten rid of—except it's the only picture I have of myself at that age.

Okay. I'll tell. If it's too much, if it turns Ruben off, well... That'll only make it easier for us to go our separate ways.

The only downside is getting through it.

As I open my mouth, it occurs to me to wonder if my worst thing, the secret emptiness at the center of me, is not so bad after all. Maybe I've made more of it than was necessary all these years.

How do other people deal with their worst things?

How does Ruben deal with his worst thing?

NOT TELLING EVERYTHING

HENRY DOESN'T SEEM able to sit still on the bed. He stands and heads back to the living room, pacing and panting a little, like a caged animal.

"Henry, look. I'm sorry I asked you about the photo. Whatever it means to you is obviously important. Of course you don't need to talk about it, but... I want to help."

Henry stops in the middle of the living room and makes an obvious effort to calm himself. In a tight, careful voice, he says, "Would you mind answering my question first? Please."

"Okay, okay. Just... give me a minute." Ruben sits on the couch and casts back for awful times. They're not hard to find. *But what's the* worst *thing?*

Henry paces two steps and turns.

"I'll tell you my worst thing," Ruben says. "But I'm going to keep it short and I don't want to discuss it afterward. I'm only telling you because it appears to be a requirement for you to tell me what's upsetting you so much."

Henry nods to confirm the condition.

"Okay. I have two sisters, Luisa and Marie. They're ten and twelve years older than me. When I was ten, Marie went missing for five days. The police tracked her down by following a trail that led to a defunct job placement center where she'd been instructed to go by a man in a mall who'd posed as a guidance counselor." Ruben swallows and hesitates. "By the time she was found, she hadn't been given food for five days and she'd been repeatedly beaten and raped."

"Oh my God," Henry says on an exhale.

"Obviously that was devastating enough. But the sick fuck did it all to a continuous replay of—and I beg you not to laugh, because there's nothing funny to me about this—*The Beach Boys' Christmas Album*. It was March."

"That is... That's grotesque. Was she...?" Henry is silent for a moment and seems to rethink his question. "How does she manage to get through the holiday season?"

Ruben smiles wryly. "That was nine years ago. For the first five years after it happened, Marie didn't do Christmas. At all. She and one or more of us in the family would take off with her during the holiday season to somewhere in the world where they don't celebrate Christmas... and also where there's no beach."

"Extremely sad, that last bit."

"No shit. But then Marie got sick of it and dug into therapy with a vengeance. She became a therapist. Now she works with abused kids."

Henry stops fidgeting and stares at Ruben like that's important news. "Really?"

Ruben nods.

After a bit Henry says, "I can guess, but I'd like to know. Why is that your worst thing?"

Ruben peers up at Henry sternly. "I told you I wasn't going to discuss it, Henry. And what are we doing here?"

Henry lifts his shoulders. "Discussing."

Ruben sighs. He considers and then says, "Marie doesn't mother me. Our mom has that role amply covered. Marie is my champion. She molded me, for lack of a better word. I think the way she treated me when I was growing up led me to develop confidence, along with compassion for people who are attracted to me. I became who I am in large part because Marie very gently but very firmly showed me how to make the most of myself without getting too big a head about it. Those are her words."

Ruben closes his eyes. "When Marie went missing, I completely freaked out. My family was trying so hard to handle what was happening to Marie, and I quickly became a second burden. I just... I *could not* imagine my life without Marie, but I felt like I was being forced to. Everyone tried to keep the sordid details from me, but I was so desperate for Marie to be found and to be okay— and I'd been an accomplished eavesdropper for a long time—that I found out anyway. That's when I freaked."

"Understandable."

"After she was found, my parents put a couple of my aunts on Ruben duty for a few weeks so Mom and Dad and Luisa could focus on Marie. I wasn't allowed to see her during that time, and rightly so. I've since seen photos of her in those first weeks after she was found, and seeing her in that state would have sent me into hysterics.

"When she finally did come home, a few weeks after they found her, she was wasted physically and mentally and just... horribly different. Seeing her again made me so overcome with gratefulness that I refused to leave her side—literally and absolutely. I even went in with her when she had doctor appointments. They tried to keep me out, but if they forced me, I threw savage, awful fits. So Marie and I both insisted we stay together. My parents even officially pulled me out of school for a while.

"At first I felt like I needed to be near Marie so I could suck life itself back into me after almost losing her, but as I gradually relaxed and it filtered through my constant panic that she was really back, I shifted to helping her..." He stops because he's weary of reliving it.

"She's... she's okay now?"

"Yeah. She is. She's really okay. She's amazing. I've always wished you two could meet. You'd love each other. You remind me of her."

"That's... Thank you. Um... what happened to the guy who did it?"

"Found, convicted, and committed suicide in prison. Turned out he was the victim of a lot of childhood abuse. That was partly what motivated Marie to become a therapist and help kids the way she does."

Ruben notices that Henry's breathing has slowed. "Okay. I'm done. Your turn."

Henry sits next to Ruben on the couch. "That must have been really hard to live through. For all of you. Thank you for telling me. I needed... It helped."

"All right. Good. Now please, Henry."

Henry looks down at his restless hands. Ruben shifts so he can cover them with his own.

"To finally answer the question you asked earlier today... the main reason Martin and I broke up was..." Henry closes his mouth then opens it to say more, but nothing comes out. He pulls his pale hands away from Ruben and hugs himself, runs his hands over his head. He's obviously trying hard to say something. Finally he turns to look at Ruben, his face full of misery.

It's driving Ruben nuts not being able to make it better. "Just... begin," he says. "Say *something*, even if it's wrong."

Henry nods, opens his mouth, and speaks in a rush. "Martin and I broke up because I wouldn't tell him my worst thing." Henry's huge eyes fix onto Ruben's. "I trusted him. I thought we were together for the long haul, but one day he asked me what the worst thing was that had ever happened to me and... and I refused to tell him. That was the beginning of the end for us."

"Why wouldn't you tell him?"

Henry gets up again to pace. "Fuck, Ruben. Most days I can't even tell *myself* my worst thing. I've never told anyone. Also I didn't want to tell him because he often complained about my 'boring stories.'"

"Witless, worthless asshat," Ruben mutters under his breath.

Henry wrings his hands. Ruben can't remember ever seeing anyone do that except as a joke.

"Henry, you're actually wringing your hands. Should I call a doctor? Get you a sedative? Spit. It. Out."

"My obsession with history is a substitute for my inability to deal with my worst thing."

"Martin's words. Not yours," Ruben guesses.

"Yes."

"But you're going to tell me your worst thing now. Why?" Ruben tries not to be flattered.

Henry opens his mouth and closes his eyes. "That's not important," he says after a long moment and shakes his head. Ruben realizes he's right.

"So what *is* important?" Ruben asks.

Henry sits back down on the couch, appears to try to pull himself together, tries to talk, and fails again. His forehead is strained and furrowed. Then he stops breathing altogether. "I can't," he says in a breathless, tight whisper. His expressive eyes fill, and he bows his head. "I'm sorry."

Ruben kneels on the floor and lifts Henry's chin until he can look into Henry's agonized eyes. "Listen, Henry." Ruben's mind churns as he tries to come up with a solution. "Can you... can you think of another way to tell me. Tell me without having to actually say it."

Henry studies Ruben's face intently and takes an infinitely small breath.

"Desk," Henry whispers. "Bottom drawer."

"Got it," says Ruben. He lunges to the desk and jerks on the drawer handle to pull it open, but it doesn't budge. "It's locked. Key?"

"Um... shit." The hand wringing starts again. "Bedroom closet. Black boots."

Ruben runs to fetch the key, unlocks the drawer, and looks over at Henry, who waves a hand and manages only to say, "Under." Ruben roots inside the drawer and excavates a slim manila envelope from the very bottom of the stack of files.

Henry nods. "Open it."

"Only if you take a big breath."

Henry complies, eyes bulging, legs jumping with anxiety.

The single sheet of paper Ruben pulls from the envelope is Henry's birth certificate. Henry was born in a town in Massachusetts Ruben has never heard of. When he sees Henry's birth date, Ruben can't keep himself from automatically doing the math. *Not ten years older than me, but fourteen.* In the blank after "Father's Name" is the typed word "Unknown." Likewise, after "Mother's Name."

"Jesus, Henry," says Ruben. "So who's the family in the photo?"

"Foster family number four."

"And Uncle Scotty and Aunt Janice and Jamie?"

"Foster family six." Six foster homes by the age of eleven.

"Shit. It must have been hell to have started your life that way."

As soon as the words are out of Ruben's mouth, he sees that they were somehow the wrong thing to say. From one moment to the next, Henry's eyes turn wild and his face twists with pain. He blinks twice and begins to cry in earnest.

Ruben tosses the birth certificate onto the floor and speed crawls across the carpet to wrap Henry in his arms.

"Sorry, sorry, sorry," Henry gasps over and over. The words judder through his chattering teeth between sobs. Ruben hugs him harder. He presses Henry's head against his shoulder with one hand and wraps the other arm around Henry's waist. *Jesus.* Ruben's heart swells in sympathy as Henry shows no signs of relaxing.

"Henry...," Ruben says.

"I'm sorry."

"Stop saying you're sorry and tell me what I can do to help you."

"I didn't..."

Ruben wraps an arm around Henry's shoulder and tries to pull more of him closer.

"I didn't think it would be this hard to tell." Henry's voice is so low Ruben almost doesn't hear.

"Well, you've said it now. So try to relax." He leans back to brush the wetness from Henry's cheeks and kisses his forehead.

"No," Henry says fiercely and shakes even harder.

Desperate, Ruben topples them sideways so they're lying with Henry's back against the back of the couch. He squeezes his arms around Henry, then wraps his legs around him too. As he does so, he realizes that his impulse is to hold Henry tight to help him find the broken pieces and put himself back together.

From three inches away, Ruben studies Henry's wracked face and wipes away more tears with a tissue he finally thought to dig out of his jeans pocket. "What do you mean, 'No'?"

"That... wasn't..." Ruben can't bear to watch the war of pain and determination on Henry's face, so he pulls Henry's head onto his chest. Henry's hands, folded between them, ball into tight fists. Henry swallows hard, and Ruben feels Henry's mouth open against his collarbone.

It's only because Ruben stops breathing that he hears Henry's whispered words.

"That wasn't the worst thing."

Inside the cocoon Ruben's made for them, Henry begins to tell his worst thing.

Though his words are few, it takes Henry a long time to get them all out. He keeps losing his voice in the apparent effort of forming words and pushing them past the panic.

TELLING EVERYTHING

I WAS FOUND in the early hours of an unusually cold July morning.
In the men's washroom at a truck stop in the middle of nowhere.
In a garbage can.
Naked. Blue with cold. Nearly dead.
I was less than a week old.

NOT TELLING EVERYTHING

THE WORDS FALL like icicles into Ruben's heart. They accumulate and reverberate and magnify inside his head.

Ruben clamps his jaw closed to lock his rage inside. There's no one to rage against.

Only Henry, spent, beaten, and shivering.

Ruben drags the blanket from the back of the couch and tents it to cover them. It creates a dark, secret, quiet space that slowly seems to warm and calm Henry enough to drop him into a damp, depleted sleep.

Henry feels small in Ruben's arms—huddled and seeking warmth and safety even as he sleeps.

With Henry's surrender into sleep, Ruben allows anger and sadness to rise up. He directs the anger at Martin and whoever was responsible for Henry's unbearable beginning. The sadness is for Henry's solitary vigil over his painful history through all the years and all the losses.

Then, because there's no one there to hit, Ruben cries too.

He cries because he suspects Henry only told him because he knows Ruben is leaving.

He cries because he can't protect Henry from the pain.

He falls asleep amid a tumble of tangled implications that twist and spin.

In his dreams Ruben holds Henry tight to steady himself.

THE HISTORIAN
TELLING EVERYTHING

I LAND SAFELY, falling into the heart of the seed, disappearing into the shadow of myself.

Becoming one.

My breaths remain long and slow, as though I'm still asleep. But I'm not.

I blink inside the tight darkness. Nourished and safe.

The next time I wake, I recognize Ruben's body wrapping me from head to toe, holding me tight within his arms and legs under the heavy blanket.

The seed pod of him makes me smile with gratitude into his neck, which wakes him up.

He shifts and sighs without releasing me, pulls me against him even more tightly, and kisses the top of my head, which is tucked under his chin.

I didn't think it was possible to be held more tightly. Or more carefully.

It was.

Where will I find the strength to let this man go?

NOT TELLING EVERYTHING

While Henry's in the bathroom, washing his face, Ruben sits at the dining table and calls his parents.

"Hey, Mom. Is there enough food for me to come for Sunday lunch tomorrow?"

"Ruben. Of course, kiddo. Shall I send Dad to pick you up at the station?"

"No. I've been in town already since Friday."

"Aha. And you're staying…"

"Yes, Mom, I'm staying with someone." He laughs. "We met in Boston before I went away to school." Ruben notes his careful avoidance of gender-necessary language and shakes his head at himself. *Yeah. It's probably time to come out to my family.*

His mom clears her throat. "Are you…?"

"No. It's not serious."

"Well, you could still invite her to join us for Sunday lunch."

"Okay. Thanks. I'll ask. Could we eat a little later than usual, though?"

"One o'clock?"

"Perfect."

"We'll see you tomorrow. I love you."

"Love you too, Mom."

When they stop at a crosswalk on the way down to the harbor, Henry turns to Ruben and says, "Thank you."

"For what?"

"I know you didn't sign up for that kind of intensity when you accepted my invitation to spend the weekend with me. But... it meant a lot to me. You were perfect—perfectly what I needed."

"You're welcome." Ruben mentally shakes his head to rid himself of Martin's presence, as the thought that he did in one day what Martin couldn't do in years threatens to trigger a bout of smugness.

The sidewalk skirts the blocks-long row of huge, old maple trees that begin outside Henry's apartment building. Their red orange leaves flicker in the light of the streetlamps.

"Are you okay?" Ruben looks away from the trees to glance at Henry, who walks with his head bowed and his hands deep in his coat pockets.

Henry nods. "Yes, but... I need to talk to you about something else."

"Me too."

They look at each other. "Is it...? Is there a chance it's the same thing?" Henry asks.

"Could be," Ruben says cautiously.

"I guess it would make things easier if it were." Henry says. "Well, let's find out." He clears his throat. "I'll go first."

Ruben nods, grateful and a little scared.

"I do want more," Henry says, "or at least the possibility of more. With... someone. I see how unrealistic it is to ask you for that possibility. You're just starting out, in so many ways. Of course I want... I want you to be free to find your own way. But I need to move on."

"You made this decision before you told me your worst thing, didn't you?"

Henry nods.

Ruben focuses on nothing in the distance, glad for the long stretches of dim dusk between streetlamps. He feels overtaxed, as if his annual quota of emoting has been far surpassed. *This is exactly what I don't want—the emotional intensity of a relationship, especially the obvious complexity of the package deal of Henry.* He remembers that he wants to keep things simple. Parting with Henry is good for them both.

"If you knew you were going to end it, you told me your worst thing because..."

"Because I don't want to make the same mistake I made with Martin, the mistake of not sharing myself with whoever I'm with. I'll admit that I used you for practice. Even if I made an utter ass of myself, the stakes weren't as high as they will be the next time I tell someone. If you had—" Henry huffs out a breath that fogs the air in front of his face. "If you had rejected me, shaken your head and left, it would have hurt, but I would have been able to let it go."

"I would only be leaving a little sooner than planned."

"Yes. Also, to confess everything, I was in danger of resenting you for… for practicing sex with me and being so spectacular at it and… and then taking your skills on the road, as it were." He waves a hand as if to dismiss that thought. "So I decided to practice something with you too. I wasn't sure I'd be able to, but your persistence and the fact that you wanted to hear it, made it possible."

Ruben nods. "A fair trade, then?"

"That was the idea."

"Great," says Ruben with cheerful bravado he doesn't feel. "Thanks for the clarity. Going cold turkey after this weekend with you will be hell, but it seems like the sensible thing to do." He stops walking and peers at Henry. "Can we be done with this part now? Is there anything else you need to say?"

"No," says Henry with a disarming smile. "But it's nice of you to offer. I'm fine. Do you need to debrief after ushering me so skillfully through my meltdown?"

"Nope. It's all good." Eager to get past the awkward ache and back to the fun, Ruben asks, "Is there decent food at this place we're headed to?"

"God, I hope so. I'm starving. Those sandwiches seem like last year."

As they near the harbor, Ruben hears the lilt of a live band—something Irish—coming through the open doors of the restaurant Henry's steering them toward. They bypass the door and head around back, where a crowd spills out onto a wide deck facing the water, and people in coats and hats sit and stand around the outside tables. The crush and babble and laughter of a Saturday-night hot spot settles over Ruben like a reunion with his normal life. His shoulders relax and his spine straightens.

Henry turns toward Ruben as they enter the crowd. The white lights strung above their heads reflect brightly in Henry's glasses as he nods for Ruben to follow him.

Ruben holds the collar of Henry's coat, the better to keep track of him, and says, too softly for Henry to hear, "I'm going to miss you."

TELLING EVERYTHING

I'VE NEVER BEEN to this pub before. I guess I've been at work or at home or on business trips, my nose flat against the grindstone since I moved to this part of town.

The lights reflected on the swaying water and the still, cool air feel like the perfect antidote, reward, and prescription to lighten the heaviness of the past few hours.

By a fluke we nab a prime table at the far back corner of the deck, right up against the pub. Ruben flops into the chair next to me. We sit with our backs against the wall so we can survey the scene. I hunch into my thick wool coat and muffler and my hat with the dorky earflaps, glad to be warm again.

Way down below the noise of music and voices, I feel my heartbeats.

A countdown ticking inside my chest.

Perhaps because we're in a social situation, or in public, or doing something other than being intense and alone together—or all of the above—Ruben's sparkling energy seems extravagant. He's all exuberance and smiles and charm as he launches into a funny story about a tryst that he botched with a guy at a bar a few weeks earlier. His eyes flash, his hands fly, and his face and body act out all the parts, flinging signs of life into the air around us… and causing men and women to steal glances at him above their glasses of wine and beer.

Ruben seems so confident in his skin, even with his newly revised sexuality. He sees me notice he's being checked out, but only winks at me and goes on telling his story.

That guy over there with the ponytail needs to close his mouth soon, or bugs will get in. It's comical, and I can't help but laugh out loud.

"What?" Ruben says with a wide grin, a hand paused aloft in midsentence.

"I'm sorry. I don't mean to interrupt, but your potent pheromones are driving the locals into a hot-blooded tizzy. For example…" I nod toward the guy with the ponytail.

Sure enough, Bug Mouth takes Ruben's glance as an invitation and saunters over. "Hi there," he says to Ruben with a bright grin.

"Hi," Ruben says, his smile open and warm.

"This seat taken?" the man asks. He rests a hand on the back of the chair next to Ruben, and his face is hopeful behind his attempt at coolness.

"Thanks for the thought," Ruben says with what appears to be genuine gratitude, "but not tonight." The man stares awhile longer. He seems unwilling to take no for an answer until Ruben lifts his feet onto the empty chair. Then the guy nods and walks away.

With a shake of his head, Ruben says, "It's still so new it takes me by surprise."

"What are you talking about?"

"You flipped my switch, Henry. It's only in the past few months that I've been getting hit on by men too." Ruben scoots closer to Henry. "It's pretty fun, actually."

The pub's menu is extensive, for which I'm grateful, because pretending to examine it gives me plenty of time to hide my reaction to the specter of Ruben saying, "Yes, please!" to a long line of eager men he considers "pretty fun, actually."

Ruben is approached again during the course of the evening, by two women and three more men—which seems like overkill. He's always polite but firmly uninterested. It's obvious he's had lots of practice at turning people away. I'm impressed by his respect for their courage.

Even so, every time he says "Not tonight," my hands clench under the table.

"Not tonight" means "Maybe another night," doesn't it?

Not my problem. Not my problem. Not my problem.

Through dinner and beyond—and in spite of the interruptions—we talk like we never have before. For the first time since we met, we're not distracted by what he wants and I won't let him have, or what we want to do with each other's bodies, or intense negotiations around emotional confessions. I'm by turns gladdened and saddened to discover that talking with Ruben is easy and enjoyable, that we have a lot to say to each other, and that all of it is interesting.

I'm delighted to make this discovery and sorry to make it so late.

He tells me things about his internship year that surprise me so much I only take them in with difficulty. I'm shocked by the vision of myself through his eyes. If my struggle to accept what he says didn't feel so pathetic, I might be flattered.

After dinner, when the waiter removes our empty plates, Ruben winds up his story and heads to the bathroom, and I sit back in a stupor. My unfocused gaze captures the light at play on the moving water of the harbor. I let the happy sounds of the crowd wash over me and try to mesh my view of myself with Ruben's view of me.

When a man approaches, I look over to Ruben to see how he'll handle yet another proposition. Then I remember he's gone to the bathroom. The man walks up to my side of the table and smiles down at me.

Maybe Ruben's right. Maybe I'm not invisible after all.

NOT TELLING EVERYTHING

Ruben is propositioned twice before the waiter delivers their drinks.

He usually enjoys the entertainment value of a parade of propositions coming his way, and he often says yes. But tonight's parade is over the top. Either he and Henry have stumbled into a freaky epicenter of extrabold folk, or their weekend of sexuality and intense emotion has amped up Ruben's natural magnetism to all-new levels. Not necessarily a bad thing, he realizes with a mental snicker and imagines the fun of being on campus with that level of pull. With luck his amped-up vibe will linger through next weekend.

"Okay. Fess up. How normal is this for you?" asks Henry after the waiter takes their orders. "This pageant of come-ons."

Ruben considers and shrugs. "Maybe double normal."

"Fascinating."

"Yeah. I must be humming or something."

"You might want to consider a body bag for getting home safely."

Ruben laughs. "I'm used to it. It's always been like this—though not quite *this* intense—ever since I was a kid."

"God. I would hate it."

Ruben gazes at Henry for a long moment. "Yeah. I can see that about you." He leans back in his chair and asks, "Are you ever hit on?"

"No. Or not unless I really want to be. I seem able to turn it on and off. I sometimes turn it on, like if I go to a gay bar and don't want to leave alone."

Ruben narrows his eyes and tries to imagine Henry trolling in a gay bar, which makes him feel cross. He folds his arms and forces himself stop thinking about it.

"I don't seem to show up on gaydar," Henry says. "That's why I was so surprised when you developed a crush on me. It was the first time ever, except for when I was in Europe, that anyone seemed to notice my gayness."

"Why was Europe different?"

Henry shakes his head. "I'm not sure. I was far away from where I'd grown up. I felt… freer, I suppose. So I left the switch on. It was nice. Then by the time I came back to Boston, I was so focused on my career I guess I slipped back into my old habit of making sure it's off."

"Why did the switch get turned off in the first place?"

"Oh, well. Harassment and terror starting at the age of seven."

"Seven!"

"What can I say? I knew what I knew."

"You flipped the switch off way back then?"

"Yes. And I got really good at keeping it off." Henry sees Ruben assessing him. "What?"

Henry's smile is out tonight, wide enough to crinkle the edges of his bright eyes and expose his crooked bottom teeth. The dark fabric of the goofy hat with the ear flaps frames and draws attention to his creamy skin and the pink flush on his cheeks. He exudes friendliness and kindness. "You know, I would hit on you if I saw you sitting here," he says.

"You certainly would *not*." Henry shifts in his chair, disbelief twisting his face.

"Yeah. Actually I think I would."

"Stop looking at me like that," Henry says.

"Like what? Like I find you hot?"

Henry nods.

Ruben doesn't stop.

"Want to hear more about my internship?" asks Ruben. "It was quite exciting. You'll like it."

"Sure. But only if you stop looking at me like that, because if you don't, I'm going to have to jump you right here. And I'm famished so I was kind of hoping to have some dinner first."

Ruben slides a hand onto Henry's thigh underneath the table. Henry stills it and laces their fingers together to stop Ruben's hand from sliding between his thighs.

"Tell me the story," Henry says.

"Hmm… Okay. Right away I noticed your crooked teeth." Henry presses his lips together. "And what I thought of as your mousy look—bald head, glasses, ears sticking out. Well, I wrote you off as no competition." Ruben laughs at the horrified expression on Henry's face. "Stop it, Henry," he says. "You already know where this story is headed."

"Yeah. But you've just described me as I see myself, so I'm curious to see how the story gets from there to here." Henry squeezes Ruben's hand under the table.

"It might be time to update your mirror."

"We'll see about that."

"Henry." Ruben bumps his shoulder against Henry's and looks at him for a long moment. "There are lots of ways to be attractive. I think you know by now how your particular brand of attractiveness really works for me."

Henry nods, and his face relaxes.

"Now," Ruben says, "I can give this tale structure, because in February I began to catalog the crush's progression and named the months according to my shifting view of you—including naming the months that had already passed."

"You have *got* to be kidding me."

Ruben cackles and shakes his head. *This is going to be so much fun.*

Ruben says, "September was The Month of Mousy Invisibility."

Henry snorts.

"After my initial assessment, I didn't notice you at all. I mean, of course I paid attention to your lectures, but you seemed sort of... I don't know... shy and... like it didn't matter to you whether we noticed *you* or not, as long as we interacted with museum patrons with respect and paid attention to the slides and artifacts and theories and whatever else you showed us and told us about."

Henry shrugs as if to say, "True. And?" which makes Ruben laugh with proud happiness that he assessed Henry so correctly way back then.

"A few weeks into the internship, I started to notice how present you were. Like..." Ruben closes his eyes. "You seemed so enamored of what you were teaching us, like you were literally in love with the information. And learning from you *felt* good. *I* felt good. You made things—concepts, objects, history itself—come alive as we saw them through your eyes and your mind and your words. At some point it crossed my mind to wonder what *I* might look like to you... through your eyes."

"What month was that? Still September?"

"No. It was right after I turned eighteen in October. The Month of Information Infatuation."

"That's ridiculous," Henry says, but he grins.

"I began to notice more about the way you teach. I didn't intend to. I didn't try to. I just did. Like, whenever you'd tell us something especially important, your body would do the opposite of what mine usually does in the same circumstances. You'd go completely still, and your voice would soften and slow down. The entire class would also become still and start paying even more attention to you. It made me wonder if you were doing it on purpose, commanding our attention like that."

Ruben looks at Henry for an answer, and Henry says, "Sorry. Superspecial teacher secret." He twists an imaginary key against his lips, and Ruben laughs.

"Well, as with so many discoveries about you last year, October's observations snowballed. Noticing more about your teaching style made me pay attention even more. It was like you were a... a treasure chest, but I only found the treasures if I paid very close attention. And the more I looked, the more I discovered."

"Meanwhile," says Henry.

"Meanwhile what?"

"During the first week of your internship, I recognized you as being the class crush, based on how your classmates treated you. I assured myself you weren't going to disrupt the class, then..."

"...then you focused on teaching us about the museum and history and hardly noticed me at all. Right?"

"Exactly right."

"I don't believe you."

The blue of Henry's eyes sparkles. "Keep telling your story."

Ruben laughs. "Okay. In November, I became aware of you as being *much* more interesting than I'd yet given you credit for."

"Do I even want to know about this?"

"You *need* to know, Henry."

Henry looks away from Ruben and leans back in his chair. The waiter shows up to deliver their dinners and to see if they need anything else. He winks at Ruben, which makes Henry snort.

They eat in silence for a few hungry minutes, until Ruben puts down his fork and grins at Henry.

Henry rolls his eyes and waves a hand. "Carry on, then."

"Okay. In September and October, I monitored you in a casual way, because it was kind of fun and a bit interesting. But in November, my idle interest shifted toward the slow burn of a crush. November was The Month of Nice-Guy Behavior. Everyone treated you with such respect. When I tried to figure out why, I learned even more about you. For example you *never* interrupted anyone, even when they blathered on *endlessly*. God. Long after I wanted to shake them to get them to *shut the fuck up*, you were still nodding and really listening. After a while the blatherer would wind down and let out this huge, deep sigh and look at you like you'd given them a pot of gold. You'd smile and say something like, 'Is there anything else?' And they'd swoon toward you, like you were the first person *ever* to care about what they had to say and then—bonus!—to ask if they had anything *else* to say. Those people treated you with... reverence. I never saw any of those people babble at you again, though they sometimes did with others. It's like... it's like your attention made them converse in a normal way. I was fascinated."

Henry blinks at Ruben.

Ruben watches Henry for a moment and then barks a laugh. "You have no idea that you do that, do you?" Ruben sees from Henry's face that it's true. "Well, I think you're extraordinary and I have a lot more to tell."

Henry puts his fork down, wipes his mouth with his napkin, leans back, and grips the arms of his chair. "Um..."

"Yeah. Hang on, Henry. You may be in for a few more shocks."

His eyes dark and skeptical, Henry looks like he wants to change the subject.

"You know there's no stopping me. Right?"

Henry lifts his wine glass to Ruben and sighs. "True. You're a force of nature."

"That's me. And—due to your insistence that I not use my fake ID—I return your toast with my wineglass of cranberry juice."

"Carry on, then."

"In November I still had you filed away as 'unremarkable-looking' and 'mousy,' but the behavioral treasures I collected about you sort of... um... accumulated, and made me feel... more and more uncomfortable. And that made me look at you again... look at your body."

Henry frowns and looks away.

"Don't presume, Henry. Hear me out." Ruben waits until Henry looks at him again.

"In December," Ruben says, "I died. December was The Month of Hands, and it outright killed me. That was the first in a long string of difficult months." Ruben puts down his fork and watches Henry eat for a few minutes. "Your hands... They were the first thing about your body I zeroed in on. Since I'd never considered being gay, I think the part of me that was already attracted to you sexually chose to zoom in on your hands because that felt less alarming to my psyche than fixating on other parts of you. Like your chest or your shoulders or... your *ass*." Ruben closes his eyes and moans. "Christ. I hadn't grown the balls to do that yet."

Henry narrows his gaze at his own hands as they hold his knife and fork. His skeptical expression makes Ruben soften his voice.

"Your hands and wrists initially seemed too skinny, but in early December, they started looking different to me. I stopped thinking *skinny* and started waxing poetic, for God's sake... to my own distress. Your hands became *slim, lovely, long-fingered, delicate*. I'd roll my eyes at myself, at the way I carried on. And you wear these cool bracelets—" Ruben stops talking to play with the leather bracelets on Henry's wrist for a moment. "—which draw attention to your hands."

Henry puts down his cutlery and unclasps one of the bracelets—a simple one made of thin strips of leather braided together. He hands it to Ruben, who doesn't understand at first.

"Take it," Henry says. "If you want it."

Ruben reaches for it slowly, not wanting to assume. "Seriously? To keep?"

"Sure."

"Thanks, Henry. Thank you." Ruben fastens the clasp and then fiddles with the bracelet, twisting it around his wrist. He beams a bright grin of gratitude at Henry.

Henry nods and says, "Go on with your story."

"Yeah." Ruben gathers his thoughts and has to take his hand away from the bracelet to find his focus. "Okay. For a couple of weeks, I was besotted with your hands to the point that I *could not* take my eyes off them. You use your hands so sparingly. Actually all your movements are spare, as if you don't want to draw attention to yourself or... as if you have a strict allowance of movements per day, and it's never quite enough, so you always have to be frugal. The minimal movements you made with your hands were—are—artistic somehow, like a dance. But then after a while, unbearably... they were like a seductive dance." Ruben shifts in his chair.

"That—my physical reaction to being mesmerized by your hands—was my first conscious awareness of my sexual attraction. It took me totally by surprise because until then, I swear, it hadn't occurred to me to be into men. For years

I'd been so focused on girls, on women, on locating a holy grail of womanhood or a sexual experience with a woman that would finally satisfy me—that I missed the mark entirely."

"Doh!"

Ruben slaps his own forehead. "*Men*. Of course."

"You adapted to that revelation fairly easily, though. Didn't you?"

"No. No. I really didn't. Not at first. I was watching your hands one day in class, zoning out, trying not to squirm, and... there it was, this information about myself that shocked me. Your hands turned me on. It confused me. I tried to reject it. Then, against my will, I began imagining what your beautiful hands might do to me." Ruben relaces his fingers with Henry's under the table and remembers some of the things Henry's beautiful hands *did* do to him.

Henry lifts his eyebrows and runs his fingernails lightly across Ruben's open palm. "Yeah," says Ruben softly. He recalls Henry doing that the night before on other parts of his body, driving him batty with need.

"Go on," says Henry with a leer.

Ruben swallows and keeps his eyes on Henry's. "Sitting in a chair in your class, elbow to elbow with my classmates, trying to be a good student, I'd have to deal with a sudden intrusive image of your palm flat and warm on my chest or my face, or... or what it might be like to hold your hand." Ruben gives Henry's hand a hard squeeze. "At the same time, I resisted imagining other, more sexual things your hands might do to me. Anyhow, the truth is... my resistance didn't last very long."

"No shit," says Henry. "Mid-December was when you aimed your first suggestive smirk my way. Dear God. I almost passed out from the surprise of it. I've never been so grateful for the holiday break."

"Er. What? I didn't think you noticed me noticing you that early."

"Oh, but I did."

Ruben tries to update his memories with that new information, but it doesn't compute.

"What did you do over the break?" asks Henry, derailing Ruben's attempts at revision.

"Let's see. I gave myself a series of stern lectures, commanding myself to get over you. But then..."

"Yeah. Then came January." Henry rubs a hand over his head and blows out an annoyed sigh.

"January," Ruben says. He stares at the table, his voice a whisper. "The Month of Eyes."

"Six long months to go," Henry murmurs.

Ruben's head snaps up. "Uh... no. Hang on. We didn't hook up until the end of August. That's nine months."

"What I mean, you clueless youngster, is that at the beginning of January I still had to get through six more months until you graduated and left."

Ruben's brow furrows. "Oh... I'm sorry."

"I made it through."

"Well, without any help from me, whatsoever. I was doing my best to break you..."

"You did. Eventually," says Henry.

"Yeah. But on your timeline, not mine."

"If we'd done it on your timeline, I'd be flipping burgers now. Go on. Keep telling."

"At a few of the parties I went to over the holidays, I found myself checking out the guys. Especially... There was a frat party where I had my first experience of thinking I was discreetly ogling a guy, only to discover him ogling me back. It was... bewildering and befuddling."

"Don't forget bewitching."

"Oh, for sure. Girls times a thousand. I was reeling. But I refused to take action. I focused on getting used to the idea that I might be bisexual. Over the holiday break, I promised myself I'd stop the thing with your hands once I was back in class, and I did. Well, sort of."

Ruben takes a deep breath. "January. Epic failure. I distracted myself from your hands by checking out your eyes. Monumental strategic idiocy. God. So much worse. Your eyes tipped me over an edge I hadn't even registered being in the vicinity of. Your face as a whole had seemed so plain to me. Yeah. All the basics were present and accounted for, but nothing I'd notice if I saw you on the street... or so I'd thought until I zeroed in on your eyes and... oh... my... God."

"January," Henry says heavily. "You started getting into my space in January, you complete and utter wanker. And I assume I'm using the term literally."

Ruben laughs and nods. "Oh yeah. Once I started thinking about you to get off, I could *not* stop myself. After taking those first few good, long looks at your face, desperate to distract myself from your hands, your eyes sucked me right in and held me." Ruben leans toward Henry's eyes. "Your eyelashes are dark and really long, and the blue of your eyes is so dark, while still being so blue, and you have these delicate age lines at the outer edges of your eyes that I could only see if I was about a foot away *and* you smiled. You wear glasses, which at first stuck you firmly into the nerd category for me, in spite of trying to pretend I'm not one to stereotype, but your glasses don't have frames, so your eyes are easy to see."

Ruben squints at Henry. "You chose that style of glasses on purpose. Didn't you? To show off your eyes?"

Henry uses his imaginary key to lock his lips again, and Ruben grins.

"But Christ. By then I didn't care," Ruben says. "I was sunk. I became stupid about you... and lost as hell. At home in my bedroom, I started fantasizing about you. It was such a relief to stop fighting it, to let myself imagine your hands touching me, your eyes looking at me."

Henry's brow furrows. "I have this uneasy feeling that I should report myself to my boss."

"Don't you dare."

Henry smiles and waves at Ruben to continue.

"Okay. By then even your crooked teeth had become dear to me, and I'd discovered your full, curvy lips. I stopped thinking you looked too pale and started noticing the smoothness of your skin and the hint of pink in your cheeks whenever you shared something with us that moved you, like some incident in history that was fraught with meaning. I noticed how hard it was for you to look people in the eye, but when you did—for example, when you looked right at me—I found such presence and depth and thoughtfulness and awareness in your eyes. I started craving direct eye contact and trying to figure out what would make you give it to me. My Holy Grail became getting you to smile directly into my eyes."

"January," Henry says bitterly. "Pure *hell*."

"I would've given anything then to know whether you noticed me or gave me a second thought." He scoots his chair closer to Henry's and rubs his hands together. "Do tell."

Henry kneads his forehead. "Yes. Dear God. Of course I noticed you. I wrestled myself through my own stages of denial, struggling first off to accept the simple fact of your attention."

"Umm, yeah. Once I admitted to myself I'd developed a full-blown crush—*on a man*—well, I stopped holding back. My natural... umm..."

"Your natural what? Aggression? Forwardness? Sense of entitlement? Foolish impetuosity?"

Ruben laughs. "Guilty on all counts. It was just such a vast relief to shrug and start treating you the way I'd treat a woman I wanted who was resisting my come-ons."

"Lucky me. Direct attack from a force of nature."

"You bet. No brakes and no holds barred. I put a lot of effort into trying to get you to respond to me the way I was responding to you. I'd been known to set my sights pretty high and I'd never failed before. But... I failed with you." Ruben looks down at this lap, and his voice softens. "You drove me around the bend, Henry."

"Do *not* expect a single ounce of sympathy from me, Ruben. You behaved so recklessly." Henry's serious voice matches the look in his eyes.

Ruben nods. "I get that now, but in my own defense, I *was* immature. Well, I still am, but I was even more immature then. I just... I *could not* accept that you either weren't interested in me or *were* but were so immune to my charms that you could resist me, even if you were only planning to resist until after the internship was over and I'd graduated. But yeah. Back to you."

"Well, I couldn't seem to get past the fact that you were interested in me at all. I felt like I was standing around blinking like a dimwit. Then once it sunk in, I spent a lot of time flipping calendar pages—at first because I was eager for you to be gone. But then I'd catch myself counting the months until you weren't my student anymore... and I'd laugh at myself for harboring stupid false hopes. Nevertheless..." Henry stares into space.

"What?"

"I did check your file at some point, to see when you'd turn eighteen."

Ruben sits up straight and stares at Henry. "Are you kidding me?"

Henry shakes his head, embarrassed.

"When?" Ruben asks. "Oh, God. I hope it was before February because..."

"During the holiday break."

"In December? But..." Ruben rubs his face with both hands, thinking back. "But it wasn't until late January that you..."

"Allowed you to see me noticing the way you were looking at me?"

"Oh, crap. You bastard. You... I'm..." Ruben takes Henry's hand under the table and draws it into his lap so Henry can feel the effect the news is having on Ruben. "I feel like I'm retroactively embarrassing myself in the middle of class with an uncontrollable hard-on because you were thinking about me in that way and that early on..."

Henry gives Ruben a hard squeeze through his jeans and withdraws his hand. "What can I say? I missed you over the holiday break. I needed to know how pervy I was being."

"In December already." Ruben shifts in his chair. "I knew there was something there, some spark coming back at me. But you were so..."

"What? Responsible? Mature? Experienced? Self-controlled?"

"All of the above, for sure. But I was going to say self-conscious. You seemed to..." Ruben thinks for a minute. "You seemed to calculate your movements and the way you presented yourself. As though you expected people to judge you and find you wanting if you weren't careful. You smiled with your lips closed, and the way you... I mean, your eyes are so damn pretty, but you keep them to yourself by not making eye contact. In January there seemed to be a new element to your self-consciousness. Like *both* of us were super attentively monitoring your movements."

"Very astute," Henry says. "Looking up your birthday was the first time I acknowledged your attention and my reaction to it. Before that it didn't seem real."

"And after that?"

"After that..." Henry swallows and gives Ruben the kind of look Ruben used to ache for—suggestive, hot, held. "When I found out that you'd turned eighteen in October, the hypervigilant, semiconscious part of me that had considered you infinitely off-limits..." He lets out a long sigh.

"Took a hike?"

"No. Backed off a fraction of an inch. You being eighteen changed the battle from a hopeless nonissue to allowing myself to wonder. Still hopeless, mind you, and without ever expecting anything to happen. There were too many possibilities for resulting awfulness."

"So why did you tolerate my flirting? Why didn't you ever... oh, I don't know... take me aside and tell me to back right off?"

"Really?"

"Yeah."

Henry puts his elbows on the table and leans forward, head bowed, hands fiddling with a napkin. Ruben waits. Finally Henry looks into Ruben's face, but still doesn't speak.

"You know I'll keep at you until you say whatever it is you don't want to say." Ruben lifts his chin and tries not to blink.

"I didn't tell you to back off, because I'd noticed your uncanny ability to keep your flirtations private. You seemed able to control yourself when others were around. But..."

"What?"

Henry looks out over the harbor, stills his hands, and says quietly, "I didn't want you to stop."

"Holy shit." Ruben forces himself to breathe.

"I was so attracted to you, to your energy and brightness. Your attention... woke me up. Stopping it would have felt like... like amputating an arm. But I didn't think anything would come of it. I never did. Not until the moment you first walked into my apartment."

"Not even when you nodded at me in your office that day—the day we got our certificates?"

"No. Not really. I only nodded so you'd leave. I was desperate for you to leave, and certain your summer on a farm, hopped up on teen hormones as you were..."

"As I am."

Henry laughs. "Right. As you are... would net you enough opportunities to get it—me—out of your system by the end of the summer."

"Like... how exactly?"

"I don't know. Farmhands? The neighbor's sons and daughters? Livestock?"

Ruben snorts. "The farmhands are, on average, about sixty. But there was this one tree."

"Oh, for God's sake, Ruben."

"Let's just say I thought about you a lot under this old fruit tree out at the end of the pasture, where the woods begin."

"Excuse me." Henry taps the arm of a passing waitress. "Would you please bring us a big glass of ice cubes?" She nods and heads off. "I'm going to wrap you up a cold compress with this nice cloth napkin," Henry says. "You need to cool down."

"How about applying a warm compress while we wait for the ice?" Ruben pulls Henry's hand onto his straining pants. Henry, teasing desire in his eyes, presses Ruben through his jeans.

"I need to know something." Ruben closes his eyes, presses his hand onto Henry's, but then stops because he can feel himself veering out of control. "Please tell me what you were thinking during those microseconds of eye contact I forced you into, all those times when I'd get too close. That look on your face before you turned away."

"You mean the surprised split second of falling toward you before I remembered who I was? And who you were? And where we were? Oh, and how much my career means to me? And pictured the looks on your parents' faces?"

"Fuck. You're right. I really, definitely didn't ever think beyond the thrill of it all. But... holy shit. I lived for those split-seconds. I counted and cataloged and replayed them endlessly. They made me so hungry for more of you."

They're both quiet for a while, staring out at the harbor, hands clasped against the hardness in Ruben's lap.

<hr>

AFTER ANOTHER ROUND of drinks, and with reluctance, Ruben gets up to go to the bathroom, his mind processing what he's learned over dinner as he makes his way into the crowded restaurant and back out again.

When he walks back onto the deck and picks out Henry through the crowd, Ruben's smile fades. Henry's talking with a good-looking man who's standing over him, leaning on his straightened arms on the back of the chair beside Henry. He's tall, with tousled, jet-black hair, wide shoulders, and a killer smile aimed right at Henry... who's smiling up at him.

What the fuck?

With a flare of irritation, Ruben hurries through the maze of chairs and tables, shoulders and elbows, and arrives in time to hear Henry say, with kindness and a spark in his eyes, "No. Not tonight, but thank you. I'm here with someone tonight. Maybe some other time." The man smiles, nods, and leaves. Ruben walks around to Henry's side of the table, stands on the exact spot where the man was standing, and glares down at Henry.

Henry studies Ruben for a long moment then says, "Are you going to hit me now?"

"What?" Ruben's voice is tight.

Henry points to Ruben's hands fisted at his sides.

"No. *Jesus.* Of course not."

"But?"

"Would you please stand up? Please?"

After another thoughtful look at Ruben, Henry stands, his back to the pub wall. Ruben stays put, breathing hard. When he speaks, his voice is low and intense. He tries hard to keep talking instead of turning around to punish the black-haired man.

Jaw clenched, Ruben says, "I'm not saying it's fair. It's not fair. You sat here all evening while people came and hit on me. I have no right to be angry when someone hits on you."

"True," says Henry with a nod.

"And... and I know we're over as of tomorrow, but..." Ruben leans toward Henry and then checks himself and leans back. "Until Martin walked through your door, I was never the jealous type. Since then... I just... I *am*. And this feeling is so strong that... I can't, I don't know how to handle it. I hate it that you told that..." He jerks his head in the direction of the black-haired man and hurries on, afraid if he catches sight of the guy, his words will disappear altogether. "I hate that you told that *fucker*, 'Maybe some other time.' I know I'm a hypocritical jerk. I've been telling people 'Not tonight' all night. But I don't care. I'm so angry I'm terrified and I'm babbling—trying to talk instead of doing any of the things my body wants me to do right now, but... but I'm running out of words and I don't feel any better yet." His voice has descended to a growl. His face is burning and throbbing, and he can feel himself trembling.

"What does your body want you to do?"

Ruben blinks. "First beat the living *shit* out of that asshole who just hit on you."

"And then?"

"And then shove you hard up against the wall and kiss the hell out of you to show everyone here that, for now, you're mine. All mine." He pauses for a moment, then, ashamed, adds in a whisper, "I'm sorry."

Henry takes a half step away from the wall toward Ruben, into what Ruben would describe as the danger zone of his barely controlled anger. "Come on, then," says Henry, tilting his head to the side.

Disbelieving, certain he's misunderstood, Ruben narrows his eyes.

"Claim me," Henry whispers through a seductive smile.

Unable to think about whether it's a good idea or not, Ruben opens a fist into a palm against Henry's chest and shoves him hard into the wall. Anger, jealousy, and desire rise in a wild, tangled surge, and Ruben clamps his mouth against Henry's and groans, forcing himself to focus on the vulnerability of Henry's lips, on how grateful he is for Henry's permission.

All mine. Ruben feels a giddy rush. He moves his hands to the wall on either side of Henry's shoulders to hold himself up against the shaking.

The scattered hoots and wolf whistles make Ruben feel even more protective of Henry.

Wanting to give Henry a dose of his own seductive medicine, Ruben concentrates on slowing his breath, slowing the kiss. He wants to drive Henry mad enough to grab him, to wrap him closer, to show whoever's watching that Henry claims Ruben too.

But trying to slow the kiss inside all his aggression feels like mainlining an impossible cocktail of vulnerability and restraint—that uniquely *Henry* combination of qualities that drew Ruben to him from the beginning. *Christ, I had no idea. Such a powerful drug.*

This is not helping.

When Henry doesn't respond the way Ruben wants him to, doesn't moan under Ruben's intensity, doesn't grab and clutch, Ruben's attention finally turns from who might be watching to what Henry's doing.

What Henry is doing, of course, is kissing Ruben as though they're alone.

Typical Henry, being shoved hard against the wall of a bar and taking it to a higher, better level. But then that thought disintegrates as Ruben falls into Henry's luscious kiss… a deeper, more intimate kiss than Ruben had intended in public.

Ruben can't take it anymore. He gives up, gives in, gives over, moves his hands from the wall to Henry's face, and presses his whole body against Henry's. He no longer cares who's watching. He wants only one thing.

More Henry.

Desperate to catch a breath, Ruben pulls back an inch to look at Henry. He notices for the first time that Henry's eyes are still red and bruised looking from crying.

Henry unbuttons Ruben's coat and tucks the tips of his warm fingers into the top of Ruben's jeans, where no else one can see, making the public moment more private. With a hand on Ruben's belt, Henry gently pulls, and his slender, beautiful, graceful fingers dip in to brush the tip of Ruben's erection.

Ruben dives back into Henry's mouth, hungry and heedless again. He holds Henry's face still—so incredibly turned on by it all. Henry's ability to restrain himself seems to grow as Ruben's self-control weakens, crushed beneath an avalanche of greedy need.

Ruben forces himself to withdraw from Henry's mouth long enough to whisper into it, "If you don't stop that this instant, I'm going to make a mess."

Henry withdraws his fingers, but keeps hold of Ruben's belt.

Through gritted teeth, Ruben says, "I'm going to step around the corner of this building while you go take care of our bill." He removes his hands from Henry's face and, without turning to face the harbor or the crowd, takes the few sideways steps necessary to get around the corner and slide away from the light, then farther, into the dim depth of a recessed service entrance. He sinks back against the heavy door, and rubs his eyes. *Christ almighty.* He has never been so out of control in public before. It scares him.

Ruben paces in the tiny alcove, tries not to touch himself, tries to wait. He can't believe he sent Henry away.

But then Henry is back.

Ruben moans an apology as he grabs Henry, presses him hard into the wall, and cushions the back of Henry's head with his hand, no longer trying to stop himself from... anything. Henry unbuckles Ruben's belt, unfastens his pants, and the back of his hand slides along the bare skin of Ruben's belly to grab him and hold him tight.

When Henry backs away from Ruben's kiss and kneels on the concrete to take Ruben into his mouth, Ruben stops breathing, can't breathe, can't wait, doesn't wait, finishes in seconds, doesn't care, doesn't care, and it feels so monumentally good.

Ruben searches for a full breath, fails, and exhales on a hard sigh. Blood pounds everywhere, and Ruben realizes with alarm that he's nowhere near sated and nowhere near calm.

"Fuck me," he mutters on an indrawn breath, meaning it in every possible sense.

TELLING EVERYTHING

I REMEMBER HOLDING Ruben in the shadowy doorway—curling my fingers into the soft hair at the back of his neck and wondering which of us was being comforted.

I remember feeling high from his stories about the way he saw me during his internship.

I remember aggression radiating off Ruben in waves, making him act impetuously and driving me to take control.

I don't remember anything between leaving the pub and getting back to my apartment.

I do remember arriving home, pushing Ruben onto the bed, and the desperate look on his face.

I suspect his aggression is confusion. When I shove him around a little to give him the message that it's okay to hand over the reins and stop protecting me, he looks up with panic in his eyes—a prisoner unaware he holds the key.

Inside his intensity is a plea for help.

He wants to be in control.

But he doesn't know how.

NOT TELLING EVERYTHING

BY THE TIME he's back in Henry's apartment, Ruben's amped-up energy and residual rage make him feel like he's going to self-combust—or maybe even hurt Henry. Not because he wants to, but because he can't control his intolerable feelings.

Thank God for Henry.

Henry shoves Ruben into the bedroom.

Ruben stumbles, willing and eager, needing direction but hating that he needs it. He knows his feelings are too strong to be just a response to what happened at the pub with the black-haired man. Anger, jealousy, yearning, defensiveness, greed, hostility, and aching aggression fly through his body without landing. They blur and block his vision, circle around, taunt and antagonize him over and over.

Keeping track of Henry's eyes seems to help the most.

The anchor beneath the waves.

At the last second, Henry flips Ruben to land on the bed on his back. Henry falls alongside him, his movements brisk and intense. He slides a leg over Ruben's thighs, tucks his foot under Ruben's knees to hold him tight.

Shades and flashbacks of Henry pinioning him at the radiator make Ruben instantly harder, and he squirms to rub himself against Henry's thigh. But Henry's having none of it. He puts Ruben's hands under his butt and gives him a look that tells him to keep them there. Ruben nods, lost.

After five long years of being the wolfish one, pushing and persuading girls and women to give him what he wants, but then not getting it anyway, after six long weeks of pushing men to get what he wants, but never getting close, Ruben can't help but compare. The last thirty seconds have amped his meter into the red, heated him to blazing, made him so giddy with arousal at Henry's torturous promise of deliverance that he doesn't recognize himself.

Sex is always about fighting for more.

Except with Henry.

Ruben drops into a willingness so trusting he never knew to imagine it. He relaxes his neck, and his head falls back into the bed, but his fingers try to clench, like they know something he doesn't—like they're not convinced it's okay to relax. He looks up and searches the tempest.

Nothing matters but holding fast to Henry's eyes and stalking the frightening itch that demands to be scratched.

Please scratch that itch right now.

But right now is not in Henry's vocabulary.

Thus begins the biggest turn-on Ruben has ever known or imagined.

Henry takes his time unbuckling Ruben's belt, unbuttoning his jeans, slowly lowering the zipper. It takes approximately thirty-five years longer than Ruben wants it to, and he squirms and wiggles and tries to increase friction where it would count the most. But Henry won't allow it and holds him close in all the wrong/right ways.

Almost there... after the zipper, he's almost there.

Ah. Henry's hand brushes Ruben's erection, sending a shooting star through Ruben's addled mind. But then with a quirk of his eyebrow, Henry takes his hand away and slowly unbuttons Ruben's shirt, which makes Ruben so demented he wants to cry and so frustrated that he groans from the intolerable mix of desire and anticipation.

Henry looks down at Ruben with an unreachable lure of a smile—a taunt Ruben suspects will feature in mental replays for years to come. It's a tolerant, all-knowing, mouthwatering smile.

A loving smile.

Ruben closes his eyes to deflect its sharp arrow.

He feels the last shirt button come undone, and Henry spreads Ruben's shirt panels aside, untucks his undershirt, runs his hand along Ruben's bare skin from his exposed underwear to his neck and stops when his long fingers spread against Ruben's jaw.

Ruben opens his eyes.

Holding his gaze Henry slides his thigh, then his leg, then his body on top of Ruben. He drops and presses his weight onto Ruben's hips at the exact moment he delivers an insistent kiss—the most enflaming kiss Ruben's mouth has ever yearned for.

This is the kiss I've been searching for.

Only... I need...

Deep inside Henry's hard kiss, the known universe breaks open and Ruben glimpses the shape of his need.

He inhales a long breath through his nose, pulls his hands from beneath his ass where Henry had put them, grips Henry's arms, and yanks him closer. He uses lips, jaw, and neck to open Henry's mouth wider, to take more of him... and Henry follows.

Ruben moans, and Henry lifts away from Ruben's mouth. The fine lines at the edges of his eyes crinkle with humor.

Oh, God. He's teaching me.

He knew what this would do to me.

Ruben shoves Henry up and off, focusing his need into precise movements.

I know what to do. I know exactly what to do.

Ruben pins Henry's shoulders, unfastens and yanks down his pants, grabs Henry's hard cock in his fist, and issues his first command. "Don't you dare move a muscle."

Henry offers no resistance. Only the sweetest smile Ruben can imagine being the cause of.

RUBEN EMERGES FROM a mind-bending climax to discover himself damp, sticky, exhausted, and enfolding Henry like he's trying to engulf him, body and soul.

Henry's blue eyes are huge and calm and full of unguarded affection. Ruben lets his guard down, and his policy—Sex, please, hold the love—becomes a victim of temporary amnesia.

In that newborn, defenseless moment, because he's no closer to being able to deliver the grown-up commitment Henry deserves, Ruben's heart breaks.

Henry sees it happen.

A shadow of suppressed regret flashes across Henry's face, tender and haunting. He strains up off the bed to reach Ruben's lips and offers a sad apology of a kiss.

A loss abbreviated to a linger.

A simple, crystal-clear, fully formed idea floats though Ruben's swirling thoughts.

I want to be the one who deserves this man.

The thought falls apart as soon as it appears.

Impossible. A dream destined to be unrequited.

Someone else will claim him before I grow up enough.

Someone else will hold Henry like this.

Not wanting Henry to sense his distress, Ruben disentangles himself and leaves the bedroom.

Henry watches him go.

Half an hour later, Ruben slips back under the covers, unable to keep arithmetic from tumbling through his head.

Twelve hours until Henry lets me go.

TELLING EVERYTHING

MY ABILITY TO turn away from Ruben—a man I want but can't have in the way I want—is an ecstasy more potent than our night of reinventions and rewards.

That ecstasy keeps me awake long after Ruben has burrowed into the warm den of covers to sleep.

I get up in the middle of the night to move our pie from the freezer to the counter. I want to finish. I want to walk away from halfheartedness free and clear.

My sleep after that is deep and peaceful and goes on for a hundred years.

In the morning, the new green sprout of my reunited self searches for fresh air, so I get up and open the living room windows, inviting the old air to leave, shivering in the cold until the kitchen timer goes off to tell me the oven is heated. I close the windows, crank up the radiator, and pat it fondly.

I slide the pie into the oven.

While I wait for Ruben to wake up, I straighten my desk, find my favorite pen, and sit. Warm and whole at last, I collect my thoughts and slide a hand back and forth across a blank sheet of paper.

NOT TELLING EVERYTHING

R UBEN WAKES TO the smell of baking apples and buries his face in the pillow to stop his nose from remembering his first kiss with Henry. He holds himself still and tight until his lungs force him to turn his head to take a breath.

The brokenhearted feelings from the night before are still with him. *Crap.*

He lies, sad and alone, willing himself to be someone else, somewhere else.

Henry appears in the bedroom doorway and comes in to sit on the edge of the bed and smooth Ruben's hair away from his face.

Ruben closes his eyes to focus on Henry's touch.

"This has got to stop," Henry says quietly.

Ruben opens his eyes. "I know. The cruel dose of sorrow at the end is too much."

"Well, sorrow's only one side of the coin."

"What's the other side?"

"Didn't you have fun?" Henry smiles. "You didn't do any of it halfway."

"Yeah," says Ruben. "But I think maybe you did."

"I've done exactly what I wanted to up to this point."

"And after this point?" Ruben asks.

Henry looks at Ruben for a long moment. "I do want more. You've helped me see that."

"Hey, now. Be nice."

Henry laughs. "I can want more without expecting it to come from you. And I can thank you for our time together." Henry takes his hand away from Ruben's forehead. "You've helped me so much, Ruben. I will never forget how you woke me up."

Ruben scoots to lean against the headboard so he can see Henry's face better. "Wow. And all I wanted was to get into your pants."

"Win-win, then?"

"Sure. Thanks for… I'm glad for you." He looks away.

"But?"

"I have to tell you… since last night…" Ruben fidgets and tries to still himself. "I'm finding it hard to stick to my decision."

Ruben can tell Henry's not buying it. He gives Ruben one of his serious, stern-teacher looks. It makes Ruben squirm.

"Have you actually changed since yesterday?" Henry asks. "Are you all of a sudden ready to give me more than you offered on Friday—like the possibility of a real relationship, or enough commitment to that possibility that we could head in that direction?" He lifts an eyebrow. "Monogamy? Really?"

Ruben scrubs his hair and wishes he could wake up more, although he's already pretty awake. So he's probably only wishing for that alternate reality. *Get a grip.* He forces himself to be still.

"No," Ruben manages to say. The word comes out on a sigh of woe, in a small, unfamiliar voice forced through a mouth that wants to bite its own tongue to keep him silent. His shoulders slump. "If I'm honest with myself, I'm not ready for that. I'm not the person you deserve. This is all so new. I don't feel…" He searches for the right words. "I don't feel like myself. Or if I do, it's a self so new I don't recognize it. And…"

Ruben checks Henry's face to see how he's reacting.

Henry smiles a little and nods.

Ruben takes a deep breath and forces himself to go on. "I like you so much, Henry. I don't want us to stop seeing each other, but I also…" He gropes again. "I don't have anything to compare you to. I'm sorry if that sounds cold, like I don't know how valuable you are."

"Ruben, those are all wonderful things to say. And to hear."

"It feels awful to tell you the truth when I know it means losing you."

"But it would feel worse not to tell the truth. This is better."

Ruben worries his bottom lip. "I've felt more like a man ever since I met you, even if I wasn't yet. But right now I just feel like a child."

"I think you're being very mature."

They sit for a while without saying anything.

"Umm," says Ruben after a while. "I'm going to ask this outright because I want to be sure I'm not missing out due to a false assumption."

"Okay. Go for it."

"Me saying no to having more of a relationship means you're saying no to more sex, right?"

Henry doesn't answer right away. Ruben fidgets as he waits, so he tucks his hands beneath the covers.

Henry scoots closer. His look is so full of calm fondness it makes Ruben miss him already. And feel even more like a child.

"What I'm saying," says Henry slowly, "is thank you very much for the extraordinary, breathtaking, long-dreamed-of, chart-topping sex, *and*, no to only sex."

Ruben nods and blinks.

"I think it will be best, when you leave here today, if you consider your exploration into having sex with a man a spectacular success."

"And continue on my merry way?"

Henry nods, but his forehead furrows and he seems to be carefully ordering his thoughts. That makes Ruben take an extra big breath in anticipation.

"You've surprised me, Ruben. When we're together I lose track of you being eighteen and me being thirty-two. I'm too busy enjoying the way we are together. I'm attracted to too many aspects of you to be able to stop at only sex." Henry looks away. When he looks back, his blue eyes hold pain. "I would *always* want all of you."

Ruben feels his body trying to lean toward Henry. He takes a hand out from under the covers, but he isn't sure what to do with it.

Henry says on a whisper, "I could love you, Ruben. I could get lost in love with you."

Ruben swallows and makes himself ask, "But?"

"But I'm done being lost and alone." Henry squeezes Ruben's hand and then stands and leaves the room.

Fuck. Ruben knocks his head back against the headboard hard enough to hurt. After fifteen minutes of reviewing the situation and finding no loopholes or acceptable ways of reversing or avoiding the past hour or the next hour, he grits his teeth and throws off the covers.

"I could love you, Ruben. I could get lost in love with you."

His heart beating too fast makes him jerk his pants up and fumble with the buttons on his shirt.

Though his appetite is gone, there's no way he's going to miss out on what he knows must be an apple pie.

How long will the smell of baking apples send me right back here? How long will I use apple pies to send me back to Henry before I've had enough? Before I let myself let him go.

When Ruben emerges from the bathroom, he finds Henry on the couch again, wrapped in the wool blanket, staring out the window and off into space. It makes Ruben think that must be Henry's default position when he's home alone.

Letting his body have its way, Ruben sits next to Henry. He can't help himself. It's like his body is magnetized to Henry's. And he's determined to take whatever closeness Henry allows before they're done for good.

Henry seems to return from a great distance. He blinks and smiles at Ruben.

"There is one thing, though," Ruben says, leaning his head onto Henry's shoulder.

"What's that?" Henry lets his head fall sideways on top of Ruben's, which feels exactly right and gives Ruben the courage to continue.

"Technically, as a top... I'm still a virgin."

After a while, Henry says, "If that bothers you, I'll bet you can find a solution soon."

"I keep thinking about last night, when I... when I was out of control, one way or another."

Ruben feels Henry's smile against the top of his head. "What happened at the pub last night really twisted your crank." Henry shifts his hips, and Ruben imagines it's because he's remembering what happened afterward in Henry's bedroom. "Kept us up all night," Henry murmurs.

"Don't distract me," Ruben says. "I have a point to make here."

"Yes?"

"After all we've done over the past two days, I couldn't believe you'd deny me that. Topping. I've imagined it and ached for it and... *aspired* to being with you that way for so long."

"And now you're sad and maybe even a little mad at me because you won't get it? Because I won't let you fuck me?"

Ruben nods, and Henry raises a hand to Ruben's face, his palm against Ruben's cheek. It feels warm and familiar.

"I'm sorry," Henry says. "I wanted it too, but I never felt—"

"Please don't say, 'safe enough.' I couldn't bear it if you felt that way."

"Only a little. It's more that I never felt..." He rubs his palm across Ruben's cheek. "I like you so much, but your out-of-control energy last night, plus knowing where this isn't headed, kept me from saying yes. It's… I don't go there casually."

"And we were officially only casual."

Henry nods against the top of Ruben's head.

"But you topped me when I wanted it this weekend."

"Yes. And it was incredible." Ruben feels Henry swallow and take a long breath. "It was beyond incredible," Henry says, his voice deep and slow.

"It's not the same."

"Obviously. And you'll have a great time discovering that. Only be careful, would you? Be safe. Okay? You're important to me, no matter what happens from here on." Henry turns to kiss the top of Ruben's head.

The loss, the could have been, the tease of ending without sharing more with Henry, keeps Ruben from responding, afraid he'll say something that will sound disrespectful of Henry's choices. He tries to focus instead on being still and taking one steady breath after another, though it's difficult with the tease of Henry's warm shoulder, Henry's gentle hand against Ruben's face, and Henry's mouth still pressing against Ruben's hair.

Eventually Henry must feel the wetness against his palm, because he turns Ruben's face so he can wipe away the tears and distract Ruben with kisses.

Which only makes it worse.

HENRY PULLS THE hot pie from the oven as Ruben drops his packed bag by the front door. When Ruben sits at the dining table, he has to press his fidgeting hands onto his thighs to still them.

For God's sake, pull yourself together.

Ruben assumed Henry made the pie fresh that morning, but it arrives at the table with two pieces already missing. "This isn't *our* pie, is it?"

Henry nods.

"I guess you and Martin ate those two pieces after I left." Try as he might, Ruben can't keep the taint of envy from his voice.

"No. Martin ate them both. I didn't have the stomach for it."

Ruben mentally swaggers and thumbs his nose at Martin's memory.

Henry lifts a big piece onto a plate and hands it to Ruben. Then he dishes himself a piece, and Ruben picks up his fork and digs in.

"Oh, dear sweet Lord have mercy," he mumbles around the first incredible bite. "Oh, *God*." Then he can't speak for a while because he doesn't want to interrupt his mouth.

"More, please." Ruben holds his empty plate out to Henry, who grins and dishes Ruben another piece.

"Henry, this is orgasmic. And I'm not even kidding. It's better than my grandmother's apple pie, and she's won all kinds of prizes." Ruben takes another bite, moans out loud, and savors the thrill of the ideal apple pie brought to life on his tongue.

They sit across from one another at the dining table, Ruben's socked feet resting on Henry's under the table for warmth, and they eat without talking. The only sounds are the scrapes of their forks as they capture the last crumbs of the last bites before the next piece hits the plate.

They finish the pie.

Ruben eats all the burned-edge bits too, his and Henry's. He reaches across the table to pluck them from the edge of Henry's plate. He needs to get everything he can before it's too late to get anything more.

Eating the apple pie feels so like kissing Henry for the first time that Ruben has to have a stern talk with himself to stay in his chair.

Even then, with his packed bag by the door, knowing their affair is over, Ruben pokes at his decision.

Daring himself to test the waters one last time, Ruben says, "Maybe you could make this pie every time we get together."

"That's your bulge talking."

Ruben laughs. "Well?"

"No thanks."

"Just like that?"

Henry's fork clatters against his plate. "You know what?" Henry's no longer smiling, not even in his eyes. "Enough already, Ruben. Give it up. You had your fun. I had fun too, but I'm not going to hang around while you taunt me with options you yourself say you can't deliver, just in case what you want turns out, somewhere down the line, to be *me* on my terms. I'm not that masochistic. And I'm through waiting."

Ruben studies his hands, feeling like a scolded boy.

When Henry stops talking, the silence stretches, and Henry does nothing to break it. Ruben listens as Henry's quick breath slows down and it becomes clear that the next bit is up to Ruben. He raises his head.

"You're right," Ruben says. "I'm sorry."

Henry sends him a tight smile.

"So... yeah." Ruben stands, his body resistant and heavy. "Off I go, then."

Ruben forces himself to keep his head up. "Thank you, Henry, for... for flipping my switch and cranking my dial. It was..." He tries to grin and feels it not working, but he seems unable to stop trying. "You're an amazing teacher." He holds out his hand to Henry.

Henry looks up and takes Ruben's hand. When Henry stands, Ruben's fake grin fades away. He reaches out to touch the delicate lines at the edges of Henry's eyes, and Henry pulls him in for what Ruben can't help but think of as a memorial kiss. They're standing in the same spot as their first kiss, surrounded by the smell of the same apple pie, and Henry's closeness makes Ruben feel the same dizziness.

A part of Ruben tenses as they kiss, waiting for Martin to ring the door buzzer. But that would be memorial overkill. Ruben doesn't need Martin to interrupt the kiss. Ruben seems to be managing that all by himself.

Henry steps back and heads to the foyer, where he puts on his coat. "I'll walk you out." He paws through the coats and scarves looped over the pegs by the door. "Where did I put my scarf?"

"What scarf?" Ruben asks as he balls Henry's blue scarf tighter, shoves it farther into his coat pocket. He uses his fingertips to make sure no part of the scarf peeks out.

"Must have left it at work," Henry mutters. He grabs another scarf from a coat peg and holds the door open for Ruben.

"Hey," Ruben says, trying to think of something to say to distract Henry from the scarf, and to distract himself from his guilt at having taken it. *Don't. I need it. I'll mail it back to him someday.*

"Hey," Ruben starts again as they walk down the stairs to the lobby. "Don't smack me. I know it's not going to happen, but I want you to know that my parents invited you to Sunday dinner today."

"That's nice of them. Will you please tell them I appreciate the invitation?"

"Sure."

Henry holds the front door open for Ruben, and then they're facing each other on the sidewalk. To Ruben's right the trees outside Henry's windows stand on a carpet of their own lost leaves.

Those didn't last either.

Henry pulls Ruben into a hug that's no longer a lover's embrace, and Ruben takes a last deep breath against the warm crook of Henry's neck. Then Henry pushes Ruben back, presses a gentle kiss onto his forehead, and turns to walk downhill toward the harbor.

When his view of Henry has shrunk to the size of a distant mirage, Ruben finds the will to turn and walk in the opposite direction.

As he walks he touches his fingers to the leather bracelet and then pulls Henry's blue scarf out of his pocket and wraps it around his neck. He tips his head down to bury his nose in it and inhales.

He was real.

The bus pulls away. Ruben presses his nose against the cold window to watch Henry's street disappear. He tries to find a steadying thought, something to hold onto.

At least I was honest. Well, except for the scarf.

It doesn't help. He tries again.

At least we woke each other up.

At least my history of Henry is mine to keep.

THE HISTORIAN

TELLING EVERYTHING

A s I w a l k away, the damp, heated spot in the crook of my neck cools, and the itch at my back diminishes and dissipates. I have a sudden vision of our story—mine and Ruben's—as told by the everyday histories of my things. My stories of us.

I touch the railing at the harbor dock as though it's a finish line, then turn around and head back home, phrases and paragraphs already forming.

The only thing I do before I sit at my desk and begin to write is strip the bedding and shove it into the washing machine.

By the time the sheets are clean and dry, my fingers are cramped from writing and my stomach demands to be fed, so I head back down to the harbor—shaking out my hands and stretching my fingers as I walk.

When I turn along the boardwalk in the opposite direction from last night's pub, I find a busy cafe with an unoccupied corner table and a view of colorful sailboat flags flapping in the wind.

I continue my date with my notebook and pen. No one bothers me while I eat and write. No one seems to notice me at all. But I notice myself.

I notice myself.

The green seedling pushes into my hand and writes me, word after word, memory after memory, back and back into histories long before Ruben. It lifts me like a curling vine on a search-and-rescue mission.

At midnight, trusting my feet on the sidewalk to take me home, I close my eyes and feel for the old space where I wasn't and the shadow self that stood beside it. I find only seed.

I sleep with my notebook under the pillow, my head on the clean pillowcase, and my newly fused pulse warming the entire bed.

In the morning I awake wrapped in everyday histories. They crowd against my knees as I walk, clamoring to be picked up and paid attention to.

On my way to work, I mentally revise my lecture notes, considering and testing ways of teaching a new group of interns about everyday history.

When I get home from work, I go straight to the desk to write without bothering to take off my coat.

I am writing myself a new womb from which to emerge.

Held and loved.

Cared for.

Wanted.

Enough.

PART IV
THE MONTHS

THE HISTORIAN
INVENTING NEW STORIES

THE EXPLORER
REVIVING OLD STORIES

REVIVING OLD STORIES

THREE MONTHS LATER
JANUARY | AMHERST

THE GUY'S NAME is Justice, which is funny because he's a law school student. He and Ruben meet on a park bench near the library. They are the only two people sitting outside in the cold.

"Nice scarf" is Justice's opening gambit.

When Ruben jokes about everything but his name, Justice asks him out.

On their second date, Ruben picks Justice up at his apartment. He pokes around in Justice's bookshelves while Justice finishes getting ready, and he finds a row of old, metal wind-up toys, a framed photo of Justice with a toddler on his shoulders, and a tiny stone replica of the Sphinx.

When Justice emerges from the bedroom zipping a sweater and carrying a pair of socks, Ruben is standing in the middle of the living room holding the Sphinx. "What's your story about this?" The hopefulness in his voice pulls the memory of Henry into the room.

"That thing?" Justice shrugs. "Who the fuck knows. My mom decorated this place. I don't even notice the stuff anymore. But it makes it all look comfortable and lived in, don't you think?"

Ruben tries again with the framed photo.

"No idea. A second cousin at some family picnic a few years ago, probably."

By the time they get into the car, Ruben can feel frostiness starting to build toward Justice. He doesn't want to feel it but he can't help it. A dozen questions later, it's obvious that Justice can't be bothered to share anything more personal than his body.

Which, Ruben is surprised to realize, is no longer enough.

Interesting.

The date deteriorates quickly through a brittle half hour and ends early when Justice drops Ruben off without a word.

Watching Justice drive away, Ruben can't seem to recall why he was attracted to the guy in the first place.

INVENTING NEW STORIES

FEBRUARY

Lieber Henry,

I was surprised to get your letter. The luxurious pajamas you ordered for me from my favorite store in Berlin were even more surprising. Thank you.

It must have been Trudi who told you I wasn't handling Mother's death very well. Your suggestion of wearing the pajamas to help me grieve sounded nutty, but I'll be damned if it's not working. Maybe on multiple fronts, because staying with you while Mother was dying doubled my grief. I have a new sense that you've forgiven me. If so, I'm grateful.

Yes. I understand the pajamas are a gift of friendship, not more.

Yes. When I visit Boston in the future, I'll arrange to stay elsewhere. I hope you know that I did my best as your guest. You were a gracious host, though I sensed something was troubling you. I'm sorry I intruded.

You'll always be the one who got away, even though we both know I was the one who pushed you. Your kindness was the thing I loved most about you.

Wishing you the best of everything,

Martin

REVIVING OLD STORIES

FIVE WEEKS LATER
MARCH | AMHERST

"WHERE DID YOU get this?" Ruben asks as he flops into the orange and red hammock strung across a corner of Danny's apartment.

"The hammock? I got it in Costa Rica."

"Go on, then. Tell me the whole story."

Asking for stories has become Ruben's favorite way of deciding who to pursue and who to drop. He laces his fingers behind his head and settles into the curve of the hammock. He's getting better at predicting who will talk and who won't. He has high hopes for Danny, a psychology graduate student he met on the soccer field a few days earlier.

Danny looks like he's not sure he heard correctly.

"Yes. Really." Ruben smiles. "I want to hear the story of this hammock. Tell already."

And Danny does. It turns out to be a long, interesting, nail-biter of a story, revolving around his parents' ugly divorce, his little sister's suicide attempts, and a vacation the four of them took to Costa Rica *after* his parents were divorced. On their first day there, each of them bought a hammock, and they ended up spending every afternoon lying in their hammocks talking. It made such a difference in all their lives that they decided to do the same trip again.

That was six years ago. The four of them have been going to that little hotel in Costa Rica every other year since the first time. Though Danny's parents have both remarried and his father has another child with his second wife, Danny's original family still spends time together in Costa Rica, lying in their hammocks for hours, catching up on each others' lives.

By the time Danny finishes telling, his face glows, his eyes flash, and Ruben is starstruck. The openness and self-deprecation that infused Danny's story make Ruben's heart feel full and at peace for the first time since the weekend he spent with Henry. He smiles at Danny and raises his eyebrows.

Danny's lingering smile of remembering becomes a smile of gratitude. After a long look at Ruben, the smile becomes a kiss as Danny leans over the edge of the hammock to get at Ruben's mouth.

———

RUBEN'S REQUESTS FOR everyday histories don't always segue into foreplay. Sometimes all he gets is a shrug and a change of topic. Sometimes memories and conversations end in tears. But always—always—Ruben learns something important about the person telling the story.

In the beginning Ruben asks for everyday histories to conjure Henry. But conjuring Henry makes him feel lonely, so he trains himself to focus all his attention on the storyteller.

Over time, question after question and story after story shift something inside Ruben. His conversations are deeper. He hustles less and connects more. He still has plenty of sex, but it's starting to mean more, and something inside that's always been wound too tight and running hot seems to loosen its grip.

When thoughts of Henry intrude, Ruben stares them down and sends them away with a prayer of thanks for Henry, the wake-up call who launched Ruben into the life he's enjoying more and more.

Thanks, Henry, for being my turning point, for making me interested in more and deeper.

For a while after their weekend together, Ruben tries to keep in touch with Henry, but e-mails from Henry are short and impersonal, and phone calls are worse. So Ruben stops initiating and… that's that.

Whenever someone asks, Ruben shares everyday histories of his own.

But he never speaks to anyone about Henry.

That's private.

INVENTING NEW STORIES

April 12

To: Henry Normand
From: Kyle Copeland, Senior Editor
Subject: Everyday History Column

Hi, Henry

Thanks for coming to the office last week to talk about your articles. I enjoyed meeting you and am happy to offer you a position as a columnist. If you'd be so kind as to make another appointment, we can go over the details and a bit of paperwork here at the office.

You mentioned that you're working on a book proposal. If you don't already have an agent, I might be able to give you a couple of good recommendations.

All the best,
Kyle
Kyle Copeland
Senior Editor, Boston Newspaper Group

REVIVING OLD STORIES

MAY | AMHERST

RUBEN PUSHES OPEN the door to his room in the house he shares with two friends. He tosses the small stack of incoming mail onto his desk and then paws through it, looking for something to lift his spirits.

Here. A letter from his mother. But the envelope contains only a newspaper clipping with a sticky note on it that says, "Look what your teacher at the museum has been up to."

The newspaper's culture editor would like to introduce readers to a new weekly column called "Everyday History," written by Henry Normand.

Ruben feels his body struggling to decide what to feel. His face grins at the sight of the words "Everyday History" in print next to Henry's name, but his lungs tighten, and he's suddenly aware of a twinge inside his pants, like his dowsing rod senses Henry's presence in the room.

Henry introduces the new column in a few paragraphs. Then there's a smaller heading with the title of this week's topic, "The Blue Pajamas." Ruben skips to the end to see if they've included a website for Henry. But no. There's only another note from the editor.

Our new columnist is not only technophobic, he's also frequently on the road. To reach Mr. Normand, please contact the editor at...

Ruben frowns at the clipping and wonders if Henry and the editor are sleeping together. *Get a grip.* He shakes his head, closes his eyes to take a big breath, and then reads.

INVENTING NEW STORIES

MAY

Everyday History
By Henry Normand

As a historian with three advanced degrees and heaps of research and teaching experience, I thought I'd reached a fine career plateau. I liked the view. I felt content to let the years ahead unfurl peacefully. Then one day an unexpected cross-pollination between my career and my personal life changed everything.

I remember the moment perfectly. At home after a series of intense conversations with a fellow historian, I picked up a pair of blue pajamas to fold them, and it hit me that the histories of the everyday things I live with give me what I always wanted from my study of history—a context for my own life that provides me with a sense of belonging.

The everyday things we live with trigger our histories—the stories of our lives.

As I write, I imagine us sitting together here in my living room, or in your living room, or in your barn or garden, telling each other stories about the everyday objects in our lives. Chatting in this way, we unfurl context to expose a more intimate understanding of the present moment.

I share the everyday histories in these articles, starting with this week's story about a pair of blue pajamas, with the hope that you'll be inspired to ask those around you to tell you their everyday histories, and that you'll tell them yours.

May you discover common ground and make your home there.

THE BLUE PAJAMAS

A PAIR OF blue pajamas once saved my life.

Years ago, after a painful breakup that made me question myself on the deepest levels, I retreated from my friends and from the world—too rough and raw to want company.

I was living in southwestern Germany at the time, attending graduate school and studying European history. Because of the breakup, I felt shifted off of whatever minimal foundations I'd had up to that point. I felt adrift and at sea.

One day, desperate to escape the walls of my tiny apartment, which mocked me with memories, I took myself to a little store nearby that I liked to visit because something about it comforted me. While passing the time there, I received an unexpected sighting of land.

An elderly woman owned and ran the store. I never did befriend her. I was afraid if I did, she'd want to talk, and I needed her store as a semiprivate musing space. But I was grateful for the choices she made about what to sell. She stocked a strange mix of modern, classical, local, and foreign items. I found unusual Asian spices, silk thread in odd colors, beautiful fountain pens, brands of crackers I'd only ever seen before in Britain, canned goods from Italy, and comical salt and pepper shakers that always made me smile. I felt as though my travels, which had been extensive by then, were summed up within the crowded space of that tiny store. It represented the cosmos of me. If I could only crack the store's code by musing and straightening and occasionally acquiring something and taking it home, I could understand myself. Or so I felt.

On that day I puttered in the salt-and-pepper-shaker corner, turning the shakers in the sets toward each other so they could have conversations—in my defense, my loneliness made me do it.

As I moved a cow salt shaker to face a farmer pepper shaker and tried to imagine their conversation, I tuned in to what the woman who ran the store was saying to a customer. "It was like she turned in on herself, like she tried to climb into her own womb."

My unexpected reaction—Oh, I could really use a womb right now—arrived on a wave of intense longing. Wanting to climb into a womb was so absurd it made me laugh out loud. Afraid my solitary cackle would make the proprietor peg me as a weirdo and bar me from the store, I grabbed the cow and farmer shakers, paid for them, and left. I'd had an idea.

Clutching my kitchen goods, I made a beeline for the most exclusive, high-end men's clothing store in town. As I stepped inside and the heavy wooden door whooshed closed behind me, a deep, silent, expensive peace settled over me.

Thirty minutes and one month's tuition later, I walked out with the perfect pair of pajamas. They were so soft I'd actually, to my deep embarrassment, groaned aloud when the store clerk placed them on my outstretched palms. The pajamas were the purest, most evocative baby blue you could imagine.

I had what I needed—baby clothes. I'd decided, in the little shop where I bought the salt and pepper shakers, that if I couldn't fight the sense of having lost everything after the breakup, then I would surrender to being defenseless. I would become a baby again. I would start over from the beginning.

I went home, turned down the heat, put on my new pajamas, piled all the blankets I owned onto the bed, climbed beneath them, and slept for three days. I emerged from my womb only when absolutely necessary.

Within a month of baby blue, scary-soft pajama therapy, I had shed my funk. It hit me one day that I was saying yes when people invited me to do things. And I was laughing again.

Seven years later, back in Boston, those pajamas were tucked away in a bottom drawer. I wore them only now and then, when I felt nostalgic, or when I wanted to remind myself that it's possible to heal and that the path of healing need not make complete sense in order to be effective.

The morning began with fog. I sat on the couch in my living room, wrapped in a blanket, eating cold take-out food from a carton, watching the trees outside the windows and trying to decide whether or not to tell someone a secret I'd kept to myself for a long time—one I'd never told anyone and couldn't imagine saying out loud. But I also could no longer imagine my future if I kept it to myself.

In my own way, I was praying for a sign. Should I tell or not? Should I risk nothing or risk too much? Should I travel through pain and out to the unknown on the other side? Or should I continue living with the pain I already knew?

Imagine my surprise when my houseguest walked into the living room wearing the baby blue pajamas, which they'd dug out of the bottom drawer of a dresser. I didn't care. My pajamas—an important symbol that represented my ability to heal and regenerate and take care of myself in times of distress—walked themselves into the room to stand in front of me. It was the exact sign I needed.

I reached for courage and told my secret. I stretched and entered the world.

REVIVING OLD STORIES

AMHERST

FOR A LONG minute after reading Henry's article about the blue pajamas, Ruben stands in the middle of his room and stares into space, holding the clipping and remembering the morning he walked into Henry's living room wearing the supersoft blue pajamas.

Then he reads the article again.

He studies the small, black-and-white photograph of Henry at the beginning of the article, and then carefully folds the clipping and slides it into his wallet.

Outside again, head down against the biting wind, Ruben takes a long walk in the wrong direction—into the sad part of town—to the tiny diner he discovered in February, where the wrinkled waitresses wear polyester uniforms with pinned-on nametags and call everyone "sweetie."

By the time Ruben takes the fourteen steps that get him from the front door of the diner to the end stool at the counter where he can sit and lean against the wall to oversee the entire place, Estelle has put a slice of apple pie under the warmer for him.

He takes it straight, as Estelle well knows. No ice cream. No whipped cream. No coffee. Just hot apple pie and a fork.

The pie is not as good as Henry's, but it's a hell of a lot closer than anything else within a thirty-mile radius.

As the young man picks up the fork for his first bite, Estelle, who's on the other side of the diner by then, pauses with the coffee pot poised over an elderly woman's cup. Estelle always likes to watch his face as he takes his first bite.

He lifts a forkful of apple pie and closes his eyes as he closes his mouth around the fork.

To Estelle he looks like he's finally found the exact thing he's been starving for.

INVENTING NEW STORIES

JUNE

Everyday History
By Henry Normand

WALNUT BOWL AND SEEDS

The summer I turned twenty-four, I spent a month at a seaside campground in Quebec. I was driving a cranky old car and ranting out loud about my life, which felt like it was falling apart, when I stumbled upon the place.

The caretaker was an old man named Jean. His kind, dark brown eyes drew me to him and calmed me. He was a small man, but tough and strong. He'd spent his life at sea or near it and had taken on his role at the campground two years earlier, after his wife died. Jean was willing to talk with me for hours on end, for which I felt an endless gratitude.

We managed to talk ourselves through the awkward first couple of days while he squinted at the European French I spoke—which often made him crack up— and I tried to process his heavily accented Quebec French.

After that we talked all day, just the two of us, no matter who else happened to be staying at the campground. We talked at the picnic table during breakfast, lunch, and dinner. We talked during our slow walks, and we talked by the campfire late into the night. We spoke about everything—our histories of pain, family members lost (both of us), boats loved and lost (Jean), opportunities missed (me), opportunities wasted (Jean), the surprise beginnings and endings of love (both of us), and much more.

We spoke with each other as though we already missed the lifetime of catching up we would never achieve in the limited time I would be at the campground.

While we talked, Jean carved. The rhythmic, practiced movements of his sharp knife against dark, hard wood and the sound of the wood becoming less of itself and more of itself at the same time soothed me. It made me want to talk and listen. I came to consider Jean's carving as the third participant in our conversations.

The wind off the water that whipped the flames of the fire, our wide-ranging talks, the old Quebec language floating around us like strings of secret passwords— all conspired to pause me at a time when I was desperate for a respite from the striving, emptiness, and breakneck speed of my life. That odd bubble of time with Jean allowed me to find a toehold, to step outside the blur and bring myself and the world back into focus. A little bit. Just enough to give my tight chest room to take a few long, deep breaths without panicking.

On my last day at the campground, I slopped my belongings into my backpack without folding anything, because I was anxious about saying good-bye to my great friend Jean. We faced each other beside the car on the dirt road leading out of the campground, and Jean surprised me by holding out in his palm the thing he'd been carving the entire month I'd been there.

I laughed out loud then, because I realized with a rush of surprise that I'd never once bothered to notice what it was. Most of my life up to that point had been about noticing details and drawing conclusions from them. I really had taken a break.

I had noticed Jean oiling the wood the day before with a yellow cloth and the oil from a tiny blue glass vial he kept tucked in the pocket of his shirt. He'd been getting it ready to give to me.

It was a bowl. I took it cautiously and looked at Jean, who nodded and pushed my hand and the bowl toward my chest. "Take it," he said. "I carved it for you." I looked down and saw a perfect, larger than life replica of half an empty walnut shell that fit comfortably in the open palm of my hand.

I remembered that I had told Jean a sad story about my lack of direction and the pressures of my self-imposed expectations. Jean looked at me with compassion and said, "Find the seed." Until he put the bowl into my hand, I hadn't realized that I had already come to a decision about where I was headed next.

He shook my hand then and he was brave enough and generous enough to continue holding my hand until my tears stopped falling from my bowed head into the bottom of the bowl.

I keep Jean's walnut bowl on my desk. Resting in the bottom are twelve tiny pieces of hard candy made by my cousin Jamie to look like poisonous jequirity beans from Indonesia.

I keep the red and black candy seeds in Jean's bowl to remind myself that tears neutralize poisonous thoughts into something sweeter and that pain is no match for the prizes that come from daring to share.

REVIVING OLD STORIES

AMHERST

RUBEN PUSHES THE last bite of pie around on the plate at Estelle's diner and closes his eyes. He remembers being in Henry's living room, picking up the walnut bowl and rolling the red and black seeds around in a beam of sunlight to distract himself from the push of his anxiety. Henry had watched with such intensity, following Ruben's every movement.

Of course he had.

Henry had been struggling over telling me his worst thing... and I stood there in his baby blue pajamas, holding Jean's bowl.

Henry had told Ruben about Jean. Ruben sets down the fork and tries to block out the sounds of the diner to remember exactly what Henry had said. On Saturday night of their weekend together, they'd gotten out of bed to forage in the kitchen and then... He squeezes his eyes closed to remember himself back into Henry's apartment.

THE WEEKEND | SATURDAY NIGHT

IN THE CHILLY hours of early morning, Ruben starts to lead Henry back to the bedroom after their rushed snack in the kitchen.

"Hang on," Henry says. He roots around in a cabinet and straightens up with two little drink boxes of chocolate milk. Ruben snorts.

"Ooh. *Sexy*," Ruben teases as he walks backward to the bedroom. He takes one of the cartons but blocks the bedroom doorway. "Kiddie stuff prohibited beyond this point."

"Why? Afraid of regressing?"

"Don't be snide or I'll call you a dirty old man," Ruben leers.

"Better not. It would only crank your dial, and you need your milk break."

Henry holds out his hand for the plastic wrap from Ruben's straw. "Stand on my feet," Henry says. "I'm freezing, and you're hot-blooded enough for us both."

"Only because you light my fire."

"Oh, for God's sake. Could you be any more of a moonstruck teenager?"

They suck on the plastic straws and slurp room-temperature milk while they roll their eyes and grin at each other. Ruben slurps until he's sucking up air.

"Disgusting," he says. "And yet it hits the spot."

Impatient and fidgety, Ruben leans into the bedroom, sets his empty carton on the bedside table, and gathers Henry in his arms. "Hurry up."

"Mmm..." Henry murmurs around the straw. For a moment he looks like a sleepy little kid, and Ruben wonders, not for the first time, what Henry was like as a boy.

"Hey. Why is your last name different from the one on your birth certificate?"

Without waiting for an answer, Ruben grabs Henry's half-empty drink box, sets it beside his own empty one, and pushes Henry underneath the covers, into the heady, damp warmth.

When Henry's silence goes on, Ruben says, "Too personal? Never mind. I've just had another idea."

He wraps his fingers around the back of Henry's neck to draw him closer, but Henry blinks and says, "I haven't thought about him in a long time."

Ruben touches his lips to Henry's and says, "Tell me."

"You're distracting me."

"You'd better focus, then." Ruben moves his lips sideways back and forth against Henry's.

"Um... I didn't... uh, the name they gave me..." Henry sighs and turns his head to the side. "The name I got at the hospital as an orphan of unknown provenance was a random pick—one more impersonal aspect of my birth. It made me lonely. When I was in my midtwenties, I met this wonderful older man, and I legally changed my last name to his."

Seeing the faraway look in Henry's eyes, Ruben maneuvers them both until they're on their sides facing one another. Ruben blows on Henry's chilled hands to warm them.

I'm here with you now, Henry. Stay with me.

"What was he like?" Ruben asks. He pictures a big man with a mane of white hair—a powerful man in an expensive suit, smirking and making eyes at Henry. Ruben squirms, and his legs start to twitch.

"We had an unusual connection," Henry says. "He gave me the exact help I needed at a time when I was really struggling." He takes a few slow breaths, his eyes focused on the past. "I would have loved him to be my father."

"Is he still around? Do you ever see him?"

"No." Henry shakes his head. "No. I only knew him for a few weeks, at a campground up the coast from Quebec City. I have no idea what happened to him after I left." He's quiet for a minute. "The time I spent with him was like a dream. It felt like… I felt like when I left the campground, I woke up. It didn't occur to me to stay in touch." He stares at Ruben, his brow furrowed. "That makes me sad."

The wistful look on Henry's face makes Ruben jealous, and he shifts his limbs as adrenaline begins to take hold. "Were you and this guy… um… lovers?" he asks, even though he doesn't want to know.

Henry laughs with surprise. "No. It wasn't like that at all. He was kind and calm and wise, like the ideal father. It was… perfect. Anyway, his last name was Normand."

Ruben pulls his knees up between Henry's legs and tightens his arms around Henry's shoulders. Henry opens his mouth to say something else, but Ruben is so relieved he doesn't need to add Mr. Normand the elder to his roster of imaginary rivals that he shuts Henry up with a hard kiss.

JUNE | AMHERST

Sitting in the diner, Ruben sighs heavily at the memory of what happened next. He turns the diner stool so his lap is hidden beneath the countertop. He peers down at his crotch. *Give it a rest already.*

Scraping the last moist bits of pie onto his fork, Ruben lingers and allows a lapse into a daydream.

What if… what if a psycho trucker stole Henry from his adoring, doting, perfect, wonderful, real parents, who were Jean Normand from Quebec and…

And Estelle. Of course.

Estelle notices Ruben watching her and comes over with the bill. Ruben smiles like she's made his day and hands her a ten-dollar bill. "Keep the change." He pats her hand, holds his smile and her hand for a moment before he leaves.

INVENTING NEW STORIES

JUNE

BOSTON MUSEUM OF HISTORY NEWSLETTER

STAFF NEWS

CURATOR AND INTERN Educator Henry Normand has signed a book deal with New Name Press, the prestigious international publishing house. The book, which will include a selection of his syndicated "Everyday History" articles, along with all-new material, will be published next spring. Congratulations, Henry!

REVIVING OLD STORIES

SEPTEMBER | AMHERST

ELLIS, ONE OF Ruben's housemates, ushers Danny out and closes the front door. Danny was over again for dinner—a casual, potluck affair that turned out to be the exact combination of people and finger foods necessary for an entertaining evening full of raunchy jokes.

"Excuse me," Ruben says. He smiles at Ellis, slips outside, and closes the door.

"Hey," Danny says. "Did I forget something?"

"No. I did. Mind if I walk you home?"

"Not at all."

But then, as they walk along, Ruben can't think of how to begin. After a couple of blocks of silence, Ruben takes a big breath and reaches for Danny's hand.

"I want to tell you some things, but I'm afraid," Ruben says.

Danny pulls Ruben's hand up to his chest and holds it there with both of his gloved ones. "Of what?" Danny asks. "Of my reaction?"

"No. Of *my* reaction. I really need to talk to someone, and you're my first choice, but starting to say these things out loud might change our relationship and... and it will mean bringing up things I've been wanting to forget."

"I think you've just passed the point of starting to say things out loud."

Ruben groans, and they walk the remaining three blocks to Danny's apartment in silence. Inside, with coats shed and the water kettle heating, Danny stands by the stove and waits patiently. They've left the lights off, as if they both think that talking in the minimal light coming in from the street will make things easier for Ruben.

The kettle whistles, and when Danny turns his back to fill their mugs, Ruben says, "I need to get someone out of my head, and I can't seem to do it." He's thinking about Henry's articles, which he knows he should stop reading.

Danny sets the mugs on the table and sits. "You know what I'm going to say by now, don't you?"

Ruben puts his head in his hands and nods.

Danny says it anyway. "So... tell me the whole story."

Ruben surprises himself by declining to tell the whole story.

Danny's undivided attention and patience are at his service, but Ruben balks, shuttered by a fresh awareness that sharing Henry could puncture the magic of his memory. He squirms and wishes he'd stomped harder on the impulse to open up.

The truth is, he doesn't want to risk removing the sheen from his history with Henry, even if it means he'll have to keep trying to get over Henry on his own.

I need to shove the Henry archive further out of sight, not drag it closer. That's the only viable solution.

Which means his meeting with Danny was a mistake. Ruben decides to finish his tea and then leave.

They sit at the table munching chocolate chip cookies, sipping tea, not talking. Unfamiliar awkwardness weighs the air until Danny asks Ruben a question that Ruben doesn't want to answer. So he doesn't.

After ten more minutes of silence, Danny sighs, and Ruben's legs twitch with the need to leave.

The half-full bag of cookies they started with is empty, but Ruben digs around inside for something more and ends up tipping the bag's last crumbs directly into his mouth.

"You're the one who wanted to talk about this," says Danny.

Ruben, frustrated with himself, his voice sharper than he means it to be, says, "Yeah, I know. And I'm avoiding your question because I don't know what he thinks of me now."

"So why not ask him, just to make sure? It could simplify things."

"No. It doesn't matter what he thinks of me now, because whatever he thinks of me, I know he's still who he is. And I'm still who I am. And that's why it didn't work out, and that's why it *can't* work out. Believe me, we covered this issue thoroughly the last time we saw each other."

"When was that?"

"About a year ago."

"Wow. That's some torch," Danny says with a brief, sympathetic smile.

"No *shit*."

"Ruben, his last words on the topic, whatever they were, might be an old story by now."

"Don't you get it, Danny? Even if he's changed his mind about what he wants, which would be extremely unlikely considering who I know him to be, I still can't deliver what he deserves."

"Are you sure you can't?"

"Yes."

"Why?" Danny asks.

"Because I respect him. Because his reasons for not wanting me were valid. Because I know myself." Ruben leans forward, defiance in his eyes. "For example, as soon as you hear what I'm going to say in the next eight seconds, this conversation will be *over* and you won't want me to stay tonight. Then I'll feel even lonelier, so I'll go home and wake up Ellis by crawling into his bed, like I often do. Because if I don't, if I go home and crawl into my own bed, alone, I'll..."

When Ruben said, "like I often do," Danny's face filled with pain. He sits still, his body rigid, and Ruben pushes the end of his sentence into the space between them.

"I'll have to feel things I don't want to feel."

After a long, heavy minute, Danny looks away from Ruben and says, "You're right. This conversation is over." He stands and begins to clear the table.

In his room alone that night, with the house quiet and heavy and dark around him, Ruben opens his laptop and begins to type an e-mail message.

Hi, Henry.

But then he can't think of anything to add.

An hour later, still staring at the blinking cursor after the word *Henry*, Ruben hears the hallway floorboards creak as his other roommate, Millie, gets up to go to the bathroom. He hits the Delete button.

When he hears Millie's bedroom door close, he shuts down the laptop and turns out the desk light. In the darkness of the quiet room, he allows his feelings to rise into view.

The wall of dark panic that overwhelms him makes him stand up and swallow hard against the tightness in his throat.

He pushes the chair away from the desk and pads next door to Ellis's room, which he enters without knocking. He knows the way in the darkness, finds the twin bed with his shins, leaves his clothes in a pile on the floor, and slides under the covers against Ellis's welcoming warmth.

"Oh, praise Jesus," Ellis mutters through a sleepy smile against Ruben's neck, his hand reaching down for Ruben as Ruben's hand reaches down for him. With their usual efficiency, they get the job done, and Ruben races toward the finish line, intent on the sedation of the afterglow.

He manages not to prolong the dangerous part, the part where Ellis falls asleep in his arms and—because it's so easy and the room is so dark and he's too tired to filter his thoughts—Ruben pretends he's holding Henry.

With effort Ruben disentangles himself from the heat and walks back to his room and his cold bed. If he's tired enough, the fickle gods of chance will deliver Henry into his arms in his dreams.

INVENTING NEW STORIES

OCTOBER

Everyday History
By Henry Normand

DOORWAYS

How often during a normal day do we cross thresholds and pass through the familiar doorways of our lives at home and at work?

Remember being a teenager and leaning too close to the object of your affection in a public doorway, when you knew you shouldn't but couldn't stop?

Remember leaning together in the bedroom doorway, standing atop each other's bare feet, grinning like goofballs?

Remember the doorway the most important person in your life passed through as they kissed you in a rush and said good-bye?

I do. I remember momentous events of my life that occurred in the slender spaces of the in-between. Between rooms. Between inside and outside. Between having someone and losing them or losing someone and finding them.

In-between spaces are the province of our archetypal threshold guardians, the constructions of our collective unconscious that test us for worthiness.

Because I am uncomfortable in the familiar, memory-charged doorways of my everyday life in Boston in October, I've flown myself far away. To Germany. Where I thought I'd be able to escape threshold guardians and anniversary memories for a while.

But halfway along a narrow walkway in Freiburg's old town, I turn my head and discover that my ruthless threshold guardians—those masters of symbols—

have tricked me into remembering anyway, as though the distance I've traveled counts for nothing at all.

I stare at the doorway and the door I first found when I lived in Germany during graduate school, but had forgotten about. The top half of the door is glass. There is a miniature museum on narrow shelves affixed to the inside.

When I lived here, the exhibit changed every month, and it probably still does. Seeing the current exhibit, I give a bark of disbelieving laughter, and then, because I suddenly can't be bothered to care who might see me, I lean my forehead against the glass and begin to bargain with this particular threshold guardian. Please stop reminding me, everywhere I look, of what I am trying to forget. Please.

I hear people pass closely behind me in the narrow walkway, and when someone taps me on the shoulder to ask if I'm okay, I manage to straighten up and reassure her. But I know by then that I have lost. There will be no way out for me but through.

With a heavy sigh, I lift my head and take a good look at the exhibit. It's time to face what I've been running from. I press the tiny button I know is half-hidden in the framework around the doorjamb on the right. When I do, little lights built into the shelves turn on.

This exhibit is bizarre. They always are. Forty-two—I count them—miniature disco balls, carefully crafted from tiny pieces of mirror, hang from the bottoms of the shelves above and subtly swing and sway in whatever drafts traverse the world on the other side of the door.

I allow myself to be drawn into the turning shards of myself. Sunlight slanting down into the passageway from high above the stone walls flashes in the mirror shards along with my face.

Myself reflected back amid sparkling razzle-dazzle.

I flatten my hands on either side of the doorway as memories rise up of the one who got away, the one I'm trying to forget, the one who helped me find myself. I force myself to turn away, refocus on the present moment, and aim for the opening at the end of the walkway.

Yes, it was love, I finally admit as I walk away, my body heavy with sadness and the relief of truth. It was love that wrecked me even as it saved me.

At the end of the walkway, I reach out to touch the corner of the building where scrolling script spells out, in a vertical stack of letters, the German words for "heaven" and "hell." In case you're not sure which is where, arrows point up and down. I place my hand between Himmel *and* Hölle *and understand for the first time that*

I will have to find a way to make peace with the shards of myself, to hold the broken pieces close, to gather lost love and found self together so they can mend each other.

It's time to become the threshold, the place where heaven and hell meet. Because I can't outrun an archetype that lives in my subconscious. It will always find a way.

As of now, I will let it.

Do you remember negotiating when I had my back to the door? I lied to you, but you let me. Then you found a way to take me home.

Do you remember when we met in the darkened doorway after you shoved me? We both assumed I was in control. I wasn't.

Do you remember walking into the same room over and over, from fall to spring, one of us believing, the other disbelieving?

What I remember the most is the final threshold we crossed. I held the door for you. I kissed you on the forehead and turned away to find freedom.

You gave me myself, though it cost you everything you wanted from me.

REVIVING OLD STORIES

AMHERST

Why is Henry doing this?

Every week's article is pure Henry—full of vulnerability, perception, wisdom, strength, self-deprecation—all the qualities Ruben was attracted to in person.

But every month or so, Henry's article sends a finely sharpened arrow straight into the meaty muscle of Ruben's heart. The combination of avoidance and connection—the urgent need to be free of Henry but reading about himself in Henry's articles—is slowly unraveling him.

Why am I still doing this?

Ruben only reads Henry's articles at Estelle's diner, where he's sure no one he knows will see him, where he can be alone without being alone, and where he feels closest to Henry. He's never told anyone about the diner. After the botched confession to Danny and Danny's subsequent insistence that they not see each other for a while, Ruben isn't willing to put himself in a situation where his struggles about Henry will be questioned.

He knows there are no answers. Only acts of will.

Ruben pulls a five-dollar bill from his coat pocket and sets it under the napkin dispenser. Then he slides the empty pie plate aside so he can lay his head down on the counter. The old laminate feels cool against his cheek.

Elbows on thighs, hands hung between his knees, chest against the hard edge of the counter, Ruben stares at the wall and allows his face to stop faking it. Inside the cheerful soundtrack of Estelle's familiar, comforting laugh and the soft clink of glasses and forks and easy conversations, sadness and frustration tighten Ruben's eyes and mouth.

What if my threshold is the fear of loving?

That question triggers the one he's been avoiding.

What if I've never fallen in love because I never let myself love Henry?

By the time he reaches the diner door, he's running, fleeing the question, unwilling to find out what will happen if he can't outrun the dead end of the answer.

THE HISTORIAN
INVENTING NEW STORIES

FEBRUARY

To: Henry Normand
From: J. P. Hanson, Director, Boston Museum of History
Subject: Leave of Absence

Henry,

The board has approved a leave of absence for your research and book tour for the dates you requested. I'll get the official hard copy to you this afternoon.

The Board also asked me to pass along their congratulations. They seemed genuinely happy for you. Of course we're all pleased with the publicity the museum is getting through you.

Thanks again for taking me out to lunch last Monday. It was nice to meet your agent. He seems like a capable fellow. It's good that he's on your side, though, as I caught a steely glint in his eye a couple of times.

Off you go, then.

Have fun,
Jocelyn

THE EXPLORER
REVIVING OLD STORIES

APRIL | BOSTON

W HEN THE GLUM weather shows signs of relenting, Ruben convinces some of his high school and college friends to meet in Boston on a weekend to check out the harbor restaurant, the busy pub where he and Henry spent their Saturday evening, though none of his friends know about that.

The restaurant is a good fit for Ruben and his friends—great indie folk bands, a phenomenal regional microbrew beer selection, and a compelling view of the harbor.

Who am I kidding?

After an hour of laughing in the chilly breeze on the back deck, Ruben stops pretending he's doing anything but trying to replace memories of Henry with the strained effervescence of his current life.

It's Ruben's attempt at an exorcism.

His friends like the restaurant, so they go back the next night, and then on subsequent weekends. Whenever Ruben's in Boston, he joins them... and notices himself keeping an eye out for Henry, though he assumes Henry's busy life and his growing fame, along with Henry's likely wish to not be reminded of Ruben, will keep him from showing up there.

That's a good thing.

Isn't it?

He argues with himself and tries to convince himself to be realistic.

Hope has no place in this equation.

After all I'm here to replace my memories, not revive them.

When he's at the restaurant, Ruben also keeps an eye out for the handsome, black-haired man who put the moves on Henry.

His first sighting occurs on an unseasonably warm Saturday night in late April. As new arrivals squeeze in around the table on the back deck, Ruben stands to move a chair and… there he is, leaning against the railing at a stand-up table, wearing Clark Kent glasses, holding a beer mug, and laughing with a man and a woman who have their arms around each other.

The heated discussion at Ruben's overcrowded table fades to silence as his vision lasers and shuts off his other senses. He wonders if hitting the guy would feel as good as he thinks it would. Dimly Ruben observes his lizard brain taking over in a logic-frying boil of jealous aggression.

Then Danny pulls Ruben down into a chair and puts his mouth against Ruben's ear to ask, "Who are you glaring at? Should I hustle the women and children inside?"

Ruben blinks and turns toward Danny.

"Seriously," Danny says, "your *High Noon* glare is giving me shivers." Although Danny's speaking to Ruben again, the weight of Ruben's untold story has kept them platonic. Ruben forces his lips to smile and forces the smile to reach his eyes because he knows Danny will take any hint of a chink in Ruben's armor as an opportunity to fish for a story.

Ruben offers to fetch the next round from the bar inside.

I was here with Henry so long ago. Why do I still care so much?

He shakes his head to rid himself of the pressure in his jaw, to stop the story of Henry from getting out.

This is only happening because Henry's damn articles keep dragging my memories into the present.

And yet Ruben can't stop reading them. His teeth clench again.

Shit. Maybe I should talk with Danny about Henry after all.

Ruben glances back at the black-haired man, and the sight of him flicks the surging buzz to life again, that tight heat in his belly that connects directly to his fists. He licks his lips, forces his hands open, and slides away into the restaurant.

The weekends wear on, and Ruben's attempt at exorcism is a resounding failure.

But it's too late to recant. His friends won't be persuaded to go elsewhere, and Ruben doesn't want to be alone, so he keeps tagging along, saying less and less, withdrawing more and more.

Henry's ghostly form, right there at the table at the edge of the deck, refuses to fade, even amid the drama and intrigue swirling around Ruben and his friends as spring arrives in earnest. Ruben goes through the motions, catalogs the flash of fake IDs, the clink of beer bottles, the gasps and gossip, the heat of innuendo and argument. He holds still amid the drama and waits for something real to change.

The black-haired man doesn't get any easier to look at.

ONE LATE SATURDAY night, after a long evening at the harbor restaurant, Danny offers to give Ruben a ride to Ruben's parents' house, but hijacks him instead to the friends' apartment where Danny is staying for the weekend.

On the stairs up to the guest room, Ruben protests, even though he knows it's too little, too late. "Why are you doing this?"

"I can't bear how sad you looked all night." Danny leads Ruben to the bed. Ruben sits, listless and uninvolved. Danny kneels to take off Ruben's shoes and socks and then stands him up and undresses him like he would a child.

The familiarity of Danny and his kindness seduce Ruben into forgetting for a while and give him one night to pretend the moving parts function the way they should.

As Danny and the dawn light push the shadows back, Ruben's thoughts clear.

He decides he's not going back to the harbor restaurant, even if it means spending evenings in Boston without his friends.

INVENTING NEW STORIES

MAY

NATIONAL ENTERTAINMENT TRENDS WEEKLY

BOOK BUZZ REVIEW OF
EVERYDAY HISTORY, BY HENRY NORMAND

How did a museum nerd like Henry Normand get onto the roster of one of the entertainment industry's most sought-after talent agents, Erik Bonaventure? It's tempting to give Bonaventure most of the credit for the buzz around Normand's work, but after doing some digging, we're resisting that temptation. There's real substance to Normand's work—enough to warrant all the kudos.

Normand's career as a historian and museum educator took a sharp turn toward the modern when he began writing his weekly "Everyday History" articles, first published in the Boston Newspaper Group's family of publications in May of last year.

Everyday History is Normand's term for stories about the stuff in our lives. Sounds boring, right? It's not. We'll fly some numbers by you to prove it.

Normand's "Everyday History" articles were nationally syndicated after four months.

Everyday History, Normand's TV show, aired two months ago and is climbing the charts.

Normand's presence on social media has so much buzz our ears hurt.

The list of local and regional awards bestowed upon Normand fills a long page on his website and continues to grow.

Hang on. What about Normand's book?

Everyday History, *the book, was released at the end of last month, but pre-sales alone were higher than the publisher's cautious first print run, and the book is already into a third printing.*

According to Bonaventure, higher education's long-held regard for Normand in multiple fields, from history to social sciences and education, has driven up bulk orders from colleges and universities across the country.

According to the press office at the Boston Museum, where Normand still holds a position as curator and educator, regional high school educators also regard Normand highly and have been placing bulk orders and spreading the word to high school colleagues in other parts of the country.

Popular reviews of the book, in venues ranging from online blogs and forums to high-circulation print magazines like Esquire *and* Elle Decor, *keep pouring out and crossbreeding, further boosting Normand's already hot link value.*

Earlier this month Normand hit the road on a six-month trip to do a combination of book and TV publicity, field research, and on-location TV show filming. Bonaventure's office reports that Normand is gathering material for a second book, one that will showcase the Everyday History stories he's currently collecting from around the country during his trip.

Even before he hit the road, Normand was as hard to reach as J.D. Salinger, but we insisted, and Bonaventure arranged a sound-byte opportunity.

Normand's aversion to modern technology meant he called us from a gas station pay phone in West Virginia. We asked him for his thoughts about the popular response he and his Everyday History message are receiving. He said, "Everyone has stuff. Everyone wants to connect. Everyday History is a permission slip to be nosy in a way that's caring. The payoff is seeing the world through someone else's eyes and discovering that your own perspective has shifted in the process."

The call was cut short when Normand ran out of quarters.

That's okay. We've heard enough. Go buy the book.

Now excuse us. We've just noticed the Elvis snow globe on our neighbor's desk and have a sudden, burning need to wrap up this article and ask for the story.

Normand's book is packed with his reprinted "Everyday History" newspaper articles, new material collected from people in the Boston area (don't miss the story of Normand's visit to the Lint Museum of Greater Boston, which caused us to flop onto our desks with laughter), thought-provoking essays, and practical tips about using Everyday History to connect with the people in your life on deeper levels.

For more information about Everyday History, Henry Normand, and his activities, visit his website. See the sidebar for details.

REVIVING OLD STORIES

MAY | AMHERST

Danny shakes Ruben's shoulder, forcing him up from a sleep so deep and a dream so real it felt like another lifetime in a parallel universe. Henry was there. Of course. *Shit.* Ruben rubs his eyes.

"Is that the guy?" Danny asks, nodding down at Ruben, who's been napping in the hammock in Danny's apartment. At first Ruben thinks Danny somehow knows what he was dreaming, but then he feels the magazine clutched against his chest with both arms.

"Um... what guy?" Ruben asks.

"Cut it out, Ruben. You were talking in your sleep about someone named Henry, and it's not the first time. You're still struggling over that someone you can't let go of, aren't you? Someone named Henry?"

Upset at having his secret guessed and not wanting to show it, Ruben says, "I don't know what you mean. It was just a dream." He tries not to move his arms, which would be a dead giveaway.

Danny rolls his eyes and gives Ruben a grim checkmate smile. He holds up a hand and folds down a finger for every point as he says, "One, you're secretive as hell. Two, you're allergic to relationships that threaten to venture past a certain point. You have so many friends with benefits I'm not sure even you can keep track of them. Three, you go for walks alone and come back more serious than when you left. And four, on your worst days, you eat apple pie."

Ruben glares at Danny and clutches the magazine closer.

Danny doesn't miss the shift. "I know about the apple pie," Danny says, "because the most intense, spine-tingling sex we have only happens after you've been unusually quiet and when your breath smells like apple pie." He folds down the last finger. "Five, we never eat apple pie together."

Ruben's heart pounds. It's true. After trips to the diner, he always craves Henry—or a reasonable facsimile thereof. And Danny's the closest he's found.

Ruben closes his eyes and tries to avoid feeling ashamed, because Danny's spine-tingling sex with Ruben is Ruben's imaginary spine-tingling sex with Henry.

I never promised Danny monogamy.

But Danny isn't finished. "Your struggle seems to be getting worse, Ruben. So even if you don't want to talk about it with me, which you're welcome to, as your friend, I suggest you talk to someone. If you don't do it soon, I'm concerned you're going to suck more of your life than you intend to into the black hole of your unfinished business with this... Henry."

Struck dumb by the uncharacteristic boldness of Danny's intervention, Ruben stares up at him. He takes a few shallow breaths and miserably admits to himself that Danny might be right.

Maybe.

"I'm worried about you, buddy." Danny smiles and tugs the magazine from Ruben's hug. Ruben doesn't want to let it go, but by the time he realizes that clutching it is a red flag, it's too late.

"*This* is your Henry?"

Ruben tries to maintain an impassive face.

"Henry *Normand*? Wow. He's quite the geek superstar these days. New book. TV show." He flips through the article for a moment. "I always enjoy his articles. Mom brings them up over dinner sometimes as conversation starters to get me and my sister talking about our lives. Usually works too. We've had some interesting conversations that started with one of Henry's articles."

Ruben's brain thrums at a hundred miles an hour, trying to find the correct answer to the question, "Is spilling my guts to Danny about Henry a good idea?"

"Still no response," Danny says with some amusement. "That bad, eh?" He leans over the edge of the hammock and kisses Ruben, as he's done many times since the first day Ruben climbed into the hammock. The gesture startles Ruben and makes him take a big breath.

What have I got to lose? I am so damn miserable. Why not try something other than hoarding Henry's memory? Why not try letting the story go... as a step toward letting Henry go?

Ruben slides a grateful hand around Danny's neck and kisses him back, until Danny laughs into his mouth and pulls away.

"That's better," Danny says. "Shove over." Ruben awkwardly shifts sideways in the hammock and Danny climbs in, puts an arm behind Ruben's neck, and pulls Ruben's head onto his chest.

Danny's comfort is so surprising and unselfish, so real and *right now*, that Ruben starts to talk.

A FEW HOURS EARLIER

DURING A BREAK in an afternoon seminar, Ruben hears someone talking about Henry and the new article, and he skips the remainder of class to find and buy the magazine.

Lying in the hammock at Danny's, he reads the review of Henry's new book three times. Then he stares at the big, full-color photo of Henry for what seems like forever.

Ruben's study of the magazine article marks the first time in a long time he's allowed himself to look at a photo of Henry. The *Everyday History* TV show, which first aired a couple of months earlier, has been a torturous temptation. But Ruben has held out, not wanting to speed his downward spiral by watching Henry in motion, radiating brilliance—and smiling at someone else.

How long *has* it been since he's taken a good, long look at a photo of Henry? He closes his eyes to figure it out. Since before he met Danny, which was a year and a few months ago.

With a sigh he takes another look at the photo. It's good. Hell. It's *great*. Henry looks exactly the same, only… happier. He's wearing a dark gray, V-neck sweater over a T-shirt the exact blue of the sky behind him.

In the photo, Henry isn't looking at the camera, but at the tiny, white-haired woman sitting next to him on a bench in a garden in Charleston, South Carolina. With both hands, the woman holds out an extravagant bouquet of fresh flowers, clearly giving it to Henry as a gift. The camera has caught her laughing with an open face. One of Henry's hands is already lifting above his black jeans to take the bouquet. He beams at the old lady with fondness, respect, and warmth.

Henry bestowed that look on each of the students in his internship class at one time or another, when they said something he seemed to consider insightful, when they finally understood something challenging, or—Ruben hasn't put words to it before, but seeing the magazine photo makes it suddenly obvious—when someone was especially kind.

Ruben knows how it feels to be on the receiving end of that look.

I can't believe how desperately I want Henry to look at me like that again.

That's what Ruben is dreaming about when Danny finds him clutching the magazine to his chest with both arms.

The thought refuses to leave.

<hr>

DANNY'S SOOTHING TREATMENT—LISTENING attentively as they lie twined together in the hammock—washes over Ruben's troubles. The vice grip of misery that tightened when Ruben encountered the magazine article begins to loosen as Ruben spills his secrets. After too long someone else in Ruben's life knows about Henry, and that feels good, like Ruben doesn't have to worry about himself all on his own anymore. It's become too big a job for one person anyway.

His story told, Ruben leaves Danny's to put in some study time at the library. Danny, who's on late hotline duty that night at the counseling center, convinced Ruben that making plans to get together the next day will provide comfort to Ruben during the intervening hours.

Alone after midnight in the emptying library, Ruben finishes the last of his homework assignments and considers his next move. Still riding the wave of Danny-induced relief, feeling pleased to have weathered the experience of looking at Henry's magazine photo, Ruben decides to brave another experiment.

Flopped in a big armchair, back to the wall, textbook on his lap, Ruben stares at a photo on his cell phone.

And forgets to breathe.

What Ruben hadn't told Henry that night at the harbor restaurant was that February of his internship year was Photos Month—or more accurately, Photo Month—because Ruben used his cell phone to secretly take photos of Henry. He explored what he could get away with without anyone realizing what he was doing—fake-checking for messages and fake-texting while building a surreptitious archive of Henry photos. Early on, in the first week in February, he took one photo that turned out to be enough.

Ruben has been studiously feigning amnesia about that photo for a long time, so the powerful hit of nostalgia makes his throat constrict as he stares at it. Or maybe it's his growing awareness that whatever it is that won't let him let Henry go isn't going to resolve itself on its own. Ruben's going to have to get to the bottom of it. Soon. With Danny's help.

But not now.

I took this photo more than two years ago.

Christ. This torch needs to be doused for good.

But not right now.

INTERNSHIP | FEBRUARY | BOSTON

ON THE EARLY February day when he takes The Photo, Ruben stands in the long hallway outside the locked classroom at the museum. Slanting afternoon sunlight pours through the hallway's tall windows, warming the air, laying rectangles of light on the old wooden floor, hanging curtains of golden brilliance along the hallway at regular intervals.

Waiting for class to start, Ruben and his classmates tease Harriet about her new haircut and blink against the bright daylight. Everyone is laughing, including Harriet—when a movement at the other end of the hallway draws Ruben's eye. He squints against the glare to see if it's Henry. His heart quickens, and he curls his hand around the phone in his pocket, just in case.

When Henry, posture perfect, the black linen of his suit pants and jacket sucking light out of the air, steps into the first wide bar of sunlight, Ruben catches his breath. He takes the phone out of his pocket, taps the buttons to call up the camera function, and slides toward the outer edge of the group of classmates to get a better view.

Henry's smooth head and big eyes rise over the tall stack of old books he holds against his chest as he walks, chin resting on the top book to steady it, his slender, pale hands supporting the bottom of the pile. He steps into a bar of darkness and then into light again as he walks toward them. By then Ruben is in his fake-texting stance and peers down at the phone that's tilted to capture Henry.

He misses that photo and then the next few too, pressing the shutter button too early or too late to catch Henry in sunlight, until—*thank God*—he nails it as Henry steps into the last spill of light.

Ruben doesn't know until later how good that photo is because, as Henry nears the last window, Ruben looks up to watch him with his own eyes before it's all over. In the instant Henry passes from shade into light, he sees Ruben, looks right at him, and smiles that smile. His blue eyes crinkle and brighten.

Ruben almost moans out loud, but he remembers to tap the shutter button. Without looking at his phone, fervently hoping it was still in the right position to capture the photo he wanted, he shoves it into his pocket so he can take the stack of books from Henry—good little student that he is—so Henry can unlock the classroom door.

"Thank you," Henry says, smiling the smile again, the one Ruben longs for, the special smile of fondness and respect and warmth. Ruben, keenly aware that the stack of books is the only thing separating them, takes their weight. In that split second, he feels Henry's breath against his face as their hands brush beneath the books, and then Henry turns away.

In Ruben's customized version of the memory, which he has often replayed, Henry's "Thank you" is for Ruben's touch.

And the books fall to the floor.

THE WEEKEND | SUNDAY | BOSTON

AT THE END of their weekend together, after Ruben tells Henry good-bye outside Henry's apartment building, Ruben makes his way to his parents' house for Sunday dinner. On the bus he takes out his phone and pulls up the February photo, which he is intimately familiar with by then. Since February he's spent months mooning over it and jacking off to it, all the while hoping for something real with Henry but certain it will never happen.

But now it has.

As the bus turns a corner, the photo loads on his phone, and...

And I can't bear to look at it.

He scrunches his eyes closed, resisting the image, needing it to go away, and the motion of the bus pulls nausea from the pain.

He turns off the phone and leaves it off.

Late that night in his bedroom at his parents' house, after everyone else has gone to sleep, he tries to look at it again.

His body still reeling from the effects of two long nights with Henry, his emotions flayed from what he learned about Henry and how it felt to be with Henry, and most of all, knowing how their story has ended, Ruben discovers that the photo means something altogether different.

Henry's sparkling blue eyes smile up at me when I lie on top of him.
Henry's slender, pale hands touch me in ways that make me desperate with need.
Henry's presence brightens and warms the air.

OVER TIME, RUBEN'S relationship with the February photo becomes a crusade of tolerance. And then a war he eventually loses. As the weeks turn into months with no contact, Ruben forces himself to look at the photo less and less and then not at all.

It reminds him of too much and too little, neither of which he wants.

INVENTING NEW STORIES

MAY

EVERYDAY HISTORY
By Henry Normand

APPLES

EVERY DAY AFTER school in fourth and fifth grade, I went to my cousin Jamie's tiny apartment in a terrible, rickety building in a part of Boston that wasn't very nice. Her apartment was only a block from my elementary school, but I ran as fast as I could the whole way. My shaking fingers fumbled the key against the lock in her door until she heard me and came to let me in.

I was teased a lot as a kid, but I could run faster than the bullies who often tried to sneak up on me after school. My heart was always pounding by the time I fell into Jamie's apartment, my back itching with fear. I felt like a persecuted action hero returning at last to his home planet, desperate for a vacation.

One day when I was ten, after I'd made it across the threshold, hugged Jamie until she laughed, and sniffed the air to see if I could guess what she was baking, I caught a glimpse of something peculiar on the couch. I bent over to look, but then scratched my head, not understanding what I saw.

"Um... Jamie?" There was the red apple corer—my apple corer, the one she'd given me the day I broke my toe the year before—but it was on the couch mostly covered by a faded red washcloth folded over along one edge and looking for all the world like a miniature blanket. Jamie saw what I was looking at, laughed her bright laugh, and came over to explain.

"Do you smell that?" she asked me.

I nodded. "Apple crisp." It was one of my all-time favorites from her extensive repertoire.

"Mrs. Frankenstein—" She had to pause while we both giggled at our secret name for the terrifying, bitchy lady across the hall. "—is in love." My giggle ended in a gape. I couldn't image anyone wanting to spend time with mean Mrs. Frankenstein, much less be so stupid as to fall in love with her.

"Wait," I said. "You mean she's in love with someone who loves her back?"

"Yeah. I know," Jamie said. "It boggles the mind, but it's true. I even saw them together."

"Yuck."

"Yes. That was my reaction too. Anyway, they apparently spent this morning strolling through an apple orchard and she brought me... Brace your little self now." I made a show of spreading my legs and bending my knees and then nodded that I was ready. "A gift—a big bag of apples. Nice ones too."

Mrs. Frankenstein was famously, clinically stingy. I toppled over onto the rug in front of the couch, too shocked to remain upright.

Suddenly light dawned. "The apple corer is resting?"

Jamie nodded and put a finger to her lips, and we tiptoed into the kitchen. Our bowls waited on the table, ready for hot apple crisp, and my glass of milk had been poured.

Jamie opened the oven door and the kitchen filled with a damp, dense, divine smell that seemed to sum up all I was grateful for about her. I sat down with care because the ancient card table was prone to fits of unauthorized folding. Jamie filled our bowls to the brim and, grinning at each other, we lifted steaming spoonfuls of apple crisp drenched in vanilla cream and blew on them. I seared a few taste buds, but I didn't mind, because Jamie's apple crisp tasted and felt like life itself, and I wasn't willing to wait.

I loved Jamie more than anyone I'd ever known. She helped me learn to like apples again.

I once spent an entire day and part of a night under an old apple tree. I was five years old. It was springtime, and the tree's pale pink blossoms fluttered all around me like magic made visible.

The first thing I did, after I made sure there was no one else anywhere in sight, was kneel down and lick the morning dew off individual blades of grass because I was thirsty. The dew tasted amazing, like bug prints and greenness. If I squinted, I could see teeny-tiny pictures of myself in individual drops of dew before I slurped them up. I stopped when I noticed that my pants were so soaked from the knees down that I was going to get into trouble.

Then I hunted around for old apples. I brushed my hands at ground level through the tall grass to find half-buried apples and then dug them out of soil that smelled like sad, tired, dead apples no one had loved. When I found an apple that was edible enough, I wiped it on the damp grass and dried it on my shirt. When I ate it, the sourness made my face do funny things. I found enough to quell my hunger.

Then I danced in the falling blossoms for a long while, imagining their swirls and turnings as magic spells I'd made with my twig wand, imagining friends and conversations, blinking as rays of sunlight warmed me and played with me in the blossoms.

When time became endless, play segued into fear, and I shouted myself hoarse, impatient to be rescued. Then I cried. I climbed the tree, but I couldn't see anyone anywhere, and I was afraid to wander away because I'd been punished for that before. Finally I slept, curled in a tight ball against the trunk of the apple tree, which I'd wanted to be friends with. But it was bumpy and hard and wouldn't put its arms around me.

When I woke, the sun was almost down to the horizon, and I panicked in earnest and wore myself out. I cried myself to sleep again, in spite of being cold and hungry and scared of the animals I sensed shuffling closer and waiting to strike as soon as I dropped off. I remember that I dreamed of those animals for what felt like a lifetime. That night and for many nights afterward.

Hours later I woke to the brightness of a flashlight in my eyes and a stinging swat on my bottom for getting lost. Deep darkness stretched all around and swallowed up the last ounce of my courage.

I cried again then, but I did it silently. I wanted to be alone after all, because I realized the truth. I hadn't gotten lost. I was right where they had left me. The truth was that the people who were supposed to care for me had left me behind and then forgotten all about me for one whole day and part of a night.

A year or so ago someone gave me a big bag of apples from a family farm. I saved every single seed. Over the past week, I've carefully threaded those seeds to make a bracelet for Jamie. I'm going away today and want to give her something to remind her of our history with apples and of how much she means to me.

Before I leave the museum tonight, I'll send this article—which you're reading weeks later—to my editor at the newspaper. Then I'll stand at the window for a long while, remembering and staring out at the blossoms drifting from the big apple *trees in the courtyard. Finally I'll sigh, turn around, grab my two big briefcases, and lock up for the last time until I return at the end of November.*

Down in the parking garage, I'll stash the briefcases in the back of the RV and then I'll hit the road, head south, and drive through the night. I'm excited about this trip, about my research and the book tour, about the adventures I hope to find and the amazing people I know I'll meet. But I can't help also feeling sad about things that were and things that might have been.

Beginning this trip in darkness feels like the right way to say good-bye to what cannot be and to honor the seed of renewal, deep in the ground of me, collecting itself, reaching for daylight.

Light will come, as it always does, but I'm not waiting any longer. I keep my foot on the gas. If I'm lucky, I'll meet you soon. Someone will introduce us. We'll shake hands, and you'll tell me your name. We'll smile at each other over slices of warm apple pie as you tell me your stories.

I can't wait to hear them.

REVIVING OLD STORIES

AMHERST

ESTELLE, REFILLING A napkin dispenser near the young man, notices when his fork stops in midair. His other hand is pressed flat against the newspaper on the counter. Then she gets a good look at his face. "Everything all right, sweetie?"

He looks up at her, his face frozen and white. When he opens his mouth to answer, the fork falls from his fingers, and he flings himself back off the stool, lunging for the bathroom door, which, thank heavens, is right there next to him.

Estelle leans over the counter a little toward the bathroom door and faintly hears him being sick. Poor thing. Curious about what could have upset him so, she takes a look at the newspaper he shoved aside as he raced away. It's only an article about apples, which she begins to read.

Someone calls for more coffee, but she doesn't hear.

RUBEN SNEAKS BACK onto his stool at the counter, too exposed and frail to go any further. Estelle has removed the empty plate and fork, but left the newspaper. He leans forward until his heavy head rests on the counter, wraps his arms around himself as his body begins to shake with anger.

What kind of people forget about a five-year-old child? What kind of government gives that kind of person a child? How can Henry be so generous and caring after all he's lived through? How many heartbreaks and cruelties has Henry lived through that I don't even know about?

Ruben stares at the old wallpaper six inches from his nose and thinks about how selfish he's been. The sadness and longing and shame he's been trying to avoid for so long rise up through the anger.

I was one of Henry's heartbreaks.

From the other side of the counter, Estelle says, "I expect you don't have anything against apples, sweetie, but something about that article sure didn't agree with you." He feels her hand rest on his head for a moment and closes his eyes, remembering how he imagined Estelle as Henry's mother.

"Please don't be nice to me right now," he whispers.

Estelle either doesn't hear him or ignores him, because a few minutes later someone drapes a blanket over his shoulders, tucks it in around him and puts a hand on his back. It's such a nice thing to do, and the warmth and weight of the blanket and the hand feel so good that Ruben starts to cry. On top of everything else, he's embarrassed because he can't seem to cry without making a racket, and the diner is so tiny. Everyone must be staring at him, wondering.

Estelle pats him. "Don't you worry, sweetheart. No one here is going to judge you for anything. You just rest a bit. You hear?" Ruben nods and keeps crying, but she takes her hand away. He hears Estelle's footsteps and then her calm voice across the room. When he hears someone order the meatloaf platter and a vanilla milkshake, he takes a big, shaky breath.

Estelle comes back after a while, leans over the counter toward him, and says softly, "I see your phone here, sweetie. Is there someone I can call for you?"

Ruben focuses his attention on a blue flower on the wallpaper and wishes he could stay right there until afternoon becomes night and Estelle closes the diner. He imagines her shooing everyone out and locking the door, then calmly clearing tables and washing dishes, counting coins at the cash register, untying her apron, turning out lights, patting Ruben on the way past, letting him be.

He'd hear her muted footsteps on the stairs as she climbed to her apartment overhead. He'd grow drowsy amid the gentle hum of appliances and idly follow the occasional sweep of headlights across the wallpaper until his eyes closed. The sleep he would have then, he imagines, would be worth waiting for—a vast cave of forgetfulness. Much later, dawn would seep through the plate glass windows. Estelle, in a fresh, perfectly pressed uniform, would come down and make Ruben a piping hot cup of peppermint tea. The smell would wake him up. He'd straighten and stretch, rub his tear-streaked face, smile a tiny smile, and blink in the sunlight beginning to brighten the diner. Estelle would smile back and unlock the door, and the bell would jingle as the first customer came in... and it would be Henry.

Fuck.

I need help.

"Danny," he tells the wallpaper, and he must say it loud enough because, although Estelle is on the other side of the room by then, her footsteps come closer and Ruben hears her pick up his phone. After a pause he hears Estelle say, "Danny...? You don't know me, but you have a friend who's having some trouble... Does he have dark, sort of curly hair?" She taps Ruben on the shoulder. "Sweetie, is your name Ruben?" Ruben nods, and his cheek rubs against the counter. Estelle says into the phone, "Danny? Yes, it's Ruben... No. He'll be okay until you get here." She gives Danny the address of the diner and says good-bye.

"He says he's leaving right now, and he'll be here in about twenty minutes. Can I get you anything in the meantime, hon?" Ruben shakes his head, but that seems rude, so he swallows against the lump in his throat and says to the flower, "No. Thank you."

Thinking about Danny having to stop whatever he's doing and come fetch him makes Ruben feel even more pathetic than he already felt, which he hadn't thought possible.

RUBEN HAS TO pee. Carefully keeping his face turned toward the wall, he stands and takes off the blanket—plaid wool with fringe—drapes it over the stool, and slips into the bathroom. He pees and then washes his hands and splashes cold water on his face. Finally he looks at himself in the mirror.

Oh crap.

His face is a wretched, red-eyed mess. He takes a few deep breaths and rolls his shoulders. *Whatever.*

But then he tosses the paper towel into the trash and... the image of newborn Henry being tossed into the garbage in a men's bathroom explodes against the screen of his mind's eye, making him double over, dizzy and nauseous with the effort of trying to push it away. He leans back against the wall, slides down, and lets his head fall onto his drawn-up knees.

The scene repeats over and over on a draining loop he can't seem to escape. His useless hands drop to the cold floor.

That's where Danny finds him. The bathroom door bangs open against Ruben's shoe, and then Danny's on the floor on his knees, pulling Ruben forward into his arms, saying something comforting against Ruben's ear. But Ruben can't make out the words.

Because Ruben's mind, tired of keeping so many secrets from itself for so long, chooses that moment to unveil another one.

Danny is in love with me. And I keep breaking his heart.

⸻

R U B E N   H A S N ' T   S A I D much in the last half hour except "yes" and "no."

"Is this about Henry?"

"Yes."

"Do you want me to take you home?"

"No."

Estelle has been catching Danny up to speed. They both turn to look at Ruben and clearly want him to say something. Ruben knows they deserve to hear something. He surveys his throbbing head to see if he can find words to send to his mouth. *Nope.* He blinks, folds his hands together on the counter, and stares at the framed photo of ducks on a lake that hangs on the wall above the coffee machine behind Estelle. His mind is a perfect blank. Danny sighs and looks at Estelle.

Estelle, without a speck of disapproval in her voice, says to Ruben, "Sweetie, you've been coming here to my little diner for more than a year. I consider you a special customer and I take special interest in my special customers. It would be nice to know why you couldn't keep my pie down today." She covers Ruben's hands with one of her soft, wrinkly ones. "Don't you think that's fair?"

Ruben decides it'll be easier to talk to Estelle than Danny, so he edits Danny out of the scene, knowing it's unfair but needing to do something to get himself to talk so they'll stop staring at him.

"You read it?" Ruben asks, nodding at the article on the counter.

Estelle nods.

Ruben can't think about the article as a whole or he'll be sick again. He clenches his jaw and tries to think of a way to tell Estelle why he hurts so much.

Estelle glances down at the paper. "You know this Henry Normand? Personally?"

Ruben nods miserably.

"Is any of this about you?"

Ruben nods again. "I gave him that bag of apples."

Estelle waits for him to go on. Her calm eyes make Ruben sigh.

"Every week," Ruben says, "there's another article by Henry. Most of them seem to include personal messages to me. *I hate them.*" Ruben shoves the newspaper away, knowing he doesn't mean it, already wanting to pull it back. He sighs again. "No. The truth is... the real truth is I love his articles. They're full of everything I liked about him."

Estelle leans over the counter and says, "You're pining for this Henry, aren't you?"

Ruben's body tenses. He'd forgotten to be cautious in case Estelle isn't as tolerant as he'd imagined her to be.

"Ease up there, hon," Estelle says gently. "My grandson is gay. I may be old, but I'm not a relic."

Ruben swallows and wills the diner and Estelle to suffuse him with their frankness and lack of pretense.

"Well?" Estelle urges.

"I can't get him out of my head. It's tearing me apart."

"Why do you need to get him out of your head?"

"He doesn't want me."

"Are you sure, sweetie? Seems to me if he's writing about you in his articles, he might still have feelings for you. Whether that's true or not, you still have feelings for him. The question is, what are you going to do about it?"

"It's not that simple, Estelle."

"Why not. What's the problem?"

"*I am.* I'm not grown-up enough for him. We... we liked each other a lot, but I'm not what he wants. These personal messages in the articles are all about how he appreciated me but he's trying to get over me."

"Who says you're not grown-up enough for him?" Estelle asks.

"*He* did...," Ruben says, but then he furrows his brow and tilts his head. *What was it Henry said about me not being grown-up enough?*

Ruben sits up straight and stares at Estelle, who smiles like she already knows the answer.

"I did," he says to himself. He slaps his forehead. "Oh my God. *He* didn't..."

Ruben closes his eyes to try harder to remember their specific conversations about why they were ending it that weekend. As each memory comes up, Ruben feels more stupid and sick.

In every instance, in every memory, in every conversation, Henry said he wanted more, and Ruben said he wanted less.

A series of truths, long cramped within the dark corners of his heart, bursts into the light of consciousness. Ruben grips the counter, afraid of tilting over in the bright glare.

I thought I only wanted Henry for sex education. I thought I wasn't capable of more. I thought I wasn't grown-up enough to say yes. But Henry thought I was grown-up enough. All I had to do was say yes. Yes. I'm in love with Henry. I'm in love with Henry.

"I'm in love with Henry," Ruben says to Estelle, like it's a simple fact she needs to know.

"Of course you are, sweetie."

Customers come in, making the bell on the door jingle, and Estelle goes to get them settled and take their drink orders. In her absence Danny and Ruben sit next to each other in awkward silence.

When he feels his heart start to pound from the tension, Ruben turns to look at Danny. Though Danny's head is bowed, Ruben can see his misery.

Afraid to touch Danny because he's not sure he can keep pity or shame out of his touch, Ruben stares at Danny until he looks up.

It seems difficult for Danny to look at Ruben, but he does it anyway, and that makes Ruben reach for him, squeeze Danny's thigh, and then let his hand rest there.

Danny covers Ruben's hand with his own and looks down at their hands together. Then he takes his hand away and looks into Ruben's eyes.

In a whisper, Danny says, "I wanted you to get over him."

RUBEN HUGS ESTELLE good-bye, promises to see her soon, and leaves with Danny. In the car Ruben struggles to gather the flapping ends of truth into something honest and caring he can offer Danny.

"I need closure," Ruben says. "Somehow. One way or another. If I'm going to move on, in whatever direction, I have to talk with Henry. Maybe he doesn't want me. Maybe he's with someone else now. But I have to stop kidding myself and resolve this for real."

Danny nods but keeps his eyes on the road. Ruben notices his tight grip on the steering wheel.

"I'm sorry it's taken me this long to sort things out," Ruben says. "I'm sorry I hurt you."

They stare out the windows for a while.

Ruben thinks of something else he wants to say. "Even if it's been a fucked-up love until now, I do love you, Danny. I'm not going to stop loving you."

"But you just want to be friends now. Right?"

"Yeah," Ruben says.

After a few miles, Danny says, "Thank you for finally telling me the truth."

* * *

THE NEXT NIGHT, as Ruben plods through the boring work of typing up the bibliography for a paper and struggles to keep his mind on task, he wonders what his life might have been like if he'd said yes to Henry during that weekend they shared.

Would he have proofread Henry's "Everyday History" articles? Would they have gone to Germany together in October? Would Ruben be out on the road with Henry, driving the RV while Henry reads the map by flashlight, looking for the turn-off to the campground?

God, it would have been fun to be on the road with Henry. Why did I assume a life with Henry would be too boring for me?

Ruben sighs at his idiocy, prints the bibliography, and closes his laptop.

It's not until he stands at the door with his hand on the doorknob, about to head to Ellis's room for habitual comfort, that he realizes he doesn't want to go. At all.

"Huh," he says as his hand falls away from the door. The end of Henry's apple article blazes across his mind.

"I'm not waiting any longer."

A spike of white-hot jealousy flashes through Ruben for a moment when he thinks of some other guy driving the RV into a campground with Henry... because Henry isn't waiting any longer.

Well, then I'm not waiting either.

I know how to grow up.

One way or another, it's time to face the truth.

PART V
THE WEEKS

THE HISTORIAN
LOOKING FOR HIMSELF

THE EXPLORER
LOOKING FOR HENRY

LOOKING FOR HIMSELF

JUNE

INTERVIEWER: When I sat down and reread the newspaper articles you've included in your book, it made me wonder all over again who the heartbreak was about. How does the love story that's in the subtext of some of your "Everyday History" articles turn out?

NORMAND: Yes, some of the articles were about someone in particular. I was... experimenting. I wanted to see if writing those articles would help me process the heartache.

INTERVIEWER: And did it?

NORMAND: Yes and no. After I wrote those articles, they... weighed on me somehow. At some point I decided to mentally archive them as my past and face the future.

INTERVIEWER: That's when you stopped writing the heartache articles?

NORMAND: Yes.

INTERVIEWER: I miss them. Of course I'm sorry for your pain, but those passionate, allusive articles were my favorites. They were evocative and hinted at mystery.

NORMAND: Geez. And I thought they were indulgent, ill-advised, mental hand wringing. To me they always seemed too cryptic not to irritate an outsider.

INTERVIEWER: By "outsider," you mean anyone apart from you and the person you were heartbroken about?

NORMAND: Yes.

INTERVIEWER: A few times in those articles, you speak directly to that person, which makes the articles read like secret letters to a secret lover, and yet you somehow provide enough contextual information that I don't feel left out. I've been talking with people about your articles for a while now, and the heartache articles often come up. People want to know more about the love story and who it's about, but they also wonder about your careful avoidance of "he" or "she." Did you do that on purpose?

NORMAND: Oh... Umm... At some point, way back when, I semiconsciously adopted a writing style that's inclusive, so different kinds of readers can relate. It's a habit by now. My friend Jamie teases me about going overboard with it. She calls me the Crusading Pluralist, because I always want to include everyone in the possibilities, even when it's awkward.

INTERVIEWER: I have to ask. Is Jamie the person the heartache is about?

NORMAND: Give me a break here, you meanie. I'm trying to handle becoming well-known without stressing myself into a crack addiction—now that I can afford one—so please don't push me on this.

INTERVIEWER: [laughs]. All right. I can change directions, though I'm not promising you'll like it any better. While preparing for this interview, I discovered that most of the funding for your activities—your TV show and many of your programs and events—comes from conservative organizations. You spoke a moment ago about inclusiveness being important to you, and your opinions and writing come across as liberal, so how does it all add up? How did you get into this conservative funding situation?

NORMAND: I'm lucky to have an agent who listens to my ideas about projects I want to do and then makes them happen. We send out proposals to see who's interested. Sometimes I do accept funding from conservative organizations, though the programs themselves reach out to people across a broad spectrum.

INTERVIEWER: You talked earlier in the show about some of the surprising results coming out of the programs you're referring to. It's pretty obvious that you're onto something.

NORMAND: To tell you the truth, I'm bowled over by the response to this simple idea.

INTERVIEWER: Frankly, Henry, I think people are responding to more than the idea. You're simply too intriguing for your own good. Let's move on to your self-described technophobia. Rumors abound. Why don't you set the record straight. When it comes to modern technology, what can and can't you do? Let's get specific.

NORMAND: Okay. I do have a computer, but I always write first and second drafts by hand. I use the computer as a typewriter. And... um... I use the Internet in a minimal way—to send material to my newspaper and book editors. What else? Oh, I have an e-mail account. But honestly I'm an unrepentant goof when it comes to e-mail. I have to psych myself up so much that I end up procrastinating until regular mail would've been faster anyway...

INTERVIEWER: Your pause is going on and on. Are you trying to organize your mental list of your other modern technology skills, or was that it? How about a cell phone? He's shaking his head, folks. MP3 player? iPod? E-book reader?

NORMAND: I don't even know what some of those things are.

INTERVIEWER: I'm shocked. Were you raised by cavemen?

NORMAND: I was, but I'm not going to talk about that.

INTERVIEWER: Explain. Why this nonrelationship with modern digital technology?

NORMAND: I became a historian in the first place because I feel an affinity for simpler times. And I seem to have a cellular-level mistrust of modern technology. I'm aces with mechanical things, but the digital world remains beyond me. It exhausts me and, if I'm honest, it creeps me out. If I can use a screwdriver to open a gadget and watch the gears turn, I'm all over it. I get how it works. I can understand what's wrong. I can even repair it. We're friendly with each other, me and that mechanical gadget. But if I were to pry the cover off of, say, a cell phone, I'd find... what? An enslaved elf or some other magical creature giving me a raspberry, probably. I can't work with that. It's too... foreign, too futuristic, too alien to the long-gone eras with which I feel a connection. My agent despairs of me. Having a Luddite for a client makes his job challenging, but he does his best. Bless his digitized New-York-City heart.

INTERVIEWER: But how are you able to do what you do—be on the road for an extended time, shoot local TV show episodes in different places, keep up with an ever-shifting schedule of interviews, all of that—without a cell phone? Is that even legal these days?

NORMAND: Sure. I have an address book—a lovely leather one I got in Rome. And I have a schedule book. I find a hotel with a business center, or a gas station with a nice view, and I use a phone card or quarters at a payphone, and if I need to update my schedule or make a note, I hold the phone in the crook of my neck and I use what they call a pen to write on stuff called paper.

How absurd. People close to me try to convince me that using a cell phone would make my life easier, but I can't seem to get my backward-viewing mind around the idea enough to persuade my body to use one. I get modern technology intellectually but not personally. Left to my own devices—pun intended—I'd walk handwritten copies of my articles to my nearest neighbor with a basket of chocolate chip cookies and sit and wait for them to read what I wrote so we could chat about it.

INTERVIEWER: But then what do you do with the many hours the rest of us spend watching TV and online videos, texting, or talking on our cell phones?

NORMAND: Probably the same things your grandparents did. I explore ideas on paper with a fountain pen. I listen to record albums. I sit on the couch and stare out the window. I read books—the old-fashioned kind. I have friends over for dinner. I fold laundry. I write letters by hand and walk them to the post office. I seem to need a lot of quiet slowness. That's why I'm doing this tour in an RV. I crave the special peace that comes with familiar surroundings, and I don't like being accessible all the time.

INTERVIEWER: It's tempting to catalog you as a reclusive scholar, except you seem to be everywhere these days, and you're not shy about getting in front of a microphone or a camera. How does that work into your whole Luddite mentality? Your TV show is gaining popularity at an alarming rate, and this book tour and road trip is heavy on personal appearances and live interviews.

NORMAND: Teaching trumps technology. I love being a teacher—interacting with people in real time to infect them with my love of history. And I love it when the walls between us come down and we connect on a deeper level.

INTERVIEWER: That kind of connecting is hard to manage when your audiences are getting bigger and bigger, I'd imagine.

NORMAND: Well, I feel very comfortable in classrooms. Auditoriums, community centers, and even radio broadcasts, are only different-sized classrooms, and I still feel a connection with the audience.

INTERVIEWER: How is it that your website and your Twitter and Facebook accounts are active to the point of causing shock waves? It's obvious now that you're not personally making that happen.

NORMAND: Apparently I'll hire someone to use modern technology for me before I'll learn to use it myself. My agent and his staff are godlike. They toss me around the digital world, accumulating publicity, and I have enough involvement to be confident they're representing me well. I'm very grateful. Their willingness to work within my geezer limitations allows me to focus on what I love most.

INTERVIEWER: *It's working. You've been accumulating coverage at a break-neck speed.*

NORMAND: *I have. It's a bit scary.*

LOOKING FOR HENRY

AMHERST

RUBEN TURNS OFF the radio and swings his feet off the bed.

What the hell?

He heads to his computer and spends a couple of hours searching for crumbs. He scours Henry's website and Twitter and Facebook feeds. He finds interviews he hadn't seen before. He pulls up reviews of Henry's book. He scans social media chatter about Henry's TV show, which Ruben's been watching since his breakdown at Estelle's diner. He checks the fan forums that have grown up around Henry's activities. But there's nothing.

Not one word about Henry being gay.

Interesting.

THREE DAYS LATER | BOSTON

WHEN RUBEN APPROACHES the main information desk at the museum, a young woman looks up from her computer to offer a professional smile.

"Abby?" he says.

"Ruben!" She leaps up and jogs around the desk to give him a hug. "How *are* you? It's so nice to see you again." Her smile flares into the megawatt range. *Uh-oh. Did my Henry fixation make me that ignorant?*

"I'm doing great," Ruben says, taking a step back.

Abby—one of the babblers Henry listened to with endless patience—takes a big breath. Then the museum phone rings. *Thank God.*

As he waits Ruben takes a turn around the information desk. Not a lot has changed since he did his internship. Being in the museum again feels nostalgic and pervy, like watching a titillating movie he was once very familiar with but hasn't seen in a long time.

When Abby hangs up, Ruben pounces, determined to try out his playing-dumb strategy. "Hey. I'm looking for Mr. Normand. Is he around?"

"Oh. Too bad. He loves it when his former students come and visit, but he doesn't work here now."

Ruben's chest empties for a moment, but he pulls himself together and keeps his voice casual. "What do you mean? He didn't move, did he?" He pictures Henry hurling himself across the Atlantic, back to Germany to relive his college years in Martin's arms. *Stop it, Ruben. Focus.*

"No, no," Abby says. "He's on a long leave of absence—on a book tour—ever since his book came out. Plus his show's taping episodes all over the country." She grins. "He visits people's weird little museums, and he does programs with kids who..." She stops and fixes Ruben with a stern look. "You *do* know about his column and his book. Right?"

Ruben nods. "Yeah. Of course. It's great to hear about his success. He must be thrilled."

"Oh, he is. We all are. It's about time he got more recognition beyond the Boston area." She huffs like a proud hen. Ruben recognizes the feeling.

"How can I get in touch with him?" Ruben gestures in the general direction of Henry's office. "Or... do you mind if I take a quick peek in his office, for old times' sake?" *Total flaming dork. What the hell am I doing?* Ruben knows it's an inappropriate request, but brazens it out. He stares at her and worries Henry's leather bracelet on his wrist. *Have mercy on me, Abby.* She takes her time fabricating another stern look.

What if I told her the truth? Can someone please, please let me into Henry's office? I need to be near something that belongs to him, and I'm desperate to lean my forehead against his window.

"Sorry. No chance." Abby shakes her head. "Why don't you e-mail him?"

"Tried that. No response."

"Well, we all reach him through the e-mail address listed on his website."

"Hmm," says Ruben. "What about a phone number?"

"No. Oh. Maybe. Calls go through his agent because..." She chuckles with her hand over her mouth. "Mr. Normand keeps losing his cell phone. How about I give you his agent's card."

Ruben opens his mouth to tell her he's seen the agent's contact information on the agency's website and even sent him an e-mail, but he stops because the card might offer more.

She rummages in a drawer. "Here you go. Nice guy, the agent. I met him a couple of times. One of those superintense, too-hunky, slick New Yorkers. But he seems to know what he's doing."

"Great, Abby. Thanks. Have you... have you been in touch with Mr. Normand directly? How is he? I mean, I can read his website, but you know..."

"No idea, really. He's never been talkative on e-mail. Or on the phone, for that matter. He calls and gets the job done, but he saves the good stuff for in person. People here were frustrated at first about having to go through the agent, but it actually seems to work just fine."

So why hasn't it worked for me?

"Interesting" is all Ruben manages to say. It's lame, but he's trying to think.

Does Abby know if Henry's out? Could I ask without outing Henry if he's not?

"Hey. Do you know...? Maybe I could reach Mr. Normand through whoever he's been... dating? Do you know if he's with anyone?" He holds his breath, hoping she won't call him on being an inappropriate ass.

Abby's pause seems to last a week.

"Uh... no," she finally says, and Ruben feels his chest relax. But then she goes on. "I wouldn't know if he's with anyone or not. That man is like Fort Knox about his personal life."

"With the obvious exception of his articles," Ruben says, his chest tightening again.

"I know. How does he do that? Share without sharing enough to keep it from still being private?"

"Hey, listen. I just thought of something. Do you remember a woman named Jamie who was maybe—"

"Oh yeah. Right. I do." She blinks and pauses. "I used to wonder why he didn't have a girlfriend."

At the word "girlfriend," Ruben feels the bite of another nail in the coffin of Henry's closet.

"Then he brought this really fun woman—Jamie—to the annual fundraiser a while back," Abby says. "We all sat at the same table. She and Mr. Normand were hilarious together. It made me happy for him, though she was quite a bit older, which surprised me."

"When was that?"

"Um... let's see. We had Mr. Normand's *Past-Modern Technology* exhibit up, so... two and a half years ago? The fundraiser dinner is always in January."

"Do you know Jamie's last name?"

"No. Sorry. I did at some point, but I've forgotten. I only met her that once."

Ruben nods, preoccupied.

"Hey," Abby says. She stands, as if prepared to preempt Ruben's retreat. "If Mr. Normand calls, I could give him your cell number... um... if you give it to me." She smiles a smile Ruben recognizes as dangerous, and he shifts his focus to managing a graceful exit.

"He's got it," he says. "Thanks a bunch, Abby."

"Sure," Abby says with an open-invitation smile.

Ruben turns and walks away, his mind busy with questions.

Why would he keep himself in the closet? How about crossing that threshold, Henry?

Thoughts swirling, Ruben takes a sharp right at the bottom of the front steps outside the museum and circles around to the arched doorway that leads to the inner courtyard.

I wish I'd thought to visit when the apple trees were still in bloom.

He stands beneath Henry's office window, peers up through breeze-flipped leaves, and allows his imagination to deliver a time-warped glimpse of Henry peering out the window from inside.

When his imagination includes himself behind Henry's shoulder, whispering into Henry's ear, and the subsequent pain on Henry's face as he leans his forehead against the window, Ruben turns to go.

I saw. I came. I left. What a child.

He bends to pluck a leaf from the grass.

How long it will take me to grow up?

What if it doesn't happen soon enough?

AT HIS PARENTS' house, Ruben reviews the e-mail he's been working on. It's not the first e-mail he's sent to Henry since his breakdown at the diner, but it's going to be the last. He's been debating for weeks about sending it, because it's going to out Henry to whoever is passing on his personal e-mails. *If Henry didn't trust his agent and this system, he wouldn't be using it. Right?*

The e-mail is simple but complete—a few short, clear, honest paragraphs that put everything on the table.

"I'm in love with you, Henry."

Ruben takes a deep breath and clicks the Send button.

Afterward he treats himself to a celebratory chocolate milkshake at a bakery a few blocks from his parents' house. Paradoxically it makes Ruben feel more grown-up than taking himself out to a bar for a celebratory beer.

HENRY'S E-MAILED REPLY arrives the next morning.

To: Ruben Harper
From: Henry Normand
Subject: Re: PERSONAL MESSAGE FOR HENRY

Ruben,

I appreciate your frankness, but I've moved on. I've been seeing someone else for a while who I really like. I wish the same for you.

Be well—and have fun,
Henry

LOOKING FOR HIMSELF

BEFORE EVERY PRESENTATION, before every radio interview, before every TV show, I offer a prayer to Phillips Thomas, my personal patron saint of amplification.

I picture him in his three-piece suit in his Westinghouse Electric lab in the 1920s, intently holding a special microphone to catch the heartbeats of a kissing couple. Or leaning back in his desk chair, contemplating ways to facilitate mental telepathy.

I appreciate the man's spirit.

In the stillness before I speak into a microphone to send the waves of my voice out into the room or across the country, I think of Phillips and offer my pint-sized prayer...

Heartbeats and telepathy.

LOOKING FOR HENRY

JULY | AMHERST

Ruben checks his cell phone beneath the table. If the professor catches him, he'll be in trouble, and yet he can't seem to stop himself.

Still no callback from Henry's agent. It's been two weeks, three voice mails, and two e-mails since Ruben started trying to reach him, with no response.

A day after the body blow of Henry's e-mail, Ruben shrugged it off, determined to find a way to see Henry anyway.

Either my intuition is trying to tell me something or I'm becoming a stalker.

He puts away his phone and turns his attention back to the lecture. But one corner of his mind never seems to stop strategizing.

Ruben straightens his legs and slouches back in his desk chair. "How would you find someone whose last name you didn't know?"

Ellis, Ruben's housemate, rolls onto his back on Ruben's bed and uses his fat biochemistry textbook as a pillow. "Well, what do you know about him... or her?"

"Her. *Nothing*," Ruben says and feels the tightness in his voice.

"Ho, there," says Ellis. "Message received. Code-red mission it is, then."

"Yeah."

"Do you know anyone else who knows her?"

"No. Well, no one I can get in touch with."

Ellis goes back to contemplating the ceiling, and then asks, "What's her occupation?"

"No idea. She lived abroad for a while and may or may not be back in Boston."

"Any disfigurement? Tattoos? Scars?"

"Oh for God's sake, Ellis."

"Well?"

"I have no idea. I've never met her."

Ellis continues to ask questions, some more thought provoking than others. As they veer more and more into the surreal, Ruben feels more and more hopeless. "Never mind," he says. "I should get some sleep."

"Okay," says Ellis. "But be alert for brain farts. You might think of something useful about her when you least expect it."

ELLIS HEADS BACK to his room, and Ruben goes to bed. His dream begins with something that really happened on the first day of his weekend with Henry—after Ruben half hoisted Henry from the front door to the bedroom and threw him onto the bed. As happened in reality, by the time Ruben falls on top of Henry and Henry wraps his arms around him, they're both hard, and their kiss, which is only their second real kiss, escalates from zero to rocket launch the first time Ruben grinds against Henry's hips.

Afraid he's going to drool into Henry's mouth because he's not willing to take time out to swallow, Ruben finally manages to pull back a fraction of an inch. But Henry's mouth follows him. Ruben straddles Henry's lap and they're still kissing, hands moving fast.

Henry reaches inside the back of Ruben's jeans and clutches his bare ass to pull him closer. Ruben's heart feels like a cartoon, pounding out of his chest, and he wonders if Henry can feel its jackhammer. *I'm going to pass out. I'm going to pass out from the shock of this much joy.*

Then the memory replay morphs into all dream—a dream in which Ruben wakes up on the floor by Henry's bed after he's fainted. He opens his eyes to see a burly, serious-faced paramedic looming over him to put an oxygen mask over his mouth and nose. Ruben tries to ask him where Henry is, but the paramedic has his hand over the mask to keep it in place, and he turns away to talk to another paramedic standing in Henry's bedroom doorway.

The paramedic in the doorway wears a red cape. *She must be the boss.* The paramedic kneeling beside Ruben shakes his head and says, "I don't think he's going to survive the trip across the threshold." Ruben watches the man's eyebrows knit with concern. "But based on these readings, we've got no choice. We've got to get him out of here stat."

Ruben's hard-on pushes painfully against the front of his jeans. "I need Henry," he shouts into the oxygen mask, but there's too much other noise for anyone to hear him. Sirens wail outside. The paramedics trade acronyms in urgent voices. A third paramedic leans over Ruben. Blue lights flash and whirl around the bedroom.

Amid the shoulders moving through his limited field of vision, past hands raised to fondle walkie-talkies, between concerned expressions, a slice of space opens up for a moment, and Ruben catches a glimpse of Henry in the hallway.

"There he is! He's right there," Ruben yells into the mask, but his voice disappears, and no one notices.

Another brief space opens, and Ruben watches Henry scrub a hand across his bald head in agitation. His other hand presses against his chest, like he's trying to keep his own cartoon heart from bursting out to get to Ruben.

The paramedics come to a decision. They roll Ruben onto his side to get a sheet beneath him. Then they count to three and lift it to carry Ruben out of the room. But when his feet reach the doorway, they all stop as if they've hit a solid wall. Henry is so close. He's right on the other side of the doorway.

The dream freezes then, as though someone pressed a Pause button. Ruben fills with dread. He knows his situation is serious. If they don't figure out a way to get him across the threshold soon, he'll die. He feels his life draining away. He's going to die a few feet from Henry, watching Henry reach for him. In the paused scene, Henry looks scared. His eyes reflect flashes of blue light.

Ruben closes his eyes in the dream, and his mind tries to wake him up, because the dream is too painful.

"Wait! Not yet," Henry implores. "Please. Not yet." Desperation evident in the tension of his shoulders, Henry pulls free of the frozen pause and steps across the threshold and into the bedroom. He weaves through and around the still-frozen paramedics to get to Ruben. He has to shove aside the paramedic's stiff hand to pull the oxygen mask away from Ruben's mouth.

"They were wrong," Henry says as he lowers his mouth to Ruben's. "I'm the one who's got what you need." As Henry's mouth presses against Ruben's, his kiss brilliant and warm, all the oxygen Ruben's been missing fills his chest with life.

The sweet breath that reanimates Ruben, that recharges the world with movement and color and vitality, tastes like apple pie.

The last dream image delivers an overhead shot of Ruben and Henry as boys, sitting across from each other at a rickety card table in a shabby apartment that Ruben knows must be Jamie's. They dig into giant bowls of apple crisp with vanilla cream and grin at each other. Beneath the table, Ruben rests his feet on top of Henry's.

RUBEN POUNDS ON the wall beside his bed with the side of his fist.

A minute later Ellis opens Ruben's door and makes his way in the dark to the bed, where he feels for Ruben, who's curled himself into a ball. Ellis lies down on top of the covers and slings an arm across Ruben.

"Hey. You're okay," Ellis smooths Ruben's hair, which helps Ruben focus.

"Where are you now?" Ellis asks, and the beautiful, quirky Ellis-ness of the question brings Ruben's focus out of the dream the rest of the way. He gulps a shaky breath and uncurls a little.

"Here. I'm right here," Ruben says. "Holy shit."

"Well, then... where *were* you?"

"You were right."

"You mean we *do* belong together, and I can get under the covers now? Praise Jesus."

Ruben groans. "No. Sorry." He rubs his eyes and scoots to sit up and lean across Ellis to turn on the bedside lamp. "I'm sorry," he says into Ellis's eyes.

Ellis nods and shrugs. "It was worth a try," he says as he adjusts his bathrobe and sits up beside Ruben. "What was I right about?"

"You were right about something coming to me when I least expect it. I've had a thought."

"That's great. So why all the wee-hour drama?"

Ruben sighs and rubs his eyes again. "The useful thought was wrapped inside a bad dream. I mean a *good* dream. *Shit.* Just... a hard dream."

"Best kind."

"Ellis, we never talk about stuff like this, but..."

Ellis studies Ruben's face for an awkward minute. "Who is he?"

Ruben doesn't attempt to avoid the question. Ellis deserves the truth, so Ruben gives it to him. Most of it.

They share a long stretch of silence after Ruben stops talking, and then Elliot unfolds the quilt from the bottom of Ruben's bed, drapes it over his legs, and says, "The odds are a bit off the chart."

"How many bakeries do you think there are in Boston?" Ruben asks.

"Hell of a lot of bakeries in the greater Boston area. But you're not looking for a bakery, you're looking for a baker. There are bakers in places like hospitals, schools, company kitchens, big hotels, factories—"

"Okay, okay. I get it."

Ellis stares into the darkness at the end of Ruben's bed. "You could check professional bakers' associations in Boston," he says. "Or in the region. If Jamie *is* in the Boston area, if she *is* working professionally as a baker, if she *is* a member of such an association, you could find her that way." He's thoughtful again for a moment. "Jamie isn't a very common name, so asking for members with a first name of Jamie probably wouldn't turn up all that big a list."

"Okay. Tomorrow I'll..." Ruben stops and tilts his head, as if to get a better look at something that flicked through his peripheral vision.

"Holy synapse fest, Batman?" Ellis asks.

"Yeah. Maybe. I wonder if Henry sublet his apartment. Maybe there's a subletter who knows something."

"Possible jackpot there."

Ruben yawns and rolls his shoulders. "Oh, man. I can't think anymore. I have to sleep." He's quiet for a moment, and neither of them moves. "Thanks. I owe you."

"Yet again."

"How about that brunch buffet at the Crackpot? My treat. In about—" Ruben leans around Ellis to check the clock. "—six hours?"

"Yeah. Sure." Ellis nods but doesn't get up. "I'm actually glad you woke me up," he says. "I was dreaming about human anatomy—and not in a good way. Remind me again why I let you persuade me to do a summer semester?"

"Stop complaining. Let's make brunch a study session and then go on a hike. It's possible to get the studying done and still have fun."

"Yeah," Ellis snorts. "Millie totally misplaced that memo. She's not home from last night's party, and I know she hasn't studied for that test she has tomorrow."

"We should do an intervention and drag her to brunch with us," Ruben says.

On a sigh that sounds like a surrender, Ellis says, "Yeah. Okay." He stands, but turns back to look down at Ruben. Seeing the pain in Ellis's eyes, Ruben opens his mouth to uninvite Millie, to apologize again, but Ellis stops him by turning out the bedside light and leaving.

In a few minutes, just as Ruben begins to descend into sleep, he hears a double knock on the wall by his bed, on the other side of which is Ellis's bed. Ruben knocks back twice to say he's okay.

He opens the fist he knocked with into a palm and presses it against the wall, holding it there with the hope that Ellis falls asleep soon and finds better dreams.

My questing heart keeps fucking up other people's lives.

My heart needs a home.

LOOKING FOR HIMSELF

JULY | DALLAS-FORT WORTH AIRPORT

Erik's instructions deliver me to a swank, members-only lounge. Stepping from the airport terminal's wearying combination of bustle and stasis into the club's ambiance of timeless opulence shocks me into fish-mouthed wonder.

I feel like a hobo crashing a high-society ball.

For weeks I've woken at dawn on the thin mattress in my RV or tossed all night on too-short couches in the homes of kind strangers. I've waited in shower line-ups at campgrounds, reread menus at tiny roadside diners trying to find something edible, refilled my water bottles at highway rest stops, and generally lived the life of a penny-pinching vagabond.

The chairs and couches in the club look so damn comfortable my eyelids droop in sleepy anticipation. From the ornate bar comes the subtle clink of expensive liquor bottles touching the rims of crystal tumblers. The decor is dark and richly textured, accented with white lilies in huge vases. I close my eyes and take a deep breath through my nose. Beyond the scent of the lilies, I discover hints of... *oh God...* steak and grilled seafood and—

"Henry?" I open my eyes to see Erik smiling at me. He claps my shoulder and leads me to one of the small, horseshoe-shaped booths. "You found me," he says as he moves his briefcase off the table.

"Crickey," I say, looking around. "Remind me what your fee is."

"It's great to see you," Erik says, still smiling, and I can't help but grin back.

"I wish I'd taken a detox shower and sprung for a new wardrobe before meeting you here," I say. "I feel so... rumpled and homely."

"And yet you're not. You look great, Henry. I keep telling you to spend more."

"What a shocking concept." I sigh and relax and slouch into the booth, trying on a sense of ownership.

"That's it," says Erik, laughing. "It looks good on you."

"What does?"

He waits until I open my eyes to say, "Luxury." The corner of his mouth quirks up and his eyes twinkle into mine.

Uh-oh.

Erik, my amazing, kick-ass agent, is happily married to a wealthy socialite bombshell. He dotes on his three kids. He's... *oh, shit.* He's *still* looking at me...

"You know what," I say. "I'm going to go freshen up. Be right back."

I always feel like a wilted flower around Erik, who exudes an intimidating mix of intense maleness and big-city boldness.

I shouldn't complain. I'm grateful for all the extra zeros on my bank statements that his bold know-how has blessed me with. Most of all I'm grateful for the way he helps me help people. I keep imagining more ways Everyday History can connect, reach, and assist. And he keeps making them happen.

What else is he trying to make happen?

Oh God. I hope I'm wrong.

Grateful for the private restroom, I bury my damp face in a fresh, fluffy towel and wonder how long I can hide until Erik comes looking for me.

Why has he not looked at me like that before? Or has he and I haven't noticed? When did I last see him in person? A month ago. In Nashville. Where I taped that TV episode and did that long radio interview that Erik said was a big success. But I'm pretty sure he didn't look at me like that then. What happened between then and now? I hold the towel against my face for a while and breathe into its darkness, but nothing comes to mind to explain Eric's look.

I lower the towel and peer at myself in the mirror. I'm surrounded by luxury I can now afford—comfort and freedom—courtesy of Erik's skills.

And it hits me. I grope for the vanity table chair, sit down with a thump, and put my head between my knees to catch my breath.

How free is a life in which I use ambiguous pronouns when I talk about love?

How free am I if I'm not free to love?

Damn it. I forgot to stay out of the closet.

"Hey," Erik says as I slide back into the booth. "Let's order." He pushes a menu toward me.

"I need to tell you something important," I say, ignoring the menu.

He puts his menu down and looks at me. "I'm listening."

"I'm gay," I say.

He doesn't look surprised. "I suspected."

"Since when?"

He shifts in his seat a tiny bit. Then he seems to catch himself and stops. "Small things piling up."

I watch his face closely. "Erik, are you attracted to me?"

"*Christ*, Henry."

But a flash of fear crosses his face. Even more disturbing, I know I saw a moment of desire soften his eyes before the fear kicked it to the curb and denial won the day.

The waiter comes by, but Erik and I both shake our heads, not taking our eyes off one another, and the waiter fades away.

"Come on," I say. "Your connecting flight leaves in two hours, and I have appointments in Austin this afternoon. We don't have time for small talk. If you're attracted to me, put it on the table so we can clear the air and move on."

Erik takes a deep breath and leans back. He studies me, his face stony. I've seen that look of his before, in meetings with lawyers. Calculating.

"I like you a lot, Henry. You're a goldmine and a wonderful person, but... I don't swing that way. I would have thought that was obvious. What made you even ask that question?"

I don't believe him for one second. The vibe I'm getting is more than mere platonic fondness. I know he's lying. But maybe he's lying to himself, not me. I also know I won't gain anything by insisting, so I shrug. "Something in the way you were looking at me a minute ago." I wave the moment aside. "Forget it."

He shifts in his seat again and stops himself. He's not as relaxed as he wants me to think he is.

"So," I say. "Let's talk about me coming out to the world at large."

This makes him even more jittery. His anxiety is barely discernable, but I feel the tiny reverberations of his leg moving up and down under the table. The parts of him I can see remain perfectly composed.

He clears his throat, takes a drink, and asks, "Why haven't you wanted to come out before?"

"Does it matter?"

"I'm curious. Was it because of the person you write about sometimes in your articles? Are you waiting for them? Him."

"Maybe," I say. "No. I was. Not anymore."

"What's his name?"

I can't think of a reason not to tell him, and I don't like hiding any more than I already am. So I say, "Ruben. His name is Ruben."

That stills Erik's agitated leg. He turns his calculating gaze on me and says, "You publicly coming out would be a problem."

I narrow my eyes inside a flare of irritation. "Excuse me? I'm not *asking* you. I'm telling you, someone I employ, so you can manage publicity around it. I want to come out. Immediately. In public. Period."

"Henry, please. Wait." His expression softens, and he says, "Hear me out." He turns the tumbler in his hand, and the ice cubes clack and crack while he ponders them.

"What's your favorite aspect of your work these days?" he finally asks.

I don't even have to think about my answer. It pushes against my teeth to get out. "Helping people."

"Like the foster kids you've been meeting with? Like the battered women and the cafeteria lunch ladies and the civil servants in the back rooms—"

"Yes. All of them."

"What do you see for yourself in the long term, way out there?"

"Everyday History programs in schools and communities, Everyday History centers, more publications and events, research and studies and... all the stuff we've been talking about for a while now—only more and bigger and better and even more helpful."

"By your own choice, you haven't been very involved in the machinery."

"No," I say cautiously, aware that I may have entered a minefield. "But I couldn't be more grateful that you handle things so well and help me be so successful at doing what I love to do."

Erik nods his acknowledgment of the compliment and then says, "You need at least a glimpse of what's behind the scenes before you make a decision about coming out right now."

It occurs to me, all of a sudden, that my habit of turning away from the details of my own livelihood has probably been childish—even detrimentally childish. A sick feeling blooms in the pit of my stomach. "Does this have to do with the conservative backers?"

"It does. Because of my wife's family and connections, I have direct access to people who control conservative television, radio stations, newspapers, magazines, and much more. Those connections are one reason for my success as an agent." He pushes his empty tumbler away. "Henry, these people are cautious. They calculate risks and act with care, and they've been instrumental in making you successful. Though I may not always agree with their politics and perspectives, I know these people very well. They like you and what you're doing, but they have made some assumptions about you."

"Like assuming I'm straight." A pang of nausea makes me put a hand on my stomach. When I close my eyes, I see that image of myself divided—the shadow me standing next to the space of me, the emptiness masquerading as a man with money who can't be bothered to understand its source.

"I'm advising you to consider the ramifications. If you come out now," Erik says, "they will pull the advertising for your show, various contracts won't be renewed, and I will come under pressure to drop you as a client."

"Are you kidding me? You can't be serious." I gape at Erik in disbelief. "What *decade* are you people living in?"

"*But...* if you wait until your show has a longer history of good ratings, until it's established enough to sustain a change to a different studio, after the current contract runs out..." He's shifting into client-placating mode. I can tell by the way he grows calmer in proportion to my agitation.

"I'm not saying *no*, Henry. I'm only saying *not yet*."

I stare at him. Blood pounds in my neck, trying to feed my brain so I can figure out what to do or ask or decide.

"I'll tell you what I would like to do," Erik continues softly, as though he's talking to a child and trying to defuse a potential tantrum, which perhaps he is. "Now that I know that you're gay and want to come out publicly, I'd like to start moving the machinery in a direction that will allow you to come out without damaging what you've already built. Will you give me some time to do that?"

I can't escape the certainty that I'm to blame for the situation. *Shit.*

I have a lot to lose if I don't do as Erik suggests. The thought of stopping the TV show, finding a new agent... My head spins. I consider the foster care kids who'll participate in the episode we're about to tape in Austin and the people all over the country who'll witness the kids' stories with me.

The truth is there's no rush for me to come out.

How horribly depressing.

"You've been forwarding any private e-mails to me. Right?" I ask. "For sure?"

"Absolutely," says Erik. "Our job is to make your life easier, not keep you from it."

I can't refrain from making absolutely sure. "So Ruben hasn't tried to contact me."

"Correct."

I'm embarrassed now by Erik's awareness of my empty reach for a ghost lover who exists only in my wishful thinking, so I pick up the menu and open it.

"I'll wait to come out," I say to the menu. "But starting now, I want to know more about the work you and your staff do on my behalf."

"No problem. I'm glad to hear that."

"I need a drink." I close the menu and try to catch the waiter's eye. "I want a timeline for coming out. God. I really am negotiating with my agent about my exit from the closet. Who *am* I?"

"Easy now. I'll do an assessment and come up with a suggested timeline. I know *your* timeline is ASAP, but we need to get you out of the closet with a plan in hand. Can you live with that?"

I nod.

"Good." He looks at his watch and lifts his briefcase onto the table. "Let's order and then go over some of this paperwork."

An hour later, when Erik excuses himself to go to the restroom, I lean back and examine the luxury all around me.

The dark, lily-scented richness feels claustrophobic. I squint into the dimness and loosen the collar of my shirt.

Where has all the light and fresh air gone?

LOOKING FOR HENRY

JULY | BOSTON

ON RUBEN'S THIRD trip to Henry's apartment, there's a light on.

"Yes?" A woman's voice wafts through the intercom.

Until that moment, Ruben hadn't realized how much he'd hoped Henry would answer. Ridiculous, especially as Henry's Twitter feed that afternoon reported him taping an episode of his show in Texas.

"Hi," Ruben says into the little speaker. "I'm a friend of Henry Normand's. I wonder if I could talk with you. It'll just take a moment."

Silence.

"Hello?" Ruben says.

"You're not a member of the press, are you?"

"Absolutely not. I promise. You could come down if you want. If that works better."

More silence.

"Please," says Ruben.

The door buzzes. Ruben takes the stairs three at a time.

The young woman who opens Henry's apartment door blinks with surprise when she sees Ruben and raises a hand as if to check her hair.

I must have dialed up the charm to get inside. But hey. That's not a bad idea.

He smiles warmly and holds out his hand.

"Hello," says the woman, returning the smile.

"I'm Ruben Harper. I've known Henry for years, but I've been out of contact, and now I'm having trouble reaching him. When I heard he had a subletter I thought I'd stop by and see if you could help. Like… maybe you'd be willing to pass a message along to him?"

"There's contact information on his website," she says.

"Yeah. Um... how well do you know Henry?"

"Not very well."

"He's a little old-fashioned when it comes to technology. Maybe you have contact information for—" He considers how to spread the widest net. "—a family member?"

"How do I know you're actually a friend of Henry's?"

Ruben glances through the foyer doorway into the living room. The little things are new, but the big pieces of furniture are still Henry's. He decides to take a chance. "There's an antique wood dresser in the bedroom with five drawers—two small drawers at the top, three big drawers below, and a bird carved around the keyhole of the bottom drawer. The oven dial on the stove looks like a smiley face. And"—he nods toward the desk in the corner of the living room—"the bottom left drawer of that desk is locked, and Henry didn't leave you a key." He raises his eyebrows, praying his guess is correct.

She grins. "Impressive. Come on in." She waves Ruben into the living room.

"Thanks."

"After all of that, I'm afraid I'm going to disappoint you, because the only contact information I have for Henry is his agent, Erik Bonaventure."

"You don't... You're not friends with Henry at all?"

"No. My boyfriend knows one of his colleagues at the museum. Except for our initial meetings with Henry, everything's been handled through his agent. Here. I'll get his business card."

"Don't bother. I've got one." Disappointed, Ruben tries to think of anything else he could ask before he goes. For inspiration and for old times' sake he wanders toward the windows and leans against the radiator.

"Did Henry or Erik ever mention a woman named Jamie?" he asks. "She's sort of a cousin of Henry's."

"Um... maybe. A friend of Henry's named Jamie helped him move stuff into storage. But I don't know anything about her or how to reach her."

"You don't know her last name?"

"Sorry, no."

"Or... or whether she lives in Boston or... anything else about her?"

She shakes her head. "I never even met her. Henry made a passing remark about her helping him move."

Ruben sighs and reaches under the windowsill to give the grill of the radiator a fond pat. "Damn it. Well, can I leave my name and number in case Henry or Jamie get in touch with you?"

"Sure."

Ruben's not hopeful enough to think it'll make a difference, but he writes his information on the notepad she hands him.

"Good luck," she says and moves toward the front door to show him out.

Ruben leaves reluctantly, taking in details as he walks across the room.

Without more of Henry in the room, without Henry's quirky, story-filled belongings and calm presence, it could be anyone's room, anywhere.

But a few stories linger.

This is where I began to grow up.

As he walks out the door, Ruben wonders about all the everyday histories he never heard.

What's it like for Henry to be separated from his family of belongings?

It makes Ruben sad to think of Henry's stuff stashed away, alone and unseen in a dark storage unit somewhere. The walnut bowl and the apple corer and...

Did Henry take his blue pajamas on the road with him?

On the way back to his parents' Beacon Hill townhouse, Ruben allows his mind to lapse into a semiconscious state to review and plot his next moves. He gets off the bus and stops to stare at the ad on the side of the bus shelter. It shows a handsome man in an expensive suit. Ruben wonders why it's captured his attention. *Well, besides the obvious.* He stands there until his brain puts all the pieces together and his face relaxes into a smile.

A minute on the Internet via his cell phone pinpoints the location of the opulent men's clothing store the ad is for. It's not far.

He takes his time considering all the variations the store offers and selects the softest, most perfect pair of baby blue pajamas.

Buying the pajamas makes Ruben feel happier than he's felt in a long time.

That night, wearing his new pajamas, Ruben dreams that Ellis and Danny and Henry are contestants in a reality TV show, and the prize is Ruben—who stands on a pedestal flaunting himself in his blue pajamas. The three contestants and the studio audience watch as Ruben begins to rub himself to arousal, eager to impress the contestants.

He wakes in the pale light of early dawn, his hands moving roughly against the soft fabric of the pajamas at his crotch, and shame floods over him. He lifts his hands away.

He gets out of bed, takes off the pajamas, folds them carefully, and puts them on top of the dresser. Then he lies awake under the covers until the sun rises high enough to bathe the bed in sunlight and warm him back to sleep.

THE HISTORIAN
LOOKING FOR HIMSELF

JULY

EVERYDAY HISTORY
By Henry Normand

THE RELUCTANT FAREWELL

I'M SPENDING THIS *morning with a small group of foster kids of various ages in Austin, Texas. For kids in foster care, history can be a touchy subject. My own childhood in foster care led me to a career in history. I'm curious to see if Everyday History appeals to these kids.*

At my request each child has brought something that reminds them of an unwanted good-bye. I chose reluctant farewells as our theme because I find myself unwilling to pussyfoot around the heart of the matter with these kids. I want to invite their stories of loss into the open and bear witness, because I know from experience that being honored and heard turns us toward strength.

We settle into a circle on the rug in one of the community center's activity rooms and introduce ourselves. I go last and tell them that I grew up in foster care. Then I briefly share the concept of Everyday History—how telling stories about the things in our lives can sometimes feel good.

When I ask who wants to start, Ricardo's hand shoots into the air. He's eight and grinning like a madman.

"What's that you've got?" I nod at the large, battered shoebox on his lap.

"It's Hector," he says. With reverence he lifts the lid off the box and picks up a huge taxidermied rat, mounted on a shellacked board. The younger girls in the

circle shriek, but Ricardo never loses his smile as he places the rat into the middle of the circle. He stares at it with fondness but doesn't say anything.

"Hi, Hector," I say to the rat, and others in the group tentatively offer their hellos too.

After a long stretch of silence while Ricardo sits with his head bowed, I ask him, "Why does Hector remind you of an unwanted good-bye?"

Ricardo sighs a little moan, like he's lovesick, and then looks up at me with tears in his eyes. Oh. He hadn't spoken yet because he couldn't speak without crying. "It's okay," I say. "I don't mind if you talk and cry at the same time." I look around the circle. "Does anyone else mind?" A seriousness descends on the group as they shake their heads and look from me to Ricardo.

He wipes his face and reaches out to pet Hector. "Hector was a rat my mom and I used to be afraid of." He looks up at me with such sorrow that I'm grateful I filled all four of my pants pockets with tissue packets. I hope I'll have enough to share. I pass him a tissue and nod for him to go on.

"After my dad and my sister died, my mom and... we lived in an old camper at the edge of a field. By a tree." He's silent for a moment, perhaps getting his thoughts together. "A big rat found out about our camper. We couldn't fix all the holes, so we couldn't keep him out. He would just walk in when we were eating dinner and stare at us. The first time, we screamed and stood on the table and hugged each other until he left. Then, after a week or so, we figured out that if we tossed him something, like a cracker, he'd leave."

Ricardo stops and looks at me like he doesn't know how to go on. Or like he knows but can't.

"How did Hector get his name?" I ask.

"One day I came home from school, but... Mom didn't come home from work. No one knew where we lived, so no one came. I got to school on my own for a few days, but she never did come home." He's crying full-out, and so are most of the rest of us. "I didn't know what to do." He raises his hands and lets them drop back into his lap. "But the rat came to check up on me every night at dinnertime. I was so stupid to want him to, but I did. I named him Hector so he'd know I thought he was my friend."

I pass Ricardo a whole pack of tissues and toss the rest of the packs into the circle.

"After about a week, someone finally came to school and... and"—the girl sitting next to him cautiously pats him on the shoulder. He nods and blows his nose— "and told me my mom was dead."

No one says anything. I try to think past the sorrow, but then I stop and let it come.

"Someone killed her behind a bar," Ricardo says in a whisper.

"I am so sorry," I say. He shrugs but looks up at me. I smile, and he swallows and says, "The people who came to school to tell me about Mom took me to the camper to help me pack up our stuff. But when they tried to take me away, I... I couldn't go. I threw a fit, I guess." He bows his head again. "I wouldn't leave Hector. I just... I couldn't." He reaches for Hector again and tugs him a little closer.

"A lady, Mrs. Tanner, made a phone call while we sat in her car by the camper, and a guy came with a net and caught Hector. But Hector died on the way into town. I think he missed my mom, and his heart attacked him. My heart was attacking me too, but I didn't die.

"Mrs. Tanner said it wouldn't be safe to keep Hector if he was dead. But then she surprised me. She came to visit me later at my foster home and... and she brought me Hector after all. She said he was my early birthday present." He leans over to pet Hector with a gentle touch of his fingertips, but then keeps leaning until his forehead touches the rug. He sobs and croaks into the carpet, "I loved Mrs. Tanner so much for that."

We sniffle as we watch Ricardo and wait for him gather himself. The girl next to him leaves her hand on his shoulder. Finally he takes a deep, shaky breath and sits up.

I lose it completely when each of the other kids—even the little girls—reach into the circle to pet Hector.

His fur is surprisingly soft and silky.

By the time we've heard from most of the other kids in the group, little piles of tissues surround us like shed skins—which I hope they are.

"What's your story of a good-bye, Mr. Normand?" Angie asks. She's six and hasn't been in foster care very long. She sits close beside me, her elbow propped on my leg.

"Well," I say, "I'll tell you, but my reminder isn't here."

"Aww," they say. "That's not fair."

"But not having it is part of my story," I say. "A while back, I had a winter scarf that was really soft and warm and the perfect color of a blue summer sky. It was my all-time favorite scarf. One day I noticed it was gone. I was at home when I noticed, so I thought I'd left it at work. But then I couldn't find it at work either."

I pull a photograph out of my back pocket. "I do have a photo of it. Here." They pass around the photo of me wearing the scarf.

"But then, a few weeks after I lost the scarf, I arrived home from work while I was thinking about a friend I liked who'd gone away."

Ricardo raises his hand. "Did your friend die?"

"No. They left because we—because I couldn't figure out how to be friends with them. The last day I'd seen my blue scarf was the day my friend left."

Angie shakes her head. "That sure was a very bad, sad day."

"Yes. It was. I remembered that I'd worn my favorite scarf the day my friend left, because I wanted to look my best that day. So if that was true, what could have happened to it?" I scratch my head, pretending to think.

"A rat ate it," Jasper says.

"Was it on the floor in the coat closet?" Sylvie offers.

"Nope," I say. "I think my friend took it."

"She stole it?"

"Well, I think it was more like taking something to remember me by."

"What did you do?"

"Were you mad?"

"No. I wasn't mad... because I had a secret of my own." I lean forward and lower my voice. "I took something too."

"You took something of hers?"

"Yes."

"What was it?"

I reach into my bag and take out a fountain pen—dark brown with silver fittings—and the kids pass it around.

"It's so heavy."

"Wow. It's pretty."

"Can I try it out?"

"Did they ever ask for it back?"

"No," I say. "No, they didn't. But then, I never asked for my scarf back either."

The wise beings around the circle nod as though they understand, and their kind eyes include me in their pain.

At the end of our time together, I ask the kids for a few more minutes of their attention.

"I know there's pain inside an unwanted good-bye, and I want to thank you for your courage to share your stories, even when it was difficult. I also want to honor

you for all the times you've had to be brave in the past and all the times you'll have to be brave in the future. Please try to remember how amazing and strong you are." I look at each of them and they nod back at me, one by one, their faces serious again.

"Now here's a question for you: Even when a good-bye carries pain with it, is it possible to say farewell? To fare well means to do well, to be well, to be okay. Is there some part of you that can say, in your heart, to the one who's gone, 'Fare well without me, and I will do my best to fare well without you'?"

The kids are quiet. The high school girl who shared about losing her school friends when she had to move to a new foster home begins to cry again.

"I think, maybe," I say, "if you can find that part of you, then you can keep track of your heart."

"That would be a very well thing," Angie says as she reaches for my hand.

———————————

Henry Normand's meeting with foster care kids in Austin, Texas, was filmed for an Everyday History *television show episode. We'll announce the airdate for that show here next week.*

LOOKING FOR HENRY

AMHERST

"I T W A S Y O U R fountain pen, wasn't it?" asks Danny. He's reading Henry's article as he eats his pie.

"Yeah."

Estelle bustles past with a full load of lunch plates. "I was glad I read that one upstairs," she says, nodding at the newspaper. "I cried like a baby."

Danny glances at Ruben.

"I'm all right," Ruben says. "Now that I no longer have my head up my own ass, reading his articles doesn't upset me like it used to. Only..."

"Sadder. More in love than ever. I get it," Danny says.

"Yeah. But not only that. These articles of Henry's where he writes about me make me wonder if something weird is going on."

"Like what?"

"It's hard to reconcile this article with that e-mail from Henry saying he doesn't want to see me."

"Okay. I see that. But isn't it possible that he still has *some* feelings for you but wants to move on anyway. That he is moving on, and is using this article to wish you well, even as he says good-bye?"

"Maybe. But somehow I don't think that's the whole story."

"Well, without being able to talk with him about it, you're only guessing."

"Exactly," Ruben says with a slap of a palm on his thigh. He tosses a few bills on the counter, grabs the newspaper, waves to Estelle, and drags Danny out of the diner and into the summer heat.

Ruben and Ellis slouch in their chairs at a table in a corner of the college library, which empties around them as the after-dinner study crowd thins.

"This is the age of communication miracles," Ruben says. "How can it be so difficult to reach Henry? It's making me feel incompetent."

"Let's review," Ellis says with the air of an imperious CEO.

"Okay." Ruben gives his head a vigorous shake to try to wake himself up. "Let's see. I got no answers to any of the e-mails I sent to Henry." Ruben hasn't told Ellis about that one terrible e-mail Henry sent more than a month ago.

"Which you staunchly continue to ignore the implications of."

"Correct. And no responses to my e-mails and phone messages to Henry's agent, that asshole of a threshold guardian."

"Can we please call him the Asshole Guardian from now on?"

Ruben snorts but continues with the review. "Henry's landline in Boston automatically forwards to his agent."

"At this juncture I offer the following provocative menu of options," says Ellis. "Either Henry's not interested or he's dropped off the face of the Earth."

Ruben folds his arms across his chest. He doesn't know where to direct his exasperation. At Henry for being so frustratingly technology resistant? At modern technology for its false promise of easy access? At Henry's success for taking Henry away from home? Except... without Henry's articles, which launched his success, Ruben might not have turned back toward him. Ruben doesn't want to think about what life might have been like in *that* horrible parallel universe.

"Huh," says Ellis. "Erik is a top-echelon agent. Why would such a prestigious agent take Henry on in the first place?"

"Yeah. Good question."

Ellis leans forward to type on his computer. Ruben taps his pen on his leg.

"Ho, then. Looky here," Ellis says.

Ruben scoots his chair closer so he can see Ellis's computer, which shows a search result for an article in the society section of *The New York Time*. Ellis scrawls something on a scrap of paper and pushes his chair back. "Be right back," he says and hurries off.

Ruben takes a closer look and clicks on the link at the end of the search-result snippet, but it only leads to a page to subscribe to *The New York Times*. He goes back to the search results to read it again. It doesn't seem to warrant Ellis's shift to red alert. The article refers to a fundraiser at the New York Archeological Society. A few of the attendees' names are listed, but Ruben doesn't recognize any of them.

Ruben yawns and turns back to his own computer to continue his search of bakery websites for a baker on staff named Jamie. It's a loser's expedition for sure, but he can't think of anything else to do. The New England Baker's Association won't allow him to search without a last name, and none of the local professional associations list a member with a first name of Jamie.

Ellis flings a hard copy edition of *The New York Times* onto the table and briskly flips through it.

"Here," he says. He punches the paper with his forefinger. "Ha. I knew it. We've got a link between Henry's museum and the Asshole Guardian."

"Eric Bonaventure."

"God-awful name. I bet he made it up."

"Ellis."

"From now on let's call him... Hang on. I know we hate him. But why? I'm doing it, but I can't remember *why* I'm doing it."

"We don't know why we hate him." Ruben thinks about it. "Maybe because he gets to see Henry now and then."

"Good enough." Ellis turns back to the paper. "Erik's wife attended this hoity-toity shindig. Look at this photo and the caption. Erik's wife is talking with Millicent Hornby, whose husband, Glenn Whitaker Hornby, is on the board of the museum."

"You know this?"

"Mind like a steel trap. I was browsing the museum site earlier. This might be how Henry got hooked up with Fuckface. Sorry, Erik."

"Okay. Stellar detective work, but where does it get us? I doubt I can reach this"—Ruben leans forward to look at the article—"Glenn Whitaker Hornby. And what would I say if I did reach him?" Ruben rubs his forehead, trying to think. "Screw it," he says. He pulls out his phone, turns away from the stern *Cell Phone Use Prohibited* sign on the wall above their table, and scans his contact list. "I swear she gave it to me. There." He taps the screen and puts the phone to his ear.

"Abby? Hey. It's me, Ruben Harper. Sorry to call you on your personal phone and so late, but I'm still trying to get hold of Mr. Normand and I've had an idea. Do you have a minute?"

"For you? Sure," Abby says.

"Yeah? Thank you. Um... do you know how I could get in touch with a member of the museum's board named Glenn Whitaker?"

Ruben grills Abby as gently as possible for a few minutes. He trolls her careful parsing of public information for a connection between the museum and Henry's agent, hoping he'll stumble on something he can follow up on. And then he does. He hangs up and smiles at Ellis, who raises his eyebrows.

"Glenny's in Italy until the end of August," says Ruben.

"Then why are you smiling?"

"We've got another lead." Ruben points at Ellis's computer, knowing Ellis will be faster. "Go to the museum's website and look at event listings from about a year ago, in June. Henry gave a lecture, and some agents were there to meet him and see him in action."

"Was that after his articles started coming out?"

"Yeah, barely. Maybe Henry already wanted to do the book by then and thought an agent would be useful."

Ellis's fingers fly over the keyboard. "Aha. 'Lecture by Henry Normand.' But it's not about Everyday History."

"It had probably already been scheduled for a while. What was it about?"

"'Modern Technology through the Ages,'" Ellis reads from the computer screen.

"Oh God. I know that lecture. Henry gave us an expanded version of it over the course of a week. It's a mind-blower. You'd have loved it."

Ellis nods. "Maybe so. I mean, his TV shows are all right. They're not about biochemistry, so I basically can't be bothered. And yet—"

"And yet you stay awake for the whole show every time. You haven't stayed awake for a whole TV show or movie since I've known you."

"Decent point."

Ellis turns back to work the computer, and a moment later, a museum newsletter article about Henry's lecture comes up on the screen. They lean against each other to read it.

Ruben finishes first. Disappointed to have found nothing useful, he sits back in his chair.

"Why *did* Erik get the job?" Ruben asks. "At that stage Henry was small fry for an agent of Erik's caliber. I suspect he would only have shown up in the first place to placate his wife's pal, Glenny."

"Well, *you* were wowed by Henry's teaching style. Right?"

Ruben snorts again. "No shit."

"Erik is married to a stinking-rich high-society woman. Right?" Ellis asks thoughtfully.

"So?"

"So is he *happily* married?"

Ruben laughs. "Come off it, Ellis. You want *every* guy to be gay. Would *you* have thought Henry's gay if I hadn't told you? Like from seeing him on the TV show?"

"Huh." Ellis blinks. "Well asked. Actually no. I'd have said he's nerdy and oddly cute, but definitely straight."

"Let's set aside your dubious idea that Erik is a closeted predatory gay who went out of his way to nab sweet Henry as a client for nefarious erotic purposes. Why *else* might he have wanted to take Henry on?"

They stare at each other until Ruben starts to twitch. He gets up and walks around the table a few times.

"Obviously," Ruben says, "Henry *does* have something special that's worth selling, or he wouldn't have gotten this famous this fast, even with the help of a deluxe agent. Maybe Erik saw dollar signs? After all, he's a superstar agent. Maybe he knew he could maximize the hell out of Henry's considerable talent and get a nice chunk of money for himself."

"You're making my point for me, doofus, in a roundabout way. Does high-society, well-wed Erik strike you as a guy desperate enough for money to take on a long shot like Henry? Plus if money were his only game, why wouldn't he answer your calls?"

"Why the hell *would* he answer my calls? I probably register as a fly buzzing in the background of his high-powered life. Some minion on Erik's staff who deems me insignificant to the Henry empire would trash my e-mails without a second thought. Except..." Ruben's voice fades and he looks away, not wanting Ellis to see his disappointment as logic's flytrap catches him.

"Except what?"

Ruben sighs heavily. "Except that Henry *did* send me an e-mail. Just one. In response to a very... revealing e-mail I sent him in June."

Ellis sits up. "Well, why in the hell didn't you tell me? What did he say?"

Embarrassed, Ruben fiddles with his pen and shakes his head.

"Spill already," Ellis says and nudges Ruben's leg. "Come on, Ruben. It might help."

Ruben puts the pen on the table, folds his hands in his lap, and looks up. "Henry said he doesn't want to talk to me or see me."

"Ooh-kay. And yet you're still trying to reach him because…?"

Ruben closes the lid of his laptop, stands, and starts to put his things in his bag.

"Just *tell* me," says Ellis.

Ruben sits back down with a huff. "Because… because I want to tell Henry I love him and watch his face as I say it. I want to see for myself if there's any hope. I just need to know."

"One way or the other."

Ruben nods.

"You do realize that what you're doing looks an awful lot like stalking."

"Yeah. I thought of that."

Ellis peers at Ruben for a while. Then he flaps a hand and says, "Whatever. What the hell. At least you know what you want. Except for the way it keeps your pants zipped, this phase is much easier to deal with than all those months you moped around insisting nothing was wrong."

"Yeah."

"So, if you do meet up with Henry—"

"*When.*"

"Okay. *When* you do meet up with Henry, if you look into his eyes and speak your piece, and he says he's not interested, and you believe he's telling the truth, could you… would you be able to walk away then?"

Ruben takes his time answering because he wants to locate the truth. "I think yes," he says. "Yeah. I could. Because knowing Henry has made me want Henry, but knowing Henry has also made me want love. Even if I can't have it with Henry, I still want it with someone."

They stare at each other through a long moment that becomes uncomfortable. Ellis blinks and turns to his laptop. "I am such an unmitigated fool," he mutters to his keyboard.

To spare them both, Ruben pretends not to have heard.

ELLIS TAPS ON Ruben's door and sticks his head into the room. "Beer?"

"Sure. Thanks." Ruben reaches for the beer without taking his eyes off his computer.

"Breakthrough?" Ellis asks as he perches on the arm of Ruben's desk chair.

"No, and I need a dose of your weird input. I'm so desperate my searches are getting pathetic."

"Like what?"

"Here. Look at this one—'massachusetts jamie apple crisp.'" Ruben flops back and raises his arms in exasperation. "What the hell am I doing?" They both stare at the computer screen.

Then Ellis takes a breath and holds it.

"What?" Ruben asks.

"Of course," Ellis murmurs. He sits forward. "Have you tried searching to see if they appear together anywhere? Like 'boston jamie henry normand'?"

"No, I haven't." Ruben enters the search, and his shoulders slump when the results come up. "Crap. Six thousand hits. Oh wait." He types in a revision—*boston jamie "henry normand"*—with quotation marks around Henry's name—and gets only twenty-two hits. "That's better."

"Hey!" they say at the same time when they see the link to a museum newsletter from a few years earlier. Ellis reaches across Ruben for the mouse and clicks the link. A PDF file of the newsletter opens up on the screen and he starts to scroll.

"Stop," Ruben says as the next headline comes up. "That's it. Abby told me weeks ago about that fundraiser dinner, but I didn't think to search the museum newsletters about it."

Ellis scrolls down a little more, and Ruben's thoughts are abruptly derailed by a photo. Black and white, too small to fully satisfy, it shows Henry in a classic tuxedo—slender, standing tall, and shyly looking past the camera. Ruben swallows and sighs. Henry looks handsome, kind, and absolutely delicious. Ruben nudges Ellis's fingers away from the mouse and downloads the newsletter to his hard drive, grateful for Ellis's patient silence.

"Check it out," says Ellis softly, pointing at the photo caption.

Beside Henry, inside the circle of his arm, is a plump, pretty, smiling woman the caption identifies as Jamie St. Clair.

"Holy crap," Ruben says on an exhale. "There she is." He takes one last look at Henry and slides the laptop to Ellis. "You do it."

"Right," Ellis says. "What if...?" And he's off, tapping keys and muttering to himself. When Ruben gets up to pace the room, Ellis slides off the armrest and into the desk chair.

Ruben shakes his hands out as he paces, but it does little to ward off his rising nerves. *What if she didn't move back to Boston after all?*

Ellis claps his hands. "Voila! 'Jamie St. Clair, Certified Master Baker.' She works at that old hotel on the harbor, The Captain. Five-star opulence. She must be good."

"Is there a phone number or e-mail for her?"

"Not yet." Ellis types some more. "Nope. Not that I see."

"Well, okay. It's okay. Yeah. I'll call the hotel tomorrow."

"It's a hotel, Ruben. Someone would answer the phone if you call now."

"No. I want to sleep first. I need to have a clear head when I call."

Ellis nods, his eyes steady on Ruben's face.

Ruben sits on the bed with his hands pinned between his knees to stop them from shaking as relief washes over him.

"Thanks, Ellis. Thank you."

"It's all good. Um… congratulations." Ellis stands and pushes the desk chair under the desk. He turns toward Ruben, but doesn't come closer. "Right, then. See you tomorrow. Get some sleep." Ellis clicks off the desk light and leaves.

As soon as he's alone, Ruben topples sideways onto the bed.

When the computer screen times out and turns off, sending the room into darkness, Ruben sighs and closes his eyes.

Early the next morning, Ruben wakes on top of the covers, still fully dressed, and goes straight to the desk, where he finds a sticky note with a phone number and "The Captain Hotel" in Ellis's handwriting.

Ruben works his cell phone between classes. By noon he has negotiated with enough gatekeepers to obtain Jamie's direct work e-mail address. But Jamie refuses to talk with Ruben on the phone.

At four thirty he receives an e-mail with an invitation to meet at Jamie's house in Boston in three weeks. She has a busy schedule with no days off for a while, and she needs to meet Ruben before she'll consider giving him any information about Henry.

How can I object to her reluctance to talk about Henry?
I know the feeling.

THE HISTORIAN
LOOKING FOR HIMSELF

AUGUST | NEW MEXICO

HEY, JAMIE. IT'S me. I'll pretend I've got the real you on the phone and talk until your machine runs out of tape or... or your voice mail runs out of... magical fairy dust or whatever. How are you? How's work? Have you buried everyone in baked goods yet? Ha ha. Just, please keep a journal so I can find out later what I'm missing. How am I, you ask? Well, I wouldn't have thought it possible to be this tired and this excited every single day. Oy. And this rumpled. God, I miss my ironing board. Let's see... I wrote a few letters to you-know-who, but lost my nerve before I sent them. Tried to call him once, but lost my nerve before I hit the Call button. If my moony articles got no response, I don't want to risk hearing the coldness in his voice or having my letters returned unread. My e-mail address is plastered all over my website. If he wanted to find me, he would have by now. So I've decided to take the manly road and move on. My body objects, but I'm trying. I'm... er... just a sec. Uh-oh. I have to hang up now. Blabbing excitedly into an outdoor pay phone on a lonely desert road at a little gas station near Roswell, New Mexico, while being stared at by three tattooed dudes carrying three cases of beer is not a healthy choice. I miss you so much. I'll be back in Boston in November, and I'll try to call again soon.

LOOKING FOR HENRY

AUGUST | AMHERST

RUBEN IS TIRED and overheated, his brain feels like mush, and he has three more finals to study for over the next three days. He's fallen into the habit of taking study breaks by staring at the wall of Henry-related documents above his desk without consciously trying to see anything.

Yeah. I'm definitely turning into a stalker.

His gaze comes to rest on a printout of the newsletter photo of Henry in the tuxedo, which is pinned next to a photocopy of the article Ellis found in *The New York Times*. Ruben stares without intent. His weary mind takes in words as *blah blah blah.*

His gaze suddenly snaps back to the article in *The New York Times*.

Edith C. Shander is listed in the caption of one of the photos. He counts off names in the caption and then counts off people in the photo to locate her. She's tiny. Ruben amuses himself by calculating that she's worth about ten million dollars a pound.

Why did my fried brain pick her out of the crowd?

Oh. The Shander Foundation Award.

Ruben taps on his computer and quickly finds the Shander Foundation website. The announcement spans the width of their home page. *Nominations for the Shander Foundation Award will be accepted through August 17.*

Ruben checks his calendar. *Holy shit. That's only two weeks from now.* He scrolls down the page to look for specifics, and he finds them.

"Every three years the Shander Foundation Award is presented to a resident of New England who has contributed to their local community in ways that have a positive impact reaching beyond New England.

"Established in 1821 by Edwin F. Shander, the Shander Foundation Award has honored a wide range of community leaders, including scientists, industrialists, entertainers, financiers, architects, farmers, and lawmakers.

"The Shander Foundation Award Selection Committee has a track record spanning almost two centuries of identifying and choosing nominees and winners who go on to carry out exemplary works benefiting communities in New England and far beyond.

"The cachet of a Shander Award has long been considered more valuable than the Award's cash prize of $500,000."

Ruben clicks and clicks some more. He loses himself in details about the foundation and the nomination process, all the while imagining Henry's Everyday History vision stoked by wealth and prestige.

"Shander Foundation Award recipients are chosen through a rigorous process that begins with community nominations of candidates via written personal recommendations. From those nominees, the Shander Foundation chooses three finalists who go through an extensive process of investigation, evaluation, and interviews.

"To be considered for the award, nominee finalists are required to give a public lecture on a topic of their choice. The Shander Foundation Award Lecture Series will take place in Boston in early October of this year, a week before the award is announced. Tickets for the lecture series will go on sale September 7, one week after the three nominee finalists are announced."

RUBEN SPENDS THE next two weeks reaching out and asking anyone he can think of who might know Henry to please send a recommendation to the Shander Foundation. By the time he finishes up his finals, he's totally tapped out. That's okay. He's got time to recover before the fall school session begins. The important thing is that he did everything he could think of to get Henry nominated.

And he aced his finals.

He keeps catching himself smiling.

After his last final, Ruben had dragged himself home, dropped his heavy bag of books, and fallen onto the bed. *Only for a minute,* he had promised himself. He woke up eighteen hours later with a smile on his face and the urge to cook dinner for his housemates.

At the kitchen table with Millie and Ellis, Ruben eats slowly and savors the luxury of tasting and chewing his food, for a change.

"You couldn't have done much more for Henry to try and get him nominated," Millie says as she dishes herself a second helping of mashed potatoes.

"Yeah. You're probably right," Ruben says. "But there's always that itchy feeling, you know? I keep wondering who that one person is I didn't think to ask who might make all the difference."

"But wasn't it great to find out you weren't Henry's only fan?" Millie says around a huge yawn. "Sorry. Didn't get home until late. I mean early."

Ruben and Ellis look at each other across the table and shake their heads.

"So how'd that last exam go?" Ellis asks Millie with a raised eyebrow.

"Don't," she says. "I already know what you two are going to say. You're like mother hens. No. You're like overly vigilant parole officers. Just leave me alone. I can afford to repeat a few classes."

"A few?" asks Ellis.

"Oops," says Millie. She looks from Ruben to Ellis and sighs. "Does it make a difference if I say I met someone really, really hot last night?"

"Nope." says Ruben. "Totally missing the point."

"If you don't shape up," Ellis says, "we're going to be forced to take disciplinary measures." He glances at Ruben, who smirks.

"Raise your hand if you're not a slut and you refuse to do the dishes tonight," Ruben says as he raises his hand.

Ellis raises his hand and gets up to kiss Millie on the cheek. "Have fun, dear."

Millie laughs at them and shouts, "Thanks for making dinner," at Ruben's retreating back.

THE WEIRDEST, MOST wonderful aspect of Ruben's campaign to get Henry nominated for the Shander Foundation Award is the discovery that he's not alone.

He began by contacting his former high school internship classmates. He then surveyed the museum's events calendars and newsletters for ideas about people he could contact. Each exploratory call and connection led to another. He tracked down and chatted up Henry's current and former students, coworkers, colleagues, workshop participants. He queried his own high school teachers. And he kept finding more people to call.

His new awareness of Henry's involvement in so many endeavors beyond the museum and how much he's appreciated makes Ruben's heart pound. Henry's low-key, unobtrusive presence belies the truth. *Quiet as a mouse. Doesn't stand out in a crowd. Listens more than he speaks. Keeps to the back of the room unless he's teaching.*

And yet Henry found his way into so many people's lives. All of whom were glad for the opportunity to recommend him for the Shander Award.

Many had already done so.

THE HISTORIAN
LOOKING FOR HIMSELF

AUGUST | NEW MEXICO

POSTCARD 1

JAMIE, BRACE YOURSELF for Drama amid the Campfire Embers. *Alternate title,* God Bless RV Mobility—A Tragedy in Three Postcards. *Two days ago I set up camp—which takes five minutes, max—near Santa Fe and got busy at the picnic table writing up my notes from a surreal + hilarious day spent touring Mr. Totenkamp's Nutcracker Museum—I'll wait while you snicker—which shares space with Mrs. Totenkamp's Poodle Wedding Photo Museum, jointly the pride of the neighborhood. Thank God they're a fun-loving couple, because I tittered uncontrollably during the entire tour and then hooted when they showed me the section of the museum where their two obsessions collide in a display that... Well. No matter what you imagine regarding the merger of nutcrackers and poodle weddings, I guarantee it's not as comical or kooky as the reality. The photos I took will make you laugh so hard you'll pee.*

POSTCARD 2

THE TOTENKAMPS' PARTICULAR mélange of bizarreness must have messed with my gay-broadcasting switch, because, as I jotted and chuckled to myself at the campground picnic table afterward, it took me a while to fully register the shadow that had fallen over me. Burly, good-looking fellow wearing a red-plaid lumberjack shirt and a kind smile, asking if this seat was taken. It turns out I didn't mind, because he was delightful to talk with. A while later, after dinner, we went into my wee RV to get away from the bugs, but there's not much room inside, and he took up an awful lot of space. So we sort of... ahem. In the morning, with the gray light of a gray day reflecting off his easy smile, I suddenly felt so sad and lonely and mistaken that I told him I had an appointment and needed to head out early—which I sort of did—and packed up and left.

POSTCARD 3

How can I be chest-poundingly proud of myself for the direction my career is heading while also being a forehead-smacking dolt shackled by unrequited love? If you get a package with "KEEP FROZEN!" scrawled across it, rejoice. It means I've clawed out my stupid, lame, good-for-nothing heart that's resisting taking no for an answer, even though I've finally decided it should. It would be funny if it weren't so crippling. Why can't I get over SRD? What puzzle did I think he was the answer to? Why am I still unable to tidy this up and put it away? You have my official permission to do an intervention to help me get over him. You're the only person I trust to advise me on this, so do what you will. Just... make it go away. I'm begging you. Also after you read this, please—I insist—burn it immediately. I miss you and love you always, Henry. P.S. I'll try to find a payphone that still works and call you soon.

LOOKING FOR HENRY

LATE AUGUST | BOSTON

To keep his nerves from getting the upper hand, Ruben leaps off the bus and jogs the two blocks to Jamie's street, a short one that the city forgot to modernize. He peers at numbers until he finds Jamie's house, which is small and painted yellow with white trim.

He walks in through the low gate at the sidewalk, down the walkway, through a messy flower garden, all the while trying hard to ignore the distraction of an inner shout—*Henry was here!*

Ruben pushes the doorbell.

A short, curvy woman with curly hair opens the door with a flourish, puts her hands on her hips, and says with mock villainy, "So the Young Twit found his way to the wolf's lair." Ruben's anxiety makes his laugh sound like a bark, but the smile he offers must seem genuine enough, because Jamie smiles back and lets him in, then leads him to the kitchen.

The air smells heavenly. "Gingerbread?" asks Ruben.

Jamie nods and pushes up her sleeves to continue kneading a lump of raisin-studded dough. With a floured hand, she waves at a stool on the other side of the island counter.

Ruben hesitates. "Is it safe to relax here?" he asks, only half joking. "I'm not sure how to take your young-twit comment." *Does she blame me as much as I blame myself?*

Jamie laughs. "Yes. You can relax. Please, have a seat. I won't bite."

"Okay," Ruben says. He sits but doesn't take off his coat.

"Shy Henry speaks about you in code," says Jamie. "It's his way of fake pretending he's not speaking about you at all." She shrugs. "Henry is the most wonderful person I know, so if he's having a challenging time and needs to speak in code to feel better, I'm going to leap in with both feet. My code name for you is Young Twit."

I don't want Henry to have a challenging time because of me.

Bit late for that, isn't it?

"Now you're frowning," says Jamie. "Drinking helps." She gestures to a bottle of white wine and a glass-fronted cabinet of wine glasses. "Help yourself. And I'll take a refill."

Grateful for something to do, Ruben busies himself with glasses and pouring. "Thanks," he says as he raises his glass to her. "Can I do something? It would help me relax."

"Nervous, are you? Sure. Here. Butter these pans for the cinnamon bread. Even on my days off, I can't seem to untether myself from the damn oven."

"Did you teach Henry how to make his...?" Ruben pauses to swallow. "Sorry, my mouth is watering just thinking about it... that incredible apple pie?"

"Oh my. Henry's apple pie. It's unbelievable, isn't it? When he was about, oh, ten or eleven, I showed him how to make a basic apple pie, but since then, he's gone his own way. I think he's closing in on pie-maker sainthood. Let's see. His most recent innovations were—what was it? Half coconut cream and half butter for the crust, a few drops of rosewater in the apple mixture along with six—no, wait—seven microflecks of freshly ground cardamom."

"He can stop already, as far as I'm concerned. Seriously. I've never tasted anything as good."

"Please don't say that. I thought the same thing a few years back. But, I swear, the current version is even better. Let's keep the lid off and see what happens."

Jamie separates the lump of dough into pieces and shapes them into the four pans Ruben buttered. When she's done, Ruben makes his way to the sink to wash his hands.

Okay. Enough small talk.

With his back to Jamie, Ruben asks, "Why did you agree to meet with me?"

Jamie bumps Ruben aside with her hip so she can get to the stovetop to set down the pans of dough. She drapes a towel over them, then bumps Ruben aside again so she can get to the sink to wash her hands. Her easy friendliness, the kitchen's comforting smells, and the presence of Henry's spirit in the room all make Ruben aware that he's probably going to overstay his welcome.

"I've been trying to get in touch with Henry for a long time," Ruben says, since she hasn't answered his question. "For all my trouble, I've only received one get-lost e-mail. I can't believe it's okay with him for you to, you know..."

"Fraternize with the enemy?"

Ruben laughs, and taps his twitchy fingers against the sink. "Something like that."

Jamie hands Ruben a towel, looks into his eyes, and nods. "This may take a while."

"I've cleared my schedule through," Ruben glances at his watch, "next week."

Jamie laughs. "I agreed to meet with you because I'm worried about him, about Henry, and... well, he doesn't have a very big team."

"You, basically?"

She shrugs and puts on an oven mitt to pull the gingerbread out of the oven. The enticing, sweet-sharp fragrance makes Ruben's stomach growl, and he resumes his spot on the stool.

Jamie notices Ruben's reaction and says, "Hang tight. We'll let it cool for a few minutes."

"Why doesn't Henry have a bigger team?" asks Ruben. "He's kind and smart and thoughtful and amazing and..."

Jamie holds up a hand. "Cease and desist, Young Twit. I know Henry's qualities very well. We could start listing them now and still be at it tomorrow. Yes. Henry is wonderful. Absolutely. But he's also extremely—"

"Complex."

"Yes. And—"

"Private."

Jamie stops and studies Ruben, then walks around the island counter and sits on the stool next to him, facing him.

"Exactly. And it's nice to discover that you see him so well, because he almost never lets people all the way into his life. The fact that he let you in tells me a lot about *you*. Henry told me about sharing his disturbing birth tale with you. *You* were obviously what he needed to finally pull that dark secret into the light. And telling you helped him be able to tell me."

Ruben tries to be still. He doesn't want to disrupt Jamie's flow of words, which feel like miracles of nourishment. He takes a sniff of gingerbread-infused air to convince himself he's not dreaming and is really talking with someone who knows Henry as well as Jamie does.

"I hope Henry told you how much getting to know you affected him," Jamie goes on. "You changed his life, even though you weren't comfortable... you know... going for more."

To Ruben's surprise Jamie reaches out and puts her hands on his shoulders, grips them, and shakes him gently. "You meant *so much* to him, Ruben. I can't thank you enough for getting past his defenses and helping him open up to you. That was monumental." She pulls Ruben into a fierce hug, and then just as suddenly pushes him back onto his own stool.

Heart pounding, uncertain of his voice, not knowing what to say, Ruben settles for nodding.

"My theory," Jamie says, "is that Henry doesn't have more people on his team because he's always struggling against the expectation that he'll be thrown away. He *was* thrown away. Much too early and much too often. Opening up to and caring for someone are big risks, because they increase the potential for pain if that someone then throws him away. I'm not saying that's healthy, but there it is."

Ruben reconnects with his despair about Henry's beginning—the despair he felt in the bathroom at Estelle's diner—and then he can't figure out what to do with his jumpy hands. They need to hit or hug or hurry ahead of him. He tucks them in his armpits and stands to circle the kitchen island, head down. It makes him sad to remember how generously Henry let him go that weekend, while Ruben only thought of himself.

"I can't believe how selfish I was," he finally says to the window over the sink, his eyes burning.

"Yep. A real twit," Jamie says, which surprises Ruben so much he laughs.

"I still don't understand why you consider it okay to talk to me like this," he says.

Jamie knocks on the counter with her knuckles. "This meeting of the Henry Adoration Society will now come to order. We have an agenda to get through. But first, how about some gingerbread?"

"I seriously thought you'd never ask."

Jamie cuts into the gingerbread and lifts a huge, steaming piece onto a plate for Ruben, who suppresses a whimper of frustration when he has to wait while she fetches a fork.

"Let me show you our first agenda item," Jamie says. She turns toward a bookshelf to shuffle through a box stuffed with postcards and envelopes. "Because

Henry's on the road, and we aren't talking as often, I've been getting more postcards from him than usual."

God. What I wouldn't give for a word from Henry.

When Ruben recognizes Henry's handwriting on an envelope sticking out of the box, he puts his fork down and sits on his hands to keep himself from shoving Jamie out of the way, grabbing the box, and running out of the house with it.

Jamie hands Ruben an envelope. "The reason I'm talking to you about Henry is because of what he says at the end of this letter. I know he didn't intend for me to show this to you, but when you read it, I think you'll understand why I'm doing it anyway."

Ruben holds the envelope but doesn't open it. He's happy for a moment just to feel Henry's words in his hand.

"Go on now," Jamie says.

Inside the envelope are three numbered postcards. Ruben takes them out and begins to read.

By the end of the first postcard, Ruben is laughing, picturing Henry touring the Totenkamps' museum.

By the end of the second postcard, his smile has become a scowl and he's stalked off to Jamie's living room because he needs to be alone.

"In the morning, with the gray light of a gray day reflecting off his easy smile…"

Pacing and fuming, Ruben tries and fails to move past waves of jealous anger he hasn't felt since that weekend with Henry. He sits in a chair, drops the postcards in his lap, and braces his hands on his knees, because he's breathing like he's been running and can't seem to get a good breath.

I have been running. Away from the truth. So stop. Face it. Get a grip. Read on.

He can barely focus, but he forces himself to pick up the third postcard. The need to hit something won't let up, but he forces himself to read.

By the end of the third postcard, Ruben's mind is screaming at him to run. Instead he stomps into the kitchen and asks Jamie through his anger, "Who the *fuck* is SRD?"

She gives him a steady look that eventually makes him see the storm of himself through her eyes.

You only just found Jamie. Do not wreck this.

He tries to rein himself in, orders himself to sit on the stool, concentrates on walking the tightrope between the only two things that matter in that moment. *I have to go. I can't run until I know.* He takes a breath and looks up at Jamie.

"It's *you*, you twit," Jamie says in a soft voice. "Henry's code name for you is Sparkling Razzle Dazzle. SRD."

Confused, Ruben puts a hand to his forehead and looks at the postcards again. The contradictory swirling pieces won't make peace with each other.

He slept with someone else! He loves me! He doesn't want to see me!

Only one thing is clear. Jamie's little house isn't nearly big enough.

He holds up the cards. "I'll bring these back, but I'm taking them with me now." He's not asking.

"Call me," Jamie yells, but Ruben barely hears because he's already beyond the front door, running as though his life depends on it.

LOOKING FOR HIMSELF

NEVADA

FOR TOO LONG now I've kept myself in cold storage, hoping for the day Ruben rushes in to melt me with his warmth and energy.

Not going to happen.

In spite of Erik's insistence that I use more of my lodging budget, in spite of invitations from event organizers to stay in hotels they pay for, I need campgrounds and back roads and silence. I need the unforgiving heat of August, the monotony of the Nevada desert.

I need to be unable to avoid myself.

I need the repair of retreat.

Between scheduled tour stops, I drive the thin roads and aim for campgrounds this side of grotty but not so nice that they're packed with rowdy families.

Because apparently I have needs.

The mayhem of my body's attempt to exorcise Ruben keeps me up most nights in more ways than one, sweating and groping as I defrost myself. If I can't have Ruben, if I can't come out yet, if I can't openly date, I have to find other ways to manage the backlog of desire.

I've found four.

First I arrive at each new campground as early in the day as possible, even if that means I leave again later to give a presentation or do an interview. I eat sandwiches for lunch at a picnic table and spend an hour or two writing, transmuting desire, rediscovering wholeness.

Second, after I write, unless there's an event to get to, I spend the afternoon lying on the bed in the back of my RV, staring out the window at the sky, trying to make sense of things and having pretend conversations with Jean beside a campfire in Quebec.

I would trade a year of my life right now to spend another month at that campground in Quebec with Jean. The flicker and burn of the campfire. The ceaseless shush of the waves. The sound of Jean's knife cutting away the unnecessary to reveal the meaningful.

I've tried to talk with Jamie, but her impatience blocks my view of myself. On our last call, she told me she thinks it's stupid for me to wait to come out. But then I lost the thread of her reasoning, saddened to think she doesn't understand me. When I felt my body turn my ears off, I apologized and hung up the phone. I stood by the gas station payphone in the heat for twenty minutes, until a woman asked me if I was okay. Jamie wants me to be someone I can't find right now, and it hurts to talk with her because it hurts to pretend.

Third, when darkness has truly fallen, I get up and walk. Direction doesn't matter. All that matters is that I walk until I'm exhausted and starving, even if I only walk circles around the campground. Then I head back to the RV and eat the take-out food I bought that morning or after whatever event I did. It's awful and congealed and sad by the time I eat it, which is why I make sure I'm starving and it's dark.

I haven't been cooking for myself, even though the RV is well equipped for it. I'm too busy rearranging my internal landscape to remember how to find a pan. Or maybe I'm punishing myself for indulging desire in the first place, and take-out food is my penance.

Fourth, I troll the campground for men who play for my team. I wouldn't have believed they'd be there, and they rarely are, but now and then I get lucky. Sometimes we sit next to each other and stare into a campfire before we get naked together. Sometimes we even talk. And then I give my body what it most craves—a semblance of what it most craves. A ghost of a foretaste of a facsimile of a life of freedom I don't know how to live. I expect every touch of skin to skin to progress my pilgrimage toward liberty. But touching anyone other than Ruben feels like chewing through my own ankle in order to shed the shackle of memory.

The moon wakes me. I groan and turn over to ease the ache in the small of my back.

Those are the worst times, when I open my eyes on a night so dark I needn't have bothered. I close my eyes again and surrender to the dream I've woken from, because it calls me with whispered seductions.

Though details change, it's always the same dream—touching and being touched by Ruben in compelling variations that are cruel in their temptations. Eventually, because I need to sleep, I succumb and move my hands.

I tip my head back so I can see the stars through the window. I grip myself and remove my mind from the equation.

Though I offer it other choices when I'm awake, my body will accept no substitutes.

I am a sex slave to my own dreams.

THE DOOR OF the Dallas-Fort Worth airport lounge closes behind me with a heavy thunk, silencing the busy airport noise. The wide-open windows fill the air inside with the smell of sun-warmed sage.

I know I'm dreaming, but the sensory relief of being in the opulent lounge again makes me push that knowledge out of sight.

In the dream I wake from a nap. I'm lying on my side on a long booth seat near the windows, my head on someone's lap. Ruben, I think with a smile, and push my hand beneath his thigh to feel his heat. But it feels... wrong. Not jeans. Expensive suit fabric.

Oh no. It's Erik.

I don't want to open my eyes.

His hand caresses my shoulder, moves with taunting slowness down my arm to rest on my hip and... Dear Lord. It feels so good, even though I know it's not Ruben. Keeping my eyes tightly closed, I turn onto my back, my heart pounding, angry at myself for pretending it's Ruben's hand when I know it's Erik's.

He teases me with his hand, tickles across my pelvis, caresses my abdomen. His fingers slide inside my pants.

He stops and waits.

He wants me to look at him before he touches me more.

I squirm, beyond ready for the more that his hand's quick pulse promises. I'm so hard I make a bargain with myself: I'll look, but it won't mean anything. I'll do it for the physical relief, only because my body wants it. I'll look into Erik's eyes, but it won't matter.

I steel myself and open my eyes.

It's Ruben.

Ruben is touching me.

When Ruben sees the calculated absence in my eyes, his radiant smile fades. He pulls his hand away, slides his legs out from under my head, walks away.

I wake in the RV, in a campground I can't remember the name of, to the smell of wild sage.

I wake to a radius of loss spreading around me for thousands of miles in every direction, pinning me at its center, incapable of movement, my sweaty palm pressed against my abdomen.

LOOKING FOR HENRY

LATE AUGUST | BOSTON

RUBEN PLOWS THROUGH the crowd outside the harbor restaurant, shoves his way inside to the bar, never still, never stopping, fueled by frustration. Henry's postcards burn a hole in his coat pocket.

The escape from Jamie's house, the sprint for the bus, and the battle through the Saturday-night crowds have made him thirsty. At least that's his excuse.

The crush at the bar is impossible, but Ruben sticks it out and finally gets the bartender's attention. He orders two beers, both for himself. He'll find a table out back, study Henry's postcards, and drink himself as stupid as possible as quickly as possible.

The rushed bartender lifts two big mugs of beer onto the bar and takes a closer look at Ruben. "I need to see some ID," she says, holding out her hand even as she half turns to take the next customer's order.

Ruben fumbles his fake driver's license from his wallet. He knows it's foolproof, but the gesture of handing it to the bartender seems to occur in the freeze-framed eye of a hurricane—a freakish, timeless moment of top-lit stillness and clarity.

I'm faking my way into a drunken stupor so I can fake forget the man I'm in love with, will never be able to forget, and am obviously—look at me—not grown up enough to be with.

Henry's calm voice echoes in Ruben's mind. "You will hurt me if you can't control yourself."

The bartender cocks her head at Ruben and raises her eyebrows, impatient. Ruben watches his arm extend to show her the fake ID.

THE HISTORIAN
LOOKING FOR HIMSELF

NEVADA

I DON'T SLEEP for most of the night. I watch the stars revolve in an otherwise pitch-black sky. In a moment of utter silence, when all the night sounds pause at once, I decide to renew my old pact.

Like a seed, I will feed on my own self and trust the process until something green grows from the absence in which I was planted.

I write in darkness and fall asleep with the pen in my hand.

LOOKING FOR HENRY

LATE AUGUST | BOSTON

DOWNING THE THIRD mug of beer makes a noticeable difference. Halfway into the fourth, Ruben decides he's regained control. It's a ridiculous lie from his fool of a mind, but he decides to go with it.

Why hasn't anyone hit on me yet?

Ruben has been saving himself for the possibility, however remote, of being with Henry. But postcard number two, which he's read thirty-seven times since he sat down, has soured his resolve.

"Burly, good-looking fellow wearing a red-plaid lumberjack shirt and a kind smile, asking if this seat is taken. It turns out I didn't mind..."

Determined not to be left out, Ruben scans the crowded deck for likely victims, hoping for trouble and desperate for a distraction.

Looks like my raging hypocrisy will require a fake ID for a while yet.

Then he spots the black-haired man.

Ruben picks up his beer mug and weaves his way through the crowd, never taking his eyes off the man.

When Ruben's about halfway to him, the black-haired man picks Ruben out of the crowd and watches his progress, an amused smile eventually turning up one side of his mouth.

"I remember you," he says when Ruben puts his beer mug on the table and sits. "You put on quite a show after I propositioned your friend a while back."

"Great memory," Ruben says. He has to fight to keep the snarl out of his voice.

"What can I do for you?" the man asks as he searches over Ruben's shoulder. "Who you looking for?"

Up close the man looks older—Henry's age, or even a little older. He's more handsome up close too, and Ruben feels the heat of an itch that needs to be scratched.

The man refocuses on Ruben. "I thought you might be here with your cute dad again tonight."

"Why?" Ruben asks. "You couldn't take no for an answer the first time?"

"No. I thought it might be time for your diaper change."

In spite of himself, Ruben laughs. The man clinks his beer mug against Ruben's in acknowledgment of the shift. They drink, and their eyes meet over the rims of their beers.

Ruben rests his elbows on the table, tiredness nudging the outer edges of his angry energy. "You would have liked him, actually."

"I already did. And my condolences."

Ruben sighs. "Oh well." He gives the man a steady look. When the look holds, Ruben says, "I don't suppose you'd be up for a spot of babysitting tonight?"

The black-haired man laughs, exposing a row of crooked bottom teeth. And Ruben finds himself really, really wanting him to say yes.

"Sure. If you show me your ID. The real one."

Ruben pulls his wallet out and shows the man his real driver's license.

"Good enough," the black-haired man says.

His name is Patrick and he lives close by. They talk as they walk at first, but Ruben is only half listening. By the time they arrive at Patrick's apartment, they've been walking in silence for a while.

An hour later, Patrick rolls onto his stomach, spreads his legs, looks back at Ruben, and, with a wry half smile still in place, raises his eyebrows to invite Ruben to return the favor. Ruben shakes his head and says, "I don't go there."

Patrick doesn't seem to mind, and they find other things to do with each other.

We're only passing the time.

Eventually Patrick falls asleep, way on the other side of the bed, and Ruben is relieved to be alone. He lies awake, feeling sated, foolish, and regretful. With a sigh, he closes his eyes and remembers what happened after he and Henry left the restaurant.

THE WEEKEND | SATURDAY NIGHT | BOSTON

Long past midnight, still riding waves of jealousy-fueled aggression left over from what happened at the restaurant, Ruben pins Henry's wrists to the bed above their heads, spreads Henry's legs with his knees, and says with a leer, "I think it's time we do something about my virginity as a top."

Henry reacts instantly. "No!" His eyebrows crash together, and he slithers back and away from Ruben, who remains frozen with shock. Henry walks fast around the bed, grabs Ruben's T-shirt, and leaves the bedroom.

Angry all over again, Ruben follows and finds Henry in the kitchen.

"I'm sorry," Henry says. "I know you want to go there, and you've been deliciously bossy tonight, but no. You're too... You'll hurt me if you can't control yourself."

"I can control myself!"

Henry, breathing fast, looks steadily at Ruben until Ruben has to admit the truth. Winding through his giddy experiments in commanding Henry, the backlash of leftover anger has been surging to the surface all night. And Henry has been handling it, using it, guiding it, deflecting and transmuting it.

With no help whatsoever from Ruben.

Did I think I was controlling him? Did I think I was doing that on my own?

He's been trying to teach inside our tempest.

Maybe it's time I paid attention.

Ruben nods and bows his head, ashamed of his selfishness.

When Henry opens the refrigerator and reaches for something, Ruben walks into the living room. He feels both ashamed and foolish, because he knows he's only turning away to avoid seeing Henry's bare ass as he bends over.

LATE AUGUST | BOSTON

Patrick gets up to go to the bathroom. Ruben pretends to be asleep, but he's wide-awake, unable to remember why he wanted to lie in a stranger's bed—unable to remember why he wanted to lie to himself.

If I were Henry, would I want to be with me?
If I loved Henry like he deserves, would I have done what I did tonight?
"You will hurt me if you can't control yourself."
I will hurt myself too.
Too late. I already have.

LOOKING FOR HIMSELF

AUGUST

"HENRY. THANK GOD you called."

"Hey, Erik. What's up?"

"Congratulations, buddy. You're a Shander Award finalist."

I stare at my stunned reflection in the silvery square on the front of the pay phone.

"Oh my God. Seriously?"

"Yes, seriously. Get ready for big leaps. This is your ticket for a rocket ride."

My mind remains a vast, surprised void. "Um... sorry not to say something intelligent right now, but I can't think past 'Oh my God.'"

Erik laughs. "No worries. Take some time to let it register and then call me back. We need to talk, but I've got—hang on, let me check—I've got back-to-back meetings today, so you'll have to call me tomorrow morning. Will you do that?"

"Yes. Sure. Of course."

"I made plans for us to meet right after you do San Francisco. I booked us a couple of rooms in a nice resort in Napa Valley. I'll want to run some new opportunities by you then, but it's also to force you to take a break. I even booked you a massage."

"Oh Lord. That sounds heavenly. Thank you."

"We'll celebrate your nomination, but you being a finalist has put other things in motion that I've had waiting in the wings. We've got a lot to talk about."

"Like what?"

"Like you coming out. And the fact that giving your Shander lecture in Boston in early October means shifting the shooting schedule in the Northwest and juggling the Oregon and Washington events you'll need to go back for after the lecture. But don't fret. We'll arrange things so your tour still ends at the end of November like we originally planned. We can deal with most things on the phone, but you'll need to call me more often between now and your lecture."

"Okay. When do we meet in Napa?"

"Three weeks from now, on September 24. I can't meet you sooner—too much else going on, and it'll take me that long anyway to prepare some of the opportunities I want to present to you. But definitely call me tomorrow morning."

And then he's gone.

Preoccupied, I hold the phone in my hand. My mind whirs as I start to piece together my Shander lecture.

LOOKING FOR HENRY

LATE AUGUST | BOSTON

RUBEN LIES AWAKE in Patrick's bed, bludgeoning himself with questions. *What now? Is Henry sleeping alone tonight? What if he isn't?*

The smell of sex and beer and a stranger's sweat makes it hard to breathe. Ruben flings back the covers, grabs his clothes, yanks them on, and leaves Patrick's apartment without a word. He rushes into the fresh air and breathes great lungfuls that threaten to never be enough.

His own beery breath makes him nauseous. When regret chokes off his air supply and his skin crawls with unwanted memories of Patrick's clutching hands, Ruben decides to walk it off, to walk into the city's midnight quiet on the chance it will deliver a cure by osmosis.

It's a long way back to his parents' house. It's going to take forever.

I can't go on like this.

Hours later Ruben realizes he's been walking in circles, and home is as out of reach as when he began. He stops to sit on a bench in a little park he's never noticed before. He rests his elbows on his knees and lowers his aching head into his hands.

Too many thoughts refuse to connect. Too many feelings refuse to sort. He's jittery, angry, sad, scared, yearning, desperate, hopeful, and he vows to sit until something—anything—arranges itself into a semblance of sense, until the pileup of feelings and thoughts sorts itself into a trail he can follow.

He sits and waits.

When it begins to rain, he gets chilled and finally wraps his arms tightly around himself to conserve whatever dryness and heat might remain. But he refuses to leave without finding at least a hint of relief.

He sits and waits some more.

As color begins to show beneath the sky's overwhelming darkness, as grays give way to a muted festival of pink at the horizon, an old man with a dog walks by and nods to Ruben, which makes Ruben realize how he must look, sitting in the dawn rain like a fool, soaking wet and wearing a too-thin jacket.

Oh.

Maybe it's not about keeping Henry for myself.

Maybe it's about protecting him from harm.

From people who want to use him for sex.

Like I did.

Like I thought I did.

THE HISTORIAN
LOOKING FOR HIMSELF

SEPTEMBER | SANTA BARBARA

TODAY'S FEDEX PACKAGE from Erik includes lecture details from the Shander Foundation. I carefully study their requirements, and I'm relieved by the time I finish. It looks like I'll have the leeway to do what I want with my lecture.

Over the past week of long nights spent staring up at the sky, I've felt puzzle pieces fitting into place as the empty shape of me reaches out again for my shadow, stretching for a reunion.

No. I can't—*won't*—come out yet. I don't want to jeopardize the Everyday History programs already up and running.

So I'll use my Shander lecture to come out about something else.

I'll tell the story of how I began.

LOOKING FOR HENRY

LATE AUGUST | BOSTON

"HELLO."

"Marie…"

Ruben's sister must hear him panting into his phone, because she asks, "Where are you?"

When he can't answer, she says, "I'm at work, but I'll leave right now and drive into town. Stay on the phone. As soon as you can, tell me where you are. Whatever this is, it'll be okay. Just don't hang up."

Relieved to know that help is on the way, Ruben folds an arm across his raised knees and drops his head onto it. He keeps the phone pressed against his ear while he waits.

"I'm crossing the bridge now," Marie says. "I need to know which way to turn to get to you."

"Harbor Hotel," Ruben croaks out. "Parking lot." He's sitting at the outer edge of the mostly empty lot, on wet pavement, shivering in the rain, his back against the wide concrete base of a light pole to block the harsh wind.

He waits another fifteen minutes, and then Marie's hand is on top of his head. She tugs his phone from his unresponsive fingers, pulls up on his arms to help him stand, wraps him in a brief, tight hug, and puts him into the car.

They circle the light pole, and Ruben turns his head to watch as long as he can. He memorizes the sight of his fake ID leaning against the concrete base. When the car straightens out, he faces forward and leans into the heat that blasts from the vent.

At home, Ruben stands in the middle of his bedroom wearing a towel, flushed from the hot bath Marie insisted he take. His limbs ache from sitting on the hard asphalt of the parking lot in the rain for so long. She hands him a pair of boxers and a long T-shirt, turns her back, and holds her hand out for his towel. Ruben feels like a little kid.

The exact opposite of how I want to feel.

He struggles to process his angry frustration, weary of its persistence. More than he's ever wanted anything in his life, he wants to be more mature.

"Sweetheart, I wish you'd tell me what's wrong," Marie says again.

Ruben shakes his head. "I have to sleep now."

She nods, but Ruben can tell from the way the edges of her mouth draw down that she doesn't like it. She gestures for him to get under the covers, and then she tucks him in and sweeps his damp hair off his forehead.

"Ruben, hey. I'm going to say this in case you need to hear it. Okay? No matter what this is, we can figure it out. Guaranteed. You know that. Right?"

He knows she means it, so he nods and closes his eyes. Marie kisses him on the forehead, which reminds him of the last kiss he received from Henry on the sidewalk that Sunday. That also felt like a kiss for a child.

Marie pats his leg but doesn't leave.

"Will you be around for a while?" Ruben manages to ask.

That seems to finally satisfy her. She stands and says, "I'm staying over for a few nights. Come get me if you need to, no matter what or when. Okay?" When he nods, she turns out the light and leaves.

Ruben reaches under the pillow for Henry's postcards. While Marie started his bathwater, he'd transferred them from the dry inner pocket of his jacket. They're cool, so he presses them between his palms to warm them and to try to assimilate some of Henry's maturity by osmosis.

He can feel deeper layers of truth stalking him like a pack of wild dogs.

I have to rescue myself.

A wave of dizziness and exhaustion tips him toward sleep. Like a drumbeat, a phantom memory of unending rain taps against the top of his head.

Lost in a storm.

In a troubled dream, he struggles beneath shifting waves, clutching Henry's postcards to his chest, peering up through heavy gray water at an outstretched hand bathed in sunlight.

He sleeps all day, misses dinner, and dives into the next night's sleep without a pause. He regains full consciousness in the perfect silence of two in the morning.

With a sigh he turns on the bedside light and sits cross-legged with his back against the headboard and the covers pulled up over his chest.

With care, he spreads the postcards in a row across the bed and then tucks his arms underneath the covers and studies them from behind half-closed eyelids.

His body's heaviness urges him to give up and lie back down, but he resists, leans his head back, and allows thoughts to come and go. He watches them run, too tired and sad to enforce order.

Fragments and moments and memories and implications parade by. He wonders about all the things he doesn't know about Henry, certain they're more interesting and complex and myriad than he can imagine. Like the fact that Henry uses code to distance himself from troublesome topics.

Henry's code for Ruben makes him smile. *Sparkling Razzle Dazzle. What would my code for Henry be?*

Hope. Home. Happy.

Eventually Ruben persuades himself to turn off the light. When he lifts his hand from the lamp, the march of random thoughts stutters to a stop.

In slow motion his memory replays the intense, thrilling moment at the restaurant when Henry said, *"Claim me,"* and granted Ruben permission to lunge, to transmute his aggression.

Something nudges at his consciousness.

An impression floats and disappears before he gets a good look at it. To court it back, he lifts his hand to the lamp again, rewinds his thoughts. Finally his memory replays that moment at the restaurant from Henry's perspective.

Ruben's head snaps up and his eyes fly open.

At the restaurant Ruben was too addled to fully notice it, but in his revisited memory, he hears the tone of Henry's voice for the first time and sees the look in his eyes when he says, *"Claim me."*

Oh God. It was a wish.

A wish Henry already knew to be impossible. A wish whispered into a pretend possibility. A wish pushed into the air against Henry's will. A wish from the thrown-away baby and the sweet man, trying to get Ruben's attention.

Beautiful Henry, wanting to be claimed. By someone. Even for a moment.

LOOKING FOR HIMSELF

SEPTEMBER | SANTA BARBARA

ERIK'S VOICE ON the phone a few days ago held more than excitement about my nomination for the Shander Award. I'm sure of it. If it wouldn't be so preposterous, I'd call his laughter giddy. But why? Maybe because I'll be meeting him in Napa at a hotel that he arranged for us. I'll have to be on guard. On the call I heard in his voice the same thing I heard in the airport lounge in July.

Napa's going to be awkward if Erik has a crush on me. If he even knows he has a crush on me. If he tries to do something about it.

I hope I'm wrong. If I'm not, I hope he's strong enough to leave the possibilities unexplored, to spare us the messiness of that choreography.

At least I think that's what I hope. I hope that's what I hope.

I stand beside the escalators and stare at the board that lists the store's departments. I can't decide whether to head for sleepwear or sporting goods.

What does one wear to an assignation that may turn out to be two parts business and one part ill-advised temptation?

One of the nice suits hanging in my RV's tiny closet?

A rumpled T-shirt and pants infused with campfire smoke?

Supersoft pajamas?

A catcher's mask?

LOOKING FOR HENRY

LATE AUGUST | BOSTON

THE LATE-NIGHT QUIET of the house and the knowledge that Marie is right down the hall give Ruben the courage to conduct an experiment. It's time to see if he can unravel the scary, unfocused aggression triggered by Henry's second postcard.

They're the same feelings the incident at the restaurant triggered.

I didn't claim Henry when I had the chance. I won't make that mistake again— even if I have to take a journey to the other side of the mirror to figure it out.

Ruben forces himself to sit up straight and stare at Henry's handwriting, at the words Henry wrote to Jamie. As Ruben allows the jealousy to burgeon and spill, his face heats, and his breathing speeds up. But he holds on inside the jitter and jangle. He reaches beyond, and hopes there's an end.

It's like reaching through a coin to the other side. *One side jealousy. The other side caring. And the coin flips.*

In a whoosh the tension drains from Ruben's muscles. It's like a canyon opens up, and all the heavy, wearying, worrying, frightening, lashing feelings slip over the edge, leaving Ruben suspended in a blank, clear space. His heart beats, strong and steady, a homing beacon that pulses a protective beam into the darkness.

On one side I'm a child, pushing everyone away from my prize. On the other side, I'm a man, allowing myself to care for Henry.

Emptied of jealousy, the cleared space around his heart fills with love.

"Ruben, hey." Marie wakes him with a gentle hand on his shoulder. Slumped sideways against the headboard, Ruben opens his eyes to see her sitting on the edge of the bed in bright sunlight. He groans and rubs his cricked neck.

"Sorry to wake you," says Marie, "but you looked uncomfortable. Mom says the big breakfast she's making you will be ready in about an hour."

"Mmm. Yeah. That means blueberry coffee cake. Thanks." Ruben scoots farther under the covers and lies down all the way, careful not to jostle Henry's postcards off the bed. Marie picks them up and hands them to him.

"Did you read them?" asks Ruben.

"No. Yes. No... um..."

Ruben laughs. "It's okay. I was going to show you anyway." He takes a look at the clock. "Aren't you going to be late for work?"

"Day off today."

Ruben nods. He suspects she's taken the day off for him. "Thanks, Marie. Thanks for—"

"Yes. Fine. You're welcome. Now *tell* me what's going on. I can't stand it for one more second."

He considers. "Okay. But it'll take a while, so you might as well get comfortable." He moves away and pulls back the covers. Marie slips off her shoes, climbs in beside him, and they pull the covers up to their chins.

Ruben turns to face her and takes a deep breath. "There's someone I love."

She nods at the postcards. "This Henry?"

"Yes."

She picks up the first postcard and rubs her thumb over Henry's writing. "Then who's Jamie?"

"She's Henry's cousin. Well sort of. Wow. This really is going to take a while."

Marie slides her foot to touch Ruben's. Then she waits. Ruben knows she'll wait as long as it takes. Her patience removes his reluctance.

"Um... I don't really know how to tell this except... Well, a bunch of stuff happened yesterday that made me realize something so paradoxical it, like, *rearranged* me. It's still rearranging me."

He pauses, aware that he's about to say the next part out loud for the first time. He takes his time to polish it a bit before he offers it up to Marie.

"I realized I'm a lost creature, a work in progress, a scared half-child—but at the same time I'm a man with a mission and a keen strategist." He swallows his heart back into his chest, touches the postcard Marie holds, and says, "I'm ready to give Henry the kind of love he said he wanted."

Marie smiles and nudges Ruben's foot again. "Tell me you have a plan and then tell me everything about this Henry. From the beginning."

"Of course I have a plan."

Marie smiles into Ruben's eyes and breathes quietly beside him.

It helps.

ONE WEEK LATER | BOSTON

ON THE LAST day of August, the day the Shander Award nominees will be announced, Ruben wakes up early to check the Shander Foundation website. He's checked fifty times by nine o'clock and the nominee finalists still haven't been announced, so he promises himself he'll wait until after lunch to check again, to spare himself the heart rate fluctuations.

Two hours later Danny calls with the news that the nominees have been posted. And Henry is one of the finalists. Ruben closes his eyes as he clutches the phone and his entire body relaxes as his mind speeds up.

Now I know how to reach him.

A week later the Shander Foundation announces the dates for the nominee lecture series in Boston. Henry's lecture will take place on Friday, October 8. According to Henry's website, that's several weeks before his road trip is scheduled to end. Even if only briefly, Henry will be in Boston earlier than planned.

Ruben clicks the Buy Now button to purchase tickets to Henry's lecture. When he sees how much the tickets cost, he pauses, but only long enough to be sure about how many tickets he wants.

THE HISTORIAN
LOOKING FOR HIMSELF

LATE SEPTEMBER | NAPA VALLEY

"Better?" Erik asks when I find him at the patio cafe.

"Dear God, yes. That was the best massage I've ever had. She was amazing." I stretch out on the deck chair and let my arms hang over the sides. Being relaxed around Erik is risky, but my scattered wits resist herding.

With my eyes closed, I notice the smell of eucalyptus and the buzz of insects.

"So, let's discuss you coming out," Erik says.

"Yes, please. But imagine me sitting up properly. I can't seem to actually do it right now."

I hear Erik's fingernail tap against his glass a few times. He's about to say something he knows I won't like. With reluctance I open my eyes and sit up a little straighter.

"It's been kept out of the press, but there's something you need to know about Edith Shander."

"Okay."

He clears his throat and taps the glass again. "Edith has a grandson, Quincy, who's nineteen. When he was ten, his parents died in a car accident. He was raised by Edith—well, Edith and her household staff—in Boston and New York. When Quincy was fifteen, he came out to his family, including Edith. Those of us who know both of them advised Quincy against coming out to her, but he wanted to risk it."

"Uh-oh. What happened?"

"Edith took a hard line. She was uncompromising. She wrote him out of her will, told him she had done so, and shipped him off to a boarding school in Europe."

"God, that's awful." I think back to the interactions I've had with Edith Shander over the past weeks. "But in her phone interviews with me and at that meeting with the award committee in Santa Barbara, she seemed... Wow. I'm surprised. Poor Quincy."

"Yes," says Erik.

And poor you. Since we arrived here at the resort, I've seen no sign of the suggestive gaze he dealt me in the airport lounge in Dallas. Not yet anyway.

"Erik, why doesn't the fact that you know Mrs. Shander personally jeopardize my eligibility for the award?"

"The award committee is into connections, believe me. Any and all connections are capitalized on by those involved in the awarding process. That most definitely includes me."

Erik puts a hand on the pitcher of margaritas and raises his eyebrows. I nod, follow my thoughts, and connect the dots. Suddenly my mouth is dry. "I don't think I like the direction this is heading."

"Unfortunately there's more," Erik says. "In the 1950s, a Shander Award winner went off the deep end and caused a massive scandal, burning through the money and grossly abusing her new prestige. The Foundation took a big hit of bad publicity, and in subsequent award years, they adopted a wait-and-see period with winners. The $500,000 prize is paid out three months to the day after the award is announced, as a way for the Foundation to... assure themselves of the winner's character."

"Are you serious? The Foundation would consider my gayness a sign of *bad character*?"

"I know these people, Henry," Erik says, his voice low, as though he's clueing me in on a secret. "The award would be passed to the runner-up, and your loss of prestige would be much more damaging than not winning the award in the first place. It would destroy much of what you've built so far."

"And after the three months?"

"Zero backlash for the Foundation. Their position is that, after a few months have passed, they can distance themselves from the brunt of any bad publicity associated with the winner. In your case, if you came out before the three months was up, I could see them coming up with a technicality that would disqualify you, so their homophobia would remain hidden."

Erik hands me the margarita, and I take it but I set it on the low table beside my lounge chair. My throat is too tight to want it after all. "Go on, then," I say, my jaw tight around the words. "Spell it out."

Erik clears his throat. "All things considered, I recommend that you don't come out. Not yet."

"Not yet," I mutter to myself, appalled by the cumulative impact that short phrase is having on my psyche.

"We'll plan for you to come out—with an official public announcement— as soon as you receive the award money."

"And if I don't win?"

"Henry, the only way you won't win is if you don't show up for the lecture."

I study him with my eyes narrowed. "You haven't rigged it, have you?"

Eric laughs. "No. Christ. I would never do that. But I've thoroughly studied your competitors, and I know your strengths."

I bow my head, drained by all the sudden plot twists.

"Anything else?" I ask, weary and ready to find the safety of my room.

"Yes. I saved the good news for last. Whether you win or not, you may be offered a show on a major network out of LA."

I gape at Erik. "You're kidding. Really?"

"It's tentative as yet, but they want to meet you in person as soon as possible. We have a few meetings scheduled with the higher-ups at the studio over the next week. That's one of the reasons we shifted your tour schedule—that and all the Los Angeles events we've added since your nomination."

"So I'll... what? Leave the RV here in Napa and fly from LA to Boston for the lecture?"

"Right. And fly back to San Francisco the day after the lecture to resume your tour."

"Uh. No. I won't. No way. A couple of days in Boston isn't nearly enough."

Erik raises his eyebrows. "If not for the lecture, you wouldn't be going to Boston at all for another month."

We stare at each other until Erik shrugs. "We committed you to some national TV appearances in LA that were out of reach until you got the Shander nomination. There's not much wiggle room for the timing of the Boston trip, so I'll say maybe. I'll see what we can arrange."

Now even more intent on making a quick getaway, I nod and reach for my margarita.

Erik taps his glass. "One more thing."

"Why do I not have a good feeling about this?" I mutter.

"You *could* have a good feeling about it."

"Just tell me, Erik."

"If the deal with the TV network goes through, you'll be moving to LA."

Where the seed of me had begun to grow again, a creeping blankness burgeons and pushes.

"I've got a headache," I say. "I'm going to have dinner in my room. I need some time to adjust."

I start to stand, but Erik puts a hand on my arm, and I stay seated.

"As you adjust this evening, Henry, consider how much more the award and the new show will allow you to do." He places a file folder on the table and taps it. "I've got figures here on potential household reach for the new show, plus other metrics I think will interest you."

Through the pebbled glass of the table, I see the tip of Erik's brown shoe moving up and down.

I pick up the folder and stand, my body heavy, the lightness of the massage a distant memory. "I'm grateful for all your work, Erik. But right now I'm just tired." I turn to go.

"Our rooms here cost nine hundred dollars a night," Erik says.

I stop but don't turn around.

"I've seen you looking around and enjoying yourself here," he says. "You're one lecture and a few key decisions away from having it all—from living very well, helping a lot of people, and coming out publicly with no worries."

"What is your point?"

"You're at a crossroads. Impress the new TV studio, be willing to move to LA, deliver your lecture, wait a few months to come out, get the award money..."

"You're saying if I do that then I can fix all the hurt, lonely, lost, forgotten people in the country? Is that your point?"

After a moment Erik says, "More or less."

I walk away, my shoulders curled beneath the burden of good news.

"Sleep well, Henry," Erik says behind me.

Who can I hire to manage my inner life?

I certainly don't seem able to do it.

Erik's file folder full of persuasive metrics has eyes that follow me around my hotel room. I escape to the bathroom and step into the shower, imagining the hot water sluicing over my shoulders scouring away the burdens I've chosen.

Everyday History was such a simple idea. It gave me such joy. It still does—when I can locate it within all the red tape and plot twists.

Where are the parts of me in charge of bold simplicity, crap eradication, and standing tall enough to shed what I don't want without losing what I do want?

I use two fingers to pick up Erik's file folder and carry it to the closet, where I push it, unopened, to the back of the top shelf. It will wait.

I'm not deluded enough to think it will wait very long. I can't repair my life by ignoring it, but I can spare this moment. One evening to reconcile and orient myself.

I order dinner early, eat on my little balcony, and look out over the neat rows of grapevines.

The air stills. Shadows gain ground. My mind empties.

Because I'm on vacation, when I turn out the light and slide between the sheets, I don't fight my dreams.

THE EXPLORER

LOOKING FOR HENRY

MID-SEPTEMBER | BOSTON

RUBEN PATS HENRY'S postcards in the breast pocket of his jacket and presses Jamie's doorbell.

"I made gingerbread again," Jamie says when she opens the door, "since you missed out on it last time."

"Sorry," he says as he follows her into the kitchen and sniffs the air. "Did Henry call?" Ruben can't keep himself from blurting it.

Jamie laughs. "Hello, Ruben. How are you? Would you like something to drink?"

Ruben blinks and frowns. Jamie sighs and takes a pitcher of iced tea from the fridge.

"No, I haven't spoken to Henry since you were here before," she says. "He's taking a time out. Or maybe we both are. Anyway he's mad at me." She hands Ruben a square of hot gingerbread on a plate.

Ruben lifts the plate to his nose. "Mmm. Thank you. So why is Henry mad at you?"

"I gave him an earful about being inaccessible, among other things, and he got bristly. Doesn't happen very often. I pointed out the futility of him trying to choose between loneliness or the dreaded cell phone."

"Why have to choose at all? I mean, I've been wondering why he agreed to be gone for so long? Wouldn't he rather be at home?"

"He told me he wanted to get away from his apartment for a while."

"But why? He seemed so comfortable there. I love his apartment."

Jamie narrows her eyes at Ruben. "Well, why do you think?"

"I don't know," he says with a shrug.

"Because being at home reminds him of being there with you."

"But I was only there for a few hours."

"And so what does that tell you?" Jamie asks, her voice crisp.

"Shit." Ruben takes a big breath and lets it out slowly. They're both quiet for a while.

"Does Henry respond to *your* e-mails?" Ruben finally asks.

Jamie snorts. "Sure. If you want to call a telegram a response."

Ruben laughs. "I always thought his e-mails were short because he's shy."

"No. He equates e-mails with telegrams. I only know what's going on with him when we talk in real time. The postcards help, but that's not a conversation."

"No." Ruben's worries about Henry make his stomach clench, and he puts down the fork. "Jamie, I've been looping through conspiracy theories lately about Henry, and I could use a reality check. You know him a lot better than I do. What do *you* think is going on?"

Jamie considers for a moment. "Henry only gets bristly and righteous when he's defending something he knows he shouldn't. That's what's bugging me. I don't think he's been getting enough… perspective."

"You mean, besides Erik's perspective?" Ruben says.

"Right."

"Are we saying Erik's bent? I mean, he's a successful, high-caliber professional. Why would he risk his reputation and his lifestyle by doing something as unethical as…?"

Jamie knocks her knuckles against the counter. "Wait. The plot thickens." She gets up and goes to the box in the bookshelf where she keeps her mail from Henry.

Henry's first set of postcards pulse against Ruben's chest. He imagines that their movements cause his heart to beat, rather than the other way around.

Slowly he takes the envelope out of his pocket and presses it to the counter with his fingertips, desperate to hang on to it even though he knows giving it back is the right thing to do.

When Jamie turns around and sees the envelope, she surprises Ruben. "You keep those," she says. "I'd treasure them, but I think you actually need them. Only… give them back if you ever don't want them anymore. I'm not a very sentimental person, except when it comes to Henry."

That reminds Ruben of something he's been wondering about. "Hey. Do you mind if I ask why your family didn't keep Henry?"

Jamie sets a new envelope on the counter between them, sits on the stool next to Ruben, and gestures to Ruben to go on eating his gingerbread. "No, I don't mind. I was eighteen and out of the house already when my parents got Henry. He was with them a couple of years, until my dad died and my mom went to live with her sister. By then I was twenty but too young in too many ways to take Henry on myself—or I would have, in a heartbeat. Even so I did what I could, especially when Henry couldn't seem to find a good fit with a foster family. I'd approach whatever foster family he was sent to and offer to babysit him for free. They always took me up on it. Henry and I both considered my place his home, though he usually slept at the home of the foster family of the moment."

"How old was he when you moved to Europe?"

"Oh, that was so hard. When he was a senior in high school, a fancy cooking school in Paris offered me a scholarship. I wasn't going to take it at first, but then Henry and I filled out endless application forms that winter. We tried to get him into the best possible situation, so I could go and he would be okay. Or as okay as possible. And that's what we did. The day he turned eighteen, we moved him into his own little bachelor apartment—with my stove—and I went off to France while he got ready for his first year of college."

"Yeah. That must have been hard."

"It was. It was a lot harder than I thought it would be. But it got better after a while. Henry managed to do some study trips in Europe, and he crammed his undergraduate degree into three years. Then he got his first graduate degree in Germany. We saw each other pretty often. By the time he was done studying in Europe, I'd been in France seven years. That's when I got the job here at the hotel. Henry moved back to Boston and got the job at the museum, where he worked while getting his second PhD."

"Amazing. He's lucky to have you in his life."

Jamie waves a dismissive hand. "*I've* been lucky to have Henry in *my* life. I've never been able to resist him." She smiles a goofy smile. "I'm only sentimental about him because he's so damned sweet."

"Yeah. Sweetness backed by incredible strength," Ruben says half to himself. "Deadly combination." He looks up at Jamie and blurts out an awkward confession. "Henry's complexity makes me feel average and boring."

"Oh knock it off. He may be complex, but he craves simplicity. I guarantee your brand of forceful decisiveness calmed him down. I should know. I've been bossing him around most of his life. Not that he always does what I—" She gets a faraway look. "Huh."

"What?" Ruben replays what she's just said. "*Shit*. Erik."

In the silence that follows, Ruben tries to get a handle on his emotions. The thought of Erik calming Henry down and telling him what to do makes Ruben's jealous aggression flare, but Ruben stares it down, focuses on his desire to protect and care for Henry. He finds the edge of the coin and slowly and steadily breathes against it until it flips.

When Ruben opens his eyes, Jamie looks at him with compassion.

"Here," Jamie says. She pushes the new envelope from Henry across the counter. "You need to read this before we talk any more about Erik."

THE HISTORIAN
LOOKING FOR HIMSELF

EARLY SEPTEMBER | SANTA CRUZ

POSTCARD 1

JAMIE, DO YOU think we could we discuss my coming out without you going all parental on me? I'm not convinced coming out now is best. And no. The consolation sex I've been having as I troll the campgrounds doesn't count as coming out. Oh stop it with your stern did-you-use-a-condom look. I'm always safe. I'm a responsible adult. And I can have fun if I want to. So there. When I tried to tell you what Erik is doing to shift the underpinnings and minimize potential backlash when I do come out, you didn't seem want to hear. Why? I need someone to talk to. I miss you.

POSTCARD 2

SPEAKING OF ERIK, I'd suspect him of giving me the once-over if I didn't know better, if he weren't straight and happily married. With kids. Too bad. He's truly hot, in a brawn-beneath-the-business-suit way, and he has a talent for taking care of me. My pitiful phase of lingering in delusion over lost love sidetracked me for way too long. But now something about Erik is making me sit up and take notice. I can sort of see how I might find a way to open up to love again soon. I'm going to ask Erik if he has a gay brother he hasn't mentioned.

POSTCARD 3

AFTER SAN FRANCISCO Erik's going to meet me in Napa Valley at a resort he booked us into for a few days. He told me he has exciting new to share, but he won't tell me over the phone. "Not yet," Erik keeps saying. ARGH. "Not yet" has been my motto for far too long. Do I have enough college degrees? "Not yet." Oops. There went a decade of higher education. Isn't it time to go on a few dates? "Not yet." I'm enjoying my work too much. Dear God, may I please, please jump SRD now? "Not yet." How about now? "Not yet." Damn. I accidently stuffed myself back into the closet. Can I come out? "Not yet." Can I go home? "Not yet." Can I start a family? "NOT YET!"

POSTCARD 4

TO WHOM AM I directing those questions? If I'm asking myself, why can't I get the foster kids' faces out of my mind whenever I try to answer "Right now" to the question of when to come out? I don't seem able to help myself AND all the other people I want to help. Except apparently I can raise my bottle of hard cider and waggle my eyebrows at the guy at the next picnic table. At least in this way, I'm helping myself while I help someone else. Heh heh. I'm so looking forward to seeing you soon. I guess I'm not very mad at you after all. I'll arrange to have a ticket to my Shander lecture sent to you. Love, Henry.

LOOKING FOR HENRY

MID-SEPTEMBER | BOSTON

THE FIRST BATCH of postcards had been bad. This batch is worse. Much, much worse.

Ruben retreats to the living room, irked that he feels the need to. He parks himself in an armchair and imagines a seat belt firmly strapping him in place so he doesn't run out the door.

With great effort he manages to keep the coin from flipping, to keep his new perspective about Henry. It's exhausting and leaves him feeling frail and drained, but it gets him through.

He reads the last postcard, sets it on his lap, grips the arms of the chair, and focuses all his attention on who he wants to be. When the coin remains flipped the right way up—the grown-up way up—for ten minutes, he stands and returns to the kitchen. He monitors his footsteps on the way to make sure he doesn't stomp.

Jamie is sitting at the counter, flipping through a newspaper.

Ruben waves the new postcards. "Is Henry still in love with me or not?"

"*That's* the question you want to be asking right now?"

Ruben drops his gaze. Jamie remains silent, but Ruben needs that question addressed before he can pay attention to anything else. He looks up at her and nods.

Jamie tilts her head. "It's hard to say. He seems willing to move on, which is not a bad thing."

Ruben glowers.

"I'm not going to sugarcoat my opinion for you," she says with a shrug. "I like you, but Henry's happiness comes first. And if he's decided to move on, I'm not going to interfere. He doesn't write about you much in his postcards anymore. And he's been sleeping around. Henry would *never, ever* do that if he thought you two might get back together. He's much too loyal, even if it's only a one-sided loyalty. Another point against you is the fact that he's admitted to being attracted to someone else for reasons that are not purely physical. Even if the guy he's attracted to is straight. Hell. Even if it's Erik, which I have to say, gives me the creeps." She shivers. "My point is that, after a long, long time of using the memory of you to close himself off, Henry is opening up again. I can't help but see that as a positive."

Ruben sets the new postcards on the counter. He doesn't want to let go of them, but he keeps catching himself starting to crush them inside the fist that wants to form. "Henry didn't actually say he's attracted to Erik." He can hear the childish petulance in his voice.

Jamie raises her eyebrows. "In Henry-speak, he did. That gay-brother comment is guilt about his attraction."

Ruben mentally commands the coin to stay put. He paces, rolls his head around, and decides to take a sideways conversational step to give himself time to cool down. He pulls up the mental list of questions he's been wanting to ask Jamie. "Do you know how Henry got Erik as an agent?"

"Of course. After his column went into syndication, Henry wrote a book proposal. I asked someone I know in publishing to take a look at it. She thought it was sharp and professional, and she had some suggestions about what Henry could do next, starting with getting an agent. He was reluctant, so I came up with a plan to show Henry's work to some agents without him knowing about it. He had a lecture coming up at the museum and, even though it wasn't on Everyday History, I knew he'd do what he does best."

"Wow the audience into mouth-gaping awe?"

"Yes, basically."

"Been there." Ruben sighs heavily and sits. "So how'd it go?"

"Well, I asked around and identified a few agents who seemed decent enough, and I invited them to the lecture. Jocelyn, Henry's boss at the museum, recommended Erik. Apparently there's a connection between one of the board members and Erik's wife. Erik showed up at the lecture but made a big point of telling me it was only as a favor to his wife's friend and not to expect anything to come of it. I nodded and let him talk. All the while I snickered to myself, because I trusted in Henry's powers."

"You really didn't tell Henry the agents were there?"

Jamie shifts uncomfortably in her chair. "Well, no. Not before the lecture. I wanted him to be his usual self, and I wasn't sure how he'd react if he knew there were agents in the audience scoping him out. I wrangled him—took him out for a nice dinner beforehand and casually mentioned, a few minutes before he went on stage, that a couple of people wanted to say hi to him after the lecture."

"That was the 'Modern Technology Through the Ages' lecture. Right?"

"Yes." Jamie looks surprised. "Were you there?"

"No. But I read about it in the museum's newsletter."

"Well, it was sold-out and standing room only, as always with Henry's lectures. I gave my seat to someone and stood off to the side so I could watch the agents' reactions. They all looked engaged and interested throughout, but Erik's transformation over the course of the lecture was truly remarkable. Oh, and hey. That lecture includes funny bits about Henry's aversion to digital technology, so Erik knew from the start what he'd be dealing with if he took Henry on."

"True... So Henry's allure changed Erik's mind. Wow."

"Could be. When we talked after the lecture, Erik had done a one-eighty. The difference in Erik after the lecture struck me initially as odd somehow." She shakes her head like she's trying to dislodge a stuck memory. "Before I invited those agents to see Henry, I read whatever I could find on the Internet about them. And I kept an eye out for personal stuff too. I guess I thought it might help me see whether they'd be a good personality match for Henry." She lifts her left eyebrow. "If I hadn't already known about Erik's devotion to his marriage and his kids because of the research I'd done on him, I would have said he developed a sudden crush on Henry during that lecture."

"No shit."

"When I introduced them, Erik's face flushed, and his smile was sort of... too personal. Then his face closed off, and he smiled a scary smile and proceeded to pull out all the stops. He power played like a linebacker. Blew straight past the competition with a deal Henry would've been a fool to pass up. One of the other agents was really disappointed. At the time, snagging such a virtuoso of an agent for Henry made me happy. But now..."

"Yeah. Now." Ruben rubs his jaw and reviews his strategy, mentally scanning for any loose ends Jamie might know how to help wrap up.

"Would you be willing to share any new postcards you get from Henry with me? I mean, obviously only if you deem them shareable."

"Sure."

Another thought rises up, and Ruben asks, "How aware do you think Henry is of the details of his business life?"

"Ugh. Not much. Another area he accuses me of nagging him about. He's not remotely stupid, but he has always preferred to hire someone he trusts to handle the business aspects. He's a delegator, not a micromanager. Henry and business? No affinity whatsoever."

Ruben nods, distracted. "He'd want to do what he loves the most, while still making sure all the business stuff is handled by someone responsible."

"Exactly."

"Shit. Jamie, we have to see Henry. In person. If we can talk to him directly, one of us may be able to tell if there's something fishy going on with Erik, if Erik's taking advantage of him."

"I'll see Henry in person at his lecture."

"That means waiting another month. Who knows what'll happen before that? I don't have a good feeling about this. You'll keep trying to contact Henry, to get him on the phone?"

Jamie nods.

"Or," Ruben says with a crooked smile, "I could crash that party in Napa."

They both know Ruben is joking. Mostly. Ruben considers the idea of crashing Henry's road trip, but stops when he realizes he's not willing to gamble any possible future he and Henry may have together on an ambush. There's too much potential for failure in the face of unexpected variables.

Jamie smiles at Ruben and gets him another piece of gingerbread. "The Shander lecture it is, then. I know it's pricey, but it would be great if you could be there too. I'd be willing to pay for half of your ticket."

"Tickets for the lectures sold out in two hours."

"Wow. Really?"

"Yeah. But I'm way ahead of you."

LOOKING FOR HIMSELF

LATE SEPTEMBER | NAPA VALLEY

I'VE BEEN FOLLOWING Erik's extraordinary ass up and down hills on a bicycle all afternoon, and my brain is no longer doing its job. I need a cold shower, a good meal, a hot bath, and a long sleep, in that order. Alone. I need to back away from the edge of this dangerous ledge.

We drop off the bikes and head to the hotel. I stumble on the flagstones, my ability to walk a distant memory for my weary thighs. "Easy there," says Erik. "Just a little farther."

From the dark corner into which I've shoved Ruben, I hear a cackle. I try to tame him and stick him back in his cage, but my imaginary Ruben feeds me a micromoment of alternate reality.

Cocky and scornful, eyes flashing, Ruben watches Erik's hand reach for my elbow to steady me. "Patronizing asshat," Ruben mutters inside my head. "Here, let me show you how it's done." He rewinds the moment, cuts Erik out, and pastes himself in. I stumble, and Ruben smirks into my eyes and says, "I think you need to lie down." He winds an arm around my waist and pulls me close against him. By the time we get to our room, I'm still hot and sweaty, and my thighs still ache, but I'm no longer tired.

I blink. Shake my head. Focus on palm trees and bright sunlight. Instruct myself to inhale and move on. Tell myself how great my life is.

Look around. This is my life. So warm. So pretty.

Inside myself, doors close and locks click. I turn away. Open my eyes. Try to see.

What I see is Erik in a way I haven't seen him before.

We sit across from each other in the hotel's fancy dining room, dinner plates scraped clean. Erik is silent, brooding, and anxious in his minimalist way. This is it. Tomorrow we fly to Los Angeles to meet with the studio, and then the Shander-Award-nominee whirlwind begins.

"Are you going to tell me what's been bothering you all day?"

He stares down at his empty plate. "Maybe," he says after a while. "Maybe not."

We wait. The waitress clears our dinner things and leaves a dessert menu that neither of us touch. I close my eyes and use my imagination to indulge the apple-pie craving that's been haunting me. *My* apple pie.

My favorite U-pick apple orchard near Boston opens for business every fall in mid-September. Crisp air. Warm woolen scarves. The trees outside the windows of my apartment changing color as the days progress. My dear oven. Hot apple pie on a snowy day.

Home.

Then I remember the radiator under the windows tick-ticking its history into my awareness all day, every day.

"I'm glad we're having those meetings with the studio in Los Angeles," I say.

Erik looks up. "Really?"

"Yes." My voice is firm. "It's time I start imagining something different for myself."

He stares. "Uh… I'm glad to hear that. I…" He swallows and says, "I'm often in LA for work."

I assume this is a non sequitur. But then I see the way he's looking at me.

When I don't look away, he signals the waitress for the check.

Outside my room I put my hand on the door uncertainly, and Erik touches the inside of my wrist with the tips of his fingers. He presses them there and holds me with his gaze. Desire and fear vie for dominance in his eyes. His denial is history.

When his pupils start to dilate and I can't get a good breath, I lean toward him.

I fall into his eyes, let the devil take me.

Ruben pounds on the locked door in my mind.

I ignore him.

LOOKING FOR HENRY

SEPTEMBER | BOSTON

Sprawled on his back on his parents' bed, Ruben stares at the family photos on his mother's dresser.

"Mom, do you remember when I was a week old?"

"Of course." Her voice is muffled by the hanging clothes in the walk-in closet as she leans over to arrange shoes in the new shoe caddy.

"How big was I? Show me with your hands."

Florence emerges from the closet, sets a padded hanger on the bed, and spreads her hands.

Tiny.

"You were my surprise baby," she says.

"I *was*?" Ruben lifts his hands off the bed. "You're telling me this *now*?"

When she sees Ruben's chagrined look, Florence dismisses his anxiety with a wave. "Oh relax, kiddo. After your sisters were born, your dad and I kept trying all those years. But nothing. Not until *you*."

Ruben looks around the bedroom, probably the room where he was conceived—conceived in love by parents who always wanted him. That thought makes him exhale hard, press his palms against his eyes, and think of Henry.

"Ruben, cool it," Florence says. "I was delirious with joy." She sits on the edge of the bed and pats Ruben's leg.

"I know, Mom. I believe you."

"Then what are you rubbing your eyes about?"

"What was I like when I was a week old?"

"Why do you want to know?"

"I'll tell you in a minute."

Florence blinks and purses her lips, a look Ruben recognizes as her remembering look. "Let's see. You had oodles of dark hair. So different from your sisters' blonde wisps. Oh, they were completely smitten with you. Every time I turned my back, they put pretty barrettes in all that hair."

Ruben snorts. "Well, that sure explains a lot."

Florence smiles, but her eyes remain unfocused. "And your grandmother came to visit."

"What? No way. She didn't even leave the farm to go to your wedding."

"It was the oddest thing." Florence shakes her head. "She showed up with no warning. It took my breath away to see her on our doorstep. She looked so... out of context."

All these doting people in my life.

"She pushed her way into the house," Florence says. "She said she couldn't wait until you were old enough to go to her."

All around me, all the time. Mother, father, sisters, grandmother, aunts. Caring for me, eager to be with me. Interested, loving, present.

Tears fall from Ruben's eyes into his ears and onto the pillow, and he doesn't bother to wipe them away.

"Sweetheart, what's wrong?"

"I can't believe how much I cry since I got gay. I'm getting pretty good at it."

"You're not crying because you're gay, and you know it." Florence wipes Ruben's face and then gets up and comes back with a box of tissues.

"I'm okay," Ruben says. He wants but doesn't want her to stop fussing over him. "Just tell me more for another minute. Okay? Do you remember anything else?"

"Oh yes," she says. She lies down next to him and takes his hand in hers. "I could talk about this all day." She looks over at him and smiles. "I missed you when you were away at school."

They're quiet for a few minutes. Ruben thinks she's sorting through memories, but then she says, "Marie told me you're going through a rough patch, but she insisted you'd need to tell me about it yourself." She pats Ruben's hand. "Now's the time, my love."

Henry created this moment.

If not for Henry, Ruben wouldn't have asked his mom for stories like he's been doing for the past couple of years. Many months earlier, if not for Henry, Ruben wouldn't have felt so calm and certain when he told his parents that he was gay. He wouldn't have transferred to a college in Boston so he could be closer to his family.

And it's because of Henry showing him how to cry that Ruben feels comfortable lying next to his mother, holding her hand, spilling over with gratitude.

There's just so much to be thankful for. Ruben has always assumed he can have whatever he wants. All he has to do is ask for it. Or reach out and take it. And with few exceptions, that's how it's always been.

Henry could assume nothing about anything—not one single source of love for years and years—not until he met Jamie. Henry had no assurances, no stability, and saw no faces in his daily life that were familiar to him since forever.

Ruben turns to look at his mother. *My mom is right here. She's always been right here.* He imagines growing up as Henry did, so fast and so alone, unwanted, his extraordinary qualities overlooked and drowned in all the circumstances he had to weather.

He studies his mother's concerned face as she looks back at him, and the unfairness of Henry's history swamps Ruben. His face twists with sorrow and pain.

Florence pulls him into her arms and holds him close. Ruben breathes in the familiar smell of her and lets himself be babied for a minute or two while he sorts himself out and gathers his courage for the next bit.

What's the flip side of this awful ache about Henry's pileup of losses? Please let that coin also have another side.

Ruben takes a few deep breaths and lets his question wind its way through him. From the far horizon of his thoughts a radiance approaches and spreads, warms him, quiets and stills him until he understands the other side.

Henry is capable of so much love.

In spite of his birth, childhood, and hard times, Henry loved Ruben with an eloquent, elegant ease. He loved Ruben with his kindness and his body, with his attention and maturity. As a teacher Henry loved his students into wonder and eagerness to learn. He loves stories, history, the museum, and what they all stand for—continuity and connection through ages, beyond lifetimes, through pain and on to what lies beyond. He obviously loves Jamie and considers her true family. Ruben knows that Henry has been loving the people he's interviewing, working with, and listening to—loving their imperfections and vulnerabilities and stories. Just... *loving.*

I've never known anyone more capable of love than Henry. His love sets people free. I didn't understand the first thing about how to do that. But now I do.

And it's time to use my love to set Henry free.

———

"Mom, you asked me if I wanted a beer." Ruben sits up to take the glass of apple juice Florence has brought him. He downs it in one long, satisfying swig. "Yum. Thank you."

"I know." She shrugs. "When I got to the kitchen, I changed my mind. I decided we're having more of an apple-juice conversation." She moves the box of tissues aside and settles on the bed with her back against the headboard. He scoots to sit up beside her, and they wiggle their toes at each other for a while.

"Mom?"

"Kiddo?"

"How would you like to have another son?"

Florence turns to inspect Ruben's face. "What do you mean?"

"I'm... I'm in love. I mean, for real."

"Ah. So that's what this is about. Well, of course. I'd adore having another son. Who is he?"

"You know him, actually. It's Henry Normand, from the museum."

Florence frowns and gives Ruben a stern look.

"Don't look at me like that. It's not like that." Ruben sighs and hugs a throw pillow to his chest. "That year I was an intern at the museum, I had a terrible... a terrible, wonderful crush on Henry. It was my first time being attracted to a man. Or maybe the first time I was consciously aware of it."

"What did he do to you?" Florence's worried eyes search Ruben's face.

"Stop it, Mom. Henry didn't do anything. And that was a real problem for me. He did absolutely *nothing*. Except he was completely, totally, comprehensively, unbelievably, staggeringly, *frustratingly* mature and responsible. I made a complete *ass* of myself, but he remained a perfect gentleman. He fended me off in the kindest of ways. And yet I *still* didn't let up."

"Lordy. I've witnessed that phase of yours. Poor Henry."

"I know." Ruben shakes his head at himself. "But he maintained. It forced me to learn him from a distance, from a perspective I wasn't used to. And then I *really* fell for him."

"But after you graduated, you went to the farm for the summer. Was that a good thing?"

"For him, probably. For me it was pure, hellish torture. Within days of being back home, I'd convinced him to have a date with me, and then I was at his apartment, and… holy crap."

"Why? What happened? I don't need details, mind you, but I do need to know what's troubling you."

"That was my first time to kiss a man. Yeah. Okay. Sorry. Too much detail." Ruben is silent for a long, still, reverential moment as he remembers. "The date was cut short because an old friend of Henry's arrived early from out of town. I left pissed off, and the damn friend stayed for *six weeks*. As soon as he left, Henry and I spent a whole weekend together." He can't stop a shiver. "That weekend altered my trajectory, Mom. Henry *evolved* me. I fought it, but…" He huffs, exasperated at his former self. "I'd just moved away from home and discovered I was gay, and—"

"And you got scared."

"Yeah. I convinced myself I didn't want what he wanted—a real relationship, or the possibility of one. But he wouldn't accept anything less, and so I had to say good-bye." Ruben laughs at himself. "God, was I deluded. I was fighting the truth. I was already in love with him by then, but that scared the hell out of me. So I convinced myself I wasn't. I didn't know how to… I'd never…"

"Maybe that's why you never really fell in love before then. Maybe that's what you were waiting for."

"What?"

"A man."

Ruben nods but then shakes his head. "If so, I really couldn't have realized it yet. I was too stuck on the idea that, even though Henry was my first, that didn't mean he was the best. So I told him flat-out that I didn't want more than sex and that I needed to do more research."

"And then you, what? Went back to Amherst to shop around?" She smiles at him fondly.

"Oh yeah." He laughs and rolls his eyes at himself. "It was fun, but only up to a point. No matter how much I… um, shopped, I couldn't find what I wanted, which was more depth or more layers or… *something*. Maybe that was because Henry shared some very personal things with me that weekend, and they affected me like… like a time-release love bomb."

"Have you reached out to Henry to tell him that?"

"No." Ruben turns his head away, ashamed. "It took me a long time to admit that what I felt for him was love. Even longer to imagine I could be enough for him. Back then, during our weekend, it was obvious to us both that it wasn't going to work out. Since then, well… there have been complications."

"Oh, honey." Florence pats his leg. "What complications? What's happened to make you so upset?"

"Long story."

"If telling takes longer than an hour, I'll have to iron while you talk. Otherwise there's not one single thing I'd rather be doing than listening to you."

It's time to lean on this gift I grew up with—my family, my mother's attention. It's enough. It's more than enough.

Ruben leans sideways to remove a worn newspaper clipping from his back pocket.

"Ah, 'The Reluctant Farewell.' I was so moved by this one," Florence says when he she sees the title. "It made me look up our local foster care program and make a donation."

"It's me, Mom. I'm the one who took his scarf."

"This is about *you*?" Florence plucks her reading glasses from the bedside table, puts them on, and scans the article. "Henry took your fountain pen?"

"Yeah. The one Dad gave me for my sixteenth birthday. I was using it to do my homework that weekend." He laughs. "Well, for about five minutes."

"Oh." She looks pensive. "Was it you in all those other articles too?"

Ruben nods, and a swell of misery makes its way to the surface when he thinks of how long it's taken to figure himself out. He allows the wave to crest and fall as he tells his mother about Henry's birth, Danny and Ellis, the breakdown at the diner, Estelle and Jamie, and Evil Agent Erik.

By the time he's done, Florence holds a crumpled tissue in her lap.

"I can't forget him," Ruben says. "Trying to forget him was like tossing a wrecking ball into my life and then heaving the rubble of my broken self off a cliff into a never-ending free fall. I may *have to* let Henry go, but I won't do it without seeing him just once more."

"What are you going to do?"

"I have a plan."

Florence snorts a laugh. "Of course you do."

"But it's a risky plan, and I'm scared." He shrugs. "I have to try it anyway."

"I know."

Ruben takes deep breaths and straightens his shoulders. It's time to get to the point, the main reason he came to find his mother in the first place.

"Mom, Henry has taught me a lot of different things about myself and life and being a good person. Even after we parted, he somehow kept on teaching me. He's amazing. Henry is who I... I'm going to... I want..."

Ruben laughs at himself.

"What's funny?"

"What's funny is what's about to come out of my mouth. Mom, I want to marry him. I want to bring him home with me and fold him into our family. I want to give him my family, our family, forever. Even if I ask and he says no, even if he never wants to see me again, I already do consider him my family. And I want to offer to be his family."

Florence rubs her forehead. "But, Ruben. Honey. You're only twenty. Don't you think—"

"I don't care, Mom. I'm *done*. I'm so done pretending to be cool. I choose Henry. I've been so wrong about so much—about love. But I finally know exactly what I want. I want to offer Henry... everything. And if he really doesn't want me, well..." He swallows back what feels like a whine. "Well, then I'll find someone else to love and I'll marry them."

As Ruben talks, Florence's expression shifts from concern to wonder.

Ruben calms himself by staring at the family photos on the dresser. "All my life, everyone has taken such good care of me. Now I want to take care of Henry."

Florence's silence goes on for so long that Ruben starts to fidget. "I'll be twenty-one next month," he offers, not sure what might help.

"So what is this plan of yours?" Florence asks. Ruben can tell from her voice that she's still not convinced.

"Henry's up for the Shander Foundation Award."

"Yes. I read about that in the paper."

"I saw the title of Henry's lecture on the Shander Foundation website. It's 'Family Photos.'"

"Oh, that's going to be interesting. And this will be the first time they film the lectures. We can watch it on TV."

"No. I'm going." Ruben looks at her defiantly. "I bought ten tickets."

"Ruben, those tickets cost more than three hundred dollars each!"

"So what. I'm going, and I'm going to be prepared in every way I can think of to reach him. Plan A, Plan B, Plan Z-squared. Whatever it takes."

"Wow," she says softly. "You're serious about this."

Ruben takes a big breath and scrubs his face with his hands. "Yeah. I really, really am. And going to Henry's lecture is the best way I can think of to bypass Evil Agent Erik."

"Who clearly has no idea what's about to hit him."

Ruben laughs. When Florence smiles, the furrows on her brow smooth a little.

"Two of the seats are for you and Dad. I'd appreciate it if you were with me." Ruben knows from the look they exchange that she knows he's talking about more than the lecture.

Florence nods her head a few times, stares down at the tissue in her hand, and then stands and turns to sit facing Ruben. With a hand on Ruben's determined face, she looks him in the eye and says in her pay-attention voice, "I am so proud of you, sweetheart. You are a brave and loving man. Henry would be a fool to say no to you."

Relieved, Ruben leans into her hand. "Hold that thought, Mom. Just hold that thought."

THE NEXT DAY | AMHERST

RUBEN STOPS AT the deli counter and takes his phone out of his pocket to try calling Millie again. He hopes she'll pick up. "Hey," he says when she does. "Your voice mail is full."

"Shit. Thanks. What's up?"

"Do you have plans for this weekend?"

"Homework," says Millie. "Tons of awful, hideous homework. Those three exams we talked about are next week, and my grade point is in the toilet."

"Yeah. Ellis told me. So here's a wacky idea. How about if you bring all your study stuff along, and Ellis and I remove you from distractions for the entire weekend?"

"Wow. Er... weirdest offer this month."

Ruben laughs. "We're going on a road trip, and I thought if you came along to help with the driving, Ellis and I could whip you into shape scholastically. I had two of those courses last year, and Ellis had the other one last semester."

There's silence on the phone. Ruben puts a tub of couscous in the cart while he waits.

"Okay," Millie says. "I guess. Yeah. You know what? That sounds pretty good."

"Can you leave tonight? It would mean missing your Friday- *and* Saturday-night bar crawls."

"Shut up. I *have to* pass these exams. So, yeah. I can leave tonight. But you're in Boston, aren't you?"

"No. I'm back. I'm with Ellis at the grocery store. We're stocking up and then taking Ellis's van for a quickie checkup at the service station. It's going to be a ridiculous marathon of a trip. We won't stop for much."

"No way in *hell* am I peeing in a jar."

"Duly noted. Now get cracking. Pack your study stuff, a warm sleeping bag, and your passport, and I'll do everything else and pay for everything. Maybe we can be on the road in... an hour?"

"An hour from *now*?" Millie says on a disbelieving laugh.

"Sure. Why not? Were you hoping to get some more *studying* in before we go?"

"Fuck off. So where the hell do you need to go in such a damn hurry?"

"We're going on a scavenger hunt."

LOOKING FOR HIMSELF

SEPTEMBER | NAPA VALLEY

POSTCARD

Jamie! Three top-secret news items plus one proposal: 1) If our meeting this week with a major TV studio goes well—prime time, baby!—I'm moving to Los Angeles. 2) Sunshine and distance promise to cauterize the SRD wound with finality. 3) Erik and I have a timeline for my coming out. Hallelujah! Proposal: If I pay for absolutely everything, will you move to LA with me? xo Henry P.S. Erik put the moves on me last night.

PART VI
THE MOMENTS

THE HISTORIAN
TAKING

THE EXPLORER
TELLING

THE HISTORIAN
TAKING

OCTOBER 8 | BOSTON

"ERIK, WHAT ARE you doing? You delayed our meetings in LA, you booked my flight into New York instead of Boston, you drove below the speed limit all the way from New York, and you stopped for gas when you didn't need to. I saw the fuel gauge. And then you parked us at the far end of the lot so it took fifteen minutes to walk to the auditorium. Do you want me to fail?"

I'm so angry I'm shaking. My fingers fumble over my tie. Erik raises a hand to help, but I turn away.

"I'm sorry," he says, but he doesn't sound sorry. He sounds scared, which confuses me. I've never needed his rock-steady support more, but at the eleventh hour, he's got nothing for me but lame excuses or stubborn silence.

You're a grown-up, Henry. You could have booked your own flight.

Great. Now I'm also arguing with myself.

I glance at the clock above the stage door and lower my voice. "In exactly fifteen minutes, I'm going out there to try to wow an awards committee headed by a known homophobe. The half-million dollars resting on my performance matters to me. The people I could help with the prize money matter to me. You, for some reason, only managed to deliver me here ten minutes ago. My jet lag is giving me a headache. My suit pants are wrinkled. I'm starving. And no. A stale gas station donut is not going to make me feel better."

I stop fiddling with my tie and force myself to take a deep breath and look at Erik. My face feels carved in granite. I need him gone so I can unlock the tension in my jaw. "Will you go now? Please."

He nods and starts toward the hallway door, and then stops when someone knocks on the stage door and walks in.

I expect it to be Edith Shander's assistant, asking me if I'm ready, but it's not. Ruben radiates into the room.

"Oh God," I say and bow my head. It's too much.

"Hey, Henry," Ruben says with a bright smile. He holds out his hand to Erik and says, "Hi."

When I say, "What are you doing here, Ruben?" Erik drops Ruben's hand like it stung him.

With steel in his voice, Erik says to Ruben, "Henry needs this time to prepare. You can't be in here." He lays a steering hand on Ruben's shoulder to push him toward the hallway door, but Ruben doesn't budge. He shrugs off the hand.

"You must be Erik," Ruben says, his voice light and pleasant. But I know that determined, focused look. I sigh and rub my forehead.

"Tick tock," I say. "You *both* need to go. Right now. Please."

Ruben nods and smiles into my eyes with such intensity that I feel the wall behind me burst into flames. "I'll look for you afterward," he says, and I can't decide whether my body registers that as a promise or a threat.

On his way out, Ruben places a heavy brown bag on the table by the door. "Apples for you," he says, "from my grandmother's farm."

All I can do is lift a hand and let it drop as my thoughts are derailed by an intrusive vision. A deluge of documents pours over me—studio contracts, an apartment-rental agreement, an auto lease, speaking-event agreements, publication contracts, a renewed agent contract. On and on and on. All signed by me in Los Angeles.

Ruben leaves through the stage door. I watch him through the two-inch gap of the slightly open door. He pauses at the lectern, looks down at my notes and then up to the far left corner of the large auditorium. When I feel Erik watching me watch Ruben, I turn to check the clock and pick up the ends of my tie to try again.

"Remember we're going to the Shander Foundation reception right after the lecture," Erik says.

I stare at him until he turns and leaves through the hallway door.

Without looking through the gap again, I close the stage door and press my back against it, grateful for something solid to lean on.

I spend nine minutes and thirty seconds of my remaining ten minutes righting myself. I picture my hand flat on top of the stack of legal documents I've signed. I signed everything with my eyes open this time. I chose my future. I know what I'm doing. And I'm thoroughly prepared for this lecture. I only need these few minutes to calm my breathing and picture the foster kids in Austin. I check my tie in the mirror one last time and mentally pet Hector for luck.

I spend the final thirty seconds with my head inside the bag of apples, inhaling everything I've been missing.

As I take my seat onstage beside Edith Shander, she smiles, pats my hand, and asks me if I'm ready. When I nod, she stands and steps up to the microphone to introduce me.

I close my eyes and offer my prayer.

Heartbeats and telepathy.

TELLING

THE AUDITORIUM IS bigger than Ruben expected. And very full. Television crews, cameras, cables, lights, and equipment crowd the edges. The audience is well dressed, beautifully coiffed, and obviously wealthy. People chatter and roam, locating their seats and then making the rounds. Hands are shaken and backs patted. Laughter. Waves and nods.

Ruben recognizes Henry's boss from the museum and a couple of museum board members right up front in seats he knows went for eight hundred dollars. Henry had sent Jamie a ticket for one of those seats, but she traded it for a cheap seat so she and Ruben could sit together. Their cheap seats are a lot farther from the stage than Ruben had hoped.

He presses his palms together between his knees and shivers. *Holy hell, it felt good to be in the same room with Henry again.*

Ruben had waited until almost time for the lecture to start before striding onstage like he knew exactly what he was doing and approaching the stage door. When he heard Henry say Erik's name, he waited a few moments, eavesdropping until he realized it felt wrong. Then he knocked and walked in.

Erik probably didn't intend to fling Ruben's hand away when he found out whose hand he was holding. But he did.

So Erik knows I'm a threat. Good.

Erik's photo on the agency website doesn't do him justice. He's bigger and more macho in person. Also a whole lot gayer, at least when he's trying to protect Henry from me.

Ruben replays Henry's tirade, his litany of Erik's inexplicable delays.

They're not inexplicable, Henry.

Erik doesn't want you *to fail.*

He wants me *to fail.*

Erik takes a seat at the end of a row in the center section of seats, right up front.

As an antidote to the sight of Erik, and because their presence calms him, Ruben grins at the backs of the heads of the two people sitting directly in front of him.

The ten seats Ruben bought, plus Jamie's seat, are arranged in three rows and filled with his supporters for his experiment. Ruben sits in the aisle seat in the middle of the three rows, with Jamie next to him, then his parents. Behind Ruben, against the back wall of the auditorium, are Ellis, Danny, and Millie. Ruben's sisters Marie and Luisa sit in front of his parents.

When Ellis pokes Ruben between the shoulder blades with the tip of his finger—Ellis-code for "Where are you right now?"—and Jamie bumps Ruben with her shoulder and says, "You okay?" he realizes how much he's fidgeting.

He tries to stop, but he can't. And then Henry walks out the stage door.

Erik leans down to rest his elbows on his knees and wrap his hands around the back of his neck.

As Ruben's mind shifts into overdrive to line up contingencies, his body stills.

Edith Shander smiles at the audience and opens her mouth.

Here we go.

TAKING

"MR. NORMAND WILL tell you, with great passion and purpose, about Everyday History. You will find yourself enthralled. But I doubt he will tell you something we on the Shander Foundation Award Committee have come to know about him.

"One of the primary reasons we chose Mr. Normand as a nominee finalist is that his heart doesn't know when to quit. We have watched him interact with and present his programs to all kinds of people, in a wide variety of situations. He is always exactly the same—open, vulnerable, compassionate, forgiving, humble, and empowering.

"Don't be fooled. Everyday History is the messenger. Henry Normand is the message."

I keep a small smile on my face throughout Mrs. Shander's lengthy introduction. When she wraps it up, I step to the podium and nod my head to acknowledge her introduction and the audience's applause.

"Thank you, Mrs. Shander. That was... Thank you. I'll do my best to live up to your view of me.

"And thanks to all of you for being here this evening. I'm honored by your interest.

"I'm going to spend a few minutes telling you what I know about Everyday History, which isn't much and won't take long. And then we're going to have some Everyday History experiences together, because an explanation won't be as satisfying as the experience of understanding each other."

I stare down at my notes for a moment, my pulse refusing to steady. Then I look up at the audience again and smile.

"When we're strangers—and we can know each other a lifetime and still be strangers—we're blank sheets of paper to each other. We're flat and sterile. But when we dare to say what we care about and why, context folds us into recognizable shapes. We become familiar to each other. We can relate.

"Caring animates us. Listening and caring animates the truth.

"I don't know exactly why Everyday History works. I only know that it does. I could offer articulate assumptions. I could explain my and other people's theories. I could show you stacks of research and studies on related topics. They might impress you, but in the end, they will only confirm what you already instinctively know. It feels good to share our truth with someone who's paying attention, and it feels good to receive the gift of someone else's true story.

"The use of things, physical objects, to prompt this kind of meaningful sharing, works the same way show-and-tell worked in grade school. We focus our attention on something that's neither me nor you. The ice over the depths is broken by staring together at this tangible *thing*, this object that's outside of us. We sit beside each other and look in the same direction. And because this thing means something to me, when I talk about it, you're going to learn something important about me.

"Everyday History is a way to sneak up on intimacy.

"I want to tell you the story of how Everyday History bloomed in my life. It's a story I haven't told before. Not like this.

"I didn't invent Everyday History, but I can pinpoint the day I recognized it in my life and found words to describe it. Everything changed for me that day.

"One of the reasons I chose family photos for this evening's theme is because my story of Everyday History began with a family photo. This one."

I glance back to confirm that the photo has come up on my cue. Yes. It's there on the big screens behind me.

"A nosy houseguest found this photo tucked on a top shelf, half-hidden by some books, and asked me to tell them about it. Well, I'm embarrassed to tell you that I didn't react very well. I snatched the photo and ran to hide it in my bedroom. Luckily for me my houseguest was not only nosy but persistent, and I ended up telling them something I'd never told anyone. Something I'd kept painfully locked inside for a long time.

"I began by telling my houseguest that the people with me in this photo were my foster family—my fourth foster family. I was seven at the time and would go through five more foster families before I turned eighteen.

"There are plenty of stories I could have told my houseguest that day about this photo, like how the boy standing behind me once gave me a little box of dried boogers."

The audience laughs, which reminds me that they're interested and listening, and the pressure in my sternum eases for a moment.

"But I chose instead to tell my oldest, most hidden secret, because my houseguest gave me a quality of attention and intense caring that made me want to relieve a burden that had weighed on me for many years.

"Until now, I've only shared this story with one other person besides that houseguest. By the time you know this story, I assure you, it won't seem worth the build-up. But it's important to me, and I want you to get to know me. That's why I want to share it. I want you to know the part of me that considers this particular story important.

"Twelve years ago, when I was in my early twenties, I went searching for answers about my origins. I began with the one document I had—my birth certificate—and started hunting down and requesting any paperwork I had legal access to about my birth. I followed leads and searched out people who might have memories or information or clues. There really wasn't much to find. I was only able to discover a few small facts, but they were... they were..."

I put a fist to my mouth and cough once, trying to make my throat work.

"My parents are not identified on my birth certificate. In the spaces for my mother's and father's names is only the word 'Unknown.' I have no idea who my parents were, and I'm not likely ever to know because..."

I have to leave the podium. I walk back and forth across the stage once and unbutton my suit jacket as I walk, because I need to rub my chest. My sternum feels locked in place, cramping my lungs.

After a slow, careful breath, I walk back to the microphone. I make myself lift my eyes before I speak. I don't want to pretend I'm not present, and I want to include everyone in what comes after we get through the pain.

I don't manage to keep my voice steady as I say the rest of it.

"I was found at a truck stop when I was about a week old. The authorities were never able to track me back any further. There was very little to go on because..."

I rub my chest again, then decide it's easier to finish before I try to find a breath.

"...because I was found in the men's bathroom, naked... in a trash can."

The audience is silent and motionless for so long it's spooky. Then a woman in the front row leans down to pull a tissue from her purse, and her movement jumpstarts me back to the present.

"Wait," I say. "*Wait.* Before you're tempted to see this as only horrible, let me tell you what happened thirty-two years later, when I finally had the courage to tell this secret to someone I cared about, when... when my beautiful, compassionate houseguest valued me for my courage.

"Immediately after telling my story that first time, I experienced the extraordinary feeling of having *survived* the sharing of my story, and something unexpected and instantaneous happened. *I mended.* The deadened, disconnected parts of me came together as mended truth. Truth that I could feel as a living presence. My weakness became my strength.

"That type of healing cause and effect is not news. Those of you who are psychiatrists and therapists routinely facilitate repairs like that. I stumbled my way into it through a photo.

"The surprise and *goodness* of that experience, which was triggered by a caring question about a family photo, so essentially realigned me that, the next day, I picked up a pen and began to write about what I'd decided to call Everyday History.

"I've been writing about, talking about, and offering the experience of Everyday History ever since. In gratitude, as hope, for strength.

"I owe my friend, that amazing houseguest, more than I can ever repay."

TELLING

MOST OF THE people seated around Ruben, his friends and family, turn to look at him during the first part of Henry's talk. *Yes*, Ruben nods. *I was the houseguest.*

Ruben can hardly believe Henry chose *that* story for his Shander nominee lecture. *Holy crap.* But it's a good choice. Powerful. The audience is hushed, and their attention remains intent on Henry.

When the time comes for Henry to say the worst part of his worst thing, he paces and rubs his chest like it hurts. Ruben's heart beats faster in sympathy, and his legs start to jump again because he knows what's coming.

Jamie reaches out, takes Ruben's hand, and holds tight. *She knows too.*

And then it's out. Right out in the open for all to see.

One big secret down.

One to go.

"I owe my friend, that amazing houseguest, more than I can ever repay."

Ruben misses the next moments of Henry's lecture because his mind keeps replaying that last line of gratitude.

With the backs of his heels, Ruben taps the satchel he's brought along, to make sure it's there, tucked under his seat. Then he turns his full attention back to Henry. Ruben's next move will count the most. He needs all the information he can get from Henry to make it work.

THE HISTORIAN
TAKING

I CAN EASILY give a talk, teach a class, present a story, and still spare enough attention to scan the audience for a face. But I don't.

Instead I glance to my left to check on Erik, who looks like he's about to throw up.

Ever since what happened at the resort in Napa, he's been both distant and more emotional, but all he'll say when I push him to tell me what's wrong is, "I don't know what you're talking about."

He catches my eye, but offers nothing. Only a haunted, hollow panic that I may have caused.

It happens as I say, "I hope you brought your family photos with you tonight, because I'm going to ask some of you to stand and share your Everyday Histories stories about them now." My eyes accidently lock onto Ruben's, way up in the back on the left, sparkling at me.

It feels like catching his eye in the classroom at the museum on a warm Monday in June. I don't hesitate or stumble over my words or lose my place or alter my breathing. But I suddenly feel the presence of him in my chest.

Heartbeats and telepathy. No. Wrong response. Face forward, damn it.

I've had lots of practice sizing up audience candidates who are likely to be good at presenting their Everyday History stories. I don't analyze much. I just reach instinctively. When I choose someone, a runner gives them a cordless microphone, picks up their family photo, and delivers the photo to the technician at the contraption that projects images onto the big screens.

The first story, from a diamond-studded elderly woman with a slight stutter, is short and poignant. By the end the cadence of her voice has slowed and her stutter has smoothed. The middle-aged man next to her stands and hugs her.

The next two stories are longer and more dramatic. More grief. More joy. More life review. While the audience's attention is not on me, I survey the crowd to assess how they're doing and to gauge their collective stamina. I don't want to drag the interactive part of my presentation past its welcome or stop before they're sated.

The people who tell their stories are scared and nervous and courageous in different ways. Their stories are all moving. I hear sniffles throughout the auditorium. The audience's attention is deep, respectful, and profound.

When applause for the man in the orange jacket has died down, I begin to feel the particular relief that signals a need to wrap things up. "We'll do two more," I say, "and then I'll answer questions."

Ruben shoots his hand into the air.

No. No way in hell.

I turn to the other side of the auditorium and point at a raised hand. "Please. The woman in the hat and the striped dress."

The runner does his work with the microphone and the family photo, and I ask a few questions to help the woman start her story.

Then I flip to the next page of my lecture notes.

THE EXPLORER
TELLING

RUBEN WATCHES HENRY at the podium, and... *Yes!* Henry flips to the next page of his notes. But he does it without looking down.

Ruben exhales hard and swallows past the dryness in his mouth. He's gambling everything on Henry's next decisions.

Legs hopping, fingers tapping, Ruben tries to listen to the woman's story.

Henry, as he's done for the past hour and a half, as he *always* does, asks questions that do the work of a velvet-wrapped crow bar. As the woman in the striped dress responds to Henry, her generic surface lifts to reveal her juicy, compelling, imperfect beauty. She leaps, and Henry catches her, values her, and gives her back to herself freshly laundered and gift wrapped.

Then she's done, and Ruben feels a shout begin at the back of his throat.

"One last story," Henry says. Ruben leaps to his feet and raises his hand. He tosses his lasso of luck and timing and prays it will catch and hold.

Henry frowns and looks away from Ruben. He looks down at his notes for the first time since he flipped that page.

THE HISTORIAN
TAKING

Henry, I sent this email to you four months ago, on June 19:

To: Henry Normand
From: Ruben Harper
Subject: PERSONAL MESSAGE FOR HENRY

Hi, Henry

After our weekend together, I was just fine, thanks... or so I kept telling myself. But then you began seducing me with your articles. I tried to resist, tried to pretend I was past you, but that was a total, messy, painful disaster. With the help of some friends, I finally stopped pretending.

I've realized I'm in love with you, Henry. Not a little bit, but all the way. I'm sorry I didn't recognize the signs sooner. They were there from the beginning.

I would have told you this in person, but I can't seem to reach you. I hope this e-mail finds you.

Whether you want me or not, I wish you happiness. That's all I've ever wished for you. It just took me a while to dig that wish out from under a load of self-deluding crap.

If you're still interested, I'll be glad to look into your eyes and tell you that I want all of you.

Any way you'll have me, I'm all yours.

Love,
Ruben

This is the reply I received from you the next day:

> To: Ruben Harper
> From: Henry Normand
> Subject: Re: PERSONAL MESSAGE FOR HENRY
>
> Ruben,
>   I appreciate your frankness, but I've moved on. I've been seeing someone else for a while who I really like. I wish the same for you.
>
> > Be well—and have fun,
> > Henry

I need to know—was this email really from you?

THE EXPLORER
TELLING

GOT HIM.

Henry's silence goes on long enough that the audience isn't sure what to make of it. Then he lifts his head and looks right at Ruben, his face an expressionless mask.

Ruben, still standing in the aisle, raises his hand again.

And then Henry sees who's sitting in front of Ruben.

Got him again.

His voice strained and rough, Henry says, "You," and points to Ruben.

Ruben takes the microphone from the runner and hands over the two photos from his satchel.

While everyone waits for Ruben's family photos to come up on the big screens, Henry stares down at the lectern.

Heads turn to look at Ruben, then Henry, then Ruben again. The air in the auditorium seems to thicken in the deepening silence, leaving only the hum of the television cameras.

"Thank you, Mr. Normand. My name is Ruben Harper. I ask for your indulgence because I've brought two family photos, but they illustrate the same story.

"A few weeks ago, my mom was cleaning out the closet in her and my dad's bedroom, and I was lying on their bed chatting with her. One topic led to another, and we got to talking about our family photos. Because I knew I'd be here tonight, I'd already been thinking about them.

"I decided to go on a tour of the house and collect all of our family photos and take them back to my parents' room. There are lots of them, and it took me several trips. I arranged the photos on the big bed in chronological order and then picked them up one by one, starting with the first one.

"Every year, starting the year they were married, my parents have had a studio portrait taken of the family. The first couple of photos are only Mom and Dad. Then come two photos of Mom, Dad, and my oldest sister, then come ten years of my parents and my two sisters. And then I finally get in on the act."

As Ruben talks he watches Henry, but Henry doesn't move. His outstretched arms grip the back corners of the podium as though to steady himself, and his head remains bowed.

But Ruben knows Henry is paying close attention.

Ruben puts everything he has into his voice and his words.

"I lined up all the photos that include me—twenty photos—and as I scanned them, I watched myself grow up. That's when Mom told me something I'd never known. She said, 'We always wanted four kids.' I came along many years after she and Dad had given up on having more than two kids, and there was never a fourth.

"And that's when the weird thing happened, the thing I most want to tell you about. I was leaning back against the headboard, looking at the photos, and thinking about the fourth member of the family who hadn't come along. And suddenly my perspective shifted, like when you stare at an optical illusion and don't get it, but then suddenly you do.

"In every single photo that includes me, there's a space where it looks like someone is missing. You can see it on the two examples I've brought that are up on the screens now. The top one was taken when I was one. See how my oldest sister, Luisa, is sitting in the middle of the bench next to my sister Marie and there's this big empty space on the bench to the right of Luisa?

"When I pointed this out to Mom, she laughed and told me that Luisa and Marie had been sharing the bench more evenly, but it was summertime and the photographer's studio had a big door—like a garage door—that was raised to let the air circulate and to bring in more light. This photo was taken just after a bird flew into the studio, chirped, and flew out again. It startled Luisa, and she scooted away from the bird and toward Marie. Of all the photos taken that day, this was the one my parents decided to have printed because, even with the odd placement of Marie and Luisa on the bench, it captured the family the best.

"Then I showed Mom the spaces in all of the other photos I'm in. One by one, she told me the stories of those empty spaces where our fourth family member wasn't. For example, in this other one I brought—from when I was eight—that big space between me and Luisa is there because, about two hours before this photo was taken, I dropped the first pie she ever made. I'd been proudly carrying her pie to the kitchen table where everyone sat waiting, and I tripped over my own feet. She was so mad no amount of cajoling or bribery would persuade her to stand any closer to me."

Ruben falters at this point, but only briefly. This is the part of his plan that involves telling a whole lot of strangers some things he considers extremely private. He mentally gives himself the pep talk he prepared and memorized.

This is between me and Henry. I can't do anything about the hundreds of witnesses here. So ignore them. Ignore the cameras, and focus. Just talk to Henry.

"The thing is... the thing is I know who the missing person is."

Jamie touches Ruben's hand as a brief gesture of support, and it helps.

"Before I went around the house to gather the family photos, Mom and I had been talking about the person I'm in love with, someone who showed me how to open up and grow up.

"There's a lot I don't know about this person, but I do know the most important things. Like how much family means to them. And how strong and loving and truly inspiring they are.

"That talk with my mom and what I saw when I considered our family photos confirmed what my heart has been trying to tell me for years: The person I'm in love with is the exact shape of the space we've been holding for them in our family.

"So." Ruben takes a huge breath. "I'm going to ask that person to marry me. I have my family's blessing. All that's left is the asking."

Ruben pauses to catch his breath, to lower the microphone and rest his arm, and to locate his mother's encouraging smile. But mostly to make damn good and sure his words reverberate through the air and fall deep into Henry's silence.

Then, heart pounding out of his chest like in a cartoon, Ruben lifts the microphone to his mouth again. *Almost there.*

"Because I'm the last person to share a story tonight, and because you're going to take questions after this, I'll go ahead and ask my question now.

"I know this is a lot to ask. I know you've said in interviews that you don't want to reveal this information. I know how much you value your privacy about your personal life. But I wonder if you'd be willing to..."

Ruben clears his throat and his voice softens and slows.

"Mr. Normand, who was your houseguest?"

THE HISTORIAN
TAKING

I CAN'T THINK. I can't think. I can't think.

So stop trying.

I am so tired. I could sleep for a hundred years.

I am so angry. I could scream until cities fall.

I am so sorry. I gambled and signed, promised and lied.

I am so lonely. I divided myself, missed the signs, lost my way.

I am so scared. My arms ache from holding still. Reaching out will ruin me. Won't it?

I am too... *sensible* to be stuck at a podium in a crowded auditorium fighting back tears.

It's *over*.

I am so hungry.

TELLING

H ENRY'S SHOULDERS BEGIN to shake.

Ruben takes a step toward Henry, needing to help, but then he remembers his goal, stops, and stays put. He knows this next bit is something Henry has to do on his own. If he's going to do it at all.

Erik gets up and strides toward Henry, who must notice him out of the corner of his eye, because he lifts a hand from the edge of the podium. *Stop right there.*

Erik stops and slowly turns to look up at Ruben.

Ha, you pathetic asshat. Henry can handle this on his own. I know that. You didn't.

Someone in the front row of the audience clears her throat and stands. It's Edith Shander.

Henry finally raises his head. His face is a total, red-eyed, tear-streaked wreck. He rubs the palms of his hands across his face and over his smooth head and straightens his spine. His nose scrunches like he's struggling to stop crying.

Oh. I'm done here. The relief flooding Ruben's body tells him he's okay, no matter what happens. *I've had my say. What happens from here on is out of my hands.* His heartbeat steadies as he waits to see what Henry will decide.

Henry looks up at Ruben again. No smile. Only the wrecked face making Henry look like he's still trying to find his way.

Then Henry looks at Edith Shander. "I'm sorry," he tells her. She doesn't move or speak. Henry waits for a long moment, then nods once and leaves the stage, a crumpled sheet of paper from the podium clutched in his fist.

For one horrible moment, Ruben thinks Henry is heading out the door to the lobby. But he stops in front of Erik—who's still standing—and pushes the crumpled sheet of paper into the pocket of Erik's suit jacket. In a deep, intense voice that carries, Henry says, "You are *so* fired."

Henry turns his back on Erik and walks up the steps toward Ruben while Ruben, the audience, and the cameras watch the agent take the paper out of his pocket and smooth it. His face works through shock, worry, and finally resignation. Erik looks up at Ruben one last time. Then he heads for the door to the lobby.

Henry must hear the door open, because he says without turning around, "Hey, Erik."

Erik stops and turns back, his hand on the door handle.

"How about now? Is *now* a good time?" Henry asks.

The look on Erik's face is indecipherable, but as the lobby door closes on his expensively clad ass, Ruben can see him already working his phone.

Don't even try. You're going down.

People murmur and shift in their seats, and the cameras turn to follow Henry, who moves with purpose up the wide, shallow steps. His hurting, beautiful eyes stay on Ruben's every step of the way.

It takes all of Ruben's willpower not to go to Henry, not to meet him halfway. The only thing keeping him in place is his memory of Henry's restraint and the gifts it bestowed, the space it gave Ruben to reach for his own control.

But as he sees Henry's determined stride and the stiff way he's holding his arms, it occurs to Ruben that he's never seen Henry angry. *Crap.* Ruben raises his hands to abandon defense. *I surrender.*

Two men at the end of a nearby row must see what Ruben sees, because they stand as Henry approaches, as if they're prepared to intervene.

Henry steps up the last step. His eyes reveal nothing. He raises a palm to Ruben's chest. Into the hush of the room, his voice deep and clear, Henry speaks two words. He pushes them into Ruben's chest with such fierceness that Ruben topples back against the wall.

"*All. Mine.*"

Ruben's cartoon heart grows wings and flies.

Staring at Ruben with the intensity of a thousand suns, Henry waits for Ruben's face to brighten and then leans forward and kisses him.

In public.

Ruben wraps his arms around Henry's shoulders and kisses him back.

For all the world to see.

THE HISTORIAN
TAKING

The taste of him, after all this time, makes everything whole again.
And I don't care. I *do not care* who knows it.
I don't care what happens after.
Only this.

THE EXPLORER
TELLING

Ruben's first thought, after an infinity of relief, is that there's nowhere for this kiss to go but into a thrust of hips. And it doesn't look like Henry's going to back off without a little help.

Ruben draws back to put his mouth against Henry's ear. "Henry, I'm all yours, and I love you so much. But in this particular moment, we need to pull ourselves together. Because right now the two choices I see are that I can lay you down on the steps and take you in epic gratitude"—Henry, thank God, snorts a laugh into Ruben's neck—"or I can let you go temporarily so you can finish up and say good-bye to these nice people who are waiting to see what you're going to do next."

Ruben feels Henry's harsh breath against his hair, and his hands on Ruben's waist tighten. Then Henry nods, and Ruben whispers, "I'm going to hold you like this for another moment while we both think of whatever terrible awfulness will do the trick of a cold shower, because the world is watching, and I forgot to bring a hat." Henry laughs outright then and they separate their hips from each other just enough to break contact.

The audience shakes off its shock with a hoot and a wolf whistle, scattered applause, and a rising murmur of voices. Ruben is glad that Henry is facing the wall, because a few people stand, glare at Ruben, and hurry out of the auditorium.

To distract Henry for another minute, and to give his pants a chance to fit better, Ruben says into Henry's ear, "What happened in Napa with Erik?"

"Ruben, please don't be jealous. He never had a chance."

Ruben squeezes his eyes shut. *Not now. Not now. Not now.* When he opens his eyes, he sees reporters coming up the stairs, so he loosens his hold on Henry. Ellis and Jamie stand to hold the reporters at bay, and Ruben steps away from Henry but keeps a hand on his shoulder.

I have to find Erik before he leaves. But not now. Not now. Not yet.

Henry turns away to kneel in the aisle beside Jean Normand, who takes Henry's hand and lets loose a barrage of French that makes Henry laugh and blush. Henry's reply, also in French, brings Ruben fully back to the present. It sounds so delicious Ruben decides he needs to learn French as soon as possible. Jean shakes his head, squeezes Henry's shoulder, and gives him a gentle push, as if to say, "Go on. Finish up. I'm not going anywhere for a while."

When Henry stands, Jamie squeezes him so hard he says, "Ow." Ruben's mom leans over to grab Henry in a long hug, and Ruben narrates. "Henry, this is my mom, Florence." She lets Henry go with a kiss on the cheek. "This gorgeous woman sitting beside Jean is my good friend, Estelle. When we have a moment, she's going to audition to be your mother. That's my dad, Edward." Henry smiles down at Estelle, his eyebrows raised in a question, and then he stretches to shake hands with Ruben's dad. Edward passes Henry's hand on to Luisa.

Marie beams at Henry, reaches out to touch his shoulder and says, "I'm Marie, your new sister. It's wonderful to finally meet you, Henry."

Before Ruben can turn Henry around to introduce him to Danny, Millie, and Ellis, Millie taps Ruben's shoulder. "Hey, check it out," she says and points to the stage.

Edith Shander, frowning and grim, approaches the podium and taps the microphone. "May I have your attention, please." She clears her throat and says in a firm, tight voice, "The Award Committee will speak to the press at the Shander Foundation offices in one hour." She says no more, only pivots and exits through the stage door. Her suited minions scurry after her.

The weight of what he's done falls hard on Ruben.

Holy fuck. I've pushed Henry into turning his back on half a million dollars.

Ruben shakes his head at Henry and mouths an "I'm sorry." He tucks his hand inside the collar at the back of Henry's dress shirt, and the heat he finds there surprises him. Ruben's fingertips jump and twitch against the pulse at Henry's neck, but Henry's eyes project only steady, calm peace.

He's trying to reassure me.

Henry pulls Ruben closer. "Stop it. You made me an offer I couldn't refuse. A much better offer than half a million dollars. I promise."

"I could have waited until you'd won. *Shit.* Why didn't I think of that?"

Henry says with a teasing smile, "Because you didn't want to wait. You did what it took to reach me as soon as you could. You reached for me. You woke me up. Again. That's what you do for me." Henry lifts Ruben's chin, his fingers curling around Ruben's jaw to tug him forward. "You gambled. I won."

The kiss surpasses all the others combined. It is tenderness without end, wrapped around enough heat to melt the soles of Ruben's shoes.

He's mine. He's really, really mine. For good. Ruben pulls away to nod at Henry. *Yes. More of that. But not here. Not yet. Soon. Let's go.*

Someone from across the auditorium yells, "Hey, Mr. Normand. Why don't you introduce us?"

Henry keeps his eyes on Ruben. When Ruben nods his okay, Henry takes him by the wrist and pulls him past Ellis and Jamie and the corralled reporters.

As they walk down the steps, Henry slides his fingers inside the leather bracelet he gave Ruben two years earlier. Ruben has never removed it. Henry's fingertips press against the pulse at Ruben's wrist. It feels like Henry saying "All. Mine." all over again.

Up on the stage, Henry waits for the crowd to settle a little. He leans toward the microphone and says in a low voice, "Folks, I think my work here is done."

This draws laughter from the crowd until Henry holds up a hand. "I'll apologize to Mrs. Shander directly, but I'd like to publicly offer her and the Shander Foundation my sincere apologies for the disruption of this evening's lecture. I'm not going to overstay my welcome here, so if you have questions for me, please... um... wow... please find me a new agent." The audience laughs again.

"Introduction already," someone shouts.

"Yes." Henry squeezes Ruben's hand and holds it up. "This amazing person is Ruben Harper. He was my nosy houseguest. He brought me a bag of apples. He walked into my living room wearing my blue pajamas and picked up Jean's walnut bowl. He took my blue scarf. He found the family photo on a top shelf in my apartment and cared enough to make me want to tell him a story that changed everything."

Henry leans into the microphone and says, "I'm going to marry him."

TAKING

RUBEN, MY FORCE of nature, undoes me, stuns me, demolishes my resistance. I feel scrubbed clean and windblown, as though I've weathered a hurricane and come away giddy and grateful to be alive. He's put every dream I pushed off the table right into my hands.

I get to *belong*.

I get to live inside the circle of his arms.

Yes and *more* and *please* and *thank you, thank you, thank you.*

THE EXPLORER

TELLING

RUBEN GIVES HIMSELF a grim smile when his guess pays off.

The door of the men's bathroom on the top floor of the auditorium complex opens. Someone comes in and—from the sound of it—throws a heavy metal briefcase onto the floor. It skids and clatters on the tile.

The water in the sink goes on. "Fuck," someone says. "Fuck. Fuck. *Fuck.*"

Ruben pushes away from the wall where he's been leaning, flushes the toilet to get Erik's attention, and opens the stall door.

"Yeah," Ruben says. "That is never going to happen."

Erik blinks and only closes his mouth when Ruben plucks a few paper towels from the dispenser and hands them to him. Ruben reaches around Erik to turn off the tap. He gives him two seconds to dry his hands and then snatches the paper towels away and tosses them into the trash can. The image of naked baby Henry lying in the garbage fast-forwards through Henry's life to today, which makes Ruben smile.

"I'm pretty sure this is the part where you tell me to fuck off," Ruben says. Curious to see what Erik will do, he takes a step and gets too close.

Erik holds Ruben's gaze but doesn't move.

"Good," Ruben says. "I'm not here to kick your ass, though somebody definitely should. Henry's lawyers will try, but Henry will have mercy on you. I am not Henry."

Erik's breath speeds up. "Get the *fuck* out of my face and say what you need to say."

Ruben nods and backs up a step. "I want to know why you did it."

"Why do you think I would tell you anything?"

"Because I'm guessing you'd like Henry to know that your original intention wasn't to screw up his life quite as thoroughly as you did. And since Henry's not going to be taking any calls or e-mails from you, this is your only chance, and I'm your only option."

Erik's glare gets old, and Ruben makes a show of looking at his watch. He folds his arms across his chest and raises an eyebrow. Erik's glare only intensifies.

"Fine, then." Ruben turns to leave.

"You were a kid. It was ridiculous that Henry couldn't get over you."

"He talked to you about me?"

"No. But he asked me every ten minutes if I was sure all his personal e-mails were being forwarded to him."

"And were they?"

Erik scowls. "Not exactly."

"I'm still waiting for a reason."

The mask of belligerent outrage slips from Erik's face for a moment, revealing unmistakable heartbreak.

Keeping his arms tightly crossed so he won't do anything rash, Ruben counts to ten. "So you thought, what? With me out of the way, you could set him up as your private bit on the side in Los Angeles? Or were you going to divorce your wife?"

The instant flush on Erik's cheeks and the fact that, for the first time, he can't meet Ruben's eyes answer for him. But Ruben wants to be sure. "You were in love with him. I want to hear you say it."

They stare at each other until Erik looks away again. His nod is almost imperceptible.

Without meaning to, Ruben unfolds his arms and jabs a finger at Erik as he says, "Henry is the nicest person you ever have or ever will throw away. I can't tell you how to live your life, but I will make a suggestion. From now on, whenever you think of Henry and what he did tonight, ask yourself what it would take to pick yourself out of the garbage and get a life that doesn't give you a rash from all the chafing."

Erik narrows his eyes.

"Consider this a public service announcement. Man up, Erik. If not for yourself, for your children. They deserve all of you, not just... pieces of fake."

Ruben knows he's said enough. If he doesn't stop, he might do something he'll regret. He picks Erik's briefcase off the floor, sets it upright between the sinks, and gives it a pat.

Then, because being in the same room as Erik without hitting him will have passed the point of tolerable in about five seconds, Ruben takes a deep breath and turns to leave. As he goes out the door, he says, his voice hard and full of threat, "And if you *ever* touch Henry again..."

He didn't intend to say it out loud. But he did. At least he finished the sentence in the privacy of his own mind. At least the anger making him tremble heeded his command to stand down.

He leaves the bathroom and steps slowly down the wide, curving stairways, needing time to decompress.

Ruben finds Henry sitting in the room behind the stage with the bag of apples on his lap. His eyes are calm and full.

"Let's go, bright eyes," Ruben says as he lifts Henry's hand. "Our family's waiting outside to take us home."

PART VII
THE NIGHT

THE HISTORIAN
FALLING

THE EXPLORER
HOLDING

THE HISTORIAN
FALLING

OCTOBER 8 | BOSTON

I SMELL RUBEN in the air.

I remember telling Jamie good-bye in the foyer when we arrived at Ruben's house, but not much else.

Disoriented and drunk on sleep and memories, I turn to bury my nose in the long-lost scent, and my hand touches something soft. In the dim light seeping in from the sitting room, I make out a row of buttons and a suggestion of blue.

Ruben has his own pair of supersoft blue pajamas. I know they're Ruben's because I left mine in the RV in California, certain that seeing them in my suitcase in Boston would provoke more memories than I could handle.

With a burst of joy, I curl myself around Ruben's pajamas and gather them to my chest as I sink back to sleep—cured, cared for, and known.

THE EXPLORER

HOLDING

DRIFTING ALONE DOWNSTAIRS in the house where he grew up, Ruben revels in the peculiar, late-night silence of a house full of people he loves. He breathes into the feeling of peace as he wanders through the ground floor, checking locks and turning off lights.

His face hurts. *I can't stop smiling.*

He makes his way upstairs again, all the way to the attic suite that he claimed when he started high school, to the foot of the bed on which he's logged endless hours fantasizing about Henry.

Henry—here in my bed.

Smiling like a fool, Ruben memorizes every detail of the view.

By the time they arrived home from the lecture, Henry looked like a rescued war refugee—dazed and beyond exhausted, but finally safe. The moment they crossed the threshold, Henry's battery failed completely. He'd stared down at the entryway rug like he'd crawl under it if he had the energy.

Ruben herded Henry to the attic, undressed him, and poured him onto the bed, where he splatted in a face-plant with his arms flung and drifted to sleep on a sigh. Ruben kissed the top of Henry's smooth head, pulled open the bottom drawer of his dresser, and retrieved his blue pajamas for the first time since the day he bought them. He set them on the bed with a fond pat and went back downstairs to visit, too wired to sleep.

Seeing Henry's protective clutch around his pajamas gives Ruben an instant full-body flush and an erection that feels like the same unrelieved hard-on he's had for Henry since they walked away from each other in front of Henry's apartment two years earlier.

Trying not to wake Henry, Ruben undresses quietly and slides under the covers, his hands twitching to reach and ravage. *It's okay. There's time. So much time.* He closes his eyes and spreads his fingers wide over his own chest, willing himself to relax and wait.

When Henry's warm hand slides up Ruben's arm, he startles.

"You're thrumming," Henry says, the grin obvious in his voice. He stretches out beside Ruben and presses close. His big, dark blue eyes—soft and full of desire—capture Ruben in their snare.

Got me.

Feasting on Henry's vulnerable look, Ruben's pounce falters. He's sideswiped by the first bashful moment of his life. Henry's warmth, Ruben's almost unmanageable hard-on, and the surprise of shyness combine to short out Ruben's circuit board until all he can do is blink at Henry and feel.

Henry's grin fades into pure heat. "God, Ruben. I can't get enough of you looking at me like that again." He props himself up on an elbow. With certainty and surgical precision, Henry leans down and takes Ruben's breath away.

The kiss feels unreal and way too perfect, like a dream sucking Ruben into intimacy too flawless to exist. He wills himself to go with it, commands himself to believe, and the clean, sweet taste of Henry's mouth moving against his— Henry's tongue slow and hot and attentive—causes Ruben's eyes to sting. Smoothing a hand over Henry's bare head from elegant eyebrows to strong neck, Ruben weaves all his feelings into the kiss and shivers at the reunion of past and present. He remembers how scary it used to be to touch Henry's exposed head, because of the intoxicating feeling it evoked—a deep, frightening, primal need to protect him.

Henry pulls back and brushes Ruben's hair off his face. When he slides his hand down Ruben's jaw and across his chest, lingers over Ruben's nipples, Ruben sighs and writhes.

With a flush in his pale cheeks, Henry whispers, "I will never, ever get enough of touching you."

Ruben's next breath is a gulp as he lifts his head to Henry's mouth. It feels like the first breath he took in that dream, when Henry pulled away the oxygen mask to give Ruben exactly what he needed and reanimated Ruben's world with motion and color and vitality.

By the time Henry's wandering hand finds Ruben's desperate cock and Ruben's lips are achy and oversensitive from Henry's unrelenting kiss, an intrusive thought has become too insistent to be ignored.

What happened in Napa?

Ruben turns his head to break the kiss and Henry loosens his grip. "Sorry," Ruben says, irritated with himself and apologizing to them both.

The curious, patient look Henry offers tugs the words from Ruben's mouth. "Erik... He had a thing for you, yeah?" Ruben aims for casual, but can't keep the worry from his voice.

Henry nods and it squeezes Ruben's heart.

"I read your postcard from Napa, but... I felt it when I saw you and Erik together. Before the lecture." Ruben swallows hard against the painful memory of how much effort it had taken to keep his reaction under control when confronted with Erik's possessiveness.

Henry nods and moves his hand away from Ruben's cock, which motivates Ruben to get to the point. He tries to smile, but it's a bad effort, so he turns his concern into a joke to make up for it. "Good thing you're a paragon of self-discipline, or you might have done something you'd regret." Ruben's fake chuckle dies when he sees the look on Henry's face.

"Well," Henry says, "I'm afraid it's rather late for that vote of confidence."

THE HISTORIAN
FALLING

Ruben slowly gathers the duvet in his hands and grips it until his knuckles turn white. I back off a few inches to prepare myself for his flip into jealous-caveman mode.

But I don't want to be calm. I want Ruben to stop talking—to stop doing anything but demolishing me with his need.

Although maybe, as it has before, his jealousy will deliver what I yearn for.

That rush when he rises up in strength and takes me.

For a long, strained moment, Ruben's face remains expressionless, then he turns toward me and takes a big breath. "What *exactly* did you and Erik do together?"

I hesitate, but I'm unwilling to dodge the truth. "I very briefly groped his ass while he groped mine, and we kissed for about five seconds outside my hotel room door."

"And?"

"And I hated it. He wasn't you. I couldn't stop thinking about you... and his wife and children. So I stopped. I went into my room without him and locked the door."

Ruben swallows and nods a few times. I brace myself. But he surprises me.

"That... yeah, that must have been difficult for Erik," he says carefully, his eyes steady on mine. I study him closely, anticipating a delayed Hulk reaction. But... *nothing*. His breathing slows. His eyes soften.

"Wait...," I say, when it's obvious he's already winding down. "Seriously? 'That must have been difficult for Erik?' That's your only reaction?"

Ruben's fists open all the way, and he brushes his hands across the duvet, smoothing out the wrinkles. "Yeah."

"Wow."

He gives me a smile. There's a hint of embarrassment in his voice when he says, "Honestly, Henry? I've done a hell of a lot more than kiss and assgrope a whole *parade* of men since we last saw each other. I'm in no position to object to what you did with Erik or with your campground flings or with anyone else. But Erik's energy at the lecture concerned me. I only... I just want you to be safe."

I stare at Ruben for a long, long time and he continues to look back at me calmly.

The boy has grown himself into a man—my man.

"You've... uh... you've been... b-busy," I say. I stumble over my words because I'm suddenly riveted by Ruben's demonstration of control.

He leers and rolls on top of me. "Guess what I want now?"

THE EXPLORER
HOLDING

ALL THOSE KISSES—AT Henry's apartment, that desperate kiss at the harbor restaurant, Henry's kisses at the lecture, the impatient kiss and handsy fumble in the backseat of Jamie's car on the way home, Henry's perfect kiss when Ruben got into bed... They were intoxicating, one and all, but none of those kisses even come close to this one.

How can the same lips, the same mouth and tongue, the same brush of stubble against stubble feel so different and so much more intense? Something has shifted. It shows in Henry's kiss.

Ruben's nerves falter and his teeth bump against Henry's.

Damn it. Fuck. I'm acting like this is my first time.

"Sorry," Ruben mutters. "Sorry *again*. Jesus. I can't believe how much I keep interrupting." He draws away and sits up, folds his legs to sit cross-legged, and touches Henry's flat stomach with his fingertips. He hopes what he has to say won't matter. He hopes it's the very last interruption before... He closes his eyes.

Henry takes Ruben's hand. "You're stalling. Stop distracting yourself and tell me."

Ruben turns Henry's hand over to press their palms together, swallows, and forces himself to look at Henry. "I... I've never done it."

"Done what?"

"Topped."

Henry looks confused. "You what? But it's been... Ruben, it's been two years since our weekend together. What have you been doing all this time?"

"Having... Yeah. Okay. Having a lot of sex. Well, until about six months ago. But I haven't topped. Not ever."

"But why?"

"Henry." It comes out as a plea. "Can't you guess?"

Henry shakes his head, his forehead furrowed with concern.

Staring down at their joined hands, Ruben laces their fingers together and clears his throat. "During our weekend together, I was a clandestine wreck. I kept having to retreat to the bathroom to reconvince myself I wasn't in love with you."

Ruben glances at Henry and laughs at the look on his face. He slides a thumb along Henry's dark eyebrow and kisses the surprise and adoration in Henry's blinking eyes, needing to memorize them with his mouth.

"I thought I was being mature, insisting I only wanted sex from you. In truth the way I felt about you scared me to death."

"I wondered what was really going on with you."

"Yeah."

Henry smiles.

"It *killed* me to walk away from you that Sunday," Ruben confesses. "But I decided to start college a free man and prove to myself you weren't all that special."

"I hope you had fun."

With a sigh Ruben squeezes Henry's hand. "Not as much as I thought I would." He meets Henry's eyes and admits the rest. "I spent what felt like a thousand years sampling other men, checking out other kisses and bodies and… and conversations, trying to locate a *shred* of what I'd felt with you."

Henry holds his breath.

"I never did. Of course I never did." Unfolding his legs to kneel beside Henry, which feels as reverent, as devotional, as the moment deserves, Ruben leans down until their lips touch. He breathes in and out against Henry's mouth for a long moment and then whispers, "I've been saving myself for you."

A blistering lucky-me look darkens Henry's blue eyes. He wraps his arms around Ruben's shoulders and tries to pull him closer. Then he huffs when Ruben resists.

"Wait," Ruben pleads. "Shit. I know I'm trying your patience, but…"

Henry drops his arms onto the bed and moans. "No. It's me." He pulls his leg out from under Ruben's hand and backs away until they're no longer touching. "I'm overeager." He rubs his forehead and his hand shakes. "You're not the only one who's been saving himself since our weekend."

Ruben shudders in anticipation of going where Henry hasn't allowed anyone else to go for that long, and his resolve threatens to weaken, but he needs Henry to go over this cliff propelled by more than just the shock of their reunion. He wants Henry to believe in him—to trust him for real.

"I'll be quick, but this is important. That weekend, when we got back from the restaurant and I pushed you to let me top, you said something that's echoed in my mind ever since. Do you remember?"

Henry shakes his head.

"You said, 'You will hurt me if you can't control yourself.' And you were right. I was too angry to focus the way I needed to. I didn't figure out until a long time later that my jealousy, which began the moment I heard Martin's voice on your intercom, was... is more of an intense need to look after you, to protect you, to help you get everything you want."

Partway through Ruben's speech, Henry's smile disappears to make way for a complex expression Ruben can't decipher—except for the aroused flush that pinks Henry's skin and blows his pupils out to *holy fuck*.

"Since that weekend," Ruben says, rushing the final words, "I've been trying to earn the right to lose my virginity as a top with you."

Henry's face tightens further and then closes off completely. Without saying a word, he backs away from Ruben's reaching arms, slides off the bed, walks unsteadily to the bathroom, and closes the door with a sharp click.

After a few minutes, Ruben hears the shower go on.

What the fuck?

He gets up to listen outside the bathroom door, but there's only the steady pulse of the shower. He knocks twice. "Henry?" When there's no answer, he opens the door a crack to see Henry sitting on the edge of the tub with his elbows on his knees and his head in his hands.

Ruben closes the door, sits next to Henry, and reaches behind them to turn off the shower. Seeing this version of Henry, so like the broken-open Henry who barely managed to tell the story of his birth, rattles Ruben. He works to remain relaxed and tries hard not to make assumptions. He trusts Henry to talk when he's ready.

His voice low and unfamiliar, Henry says, "You should go. You need to go. Now. Right now."

Ruben lays a hand lightly on Henry's back, but Henry flinches and shrugs it off. "*No*. Please don't."

Certain that leaving won't help, Ruben tries to think of what to do instead.

"Okay then. Here's the thing, Henry. If you don't tell me, this instant, exactly what's going on, I'm going to assume the worst, and we'll get ourselves into a mess."

After a long moment, Henry turns the shower back on and looks at Ruben, who's shocked to see panic in Henry's wide eyes.

Over the rattle of water hitting the bottom of the tub, Henry says, "I need you to leave so I can take a cold shower."

"Um... *now?*"

"Yes. You... God, Ruben, you don't get it." He rubs roughly at the back of his neck. "I've wanted you to top me for... for so damn long. You have no idea. But after today, after all the... the love bombs you've dropped on me and the major swerve toward perfect my life has taken because of you... Right now I can't. I just can't."

Ruben fights back tears of confusion. "Because of me you can't what?"

With a shiver, Henry says, "I want you way too much."

Oh, thank holy fuck. Ruben almost laughs with relief, but holds it back because Henry's legs are shaking, his breath is ragged, and he's gritting his teeth. "And why is that a problem?"

"Your first time shouldn't be like this. I can't control myself around you right now because you're so... because I feel so... I need to..." He looks down at the evidence in his lap and closes his eyes tight. "Ruben, just go, damn it."

It's not me who doesn't understand.

Ruben turns off the shower again, then reaches between Henry's legs and squeezes his cock firmly, which makes Henry yelp, jump up, and push at Ruben's hand to try to get away. Ruben follows and holds on tight until Henry groans and falls back against the sink.

Pinning Henry against the sink with his thighs and chest, Ruben says, "*You* don't have to be in control." He gives the head of Henry's cock a firm rub with his thumb. "Because *I am.*"

Henry shudders and groans out a harsh, frustrated breath, but he stops squirming to get away.

Ruben feels Henry's already-hard cock turn to solid granite. He studies Henry's face and sees the truth of his words sink in.

"Then please," Henry croaks, his voice catching, "I'm begging you."

Ruben takes Henry by the hand and leads him out of the bathroom.

Back in bed, stretched out beside the furnace of Henry, Ruben rolls on a condom, raises an index finger, and waggles his eyebrows. His goofy antics betray his nervousness.

"I trust you," Henry says and folds his hot hands around Ruben's neck to haul him closer. His movements and gaze are insistent, so unlike Henry's calm, educational patience all the other times they've been together. It prods a mighty wildness that Ruben has studiously kept locked away. Tentatively he slides off the shackles and invites the untapped power to explore beyond the edges of its cage.

Rubens fingers shake and he slops lube onto the sheets, but doesn't care. He reaches between Henry's legs and touches, watching Henry's face, feeding on the abandoned way Henry spreads his legs.

Ruben must be doing something right, because Henry pushes against Ruben's finger, and his head rolls back on a moan that's so urgent Ruben thinks he's hurt Henry already. But when Ruben starts to pull his hand away, Henry hisses and follows.

God. Henry's open-mouthed, scrabbling, unhinged eagerness turns Ruben on so much he has to stop moving to get himself back under control.

Because if he can't stay in control, it will end.

And that is not an option. *Not now that I feel... this. Henry undone beneath my hands.*

Ruben moves his finger against Henry's tight hole and then into the heat. That evokes a squirm and a low, wordless moan—uninhibited and fervent—a begging sound that alters Ruben's worldview and obliterates the cage in an explosion of desire.

Henry in control was heaven on earth. Me in control is a rocket ride to the moon.

Adding a second finger, then another, moving a part of himself in and out of Henry calls the wildness to the foreground, and Ruben discovers that he needs more—much more. Heart pounding, he pulls his hand away and raises up on one arm to steady his cock at Henry's entrance. Henry lifts his body and strains up to meet him.

Ruben watches his cock push slowly into Henry. *Jesus fucking hell, that's beautiful. And tight.* Ruben allows himself to be mesmerized for an eternal moment by the enthralling sight and then tears his eyes away to look up and make sure Henry's okay.

Love pours from Henry's eyes.

Drawing from the well of Henry's gaze, Ruben freezes as the look holds and holds.

Henry's hands come to life and roam over Ruben. When Henry twists his hips and begins to mutter, Ruben lowers to his elbows and turns his head sideways to try to hear Henry's words.

"So gorgeous taking me. So dazzling. Knew you would be."

Ruben smashes his mouth onto Henry's words and presses his tongue past Henry's teeth. He fills him, fills more of him, presses all of himself into Henry.

Groaning deep in his chest, Henry pulls up his knees, puts his feet flat on the bed, and lifts his torso. Ruben scrambles to find a balance between waiting and moving, between caution and roar. He releases Henry's mouth and angles his hips to move a cautious inch farther inside Henry, then forces himself to stop and wait again, legs and arms trembling from the effort.

Love continues to pour from Henry's eyes.

If he keeps looking at me like that, like he trusts me to love him, I can wait like this forever.

Henry releases a long sigh, and Ruben feels the muscles around his cock relax. He needs to move. He can't *not* move. But he waits because he wants to be sure.

"Ruben," Henry gasps, "Go. Please. I trust you." He wraps his legs around Ruben's back to hold their bodies together and force Ruben closer. And the part of Ruben's brain in charge of action screams for mercy until the part that hasn't allowed a millimeter of leeway grants a centimeter of freedom and then another and...

Way too much. Not nearly enough.

That feral force unfolds inside Ruben—unlocked, unleashed, untamed—and zeros in on Henry's face. He dares to push his cock all the way into the heat until there's nowhere left to go. He pulls out, pushes in again, revs the engine, aims for the horizon in the depths of Henry's eyes, and releases the brake.

God. Oh God. Oh God. Nothing ever felt like this. Wrapped up in Henry and moving.

Henry's escalating loss of control sends Ruben into overamped, gasping desperation, and the sudden fear that Ruben is going to ruin it for both of them.

How did Henry ever manage this? Brakes or accelerator? I can't wait. I have to wait.

The opposing forces strengthen and weaken Ruben's resolve over and over. He whines with the effort of balancing it all and starts to panic.

Can't wait. Must fuck him harder. Can't wait. I'm going to hurt him now. I can't keep him safe after all.

"I'm so sorry," Ruben blurts as he feels his body taking over.

"*Hey…,*" Henry says between a gulp and a sigh, his voice hoarse. "No. You're perfect…" Henry's eyes roll up in his head for a moment, but he brings them back to Ruben's. "Trust yourself."

Ruben stops trying to think his way through, stops trying to find a balance, stops doing anything but moving and feeling and moving. He stumbles into a rhythmic paradox of possession and release that goes on and on *and on*. It fries his brain, lifts them higher, punches through strain into pure music, and Henry climaxes with a shout that flings Ruben into a new dimension.

They spin over the edge together, holding each other tight as the earth releases them into brightness too hot to sustain without a flame of wings and a long fall onto the softness of the duvet.

Smoking feathers fill the air above the bed.

Long, shuddering minutes later, as they hold each other close and pant, Henry is the first to locate the part of his mind that forms words. He finds a ragged whisper to exhale against Ruben's ear.

"Don't you ever, *ever* not do that to me again."

Ruben gasps and laughs and then can't stop.

He gives up for eternity.

Lost and found.

Reborn.

True at last.

"SHIT. HENRY. I'M in so much trouble." Ruben gathers Henry closer. The *mine* that took over Ruben's soul during that epic orgasm still reverberates through his body. "I already wanted you more than anything I've ever wanted in my life, but *now…*"

"Yes, my man, I think you've found your calling."

My calling is you, Henry.

Henry's breath speeds up under Ruben's unfaltering gaze. He squirms and slides his hand down from Ruben's neck until his wrist brushes Ruben's cock. "Umm… Ruben, are you done talking yet?"

"Run out of restraint again already, have you?" Ruben swivels his hips and gives Henry a smirk. "Relax. I'm your new cruise director."

"Now you're pandering."

"Yeah?" Ruben whispers, wildness prowling closer. "It's working."

Plastered to Ruben's side, hard again, his pupils darkening, Henry flushes. His pale skin pinks toward red under Ruben's focused gaze.

"You're sparkling at me again," Henry whispers.

"Get used to it. This amazing power I have to light you up like a supernova means I'm going to keep doing it forever. I'm going to screw you silly for the rest of our lives, you mature, secretive, self-restrained bastard."

Henry leans closer. "Takes one to know one."

Ruben opens his mouth to say something else, to ask or tease, but Henry's hungry kiss and ardent, roving hands disintegrate Ruben's words.

"Now. Again," Henry gasps against Ruben's lips. "I've waited for you for so long."

Ruben growls, tucks himself around Henry, envelops him, spreads his hands across Henry's bare head, flexes his hips, and runs free.

PART VIII
THE AFTERNOON

THE EXPLORER
MORE THAN ENOUGH

MORE THAN ENOUGH

THREE YEARS LATER
NOVEMBER | BOSTON

RUBEN AND HENRY lean against the car in front of their Beacon Hill townhouse, taking advantage of the day's unseasonable warmth. With a lingering palm, Henry smooths the lapels of Ruben's new suit. The gesture calms Ruben a little, but not enough.

"Where did Mike and Cricket get to?" Ruben checks his watch again. The antsy feeling of missing their oldest and youngest children is ridiculous. He saw them only a few minutes earlier.

"You're going into sheepdog mode," Henry says.

"We'll be late."

"Stop pretending you care if we're late." Henry tugs on Ruben's hips and gathers him close until Ruben has to look at him.

"Yeah. Okay," Ruben says. For the past week, ever since Henry's adopted father finally died, Ruben's had trouble letting Henry and the kids out of his sight.

"I happen to like it that you feel better when we're all together," Henry says. "Jean would have liked it too."

Ruben examines the current level of grief on Henry's face and kisses the new lines at the corners of his eyes. He wishes his kisses could erase the sorrow altogether.

"Get a room, Dads!" Adrian, their middle child, calls out from the backseat where he's hiding behind a soccer magazine.

Henry laughs but doesn't pull away. "Let's give them three more minutes," he says to Ruben. "Cricket was having trouble with her outfit."

"Okay. But distract me."

Henry smiles, and fondness changes the lines at the corners of his eyes from sorrowful to joyful. "I can't tell you how much I love it that we've found an antidote for your anxieties."

Embarrassed, Ruben closes his eyes and turns away. "Just get on with it."

"Look at me." Henry puts a hand on Ruben's face and turns him back.

Ruben opens his eyes and whispers, "You're not the boss of me." But the strain of the past few weeks, as Jean worsened and finally died, tightens its hold. He pleads with his eyes.

"No. I'm not the boss of you," Henry whispers back. "More often than not, you're the boss of me, but with a few notable exceptions. Like when you need your medicine. Now stand still and let me praise you. Pay attention. There's much to distract you with these days."

Henry leans back a little and pretends to hold up a microphone. "How does it feel to be you right now, Mr. Harper? Because you've been very busy indeed. Cocaptain of the newly launched Everyday Inclusion Foundation."

"Yeah," Ruben says, rolling his shoulders, testing the tightness there. "Who needs a damn Shander Award when you have enough mojo on your own to buy the bank?"

Henry grins. "Aw. Don't hold a grudge. You're in no position to complain. And shush. There's a lot more medicine to get down you." He raises the imaginary microphone again, clears his throat, and gives Ruben a triumphant smirk. "How does it feel to be Ruben Harper, the youngest—definitely the gayest—Shander Award Committee member since its inception almost two hundred years ago?"

Ruben's shoulders begin to relax beneath Henry's hand. "Yeah," he says. "That's me, Ruben Harper, luckiest husband of all time to celebrate a three-year anniversary."

"Most adored adopted son-in-law of all time," Estelle, Henry's adopted mother, calls out from the front seat.

"New father of a strange and wonderful little girl," continues Henry.

"Old father of two teenaged boys, one regular, and one strangely gay," Adrian contributes.

Ruben leans down to look at Adrian through the open window. "And the strangely gay boy pretending to read a soccer magazine isn't helping Cricket because...?"

"Mikey's desperate to get this over with. He thinks he'll be faster." He shakes his head. "So, *so* wrong."

Henry pulls Ruben back up, raises his eyebrows, and waits for an answer.

"How does it feel to be me?" Ruben asks.

Henry nods.

"Well, Mr. Normand, it feels…" Ruben sighs and thinks about his life, and more tension falls away. "It feels spectacular."

"But wait. There's more," Henry says. "Your full dosage requires the full list."

"Yeah." Ruben says on an indrawn breath. "Oh yeah. There's more." He puts his hands on Henry's ass and briefly pulls him closer—just long enough for Henry's eyes to darken.

"Good Lord," Henry murmurs. "How lucky am I? Groped by a Harvard graduate."

"You're damn lucky," Ruben says with fake arrogance, "as I am now MBA qualified to carry your briefcase, type your letters, and fend off your hordes of swooning, adoring, young, old, gay, straight, regular, spicy, purple, foreign, and domestic groupies and fans."

"Hmm. Let me consider that offer for half a second. Umm. Nope. We already have people to do all those things. How about you do what you do best and stick to being—"

"Really, really bossy?" Ruben raises an eyebrow.

Henry's smile morphs into a look Ruben doesn't usually get in public.

"Yes. My bossy muse."

MIKE COMES OUT of the house shaking his head. "She changed five times, and she *still* looks ridiculous."

Henry goes inside to get Cricket, and after five more minutes of fidgety waiting, Ruben takes out his cell phone. When the call goes to voice mail, he leaves a message. "Hi, Mom. We're running late. Is everyone else there already? I hope Jamie remembered to bring her goldfish. Cricket asked if she could sit next to it. Okay. See you soon."

Ruben comforts himself by leaning down to watch his boys in the backseat.

"This is taking forever," Mike says, flapping his arms in frustration. "Gran, do you have any gum?"

"I just might, sweetie," Estelle says and starts digging around in her purse.

Adrian pushes the soccer magazine across the seat to Mike. "Here. Distract yourself. I highly recommend the sweaty hunk on page twenty."

"Thanks for the warning." Mike picks up the magazine and flips through it.

"Watch out," Adrian says, leaning over to check the page numbers. "It's the next page. You'd better skip it unless you want to be grossed out by my dream man."

Mike turns the page and finds… a boring, full-page ad for foot powder.

"Made you look," Adrian says with a smirk very like Ruben's. Mike swats Adrian with the magazine.

With a pat on Mike's shoulder, Ruben says, "Hold the fort, guys. I'm going in."

"Good luck with that," Mike grumbles.

⸺ ⸺ ⸺

RUBEN HEARS HENRY and Cricket talking on the back stairway before he sees them. He hangs back, not wanting to interrupt what might be a tricky negotiation. Cricket's five. She's feisty and unique and all heart, but she had a tough life before Ruben and Henry got her at the beginning of the year, and she's still adjusting.

From the relative darkness of the library doorway, Ruben sees Cricket standing a few steps up the staircase, a huge grin on her face as she talks to Henry. She's wearing shiny green galoshes with yellow polka-dots, Adrian's orange "ROCK THIS" T-shirt—which is so big on her it covers the tops of her boots—and the neon-red tutu Henry gave her for her birthday.

"I *am* ready already," she tells Henry and waves her arms like it's a hard sell. She's so excited she's hopping up and down. It's her first official family photo. She's been looking forward to it for months.

"Sweetheart," Henry says, but he doesn't say any more. He just turns and sits on the second step and squeezes his eyes shut.

What the fuck?

Henry looks like he's aged a year in the five minutes since he came inside. Ruben forces himself to stay back. As much as he wants to comfort Henry, he knows enough to wait and see—to trust that Henry's got it covered.

On the stair behind Henry, Cricket stamps her foot. "Papa, give me the key right now. Grandpa Jean didn't mean to lock his door. I *always* help him with his tie. He... he..."

Oh shit.

For as long as he lives, Ruben will never forget the look on Cricket's face as she watches Henry's head fall into his hands, and the memory that Grandpa Jean is dead crashes onto Cricket's fragile frame.

Henry hears it happen and turns around. Cricket takes a gigantic gulp of air and flings herself into his arms with a cry of *"No!"* She wraps her arms and legs around Henry and wails, her heart breaking all over again. Henry detaches her for a moment so he can open his suit jacket and tuck her further inside the warmth of his enfolding arms. She clamps onto him, and her sobs escalate, shaking them both. Henry turns his head so he can rest his cheek on her silky black hair.

When Ruben sits on the stair beside them, Henry opens his eyes.

Please. Please may I go the rest of my life without seeing Henry's face wrecked with sorrow ever again.

Ruben wipes tears from Henry's face and rubs Cricket's back for a few minutes until Henry sighs and smiles and stands.

"You okay?" Ruben asks Henry as Cricket sobs "Papa, Papa, Papa." Henry nods, and the most beautiful, serene look comes over his face.

"Yeah," Ruben says and smiles, "I know what you mean." And he does.

With a hand on Henry's back, Ruben shepherds two precious pieces of his heart outside.

We're enough. We're more than enough. We'll always be more than enough.

Ruben takes his time locking the townhouse door with his back to the car. He needs a moment to adjust to the heady rush of good, clean medicine righting his world.

"Where's Daddy?" Cricket says, her voice wobbly and wet.

"Here, sugar," Ruben says. "I'm right here."

Here. Home. Happy.

JOIN FOR A
FREE STORY

JOIN ALICE'S READER list and get the free story *Executive Decision*.

**Dar loved his career...
until he did his job too well.**

THE STRANGER IN the electric blue suit who compliments Dar's work is Pierre Catalan, owner of a multi-planet transportation empire—a polished, powerful man Dar considers way out of his league.

Alice Archer's reader list members get this free story, peeks behind the scenes, and unique items to accompany the books. Members are always the first to hear about Alice's new books and giveaways.

Get your free story at
ALICEARCHER.INFO/EDPR

REVIEW

THANK YOU FOR reading! Please consider leaving a review of *Everyday History* on your preferred platform. Honest reviews increase visibility and bring stories to the attention of other readers who may enjoy them. Your thoughts are appreciated and welcome.

ACKNOWLEDGMENTS

MY MIND AND heart sorted through a galaxy of information to create this novel. I'm grateful for the generosity and encouragement of the beta readers who helped the story find its way home: C.C., Chris E., A. J. Henderson, A. B., Andrea Dalling, and Armi.

Dreamspinner Press originally published *Everyday History*, for which I'm grateful. It was a pleasure to work with senior editor Liz Fitzgerald, whose expertise and kindness made me want to do whatever she asked.

Formatter Colleen Sheehan is an artist and a saint. She has my utmost respect. Bree Archer's original front cover design garnered many kudos, and I'm glad to have her permission to use it for this second edition as well. Big thanks to cover designer Tracy Kopsachilis for creating the remainder of the print cover for this edition.

They won't have known it, because I lurked without speaking up much, but the authors in the Rainbow Romance Writers chapter of Romance Writers of America have been guiding lights. Their comments and discussions on the forums, their articles and stories, their books, and their ways of being have shown me much about how I want to be as a writer in this genre and in general.

I'm convinced *Everyday History* would be a different novel if not for James Morrison's album *The Awakening*, which I listened to every day for hours as I wrote. The flavor of that music and those songs made its way into the bones of this story.

ABOUT
ALICE ARCHER

ALICE ARCHER HAS questions. Lots of questions. Scheming to put fictional characters through the muck so they can get to a better place helps her heal and find answers. She shares her stories with the hope that others might find some healing too.

Archer's first novel, *Everyday History*, was named a Top Book of 2016 in the *HEA USA Today* column *Rainbow Trends*.

For decades, Alice has messed about with words professionally, as an editor and writing coach. She also travels a bunch. Her home base is Eugene, Oregon.

To find out more, visit
ALICEARCHER.COM